THE
FATHOMS
BELOW

JACKIE SONNENBERG

Crystal Cove Press
A Young Adult Speculative Fiction Imprint
of Crystal Lake Publishing

www.crystalcovepress.com

Prologue

Twelve Years Ago

She moved her legs around in the water, trying to imagine what they would be like once the scales started to grow.

The tub was filled almost to the top, and when she moved beneath the surface, she felt hints of something grainy and textured on her skin. She kept touching it to feel the texture, freezing when she heard the bathroom door open and someone come in.

"Dally?"

The shower curtain moved, and her big sister stood there, instantly furrowing her brow. She looked at the water, and her face changed when she saw how clouded it was.

"What are you doing?"

"Ally," Dally said in a low whisper. "I'm going to change!"

Ally stood before the bathtub with her eyes wide open. She tentatively walked closer, peering into the water.

Dally moved her legs, bending them at the knees so that the caps were visible at the surface, revealing flesh-colored disks.

Ally saw the container behind her, reached over, and picked it up, shaking her head.

"It has to be real sea salt, you know," Ally said, possessing more wisdom at nine years old than she had at seven. She sat on the edge of the tub, still holding the Morton container. "And that's not until after you take the DNA test and then get the shot. And then you have to be in the water for a really, really long time."

"It's been a million hours," insisted Dally. She held up her fingers, deep lines and grooves that looked like the branches on their backyard tree. "See? Look how wrinkled I am."

"The only thing you're gonna turn into is a raisin."

Ally considered the Morton container, giving it a shake.

"Mom's gonna kill you for using it all."

"Are you gonna tell on me?"

Ally considered it.

"Nah."

Dally leaned up far enough to see that her sister was holding her social studies book.

"She said to tell you it's time to do homework and get ready for bed."

Dally moved her legs in the tub again, merging them together and lifting them up and down as one.

"Do you think it will be as long as my legs are, or do they get longer when you turn? Do your fins get really big?"

"I don't know," Ally answered honestly. "Mom and Dad say we can't take the test until we're older. And that's even if we test high enough."

"I think we will."

Dally kept imagining how she would look, her tail bright as the sun hitting the surface of the ocean. Her sister brushed her teeth and then left the bathroom, leaving Dally to return to her daydreaming. She would be one of those creatures, dashing through the ocean, flipping those long fins. After another moment, she sat up and searched for the bathtub plug to pull.

Dally relaxed while she waited for the water to drain, then got out to attend to her own homework.

The pictures of their ancient ancestors in her social studies book looked like aliens with their long heads and tails. Their fins curled around the sides and ended in sharp edges like fanned-out knives. Even the fins on their arms were long, mimicking the flippers of dolphins, which was her favorite animal.

> *Six hundred million years ago, most of the Earth was just ocean. This was the Devonian period and it was the turning point for our evolution because it paved the way for vertebrates in the sea to become dominant. Even though it is known as the "age of the fish," we all know this means this was the age of the fish evolving into something more.*

Dally flipped to the next page with pictures of fish classification charts with different colored lines connecting various groups.

> *The most important type of fish here is the placoderm, which refers to the first fish with a bony head plate and jaw. All signs point to this grouping of fish as the source from which all vertebrates came, including and especially us. Research and studies have linked us to the ancient fish going back millions of years, and our teeth actually come from our fish ancestors.*

The photo of a fish's mouth was wide enough, like when the dentist would tell her to open her mouth really wide so he could see all of her teeth.

> *Ancient fish had what were called "dermal denticles." These were small, spike-shaped scales that many fish today still have, like sharks and mantas. Scientists studying these dermal denticles say that once our ancestor fish evolved on land, the denticles moved from the skin into the mouth, which marked the birth of teeth.*

The next page had more charts showing fish and amphibian evolution.

> *Eventually, during this time, the fish that became vertebrates colonized the land, among them our Mer ancestors. We learned about the early lobe-finned amphibians that first made their way onto land and how our Mer ancestors learned to do the same.*

> *It is said that the second round of extinction took place at the end of the Devonian period, which paved the way for us to come on land. The big beasts up there were all wiped out, creating space and time for a new pecking order.*

The next pictures had lobe-finned fish on land, and the prehistoric merpeople themselves on their stomachs with their fins holding them up. The photos depicted the tails step-by-step splitting into two, all the way up the evolution chart to the first upright walking Neanderthal: scales fading to skin and hair.

Dally had a sharpened pencil ready to fill in the answers to the questions in her first-grade workbook, knowing all the answers by heart. She even wrote outside of the paragraph lines and onto the drawings she did in class that day, a disproportionate figure with a fat head, big tail, and lopsided smile.

After finishing the study questions at the end of the chapter, Dally flipped the pages to the next chapter about present-day advancements. There was a picture of a human arm with ice-blue scales running from the elbow to the top of the knuckle. This page talked about the first successful scale growth on human skin, a major development for human and Mer kind, and just how far scientists had come since then.

The next page showed a comparison of the early Mer Neanderthal to the more modern Mer people. One showed a Mer person swimming alongside a giant turtle, while the other depicted a Mer person as a tiny speck next to the giant. It looked like a regular fish, but the ancient Dunkleosteus was the king of the seas in the prehistoric Devonian period. It resembled a twenty-foot bullet in the shape of a fish, covered in natural hard armor.

Dally stared at the ancient sea monster, her little eyes marveling at the creatures with which her people used to coexist before they moved on land. This early Mer Neanderthal held a spear made of long, curving teeth and wore a helmet of hard shell. Dally wondered how they had been able to fight these big creatures enough to dominate them and wear their natural armor for themselves.

There were more sea dinosaurs on the next page, and these were just as big and scary looking. She loved sea dinosaurs; she even had a stuffed Liopleurodon on her bed, but that one was soft and squishy and the size of her pillow. The real ones would eat her up in one bite, and they would if she lived in the ocean then.

But they are all gone now.

She turned the page to images of more modern-day Mer folk in the open blue. Nowadays, they do not have to worry as much. There were fewer beasts living in the water, they said, insisting they were all gone. But how did they know that?

CHAPTER 1

PRESENT

THERE IT WAS: THE little white stick figure against a blue background. The very symbol for both human and Merkind. The universal symbol for the Movement was everywhere, the image she grew up with and could embrace for herself. It appeared at the end of every poster and hung as flags.

Dallas walked back from class, passing by more campus bulletin boards that displayed how much more of the Movement was everywhere. It seemed like people were putting up more and more things every day, as more news and updates emerged, and more people made their transitions.

She passed a bulletin board decorated with various flyers and announcements, including Stick Figure Movement pride and propaganda. There was one for a Mer transitioning support group and another for a used clothing drive for new Mer people. Some notices warning people about fake DNA tests from China and not to fall for them.

There were promotional posters encouraging people to take their DNA tests and support for those who did not test high enough.

There were websites, hotlines, and even those old-school sheets with tear-away slips offering swimming lessons.

There were warning notices featuring giant pictures of sharks with open jaws and bold lettering:

Predators still live in the deep!
Protect yourself and your home!

There were lists and lists of companies and organizations fighting to control the predator population, with several stating they had already done so.

There were flyers stating that because of the Oceanic Civilization Act, several breeds of sea creatures were now on the brink of extinction.

There was, of course, so much more here on this college campus than what she had at high school. She saw plenty of it and would see plenty more. Especially now that she was of legal age.

She reached the dorms, where similar decorations were everywhere. Students all had their own décor, though it was evident they carried the same declaration of pride. While varied in size, flags and posters displayed the same familiar image: the same cerulean rectangle with the stick figure symbol in the middle stamped on every other dorm window like a checkerboard.

One of the windows was open all the way, with a flag hanging like a long banner. As the wind blew it back and forth, the wavering stick figure looked as though it could be either running or swimming, just as intended.

Dallas had a matching pin she got at the mall on her backpack. Although the plastic had peeled away in age, it held up. She would give it a rub every time she put her backpack on for luck, for support, for manifestation. The waiting list was supposed to be six months, though others claimed it sometimes took longer.

She took out her phone from her backpack side pocket and saw one new text message from Albany. But there were other things she missed in class.

One missed call from home.

One new voicemail.

Two text messages from Mom and Dad.

Dallas only needed to open the most recent message from her sister to know that all the messages would be the same.

> We got them! Yours was sent to your mailbox!

Dallas almost dropped her phone as she broke into a run. All she had to do was veer to the right to the mailroom by her dorm. She shoved her key into it, opened her mailbox, and pulled everything out. She ignored flyers for $1 pizza and clothing drives as the little box fell into her hand where it belonged, the forward label from Hugh and Naomi Dwight from her home address. She squeezed it in her palm and kept it in the same grip until she reached her room. Then she held it in front of her face, staring at the Oceanic Ancestry Commission logo and label in the top left corner. Dallas's fingers found her phone as she stared at it and dialed.

"*Dallas!*" her mom cried. "*Did you get it?*"

"I did!"

She heard muffled voices through the phone of her father and sister in the background joining the call.

"*She got it!*"

"*Hey, Dally!*"

"I can't believe it," Dallas started. "We got it so soon?"

"Your father got an email from the OAC saying that we were next in line to receive them, and they came this morning."

"This is it," came her dad's voice. *"It's official."*

"Yeah, and all you need to do is put a piece of your hair in a tube!" shouted Albany in the background.

"Did you guys do it already?"

"We did, it's that simple."

"And we just sent ours out in today's mail, along with yours to your dorm. It comes with the postage all set so you can just put it in the post box."

All three voices sounded at once. Dallas imagined them all huddled around the island in their kitchen with her mom's phone on speaker.

"I will, I just...wow."

"Hey, we have a good chance."

Dallas just listened, absorbing as they all went back and forth.

It wasn't until they hung up that she started to form a million questions.

Dallas opened the package and spread out everything.

There was a little tube and plastic baggie to put it in, along with a paper of instructions and a small cardboard box already addressed to the OAC testing labs. She flipped the paper over and looked back at the little tube, in disbelief that this was it. She had expected to prick her finger and draw enough blood to smear across a glass slide, just enough so that when it was placed under a microscope, it would reveal whether there were enough of those thousands of tiny aquatic cells swimming around.

She imagined they looked like seahorses and wondered how many little seahorses she had swimming around in her blood. She wondered if there were enough to turn her into one big fish.

Dallas felt the pull of her reflection from the mirror on her dresser; the same one she had used to cut her hair last week due to boredom. It was a choppy brown mess now, the attempt at a pixie cut, the attempt at a prerequisite change. With the help of some hair gel, she managed to give it some spikes, and now she looked like sea vegetation.

She pulled out a single strand of hair and put it in the tube.

After what seemed like weeks of roughly opening her mailbox so hard she nearly snapped her key inside it, the day came when she felt the warm flutter in her stomach.

This time, it was there.

She held the envelope from the Oceanic Ancestry Commission addressed to her in front of her, staring at it. What she had been awaiting for weeks was right here, right behind that envelope, and yet Dallas lingered. It was the anticipation, the finality of it all, she supposed, but she could hear her family's encouraging words as though they were standing right next to her. So, Dallas slid a finger under the envelope and tore it open.

All the words blurred together as her eyes scanned for nothing but a number.

Dallas let the empty envelope fall to the floor as she found it, forming a tight grip on the paper. She reached for her phone and dialed home immediately. Each ring that went through sent her heart pounding faster.

"Dally?"

"Mom, I—I got it."

"You did? Hugh, come here! Ally! Ally, your sister got her results! What was it, honey? Tell us!"

Dallas suddenly became very thirsty, and her mouth felt drier than ever.

"Ninety-one. I'm ninety-one percent."

She heard the excited screaming and shouting coming from all of them, so much so that she had to pull the phone away from her ear.

"Ninety-one!?" Her father came on the phone. *"Ninety-one? You beat all of us!"*

"What are you?" Dallas asked, her voice rising in pitch.

"I'm eighty-eight, and your mother and sister are eighty-nine."

"That's great!" Dallas cried. "Oh no way. Oh wow."

"Well, Dally, looks like it's time to initiate that Plan B."

CHAPTER 2

THE PAPERWORK BECAME DOG-EARED from the number of times she'd handled it, now positioned in front of her laptop. She scrolled through the YMCA website until she found her location, then clicked on it to find the sign-up times. A variety of time slots spread across a calendar and mostly clashed with her class schedule, but she was able to grab a day when she did not have classes.

Dallas kept one finger above the keypad mouse while the other hand flattened her bent-up class schedule, soon to be gone, but academic credit should she ever need it again elsewhere. If she would even bother going back to school. Her email dinged with the confirmation, sign-up time, and the directions to the place in case she did not already know.

Dallas sat back against her pillows to process it, stretching her legs out across her bed. She probably should do more stretching in preparation, but instead responded to the urge to get up and rummage through her drawers. She did not even remember the last time she went swimming, but she knew she had to have at least one or two decent swimsuits somewhere. She pulled a black and yellow one-piece with a cringe. It was not like she was going to the beach, but that was what she was stuck with.

When she last talked to Albany by phone, she said it was not really a test, but rather a practice. It was not a pass-or-fail type of thing, as the DNA test already did that. The swimming portion was to see how "rusty" someone was and help awaken the natural ability a little bit more to make the next part easier. One could sign up for as many sessions as needed, but really, those that were given the green light did not need so many. She got the one; next was to figure out the rest of it.

Dallas took the dog-eared paperwork now and rewound it back to its stapled starting position, curling it into a paper cylinder and securing it in her backpack for the ultimate trip to make.

The campus was at its normal foot traffic, noise, and littering with students coming and going to classes. Dallas knew there was a growing foot traffic shortage due to the shortage of feet. She passed those same residential buildings to discover more Stick Figure flags flapping in the breeze. Up in one corner window, she spotted two boys unraveling a brand new one, the creases still in the corners. She watched them for a moment, smoothing out that stick figure humanoid and placing it right next to another rectangle displaying the rainbow.

Two flags of pride. Identities gained, discovered, accepted, and showcased. The boys behind the two flags embraced the belief they were not seen or did not care. To them, nothing else mattered.

To Dallas, it was about to matter.

She kept that number in her head and made sure it always stuck to the front, because it was a number she could count on. Ninety-one. As a student, one is conditioned to feel happy when seeing those high numbers. It meant passing, and the higher the number, the more it meant exceeding expectations. Dallas apparently exceeded expectations on this test, and it was not skill.

Perhaps when the time came to test her skill, she would be able to deliver this naturally, with no useless academia getting in the way.

She pushed open the doors and made her way to the offices, following the scent of newly brewed coffee that seemed to run twenty-four-seven, the ongoing fuel of working in administration. The door to the counselor's office was open, and she stepped to the threshold with a hand raised for a little knock.

"Come in," the woman said, middle-aged with her hair pulled back way too tight, looking like she was already tired of everything. She held a cup with three red lipstick stains across the rim. Dallas already pulled out the paper cylinder and unraveled it while the woman watched her, forming a small smirk in recognition.

"You too, huh?"

Dallas nodded and handed her the paper. "I just got my paperwork in the mail."

All Dallas could do was stand there while the school took care of what they needed to for the remainder of her classes, up until her excusal for Orientation, and then her departure from the campus. Just as they did for thousands of students leaving for the same reason. The woman put it down for a moment to type something on the computer, the paper reverting to its formed cylinder shape on its own.

She took the cylinder roll and handed it back to Dallas, all done. Dallas exhaled through her teeth in relief. She had never even chosen a major. As far as she was concerned, it was far easier for a freshman with no direction.

When Dallas walked into the YMCA, there was already signage indicating where to go, but she didn't need it. She could tell by the type of people that were going the same way. She laughed to herself at the number of wetsuits and fin shoes she saw. Another part of her was a tad concerned. Just how intense was this?

The couple who walked ahead of her wore matching surf suits and goggles on top of their heads. The amount of muscle they had was impressive, as well as their very long legs. Dallas imagined what they would look like under the sea. They would be the graceful ones to ride the waves underwater instead of on top, always balanced and diving through each undercurrent as if they could control it and never let it control them.

It suddenly reminded her of how everyone was sized up in gym class. She realized that in this world, some things would not change. She tried not to feel inferior with her less-than-athletic build.

Dallas followed this couple through the set of doors and past the sign with bright blue lettering, where a group of people of varying ages gathered by the swimming pool.

No one was in the pool and instead stood around waiting.

After a few moments, the doors opposite them opened, and a man came out who put the athletic couple to shame. The mounds in his arms, legs, chest, and stomach could have been pounded in with clay and blended before drying in the sun. The rich cocoa color of his skin made him look smooth. His hair was dreadlocked and pulled back in an artistic twist that trailed all the way down his back.

Dallas could see the tattoos snaking around his arms, but there were too many to discern what they were. He approached the pool area looking like a lifeguard, with red shorts and a whistle around his neck, flashing the group a big smile.

"Hi, humans!" He announced.

There was some murmuring among the group and some nervous giggles.

"Welcome to your first swim endurance test. This isn't really a test, and no one is going to fail. You're just going to hone your skills a little bit, and this is where I come in. So, why don't we all come together over here, and we can get started?"

He picked up a plastic bin by the door and dragged it to the pool, kicking a pair of flip-flops under a lounge chair and backing up a little, assessing the group.

"I'm Marcus, and I have worked as a lifeguard and swim instructor for as long as I can remember, until I joined the military. Now I do both, in both parts, for certain periods of time. That's the Dual Citizenship life." He held his hands up as if to stop something. "First things first, let me just go ahead and get this out of the way."

Without a beat, Marcus turned and dove straight into the pool, the disturbance of the reflected lights on the water shimmering on the walls and ceiling. He stayed under for a few moments and did not come up, causing the entire group to move closer to the edge in panic and interest. The people behind Dallas leaned forward so much, they almost pushed her over.

Marcus emerged to the surface and acknowledged the group, waiting. He held his arms up and stood on the pool floor in the shallower area, where the water came up past his navel, in mockery of some extraordinary result.

"Notice anything?"

There was silence.

"That's right, nothing happened. It's a very common misconception, and we have movies and TV shows to thank for that. News flash: this is pool water, people."

Several laughed.

"I had a guy in one of my last classes who immediately asked if they were going to watch me change. Everyone wants to see that up-close and personal horror show of morphing like the Wolfman, but it doesn't happen here. People say they want to know what color my tail is."

Marcus smiled. "For the record, it's a nice shimmery black, with some silver in the fins."

There were excited murmurs in the crowd. Marcus waved them over.

"All right, your turn. Everyone get in here."

There was a collective shedding of outer clothing and shoes, tossing them on the lounge chairs. Most people sat on the ledges and dropped into the pool, while others jumped in. Dallas was a sitter, seeing her legs disappear underwater got her excited. She got in and awkwardly jumped up on her toes to adjust to the cold temperature against her stomach.

"Everyone gather around here while we do some simple warm-up exercises. It's like a regular swim class. Nice and easy to awaken those aquatic muscles in you."

They did wall stretches, kicks, timed treading water, and floating. It was all very similar to the swimming lessons she had when she was a kid.

Next, he had everyone line up across the pool in rows to swim laps. It wasn't a race, but subconsciously everyone made it so. Dallas watched the rows ahead of her swim across the pool to the deep end, kick off the wall, and then swim right back. People used their arms in high parentheses and kicked their legs as straight as they could, all in the effort to be first or among the first to make it back to boost their own egos.

Dallas was definitely not the fastest. When she made it back to the shallow end, she watched the rest of her row stand up on the pool floor in victory while she was still making splashes. She avoided their victorious smiles for a reason. These would not be the bodies they would be swimming with. There was no need for any of that.

"Now, it's time for a little friendly competition." Marcus put the kibosh on her thoughts. "We're going to have you all get out for a while and come in groups to watch what we're going to do in the deep end."

This time when they lined up, they did so near the pool edge. Marcus had a little bucket he reached into, and then he threw a handful of something into the pool that produced hard droplets of rain, but Dallas couldn't see what sank to the bottom.

"Those are some little pearls that you are going to dive for. Let's see who can collect the most in each group."

He tossed in some more handfuls and called forth the first group.

Dallas watched the first group launch into the deep end and go hunting for those pearls. All she could see were legs whipping every which way until all the pearls were picked up, and the divers came out. They all had a few to a decent number. The second group fared just as well, with some having collected more than others. Dallas was in the third group.

She positioned her goggles over her eyes, making sure to tighten the side adjustments. When she stood at the ledge, she tried in vain to make out those pearls but could not see them until Marcus blew the whistle. She jumped in with her group and began her search. They were tiny and drab gray, but she had already picked up a few and balled them in her left hand while she swam.

She surfaced for air before diving back down to search for more. She could see the other members of her group swimming lower and lower into the depths, coming up for air and repeating the process. Dallas swam all the way down to the bottom and let the pool floor scrape her stomach once as she swam by, a trait she had always loved as a kid to signal that she met her goal of touching the bottom.

There were a few pearls in her hand now, though all the others were still searching. After taking her last breath of air, she dove back down and swam toward the ladders at the far end of the deep end, catching a glint or two.

She swam to the deepest part and snatched a few more pearls. When she turned around, she spotted the ladder nearest to her, which camouflaged well with the silver background. It was there, sitting on the lowest ladder step. Dallas didn't know if it was intentional or accidental, but she snatched it up before stepping on the ladder herself and surfacing. Marcus blew the whistle.

Dallas was the first one out from the ladder but took a moment longer to walk down to the shallow end where the rest of the group was. Her fingers were numb from being scrunched up, but she emptied them at her feet and waited for Marcus to tally everyone's counts. She had a nice little pile there, so when Marcus came to her, he stopped and raised his eyebrows in praise.

"And you have the most," he said to her surprise. "Out of everyone, and I think you were the one who collected the most total."

"I did?"

"Yep, you did. You were the fastest, and you have a keen eye, often looking in places no one else would. Kudos to you!"

"Wait, out of everyone?"

Marcus nodded. "Yeah, you did."

The others regarded her casually, but no one was more surprised than Dallas herself, who looked from her pile of pearls to the others to confirm it.

CHAPTER 3

DALLAS WALKED INTO THE lecture room with her folder and paperwork after checking in. For a moment, she felt like she would never leave school. She walked down the rows and found a seat closer to the front, where the screen displayed a large "Welcome!" message, complete with the Stick Figure Movement symbol right underneath it. She was early, but so were many others. This was a class actually worth attending.

She rested her paperwork and folder on the desk in front of her and opened it. Everything about the folder was thematically strong: It had a dark blue design with a few shimmers of light here and there, mimicking the look of underwater scenes. Dallas tried to imagine what it was like to see nothing but that in her surroundings. Was it always surrounded by thick blue darkness? Would it feel like night all the time without the sun?

Inside the folder were thick packets stapled together, along with brochures, FAQs, and the basics. One of them contained information on dual citizenship IDs and the steps to obtaining one. Dallas looked forward to changing her ID picture. Her last one was taken when she first got her driver's license; her hair was long and plain brown, resembling an unhappy curtain covering half her face. Dallas read and flipped through the materials several times, knowing most of the basics, but she was still anxious to hear more. She was even more eager to see visual proof.

A side door opened, and a springy young woman walked in. So tall and skinny, she resembled a bean pole split in half. Her dark golden hair was tied in a short ponytail. Dallas expected a university professor in a tweed coat and tie, but here was a camp counselor in leggings and ballet flats. She had a familiar and comforting smile.

"Good morning, everyone," she waved as she walked to the front of the room, making a point to look at as many people in the crowd as she could. Those talking stopped and faced forward.

"Welcome to your first day of Orientation! My name is Dana, and I have been a trainer here for four years. I have my bachelor's in marketing and media relations, and this is the best job I have ever had. Everyone is always excited, and I love helping new recruits learn everything they can about their new world...and their new selves. It's going to cover the basics, and you will have plenty of help to get you all transitioned and situated smoothly.

So, why don't we start by taking a poll? I want you to raise your hand if you are in the 50th percentile."

A few people raised their hands, albeit hesitantly.

"Okay," Dana said with a supportive smile. "The first thing I'm going to tell you is that your percentage does not matter. Your percentage is not a reflection of you. It does not mean that you will do poorly as a merman or mermaid if you are in the lower percentile. All it is is how far back your ancestry goes. Those of you in the 50th percentile had more generations on land than in the sea. You will take the time you need to transition, and once you do, you're in, and you will adapt naturally and become the best swimmers you can be."

There were nods and smiles in the audience, and Dana continued with the survey. When she reached the 90th percentile, Dallas raised her hand and looked around. There were a fair number like her—neither too many nor too few.

"So, you 90-percenters will naturally adapt a little quicker, because that's just your DNA. Your ancestors were the later immigrants to land and had quite a bit of catching up to do. So, these individuals needed more time to adapt to land. But no matter how far we have come in our evolution, our roots will always be there because our roots were always there."

She paused for a moment and assessed the group.

"Why do you think we like to go swimming?"

The room was quiet.

"There is something inside us that tells us we like the water and want to play in it. We invented sports like waterskiing, surfing, and diving. Swimming itself is an Olympic sport. Human beings decided somewhere that we can still handle the water in our new form on land and have done all of that to prove it. And no one thinks anything of it except that it is fun and because we want to. And up until now, no one understood why."

Dana had a clicker in her hand that she pressed, turning slightly to view the screen behind her. The slide changed to a screen that read, "The Basics."

Dana led the college-style lecture, the slides going in order of evolution from the ancient merpeople to the more modern ones. After a few slides, the lecture hall doors opened, and they were joined by an older woman.

"Everyone, this is Pat, another trainer who specializes in the science side of things."

Pat's unparticular gray hair color caught Dallas's attention right away. It had a light purple tint to it, so when Dallas saw her move in the light, it actually looked like a frosted grape. She liked that subtlety very much, reminding her of the shine of the side of a fish under the ocean's light.

"Everyone calls me Pat. Even my students," Pat started. "I am a science teacher, and I used to teach in two different high schools in the district but now have migrated to a new district in the West Atlantic Province, where I teach middle schoolers. I also come up on land occasionally to teach the science side to all newcomers as well. We are going to get into the practical details of our anatomy and transformation. You get the general idea of what happens, and you are going to learn more about it."

Dana pressed on her clicker, and the screen behind Pat turned to the human skeletal form, scaled large enough for everyone to see.

"Now, you may remember learning about the process when a living thing changes into another form as it grows. Caterpillars turn into butterflies, tadpoles turn into frogs, and that is called metamorphosis. Although that's a maturing transformation, ours is similar but different in the fact that while caterpillars and tadpoles change only once, people can change into merpeople and back into humans at will when they go from one environment to the other."

Dana changed the slide so that it was now the merman skeletal form, the vertebrae connecting the one big, long fish bone and branching off to smaller, separate bones in the fins.

"When your bottom half changes, your leg bones will merge together to form one tail bone and then drift apart when they change to legs again. The answer is no; it does not hurt."

Pat paused to reassure the group.

"It is more like a tingling sensation, like when your legs fall asleep and you move around to get the life back in them. It will feel weird when you do it the first few times, but I assure you, you will get used to it. It is very natural."

Pat pointed to the tailbone and the fins.

"You can see here the humerus, tibia, and fibula just come together. They don't disappear. They really turn into one big thick bone. Now, the feet? That is the easy part. You can see here your tarsals and metatarsals—foot bones that do not change that much. And your toes, your phalanges, stretch out a little bit longer to make your fins."

Dallas wiggled her toes inside her shoes, trying to imagine the equivalent of moving that fin.

"Everything else is basic and self-explanatory as far as the bone structure goes," said Pat, gesturing to the rest of the skeleton.

The next slide showed the human form, reminding Dallas of the "Operation" game.

"The next big change is your skin. Your epidermis, or top part of the skin layer, is what will change to adapt to water, forming another top layer of scales in some areas like your chest and hips, as well as changing color. You don't just develop fins on your feet; you will be getting a few on your arms as well."

Pat pointed to the forearms. "They will be here where the elbow is. And another thing that people don't know about: your hands. You will have webbing in between your fingers. You can't swim as well with the ones you have now, can you?"

Dana changed the slide, so now it looked like the game of Operation with a merperson—gender neutral—and the only thing missing was the big red nose. The picture showed a blue tail and fin with matching fins on the forearms and a scale-printed upper body. Pat stood before the screen, still describing the body while Dana left through a side door. When she came back, she was carrying a fish tank filled with water. Everyone already knew what type of water it was.

"Now," Pat said while Dana set the tank down on the table in front of her. "The only thing that's left to do here is a demonstration. You've seen it in pictures and videos, but you're going to want to see it up close and personal...before you do it yourselves with your own bodies once you are ready. Those of you in the back, if you would like to come up closer, you may."

Some people in the back rows got up and stood in the aisles near the front.

Everyone in the audience sat up a little straighter and leaned in just a bit more when Pat submerged her arm in the tank. The waters rippled in a responsive way to her, but the change was not instant. It took a couple of seconds before there was any change, and then there came some general reactions of awe and interest from the crowd.

Pat's skin color dulled to a bluish-violet, almost like it was put under fluorescent lighting, and then small bumps started to form all the way up her arm like goosebumps until they shaped into scales. The fin on her forearm fanned out into a perfect unfold. When she spread her fingers apart, transparent webbing appeared that one could make out only so far away.

Pat removed her arm from the tank, now a full-formed aquatic limb, and held it up. She waved her arm casually through the air as though it were still in water.

"Pictures and videos only do it so much justice, but here we are. The rest of your body will be similar to this, even though we know the major changes will be to the bottom."

Pat walked around the room, showing her arm to everyone. At one point, she returned to the center and began to wipe it with a towel.

"Now, everyone watch as my arm dries. Your transformation from your mer arm back to your human one takes the same amount of time, depending on how fast it dries. What happens is the mer parts are responding to the lack of water and shrinking back, disappearing back inside your markup for when it meets the seawater again. It seems very magical and supernatural, and sometimes, science just is."

Pat stood back at the center of the room as the aquatic elements on her arm disappeared down to nothing. She used the towel to wipe between each human finger. Dana took up the tank and carried it out of the room while Pat resumed.

"So yes, your transformation will be that fast. Your upper body, since it has minimal markup, will have little to change into and change out of. Your bottom body, as you know, is going to have more involvement."

Pat nodded to Dana, who clicked on the next slide, showing an animated GIF of human legs turning into a merman tail and reverting.

"So, when your legs come together, first your skin is going to fuse, and the scales will develop. Your feet will stretch down to become the fins. The opposite has your tail separating into two and the scales melting away until you are skin again. It will still be quick enough to change going from air to seawater. Are there any questions so far?"

A guy near the middle raised his hand. "So, you can wear clothing that works with both forms?"

Dana nodded. "Yes. Why don't we jump to that slide right now?"

⁂

Dallas ended the call with her parents to make her next.

"Hey! How's it going?" came her sister's excited voice.

"I just got off with Mom and Dad, and they gave me the update."

"Oh, okay. I'm so sorry; are you mad?"

"No, no. I mean, I'm a little disappointed, but it's no big deal. I know you guys did your orientation and all that already anyway, so it makes sense to get going sooner than me."

"Did you have yours yet?"

"Day one in the books."

"Well, the first few days are simple and cover the important stuff like the more interesting topics. After that, it gets a little more involved with things like registering your ID and the steps you have to take to have dual citizenship."

"Yeah, how does that work? Did you do yours yet?"

"Oh no, not until later, because you have to have your Oceanic address registered. Mom and Dad still have to get their paperwork processed for the new company location after they made that assistant manager the general manager for the one here. They have a lot going on!"

"I understand. Still, I can't wait to see this, and all of you."

"But could you imagine, Dally? The next time we see each other, we'll all...look a little different."

CHAPTER 4

DALLAS PICKED UP HER lunch on her way back from orientation, and it was, as she told herself, something she would have to get used to and acquire a taste for. She already liked the avocado crab rolls and spicy tuna, but opted for something a little braver this time. She did not remember the names of the types of rolls she ordered, only that she chose the ones with the main course sitting right on top and facing her head-on.

They looked like slices of grapefruit with the skin peeled off—pink and shiny with natural moisture, sunbathing on top of each seaweed rice roll. They smashed against the top of the clear plastic container when she closed it, already some flecks of rice having fallen off on her walk back.

Dallas only popped into her room to put her food on the counter, circling back to hit the bathroom. Inside her stall her thoughts trailed away with her, the human to Mer transformation images on the slideshow resurfacing like she could project them on the bathroom stall. The door to the bathroom opened just then, pushed in a rush, two pairs of sneakers squeaking on the floor and stopping in front of the mirror, right in front of Dallas's stall.

"This isn't normal."

"How do you know?"

"Well just *look* at this!"

Through the narrow space on the stall door, Dallas could see just enough of the girl's face and neck and the reddening, circular indents.

"It looks worse than a rash," the girl said, running her fingers under the sink water and dousing the spaces on her neck and chin. "And you're no better."

Dallas leaned to her left to see the girl next to her through the door space, a slimmer view, but this one was peeling away at skin flakes on her cheeks.

"Mine are rougher," the second girl was saying. "And like, you're supposed to shed so maybe eventually that means the scales will develop."

"*Maybe.* But we still don't know that."

The first girl continued to scoop more water on her neck and face, wiping it down and staring at her red-faced, dripping reflection while the second started to peel at her face.

"You probably shouldn't do that."

"Well what else am I supposed to do?"

"I seriously think we need to see the nurse. We took it too far."

"No, we didn't!"

"Yes, we did. It's not going to work. We *did* get scammed."

"We're only forty-five percent; it's not like we're two percent or anything and didn't stand a chance. Maybe we still do!"

"Not from knockoff pills from China or wherever they're from."

Dallas shifted her feet under and around the toilet, praying they would leave.

"It's a minor side effect."

"For now."

They both ran the sinks, washing and re-washing and over-washing and talking and over-talking.

Dallas eventually flushed and got up, exiting like she heard nothing and knew nothing, going to the next sink and seeing the girls in full view now. She tried not to stare, running her fingers through her hair as she caught the full botchery. It was like they both went tanning and fell asleep under a net or something that had holes in it, sunburning the design on their faces and necks and a few places on their arms in flaky red blotches. Dallas's arms itched looking at them, but she kept her eyes away, telling herself not to stare.

The girls gave her side views themselves, almost trying to conceal themselves. They were not people she knew, but saw them in the dorm a few times, not acquainted enough to force an uncomfortable conversation. Dallas reached for paper towels and saw the pill container on the counter between them.

The text was all in the characters of a different language, most likely Asian, with one picture that said exactly what the pills were supposed to be for. The cartoon mermaid was cheesy enough to be from a children's tv show, big eyes and smiling face to give that illusion of positivity. The girls hastily took paper towels after Dallas and wiped their arms down, one grabbing the container and shoving it in her bag and the other casting a side glance at Dallas.

They rushed out of the bathroom, leaving Dallas with the aftermath that remained in the sinks they used. The tiny skin flakes were dark pink, chunky now from being scrubbed off, looking like torn tissue after wiping a bloody nose.

She waited until she was sure they were long gone, then left the bathroom herself.

On the way back to her dorm, she passed the bulletin board full of flyers and papers, the Stick Figure one being the largest. There were dozens of smaller Stick Figures stuck all around it, bits of sticky residue left over from others that were taken off. Dallas stopped before it and took one nearest to her, pulling it off and taking it with her to her dorm, where she promptly pressed and stuck it on her door, right under her name.

One of her dorm neighbors was standing in her doorway when she came in from class. Amy was also a freshman, but she often got mistaken for younger. The way this girl carried herself made people think she was insecure and overly opinionated of the world, and when she stepped into the room, Dallas cringed.

"So, your door has a Stick Figure now, huh."

Dallas smiled at her. "Yeah."

"Are you real Mer or still trying to be?"

Dallas blinked. "Um, no, I'm real. I'm ninety-one percent."

"Oh wow! Congrats."

"Thanks."

Amy's eyes darted around the room like a rabbit scared to find a predator in the bushes. "I didn't know, because you don't have any other Stick Figure stuff up. I didn't think you were..."

"Well, I don't have much stuff. I just found out. And why would I decorate when I'm getting out of here soon anyway?"

Amy shrugged.

"So... when are you going to do it?"

Dallas raised a brow. "Do what?"

"When are you going to, like, turn?"

Dallas stared at her, noticing the way her bottom lip hung to reveal the extra wiring woven into the braces on her teeth. It certainly looked and sounded like talking with her was painful, as if she used whatever came out of her mouth to effectively trap anyone into an uncomfortable conversation.

"That doesn't happen until you're given the serum," she explained. "After you finish the first course in Orientation, it needs twenty-four hours to kick in before you do anything."

"But what if it doesn't go right?" Amy's mouth trap ensnared her. "Did you hear about that girl whose spine stretched too much while she was changing and then broke her in half?"

"You seriously can't believe everything you read," Dallas spat. "And I'm not stupid; I think I'll believe in science for my sake."

"There are a lot of cases of it going wrong," Amy added, bringing her voice just low enough. "People's skin falling off and they have to be treated."

"That's when people get some illegal knockoffs," Dallas blurted out, then bit her tongue, careful not to say too much of the girls from the bathroom. "Which are illegal, and unsafe, especially if someone doesn't test high enough to be able to change."

"You think you're still safe? Like, still, the ocean isn't safe."

"Of course it is."

"Well, my neighbor knows this guy whose cousin got killed by a shark recently," she continued, the trap wires pulling her in.

That you probably just made up on the spot, Dallas thought.

"I just heard about it," Amy continued. "He was completely ripped to shreds and was probably long dead from the loss of blood before he got eaten. Just like that. It's still not completely figured out down there, you know."

"What do you mean?"

"I mean they have civilized cities, towns, homes, and buildings, along with general protection from wildlife, but things are still out there that aren't used to humans. Well, merpeople. So, anyone who ventures out into the wilder ocean areas is at risk."

"But that's just being in the wild," Dallas noted. "Jungles, savannas, things like that where there are wild animals. It's not like anyone is living out in the open sea and sleeping between coral reefs or anything. There are safe places."

"Yeah, but it's still not as safe as it could be. Even in the places that have been turned into residences. There are still sharks, and things worse than sharks, that are around all the time! My neighbor says that they are pulling out of there. They're going to come back to land. It's not safe. You're basically asking to be eaten alive."

Dallas rolled her eyes.

"He says they aren't going to go back until it's safer, even if it takes a couple of years to really clear predators away. They are keeping their dual citizenship, but it's not going to be for a while until they recover a little bit." Amy slid one foot in and out of her flip-flop. "So, I don't know; just thought I'd warn you."

Dallas's eyebrows jumped a little. "Um, thanks, but I mean, shit happens. That's awful, but it's kind of like getting hit by a car."

"At least you know where cars are. The ocean is still a huge mystery and is so much more dangerous. And sharks and giant squid don't have brakes." Amy eyed her, chin slightly raised so her pupils aimed lower, trying to make Dallas lower her gaze.

Dallas forced a smile. "I appreciate it, but I've read a lot about it. I know what I'm getting into. It's not like I'm going to be going out hunting for sharks."

CHAPTER 5

SHE BIT THE INSIDE of her cheek as she sat in the waiting room with some of the others, her heart rate jumping faster than the beat of music coming from someone's earbuds.

Dallas hadn't done this since she was a kid, and perhaps that was what mostly made her nervous. Mostly. She slid her palms down her shirt to steady them, dry them, as she told herself over and over that the internet videos were exaggerated and would not happen.

Even though they played on repeat in her head.

She saw those images of someone screaming, their mouth opening as wide as it could before it stretched into a nozzle the size of a werewolf, lips fattening to pink inflatables before breaking out into millions of tiny bumps. She saw someone whose skin had completely hardened to rock...and another where someone's legs fused together, and they stayed that way, forever a mermaid of melted skin. But those were people who did not test high. Those were people who were not and could not be Mer. They were not her and her group.

Before, in the orientation room, Pat showed them all the slides of how it would work.

They displayed the outline of the human body with the circulatory system highlighted, and an animation of the serum injection lighting up bright green throughout the body. She could almost feel it right then and there, scratching her shoulder for good measure.

"Now, it's going to take some time for it to settle in and 'awaken' those old Mer cells of yours," Pat explained. "The serum is made with a good amount of sea salt water to help that process along. What is happening here is that it needs to pass through your circulatory system and sort of seep its way into every nook and cranny. Once it is settled in, and you come in contact with seawater for the first time, it is still going to take some time before all your Mer elements come back out."

The next slide showed an animation of the body changing from the inside out, the veins still running bright green liquid through them, with the Mer transformations taking place.

Pat and Dana reassured the group by telling them they would have lunch provided that day and they would have a longer break when they all came back. Dallas kept that thought in mind as she waited for her turn, telling herself it was no big deal, and it would be over in seconds.

The door in front of them opened, and a guy came out with his t-shirt sleeve still rolled up at the shoulder, a band-aid stuck across a tuft of cotton. Dallas saw a single dot of blue liquid seeping through the middle. The guy walked on like normal and did not appear to be in pain or light-headed or feeling anything that was now running through his body. Dallas watched him walk away without any sudden body modifications, not a single-color tint or bump on his skin. He left the waiting room to go back to the main orientation room, and Dallas turned her head to the door opening again.

"Next!"

She felt her heart flutter and got up, joining the nurse in the private room. There was a simple chair inside along with packages of bottled water. The nurse turned to the table to prepare for the next person, inviting Dallas to take a seat.

"Okay, hun, roll your sleeve up for me."

The nurse returned with a wad of cotton with a very strong alcoholic smell to it, wiping a circle around her arm. Dallas kept her focus on the wall in front of her, staring at a few holes that were poorly filled in with drywall. What did this room used to be? Someone's office? Storage? The tan paint job was covering up what looked like a pinkish color—

Dallas's natural reaction was to tense a little, but just a little. The nurse had another cotton wad ready and immediately put it on Dallas's arm after removing the syringe. She smoothed the band-aid around it and adjusted the sleeve. Dallas heard a ringing in her ear, and she moved her head slightly to try to shake it off. The nurse approached her again with a bottle of water already opened. Dallas took a few sips.

"You're all set. How do you feel?"

Dallas swallowed a bigger gulp. "All right, I guess."

"Good, because you don't feel anything and aren't supposed to. Some people get light-headed at first, but you guys are getting lunch now, and it will help. You can go now."

Dallas got off the chair and walked those few steps to the door, instantly imagining what was waking up in her legs. Her roots, her true roots, were probably protesting her walking on two legs and wanted to fuse together to get to the sea. The denim leggings she was wearing gave her the visual already... she thought perhaps her own tail would be that color.

In the main room, Dana was among a pile of boxes at the front, busy opening them and checking things off on a sheet of paper. Dallas saw a label on one that said, "Adult size medium."

Pat came in moments later with another box, dragging a large cooler behind her. The others who were back in the room were lining up, and Dallas joined them. She watched everyone give their size to Dana and come away with what looked like a blue bodysuit combined with a robe, a skirt cut in sections around the legs. It reminded her of the fancy tails that hung in the back of jackets.

"Size?"

"Medium," Dallas answered. She took her very own suit, feeling immediately that it was not quite swimsuit material but something thicker. It was not leather, but it was smooth. If she did not know any better, she would think it was made from the blubber of a whale. She almost opened her mouth to ask but instead immediately joined the others at the table where Pat waited to give her lunch.

The sandwich box sets were adorable and reminded her of school field trips with bags of chips and cookies in plastic bags. Dallas helped herself to a Pepsi and went back to her seat with her food. On the screen above her was a movie that was only appropriate, a documentary showcasing the development of underwater towns and cities.

It felt tight at first, but only at first, as the material was very stretchy. Dallas put her arms through the holes that were wider than she thought. The material fell along her body as if it were molding itself to her, ready to adjust in shape once she did. The sections hung loosely in front, by the sides, and in the back but provided weight. Across her chest was a laced-up tunic-type shirt that opened and closed where needed. There was also the part that went across her groin, complete with snaps underneath.

Dallas adjusted that under her legs and around, impressed. It even had built-in underwear for easy changes in and out of transformation. She turned in the mirror a few times for the full dressing-room view. It was a fashion statement to be made both on land and sea. Her eyes were still fuzzy from when she took out her contacts, assuring herself she would only be partially blind for a little while, until her eyes adjusted.

Dallas picked up her clothes, stuffing her socks back into her shoes, and left the dressing room to join the rest. This time, when Dallas entered the pool room, she was not hit with the familiar smell of chlorine. It was the sea—salty and fishy and—natural. And it was the best thing she had ever smelled in her whole life.

It called to her faster than bread baking in the oven, the smell of rain hitting fat leaves on trees, and even the burn of a glowing bonfire on a fall night. Dallas didn't even reach the doors; the scent stopped her right in her tracks and made her imagine those waters. She already knew what it would feel like to be surrounded by them, blanketed in that comfort, running through every pore in her skin, through each thread of hair. And it would be running through her lungs via her new gills.

Other people came behind her and broke her out of her trance. They walked through the double doors together. Here was a makeshift pool that went deeper than the average indoor pool. Dallas could barely read from the numbers on the floor; it went as far as twelve—to twenty—feet. Dana and Pat were both waiting for them, clad in the same wetsuits. When she saw them, she noticed that their hair was still a little wet, and she could make out the thin fins that had begun shrinking on their arms.

"Everybody, come on in," Pat called, having the group stretch out across the room.

"We know you're all anxious and nervous, and that's normal," Dana said.

As her eyes scanned the room, Dallas could tell they were still not quite white. The bluish color there was shrinking just as pupils would in exposure to light. They both must have gone for a little swim and then changed while everyone was changing, but how long ago? Was it something to master the more you did it?

"So, we are going to take this slowly. You are going to get in the water—this lovely ocean pool we have here. There is nothing in there besides some seaweed here and there, but it's still the real thing. It's enough to feel at home. It will take a couple minutes for your body to start reacting. Your gills will come in first, and then you can start doing the breathing exercises. Pat and I are here to help, and we're all doing this together as a group, which makes the transition easier. Okay, line up around the ocean pool, and when you're ready... get in."

Dallas took a deep breath, looking into the murky waters that resembled a mirror cast in darkness with no reflection—the kind where you thought if you stared at it long enough, your doppelganger from the other side would emerge and pull you inside.

She leapt off the edge and met that dark portal, welcoming that other self to swallow her whole.

The last time Dallas was at the beach, she felt that first icy rush of the waves when they hit her. This time, she felt a cool rush that gradually graduated into a warm rush, and then the water just...reacted to her. And then she reacted to it.

Tiny bubbles escaped from her nose, but she held on to the air inside her lungs, preserving it so that her new programming could do its work. She fluttered her eyes, opening them just a crack, and a little more each time until she didn't squint and looked at the ocean water with fully open eyes. As it was on land, her vision was still blurry without her contact lenses, but she could make out the fuzzy shapes of all the other legs kicking and treading water all around her.

The dark matter swallowed her eyes first. It started at the edges and pooled in inch by inch until her vision became narrower, down to the pinpricks of her pupils.

Dallas felt something slimy between her fingers at the same time her forearms began itching. It was nothing, however, compared to what was going on with the spaces on her neck underneath her ears. One side of her was yelling at her to surface for air; her lungs exhaled the last of the breath she had, and now they were telling her she needed to take in more. But there was another side to her that was saying it was all right; she did not need to do so.

For the slight itching she felt on her arms, it came across tenfold on her neck, so much that it was actually starting to hurt. She could feel the skin there moving, warping, and stretching to try to form something else or to make room for something else. By instinct, she raised her fingers to her neck and felt them forming, felt the slit-like holes in her neck. And then she felt them stretching, the edges of skin folding over into rough-textured rolls.

Dallas felt the bubbles come out of those slit holes and realized that her lungs were already moving in and out in breath like they usually would.

She took a breath and felt it escape from the spaces right below her ears. Dallas also touched her ears to note the tiny little fins along the top. It gave her ears a new ruffled shape that was not quite Elven but amused her to think they were similar.

As Dallas moved her arms around in the water, she could see the faint outline of their new shape as those forearm fins were starting to come in, and the gossamer webbing between her fingers. They were still too blurry to make out as her eyes desperately tried to blink away the black pools they were drowning in. But as she moved her hands in front of her face to see those changes, to make out her skin color turning a diffused shade of blue, her eyes began to sharpen.

Suddenly, every spare inch became clear. Like ink droplets on a watercolor painting, she could see those scales. They sprouted up and down her skin in iridescent blue and green, reflected in the water. Dallas moved her sight beyond to gauge how her far-distance vision was now focusing, and she was filled with wonder at the scene before her.

All those same pairs of legs that only moments ago kicked had now come together, pumping as one. The feet fanned out into fins, slowly recognizing their movement. She glanced from one to the next, to the ones closer and the ones further away, all in various stages of leg and tail hybrids but all with one thing in common: They were no longer human.

As though the ends of magnets, her own legs joined together in a diffusion of skin. Dallas flew her hands down to her groin, remembering unsnapping that fabric, although her body was already two steps ahead of her and had started to come undone on its own. Her robe garments danced around her as though they were a part of her as well, learning to move in accordance with her new form.

There was another thing she could pick up now. For all the images dancing in her vision, some were merely replicas.

Dallas caught her own reflection and did not recognize herself. She was a painting, a creature born from the smears on a palette that translated to every part of her. Even her hair, the old wood brown, was now washed with a blue darker than her skin.

She watched her slightly longer legs wave as one, the very same iridescent blue-green scales on her arms popping up all throughout her body, matching all the way down to her very own fins. She continued to waver in place, allowing the water to flow all around her, brushing every scale and running through each strand of her hair. And she breathed that water, in and out, in and out, feeling an unidentified power somewhere in the deepest parts of her diaphragm.

CHAPTER 6

To GET TO THE sea, she first had to travel through air.

There were normally large groups going from the Midwest to Florida for touring, so they all seemed to fit in their own way. Dallas met up with the group, her overflowing backpack bouncing at her backside, and checked in with Dana.

Once they all boarded the non-stop plane to Miami, the sliver of land separating them from their new home, Dallas reached out to touch her backpack, specifically to find and touch the Stick Figure button for luck and support. She relaxed against her seat as the plane produced those familiar rumbling noises and tried to make herself comfortable.

She opted for a *National Geographic*, immersing herself in the issue's cover article. Apparently, colonizing in the Arctic Sea proved to be challenging due to the cold. Go figure. Since the earlier sea-groundbreaking officials had built a number of homes designed to withstand it and provide the right amount of warmth while at the same time not interfering with natural temperatures. She moved on to the next page.

Across the first page was a single photo of a large jaw with rows of sharp teeth. The article continued on the second page, along with smaller photos of merpeople wearing wetsuit uniforms for some marine life group, an abbreviated name she did not know.

> ...over the years they have been putting their best practices to use to control predator populations. The ever-growing controversy continues with endangered species and wildlife protection, but with the advancement of oceanic civilization, it has become clear that it is necessary to eliminate the present dangers. Many have worked on moving certain species to aquariums both in sea and on land in safe separation. Hunter/Gatherers have rights of natural survival to abide by and are trained to do so by any means necessary.

Dallas looked at another picture of merpeople holding long spears, polished in silver and ending in a single sharpened triangle. They reminded her of the photos of ancient ancestors with their tooth spears, the very first hunter/gatherers, and just how similar they looked.

Her tablet was still out with messages sent and messages in queue to be received, so when the shuttle doors opened, she stepped out with her eyes still on it.

Okay, when you get to the docking area, have your ID ready and then they will bring you underneath to those transition areas.

Almost immediately after her dad's text came another one from her mom:

You'll be going in with your group, and you'll all do it together again.

And then, of course, her sister:

You'll be in a submarine, and you'll see fish and stuff through the windows!

Dallas got out of the shuttle with her tablet in her hands while she eyed the other people moving like a school of fish to the docks. The way their heads bobbed up and down due to the different heights and levels of terrain, they almost looked like they were actually swimming.

About to go in! Text you guys once we're there and I get my address!

She texted back to all before flipping her tablet shut and putting it in the pocket of her robe. Yes, they also had pockets. Zippered ones.

Dallas joined the ranks in the march to new beginnings. It was almost ceremonial, the way the morning sun climbed in the sky just as they would be descending down. It was as if they were bypassing the day on land since they would be beginning their own day under the sea, far below where the dawning sun would never touch and would not manage them.

She watched the people ahead of her start to make preparations, sitting down to take off shoes and socks and put away backpacks. Many had their aquatic clothes underneath their land clothes and simply took off those outer layers. Dallas had taken care of that already in the shuttle. She had her own set in her backpack and was glad not to have to fumble with the protective outer bubble they all had to get.

She wondered, once she got under there, how much her backpack would float, and in general wondered a lot about how dry things functioned underwater with their protective coverings. She wondered how many things would function underwater.

"Right this way, people!" called a familiar voice ahead, and Dallas saw Pat waving the group closer, her arm as high as it could go. The group inched forward before the docks where the submarine waited, its door open all the way, ready to close its mouth around the school of fish. There were two men beside Pat with their own tablets open and attachable scanners.

"Everyone gather around here. I need to do a roll call, so when I call your name, come forward so I can check you off, then go see either one of these guys to scan your ID."

Dallas formed a smile that did not falter. When Pat called her name, she was proud to present her new ID, her picture a mirror image of herself. When she was in the sea, there would only be a few subtle differences. Dallas looked at her photo again, visualizing the blue skin, the sporadic stipple of green scales, finned ears, gills, and, of course, those aquatic-dyed eyes, irises a darker shade of sapphire, almost black. An image that would be recreated in a short amount of time. The new self to greet the new world.

When Dallas found a seat in the submarine, she buckled her seatbelt as instructed. Pat came in last to the front-most seat that was assigned to her, counting heads with the tip of a pen. Dallas had to laugh at the whole scene, taking her back-to-school field trips. Everyone was anxious and full of excitable energy, moving around every which way in their seats to share their excitement with each other. The only real difference here was that those along for the ride were not children but teens and adults.

"Settle down," Pat, the teacher chaperone, called down the unruly rows. "We are going to launch off and then dive under to meet the ocean very soon. It is a very slow and smooth and pleasant ride, but your seatbelts are there for your safety and comfort, as we don't need you all floating all over the place once we're traveling. You'll have enough room to stretch anyway. And, of course, you know the view will be very scenic."

Pat and the assistants sat down as the driver started the engine, pulling away from the docks. Dallas's seat was in the middle row, closer to the aisle, so she looked to both her left and right as the submarine drifted out a little further and then began its descent.

CHAPTER 7

Dallas relaxed while she waited for the water to rise.

She heard it begin to pour in from the vents on the sides of the submarine, and soon it would fill the entire space.

She looked out the window for one last glance at the clear, open sky...shrinking in size as they descended. That vibrant blue scene merged into another, shifting from crisp cobalt to a wavering shimmer...and then finally darkening to a thick opacity when the sky was officially gone. Just as the water seeped over the window above and filled the horizontal panes, it began to fill the interior.

They braced themselves, just as instructed, preparing for what they had already experienced once before.

The water pooled in at a leisurely pace, washing over their feet and making its way up their legs. Following instructions, they all loosened their seatbelts slightly to allow room. Dallas tugged on hers as she adjusted the snaps on her tunic, feeling the water rise up to her knees, then to her stomach, sending chills across her skin until it reached her neck. She pinched her lips as the water line tingled them, then went past her nose and eyes, finally enveloping her head completely.

She shut her eyes as she felt that first icy rush of the waves. This time, the cool sensation gradually transformed into warmth, and the water seemed to react to her. And then she reacted to it.

Tiny bubbles escaped from her nose, but she held onto the air inside her lungs, preserving it so her new programming could take effect. She held on to it, just as the sides of her neck began to itch.

Her body tingled in the now familiar sensation, the second time. Dallas let her legs drift lifelessly in the water and let them do their work all while feeling like she was in a hot tub with actively flowing jets hitting every inch of her body. When she was little, she remembered being in a jacuzzi and completely submerging underneath it to feel what it was like. Warm, welcoming, massaging. The cool-hot tingles all over her body were making their own cocoon they were engulfing her in, the privacy of the transformation, her equivalent of wings fanning out from her arms, and then bigger ones at her feet.

Dallas's fingers loosened on the seat, allowing more bubbles to exhale.

As the sub dipped, and the tingling sensation strengthened, Dallas got the urge to open her eyes, though her eyes were still human. They were blinded to the darkness of the deepening ocean; not able to make out any kind of silhouette at all, but she could hear the release of bubbles around her to signal the others were all breathing, learning to breathe, the gentle hum here and there of those that were trying to find their voice.

She blinked, she fluttered her eyes, watching that deep blue-black lighten, sharpening the seats of the submarine in front of her to all the heads of floating hair all around her. And then Dallas felt a rush of something wash over her, something cold-hot, something that awakened everything inside her at the same time it lulled her to want to sleep. She blinked her eyes again to focus as the waters again shifted colors, the shades of blue only the creatures of the deep could see.

The vessel dipped slightly as it slid down a slope, like a toboggan riding down snow, and the fish began to swim away the deeper they went. Dallas watched out the window as the water deepened to midnight, and any dark shapes on the ocean floor could have been rock formations or the outlines of some sea beast waiting to awaken. Dallas could not see much ahead of her, but she could feel when the sub was no longer touching the sandy bottom...suddenly floating, floating somewhere below.

The last time she looked up at the window, she could see the outline of the sea floor they had just left, a wide-open mouth that had swallowed them whole. As they moved further in, that hole shrank until it closed and disappeared.

She saw the life-sized aquarium that was now their landscape: the ocean floor, gliding along a sandy road and passing bushes of coral and trees of stone. Everyone made cries of awe and delight at the colorful fish that swam by occasionally, the creatures in return flashing their slime-green eyes before darting away into the coral.

"We're making good time," Pat said to all of them, jolting Dallas out of her reverie as she heard what speech sounded like underwater for the first time. She pulled out one of her earbuds, surprised.

She expected it to sound somewhat muffled, like something over a PA system, their voices like the rest of them having to learn to swim through. But Dallas heard Pat's voice hit her like it went through her earbud.

It was true, then, that sound did carry faster underwater, the sure opposite of what she believed. Even so, their voices were still somewhat bubbly but with a hint of vibrato, a merperson's own equivalent purr of a cat and hum of a bee—both pleasant in sound and feel. It was as if Dallas could feel the words swimming right inside her head, gently nudging to ensure they were received.

She loved that Pat's tail was a vibrant violet, complementing the lighter shade of her hair. Or, more accurately, her hair had changed to complement her tail, much like her own.

Dallas waved her fins casually from her seat, fumbling with her music device and earbuds. It looked like a regular media player one could find at an electronics store, and she almost thought it might become popular enough to sell in brick-and-mortar stores on land because of its design.

The backlight was programmed to withstand darker surroundings, illuminating her thumbs as she scrolled through her latest downloads. It was similar to her new tablet, but this equipment was marvelously built to function underwater.

She opened her email to find her welcome letter with her new address:

806042 Gneiss Underway
West Province, West Atlantic

It looked both familiar and foreign, like an address one wouldn't expect to see. West Atlantic. The welcome sub had carried them down that road in the West Atlantic, with the occasional bundles of sea tumbleweed rolling past the windows. Once Dallas's eyes adjusted, it was almost as if it weren't dark at all. The blue around them lightened to a tranquil yet vivid sapphire, and even the different colored fish appeared brighter than before.

She could see small scuffles in the sand, particles kicked up in bursts as whatever was down there buried itself deeper. Things too small for Dallas to see zigzagged between tufts of seaweed. Ahead, people craned their heads this way and that to see the towering structures that loomed in the distance. Other places. Dallas remembered them from the maps in their email packets but hadn't memorized the names. She only remembered one.

Soon enough, that one came into sight, but they didn't need to get close to see that it was not just one. It was one city but could easily be mistaken for several large factories networked together. It resembled a cluster of gracefully sculpted ice cubes rounded at the edges, held together with iron foundations and frameworks, all layered on top of one another in every direction.

Each building was made to reflect that permanent live aquarium view. Dallas stared at the pipes connecting each around the sides: long and curved, with the rush of water flowing through each one.

They looked exactly like waterslides.

The vessel stopped directly in front of what would be the front of these many connecting circuits. There were large, rounded holes on both the bottom and the top, which soon revealed themselves to be doors. A panel slid open on the uppermost right, and a merwoman swam out holding a box, heading toward a canyon with a building nestled among it. Everyone was then allowed to unbuckle their seatbelts, floating an inch or two above their seats before pressing against the windows like packed sardines.

Pat got up and opened the doors. All the merpeople filtered out in an irregular single-file line. Dallas drifted down the sub stairs without ever touching them, equally stunned by the two things she was simultaneously being introduced to. First, naturally, was the revolutionary civilization that was her new home. Second was the open ocean, already welcoming yet still vast, and too quiet, like an open trap.

"Welcome to Gneiss Underway, everyone," Pat announced.

CHAPTER 8

THEY FILTERED OUT, IMMEDIATELY distracted by the goldfish bowl turned multi-layered metropolis. It resembled a welcome brochure for upscale condominiums or a top-of-the-line shopping mall. The hallways stretched down with various rooms scattered throughout. Without the necessity of gravity, as they had seen outside, there was no need to keep everything confined to ground level. Above their heads, merpeople swam in and went down different corridors in those waterslide pipes.

Dallas and the rest of the launchies swam up to the entrance, talking excitedly amongst themselves as Pat led the way.

"Get out your IDs and be ready to scan at the door," she told them.

In a somewhat automatic rhythm, the tails of all the merpeople in the group began to sync together and pump as one. Pat opened the door first, and they all scanned their IDs in an orderly fashion. Once the doors slid open, they went right in. Dallas watched as those moving through the tubes did so with fluidity, wondering if the end of those tubes would cause an outburst into a pool, just like those in water parks.

Pat took a moment to talk with other merpeople nearby who seemed to be waiting for the new launchies. One was a thirty-something woman, another a smiley younger man, and the last a middle-aged man with an impressive Santa beard. They watched the group with interest.

"Everyone, I'd like to introduce your envoys: Rebecca, Henry, and Liam. They serve as your leaders and guides in the residential and community areas and are your go-tos for pretty much everything you need. They all have their specialties in different areas. I leave you with them now to guide you on your official tours, as I must get back to what I do best: teaching middle schoolers."

Pat smiled as she handed the last of the folder files to the leaders. "You are all official West Atlantic residents, so it's time to explore your new homes!"

The three leaders came forward with the folders, dividing the group into alphabetical sections. The middle-aged envoy swam forward with his folder of names.

"Last names beginning A-H, come to me."

If anyone could be descended from Poseidon or Neptune, it was this merman. He was of medium build with a tummy of blubber, but when he moved the right way, he revealed some muscle hidden underneath. His arms had the knots in the right places, with tattoos in planned spots and hints of scars in unplanned ones.

He looked at the group with cool yet perceptive eyes, a pale mixture of blue and gray. They matched his hair and beard, which looked like chalk drawings that ran together in the rain, blue, gray, and white cascading all the way down to his tail. He addressed the group in a tone as authoritative as a drill sergeant, but Dallas immediately saw through that to the paternal core. This was a guy who, as a human, definitely carried his kids on his shoulders and bounced them on his knee with a big Santa Claus laugh.

"I'm Liam, and the first thing I want to tell you about me is that I have no problem kicking any one of your asses when I have to and loving the hell out of you when I want to. Don't listen to what anybody says about me being a softie because it's not true. I eat trouble for breakfast. Now, we've got a lot to show you, and there's a lot to see, so you will need to keep up the best you can."

Liam led the small group down a hallway with a rock texture that was lime green and appeared to be very smooth. Dallas recognized it as serpentine from reading about oceanic architecture, and she really liked the color. She ran a hand down it as she swam past to confirm its smoothness, tracing the lines with her fingernail.

They passed through other corridors and open areas that looked inviting and recreational. There were abundant seating areas that looked like living room sets that simply sank all the way down there. The chairs were cushioned and plush, long enough to fit a merperson laying there.

Dallas was dying to scoot over and feel one, to squeeze that cushion to see if tiny bubbles came out. She soon saw that those seating areas were there to accommodate the place everyone now gathered near, something straight out of a college campus.

"As you can see, this is one of our Fast Eats. There is one on every floor, and they're great when you just want to grab a quick bite or drink."

Dallas craned her neck to try to scope out the menu and see what was in the little take-out cartons in the windows. Liam seemed like he was going to take the group in to tour the place, but he stopped when another merman appeared close to him and mumbled something in his ear. Liam nodded, and they mumbled some more.

"...why, what about—"

"Just take them somewhere else. We can't go this way now. That exit over there is being blocked off."

Liam's face changed, his eyes betraying alarm as he blinked them away once he faced the group again.

"Sorry, gang, looks like they're doing maintenance over here or something. Come this way, and I'll show you around over here."

The group complied, though when they swam away, Dallas saw that merman dash over to another merman and a mermaid floating nearby, looking like they were wearing special uniforms.

"Was someone else hurt?"

"Shhh, don't let any of them hear you."

They swam away before Dallas could hear anything else, heading out the exit that was supposedly blocked off.

Liam swam faster than before, leading the group down the corridor until they came to an open area, where different levels circled above them.

Traffic in the area was high. Merpeople swam around them and above them, darting in and out of tubes and gliding down corridors. Some wore clothing—long tunics designed to wrap around long tails—while others wore nothing at all, fully embracing their new, natural forms.

Dallas noticed the ones wearing black tunics right away because they all looked the same and were with a larger pod of merpeople. They had to be important, because when they swam down from a higher level, everyone else got out of their way. Liam extended an arm and gestured for the launchies to do the same.

"Out of the way, please," one of them near the front said.

They all complied without question, though with quizzical expressions. Dallas caught sight of the emblems on the uniforms, noting how some had stripes. Like ranks. The last merman in line had several stripes...and a holster around his waist holding several weapons.

"Official business," was all Liam said. And with that, he pumped his tail to swim upward.

The group followed, watching both their tails propel them through the water and the parts of the building that passed them by. Other passing merpeople watched them approach, some with raised eyebrows. Others had their backs turned to the glass walls, the open windows, crowding over one another to see what was happening outside.

"Keep moving, people."

Liam led them to one of those tubes once they reached the second level. Wide-open shelves stacked on top of one another created three stories, with no need for barricades or railings. The circular hole before them was wide, and Dallas didn't need to be close to hear the roar passing through it.

"Now these are our pipelines, and they can get you to wherever you want to go in town. The ones connecting other buildings are opaque, while the ones leading out to sea are clear. Sometimes, if you're lucky, there'll be some fin friends to race with you. For any outside travel, we have our subs to take you to other places."

Liam ducked into the hole, seeming to swim faster into it. But once Dallas entered, she realized that wasn't the case. Something seemed to pick her up and do the swimming for her. The current. The literal "go with the flow." She lifted her arms and waved her fins against the current as she was body-surfed through the giant tube.

The current made her go faster, and she felt a numbness in her cheeks as she dashed through. The release at the end felt like a slide as Dallas tumbled, her head ducking under and sending her tail into a whirlwind of flips. She struggled to gain control and see where she was, but before she could do anything, a strong hand grasped hers and pulled her down.

"Easy now," came Liam's voice, steadying her. "You still don't have your sea legs yet. Well, you know what I mean."

Once Dallas's head stopped spinning, she was able to see where they were in an upright position. Many merpeople were slowing down and rubbing their heads, with some drifting down from a higher launch. Liam looked at all of them.

"You always go with the current, not against it. Should you find yourself wanting to break off and go in a different direction, swim in the direction of the current to gain control, then move to the side. Never about-face and try to swim directly against it."

Liam made sure he had the entire group together and brought them away from the tube opening. "As you saw, sometimes merpeople come flying out of there like cannons shot off. More experienced ones know how to slow themselves down but always keep that in mind to avoid collision."

Dallas looked around the room they were in, the wide-open space with more corridors. This area had its own cushioned seating and, sure enough, underwater vending machines, letters glowing white and yellow advertising familiar brands. Of course, Dallas realized exactly where they were, because she had seen plenty of welcome reception areas before...but none were this nice. "Nice" had always been something out of her price range. Liam told them what was down the corridors, but Dallas already knew, already felt it.

She was home.

They opened into an area where the mound of rock had various holes carved into it, stretching around the bend, sharp and chiseled, then smoothed to resemble individual little caves, sealed with rounded doors.

It turned out, they were just that. Inviting, yet private. Various, yet patterned and strategically placed like the architecture of any apartment complex. Dallas shook her head at the sight.

No, it was better.

And when they received their folders with their apartment numbers on them, Dallas did not hesitate. They would have thirty minutes to get acquainted with their new homes, put things away, and meet Liam back where they arrived.

She swam toward the door with her number on it, reminding her of the rounded top of a barrel. The only thing missing was a knob. Dallas held out her ID to the pad on the right, and the gold lights surrounding it lit up, raising the door in seconds. She swam in, expecting to find a light switch for darkness, but she was not completely in the dark.

The golden hues lighting up her door radiated from the rock walls in shimmering colors of yellow, light green, and turquoise. She ran her hands down the walls, smooth as gemstones, just like those in the main building. She had seen a picture in a magazine once of someone standing on a driveway above what looked like some gasoline spill, reflecting rainbow colors across the pavement.

This reminded her of that photo—a beautiful phenomenon that could only be explained by science. Science had a word for this, and it was bioluminescence.

And it charged up the entire cave home.

Dallas turned the corner to the kitchen and dining area first. The little table there was an actual table, or perhaps one made so well it resembled one—smooth and cylindrical with matching chairs. Next, she turned to the kitchen area, which had appliances that appeared to be made out of some kind of rock, and on the table was a plate of something and a note.

"Welcome home, Dallas Dwight!"

On the plate were two slabs of brown squares. Dallas picked one up and sniffed it, curious to discover that her sense of smell was actually stronger underwater. Then she took a big bite of the chocolate and already knew it was the best she'd ever had. She carried the bar with her as she swam down the other little hallway to locate everything else, including the bathroom, which held appliances that looked nothing like the ones she knew. If they stood alone, she would never guess what they were for.

Finally, she arrived at what was her bedroom, scanning her eyes up to the oversized hammock stretched across the cave-like walls. It really did look like a cave—a cozy little nook hollowed out for hibernation. Dallas swam up to this hammock, pulling at the ends of the soft, thick material before rolling into it, instantly swinging into a rocking burrito.

She wrapped it around herself with pleasant surprise at how abundant the material was, and that's when she noticed the window. The waters waved as far as the light stretched, with outlines of fish swimming in the distance. She wondered what she would discover greeting her every morning when she woke up.

CHAPTER 9

SHE SWAM BACK THROUGH the kitchen to grab the last square of chocolate before heading back out, tucking her ID back into her pocket. The door closed behind her without further action.

Naturally, many of the others were happily snacking on their welcome treat. Liam stood nearby, grinning at everyone.

"Tastes almost the same, if not better, huh? Well, we grow our own cacao beans, along with everything else. Now, follow me while I take you somewhere very important."

Dallas gobbled the rest of her chocolate as they went down more corridors and then into another pipeline. This one went on longer, so much longer that they were no longer in the same building. The tube was clear, showing their travel across the ocean, their shadows broadcasted on rock structures beneath and to the right.

To the left, what looked like a mirrored image was another pipe going in the opposite direction, another pod of merpeople going about their own business. Where they landed was somewhere quite different and advanced. The stone had a white marble polish mixed with complementary light and dark colors.

Dallas noticed that the merpeople swimming around wore different kinds of garments in silver and peach colors. The ceiling soared higher here, no doubt pointed at the top, giving it the outline of a palace.

"This is the viceroy's headquarters," Liam explained. "All the envoys work around here. His office is just up this way."

Dallas was taken aback. They would be meeting the viceroy? She remembered meeting the town mayor on school field trips and taking class photos, but this was different. The viceroy would have the paperwork for all the new launchies entering society. What would he say to them based on it?

Liam greeted a few merwomen and mermen who passed by them in a corridor filled with closed doors and another pipeline at the end. They went down another one and into a room where a merwoman dressed in a sharp gown worked at a glowing desk with computer monitors.

"Hello, Liam. He is speaking with some Marine Force officers right now, so if you wouldn't mind waiting here, I'll tell him you're here."

"Thank you," Liam said, turning to the group. "Viceroy Westburn is a good merman. He values order and organization, ensuring everything and everyone is in their proper place. He believes in and cares about each working cog and wheel to create a well-oiled machine."

The group lingered in the waiting area, although the envoy stayed at the front desk, continuing to talk privately with the merwoman there, his back turned. Dallas saw the merwoman's eyes widen a little while she spoke, although Dallas could not hear what she was saying. Every now and then, the merwoman would look back at the group as if she wanted to ensure no one was listening.

A door to a nearby office opened, and an envoy merman came out holding a stack of papers. A photo of a young mermaid with the word "missing" across the top in large red letters was visible.

A pink light illuminated the reception desk, and the merwoman there indicated to Liam and the group.

"All right, folks, fins in line now."

They swam down to another room that was already open for them, one much larger and round-shaped on the inside. As they entered, a small pod of Marine Force officers passed by on their way out, appearing to be in a hurry. They waited until they were out of earshot and grouped together at the far end of the hallway to talk. Liam ushered the group inside the office.

Furniture dotted along the sides, but the center of focus was the desk panel that horseshoed around a merman sitting there. He was younger than Liam, but his exact age was unknown, with slick blue-black hair that reached the nape of his neck.

Viceroy Warren Westburn looked as he did in their packets with the welcome letter; in his picture, he had a small smile that conveyed seriousness but also kindness. Now, as he looked up at the incoming group, he produced that same smile and swam up to meet them. His own tail was jet black, and when the light bounced off it, it revealed hints of silver.

"Welcome to Gneiss Underway, everyone. We hope you got to see everything—well, mostly everything, as there is still plenty to see and learn about in our town. I am Warren Westburn, and I've been the viceroy here for eight years. We are a growing community and continue to expand, and each new merperson who joins us will bring something new to the table."

Behind him was the span of a rectangular window, where Dallas could see more pipelines and even some additional buildings in the background. Beyond that, she noticed places that were not connected via the pipelines at all, almost hidden by a garden of long-grass kelp.

"I want you to take your time getting settled, exploring everything, and learning as much as you can. There is plenty to become involved in once you find what you want to do. Many merpeople are bringing their experience from their education and jobs on land down here, and those can definitely be accommodated in whatever you put on your file."

Dallas felt a tiny chill start in her stomach; afraid someone would catch on to the things she had fabricated.

"But merpeople are also getting involved in new things and trying things they have always wanted to try. We are going to help you, as many have needed this society as an opportunity to start over. If you think about it, that is exactly what we, as a species, are doing."

The viceroy emitted a glowing demeanor when delivering this sentence, caught up in the high of addressing fresh-faced new residents, but this glow quickly diminished with the interruption of a Marine Force merman.

"Sir," he spat, the word sharp enough to cut into the soft and cheery atmosphere. "Sir, I apologize for interrupting, but I need a word."

Viceroy Westburn's smile faltered as he immediately floated out of his seat.

"Excuse me," he addressed the group now with forced cheer and an equally forced smile. He went with the Marine Force to the other side of the room, where they bowed their heads. Although Liam took the time to stall and distract the group by telling them interesting facts about the town's history and development, Dallas mostly tuned in and caught a word or two of the private discussion.

"...blood that was found matched the DNA of the missing mermaid...have gone out to diffuse the waters immediately to throw off the trail...predator in question still unknown. No predators at all have been spotted."

The viceroy spoke in quieter tones.

"...to increase forces at once. Nothing should be so close to civilized areas and whatever you do, do not raise any alarm."

"...will put in the call to marine life conservationists..."

"I ask that you please keep your voice down and keep this out of the public ear. You understand?"

"Yes sir."

After a few more murmurs, the Marine Force merman left the office, and Viceroy Westburn returned, his face slightly pale, but he forced it to make that very same smile from earlier.

"Yes, well... where were we now?"

Dallas finished putting her things away in her bedroom furniture, which served as a dresser and cabinets, enjoying finding the various compartments that opened and what would fit. She had a few of her favorite books, water-bound for a cheap price, and placed them inside the nooks.

For the one in her bathroom, she already filled it with necessities, finding comfort in the familiarity of routine. Dallas put everything away except for the long comb, running it through her water-logged hair. She smiled at herself in the mirror, still unable to process that the art form before her was her reflection, for even her hair changed with the rest of her. The brown turned blue, and her formerly bleached ends were now green. She combed through her hair, watching each strand fall in line together and swim back into formation after being combed. She waved her whole head, watching all of them dance, promising they would never frizz out or give her bad bed head ever again.

She swam back out to the living room area, where her tablet rested on the big, cushioned oval.

> You know where to find us, right? You know which pipeline to use?

Dallas picked up the tablet and typed away.

> Yeah, I know where it is. 516?

The text box lit up as her mom and dad were typing.

> That's it!

> If you get lost, we'll come out there and find you.

> We can't wait to see you and hear all about it!

> Safe swimming!

Dallas responded with a smiley face and flipped her tablet shut. She dashed out of her house as the door clicked shut behind her and navigated this caved neighborhood.

Déjà vu struck her as she took in the residences, the very scene she left on land but flipped upside down. The Stick

Figure Movement banners were the same, though many were personalized, graffiti-drawn on wavy lines below the torso indicating what the figure should remain as. There were bulletin boards holding flyers for mer-transitioning support groups and self-care guides, and another one for a used marine clothing drive for new merpeople.

What stood out on this information pegboard were other flyers that were handmade, spread out and scrawled in bright red lettering like bad acne:

DANGER

ATTACKS ON THE RISE.

Sharks still live here!

Marine Force is now recruiting. Join today!

There was another flyer that was torn off, but one part of it still remained: part of the red letter "M" that Dallas recognized from the viceroy's office. She knew what the rest of that word said, but another flyer advertising safe swimming procedures was stapled right on top of it as though to erase it from existence.

CHAPTER 10

She went through one pipeline and then took a moment to locate the others and where they connected. Dallas swam through what looked like a shopping mall, with caverns opening up into various types of shops.

There was another pipeline ahead that would take her opposite the viceroy's office and even further. She zipped through that pipeline and could tell she was going the right way once those makeshift greenhouses came into view. She smiled as they became more plentiful, popping up beneath her in that tube as she sailed through the ocean.

It brought her to the Queen Mother of those little greenhouses: a room with clear domes housing fat-fanned leaves of plants she had never seen before. They lined the walls in what looked like decoration or both decoration and purpose. She took out her tablet.

> Okay, I am in the center of this building, I guess, which looks like a mini town on its own for gardening! Which tube should I take?

While waiting for a response, she swam over to the "houseplants" in their own little trough by a window. They looked like long waves of lasagna. Although green, she sensed they were actually more flowers than plants. The edges of those waves hid stripes of pink and red.

Her tablet buzzed, and she read the message:

> Keep going to the one to the far left, #12.

Dallas swam down the corridors to the pipeline of choice, where two mermen had already opened the door and swam in. She ducked in behind them and rode the current to another suburb, greeted by lanterns speckled across the rock, lighting up each door to the homes. They were a little different than the ones by her, encased in balls of twine with light peeking through. After some scanning, she finally came to the right one and pressed the intercom button.

Seconds later, she was buzzed in, and no sooner did that door open than she was tackled in a backwards tumble.

She scrambled to gain control of the momentum as a flash of purple-pink smeared her vision.

"Dally!"

Dallas hugged her tightly, and when they righted themselves, she got a good look at the new mermaid that was her big sister. Her long, once-brown hair was now a light purple that almost looked pink, matching her bright eyes and tail, which combined this purple with a subtle hint of blue that was in Dallas's. Her sister's hands went to her face as she looked her up and down, fingernails already painted to match. A pleasant, flowery scent dabbled in the webbing between her fingers, also purple, the same shade that reflected off her skin.

"Dally, you look great!"

"So do you!"

"Oh my God, look at your hair! I love it! And look how much it matches your tail! Dad's is the same color! And Mom's is purple too, like mine!"

Dallas laughed at the excitement they were both projecting, and it didn't take long for her to see how her parents turned out for herself. Dallas's mouth opened in awe at the same time theirs did upon seeing one another.

She saw their familiar faces. They were morphed, but the recognition in their familiarity did not fail to shine through. She saw their eyes dyed with little drops of ink, but the centers were still the same eyes that had looked upon her as she grew up, and they were now the same ones that looked upon her newfound growth with pride.

The scales that lined the sides of their faces replaced any wrinkles etched into their human skin before. But when they smiled, the hints of those former wrinkles showed themselves, performing the joy that was more than skin deep.

When Hugh was younger, he told them the story of how he dyed his hair bright green and got grounded, recalling how he took hours scrubbing the spills and stains in the bathroom sink. The only thing that dye ended up coloring for good was the washcloth. Now, he got to wear that color naturally, but the deeper emerald easily beat out the slime color from his youth. In his face, she could see the subtle green wash that was his new skin tone.

Naomi's was the same, though her blue was akin to a denim color, lightly spread in all the right places. Her hair was just as dark, but hers had turned the color of midnight blue, matching the irises in her eyes. She wore it loose around her shoulders now, and Dallas realized she mostly only saw her with a neatly coiled bun at the back of her head. Her hair floated freely on its own, doing as it pleased, and she was letting it do just that.

"Dallas, oh my, look at you!"

"You made it!"

"Look at you!"

"Look at you!"

This, of course, led to another round of hugging.

"Amazing. Just amazing."

"Come on in, we have quite a bit to catch up on!"

Dallas was led to the living room, taking in all the décor and conversations. She noted some things they had in their home on land—little treasures they could not leave behind, old family photos in waterproof frames. Photos of them when they first opened their business, standing outside a greenhouse, Dallas being the little swollen ball in Naomi's abdomen.

"I just love the new greenhouses," Dallas proclaimed. "I saw a few of them in the pipeline."

"It really is amazing," Naomi said. "We grow our produce in the ones a little further back. We mostly do fruit for now, and oh, we can't wait to show you. We have learned so much."

Hugh ducked into the kitchen area as Dallas was led to the living room. While she sat down on the long couch and propped her tail up, her dad came back around holding strawberries bigger than his hands.

"Whoa."

"Aren't they beauties? Biggest apples and strawberries you'll have! We've learned so much about how aquaculture has developed, and how growing has converted to underwater measures. The advancements in technology to make this happen are unbelievable! We're going to cut these up and drizzle chocolate over them for dessert later."

"So, are you getting settled, okay?" Naomi asked as she and her sister joined her on the couch. Dallas almost didn't answer the question at first, still distracted by the smoothness of both their faces. The last time she saw her mother, she had long crow's feet at her eyes, and her sister's chin was covered with blemishes, and now those things seemed to have been erased.

"I am!" she told them. "I mean, I just got here, so there is so much I have to figure out."

"Oh, you've seen nothing yet," Hugh replied, joining them. "Before dinner, we'll show you the gardens we manage."

"Our corporate office was giddy to get us down here. They couldn't wait to put 'undersea expansion' on the website with the Gneiss Underway location. And they're already talking about a location in Glugg's Path in the North Atlantic!"

"We've had an easy time transitioning, but what about you?"

Dallas waved her hand. "It was nothing. Weird at first, but after we all went into the tanks at Orientation, it wasn't so bad."

"Looks great on you," Naomi agreed. "Did you meet your envoys and neighbors?"

"I did. I've seen a few neighbors in passing, only when we went to see the viceroy."

"You got to see him?" Hugh asked.

Dallas crossed her brow at the shock in his voice. "Yeah, why?"

"Oh, he's been busy lately. Been hiding in his office. Barely had time to do his rounds at the center, let alone see new launchies. He's a good man. He seems very tense and serious, but he is a very nice man."

"So, Dally!" Albany cut in. "What do you think you want to do here?"

Dallas waved her fins a little, knowing she couldn't avoid that question forever. "Well, I haven't thought too much about it yet, actually. How's your stuff going?"

"I have to say I love that I started this thing before I got down here," Albany said. "So really, it's not like I am starting over, but I still need to get all new clients. I got new business cards a while back. So far, I just helped plan a bunch of small parties, but in no time, I'll be doing those huge weddings."

"That's so you, Ally. I'm not quite sure about myself yet."

"The thing to remember is that this is a place to start over," Naomi chimed in. "You can get involved in whatever you want, whether you want to go to a new school or not. Or you can look into jobs right away."

"Take your time to explore everything," Hugh suggested. "There are plenty of people to talk to and help."

"Do you think you want to go back to school?" Naomi asked.

"Actually," Dallas started. "I have already signed up for the Job Trials. I want to figure out where I fit in."

"That's great," said her father.

"Good for you," Naomi agreed. "That's what they're there for. Just put down the activities you did in school. You remember when you did the newspaper?"

Dallas smirked. She only did the class elective senior year, but she put on her resume that she did the paper for four years.

"Yeah."

"You're going to see so much here. The technology they have is ahead of its time," her dad added. "You've noticed the TVs in the main areas?"

"Yeah, the President came on to welcome new citizens. She seems like an enthusiastic soccer mom that just roots for all the teams."

"She is wonderful."

"When do your Job Trials start?"

"Monday, so two days from now. I'll have to see where I want to go."

Dallas was happy when they decided to show her their gardens for a change of conversation. The only decision she wanted to make was what beverage she wanted to try with her first underwater dinner.

They left through the front door and swam through the caved neighborhood. Dallas noticed they were going in the opposite direction of the main pipelines, or any pipelines for that matter.

"These greenhouses are kept away from the main building in a rural area," her mother explained. "Naturally, that is why we got housing here, so we can have access to it."

"Wait, why not just have houses built with it?" Dallas inquired. "Like, a regular farm?"

"It is not allowed to have separate housing out in the open," Hugh said. He let his sentence trail off as if he were unsure how to finish it. "It's not considered safe."

"Everything needed to be in a very fertile area anyway," explained Naomi. "And then the greenhouses were built around them. You'll see."

They led her down a nook, a corridor in the cave that had a less populous pipeline. In fact, they were the only ones. Her dad swiped his ID first, and they all went in one after the other, Albany giving her a look that was equal parts excitement and caution. Unlike the other pipelines in the main district, this one did not connect to any building on the other side. They soared through this tube with nothing on either side of them but the wide blue of the ocean, and that was the only thing to greet them at the end.

Her parents and sister slid out first, and she followed, stopping dead in mid-float. When she first arrived at Gneiss Underway and swam off that sub, she was immediately taken inside, so most of her views of the surrounding ocean were through aquarium glass. This time, she was smack dab in the middle of it. No walls.

Her fins brushed the sands beneath her out of subconscious habit, giving her the sense of feeling grounded in an abyss. Her parents stayed to her side, and her sister put her arm around her.

"My reaction exactly when I saw it for the first time."

"Beautiful, isn't it?" remarked Naomi.

"We have never seen anything like this before," Hugh said. "And now we get to live in it."

The waters here seemed a little darker, deeper, although she caught the light reflections off of stones here and there. They passed a coral reef and other plants she did not recognize, with small fish swimming in and out of them. Dallas could not stop staring at them, looking around for any other signs of life. Her family took her over to what she thought were more rocks, but as they came into view, she noticed those rocks had square-shaped panels. Doors.

Hugh IDed one to open it and ducked in, Naomi doing the same, but her sister stayed with her.

"What's in there?"

"Equipment and stuff," Albany answered. Dallas was able to peek her head in and see this aquatic toolshed, filled with things that had long handles, short handles, shovels, and picks at the end. Her parents got out and closed the shed before she could see more, including the tools that ended in things much sharper than shovels.

She followed them to other huts and saw for herself the laboratories of botany, fruits, and vegetables. These rooms had their own shade of lighting, something that had to have been created out of lava core, bright yellows that faded into whites like runny eggs pouring over various troughs. Every plant was protected by its own dome, and here and there her parents lifted them to view the products.

"Going to pick some fresh ones," her mother said, handling a few very large green peppers. Next to her, her father did the same with long, bumpy string beans. They looked just like the strawberries did in their home—gigantic versions of what they had on land. It was as though there were steroids for produce.

"Who knew salt water was so good?" said her sister as she helped carry a basket. They swam out of the huts to take the pipeline home, where Dallas got to have her first home-cooked under-the-sea meal.

Paired with a green tea latte, Dallas enjoyed the fresh vegetables along with baked salmon, not at all surprised that fish would be on the menu. And despite all the evident differences—from the scenery to appearances, form, and dress—everything about that dinner scene was as comfortable and familiar to her as it had been in a different atmosphere. That was one thing that was the same and the one thing that would always be the same.

Dallas struggled a little bit with the bags she strung on her arms, using more effort to stay swimming upward with such added weight. And that was only a few bags. She promised her parents she would take more later, still needing to save room for anything else she would get at the market whenever she went.

So, she swam back through the pipelines with a full stomach and four full bags of fresh picks, not caring at all that the handles were digging into her arms and fins. She did not stop smiling, and really, it was joy that wound up her swimming tail.

It was the bliss that kept her in the moment, so much so that she didn't notice the other merpeople moving in her direction when she came out of the pipeline. Some were moving fast, and some were moving even faster. And as Dallas learned the hard way, neither noticed the other.

The merman slammed right into her, and she spun into a whirlwind, spinning fast and landing hard against the wall. She heard the merman yell "sorry!" at her from what seemed like ten feet ahead. As soon as Dallas shook it off and hoisted her bags back up her arms, she noticed the small stampede that had formed.

Merpeople were swimming around her in flashes. She looked in the direction they came from and saw a small pod of merpeople rushing toward something at a pipeline.

"He's down!" someone yelled. "Hurry, get bandages!"

"Someone call the medics!"

Curiosity easily won Dallas over, and she floated over enough to see what was happening. She caught the flash of a tail waving on the ground, and when it came down, it produced a storm cloud of blood diffusing through the water. The merman on the ground was breathing heavily, wincing and moaning, and when he shifted, Dallas could see the deep red gash in his tail. A mermaid came to him holding a bandage while another leaned over him.

"How far away? What was it? Did it follow you?"

Some merman exited the pipeline he had just come out of, having a panicked and heated conversation about the trail of blood.

The same merpeople who rushed past Dallas were back, carrying a stretcher and going over to help the merman on it. They were joined by merpeople wearing white uniformed robes. He cried out as they lifted and steadied him on the stretcher, covering him with a blanket and dashing on to a pipeline down the corridor.

Two mermen in dark robes held cans that instantly diffused something through the surrounding waters, the swirls of red and dark pink blowing away until they disappeared. The mermen talked with a few others nearby whom Dallas thought to be the envoys. The mermen agreed and obeyed aggressively before spraying the substance through the surrounding water once again and exiting through the pipeline that led outside.

By that time, most merpeople simply moved on without saying another word about it, the train wreck everyone wanted to watch over. Dallas shuffled her bags on her arms and started to weave her way through the moving crowd, and that was when she noticed there were more envoys standing around one another talking in a huddle. She recognized the only one she knew, and he recognized her, too.

At first, Liam just took a cursory glance at anyone else still in the room, but something made him look at Dallas again. He crossed his brow, excusing himself from the huddle and swimming over to her in what turned into a hurry.

Dallas froze in place with her bags still in her arms, shuffling the weight as he approached her.

"You, which way did you come from?"

"South exit," Dallas said, moving an arm to point but changing her mind so as not to lose a bag.

"You went out to sea? How far?"

"I went to see my family in the southern neighborhood."

He was staring at her and what she had in the bags.

"The marketplace has been closed for a while now..." he said as though he were making a point, but it was lost on Dallas, and she stood there. Liam had his chin down and looked at her with pointed eyes. The only time Dallas saw that look was from her teacher when she was disruptive in class.

"Can I ask who gave you permission to go out to the greenhouses and help yourself? The only ones who can are hunter/gatherers during select hours."

"My parents," Dallas said right away. "They work for a produce company and had me over for dinner, and they insisted on giving me leftovers."

"Oh, that's right, Dallas Dwight," Liam said. "Hugh and Naomi Dwight. Yes, that's right."

"You remembered my name," Dallas said as more of a statement than a question.

Liam smirked but did not drop his authority. "Of course I did, Miss Dallas. There's always at least one launchie that goes shooting out of the pipeline the first time they use it, and this time it was you. I ought to carry one of those squeegees with me from now on so I can scrape them down from the ceiling."

Dallas smiled at the visual.

"But I'm glad to know that you were with your family, safe."

"Of course," Dallas replied, alarmed. "What's... I mean, did something happen?"

Liam cut her off before she could ask any detailed questions. "Safety has been the number one thing drilled into everyone the minute they take the plunge. We always do everything we can and always strive to do more, but merpeople can still get themselves hurt. We still have to practice some common sense."

"What happened to that merman?"

Liam leaned in. "Well, he's a hunter/gatherer, and while he was going to get the fishnets in, he...might have had an encounter with something."

Dallas's eyes widened.

"Like an animal attack? What was it?"

"I don't know; he had gone to a deeper part where it was hard to see. But it is part of his job to go to places like that, no one else's. They are saying it might have been something that just saw the school of fish and wanted to claim it from us. Those that have jobs out-sea have special training for it and it is not something everyone is allowed to do. The thing is we're still young in civilization. The wild is still wild, and some things still believe they are the top of the food chain down here. The rules are the way they are for a reason."

"I know. Like I said, my family just wanted to show me the greenhouses where they grow everything, and we did not even stay out there long. I mean, my parents are pretty cautious, and they told me about this diffuser they use that would keep anything away."

"Good, and I'm glad it is. If you truly were out in the wild alone picking from the gardens, you'd be in serious trouble, my dear."

"I'll be careful," Dallas promised. "Have merpeople done that?"

"The romantic notion and desire for exploration of new surroundings is not lost on anyone, and some seriously think they're immune to danger and go searching for it."

He gave her a soft smile.

"I don't want to see any more accidents."

There was a beat where Liam and Dallas looked to the spot where moments ago there was one, and all evidence of red in the blue had since disappeared completely. Outside the main pipeline, there was a small pod of merpeople having a discussion, carrying long, spear-like weapons on their shoulders.

One of them held a large jug and pointed in the direction ahead, and then they all followed suit. Dallas could make out from there the dark spreads in the sea where the red was still intact, and whatever trail it came from was the trail that pod purposely took.

"Do you need a hand?"

"Oh," Dallas said, snapping back to reality. "No, they're not that heavy. I appreciate it, though."

"Okay, Miss Dwight. Take care."

She took her pipeline back home, passing other merpeople and envoys that paid her no attention. When passing through the tube, there were three merpeople huddled closely together, hushing themselves when she came through the pipeline, but she still heard them.

"Westburn is full of it!"

"Someone said they saw a giant eel and he won't believe anyone."

"A giant eel? There's no such thing."

"Does it matter? *Something* attacked a merman. How can they possibly tell us we're safe here?"

CHAPTER 11

SHE LOOKED FROM HER tablet to the open cavern ahead. Nothing was particularly labeled, at least as far as she could tell from where she floated. She read the description again with a perplexed shake of her head. The next time Dallas looked up, she immediately spotted five people around a seated area and a merman talking to them, seeming to be leading this particular group. The merman looked at her, stopping the discussion.

"I think you're my missing piece," he said with a sly smirk.

Dallas put her tablet away, wondering if it were possible to blush underwater.

"Late for your first day of Job Trials," the merman said as she swam over to the group. He tsk-tsked her and asked her to take a seat on a horseshoe-shaped cushion centered around what looked like a small desk. A few tablets sat there plugged into a glowing green control panel, and she had the half-thought to plug hers in if it weren't for the spotlight on her.

"Sorry," she said. "I got a bit lost."

"You get one."

The merman was older than her but did not seem like much, with the beginning of a dark goatee around his slim chin. His eyes were a deep mixture of blue and black, matching his tail, the shades the midnight sky took when the night reached its peak. She immediately thought that he wore glasses on land from the subtle dents near his eyes and the top of his nose, as if the parts knew something was missing and were not quite used to it.

"Dallas Dwight, then," he said.

She nodded. "Yeah."

"I'm Noah Fendelman. Welcome. I am an envoy specializing in job placement and career growth. I am both a headhunter and a career guidance counselor, so to speak. I am the one in charge of all your Job Trials and helping you grow wherever you want to go. Now, as I said, you all are here to do the things you ranked the highest as most experienced or most interested on your application forms. These Job Trials are like short internships. You will spend a week at each one and determine which one could be the best fit for you. It is also like taking a class in which you are learning about the job, and at the end of your trial, you will be graded on how well you fit. Don't worry; there is no failing unless you work hard to mess up. Now, shall we get a move on?"

Noah unplugged his tablet from the table, prompting others to do the same, and he led them away. They passed through a corridor with a window stretched down the ceiling, and Dallas followed the others, arching her head all the way back so she could marvel at the green sea turtles passing by above, large, rounded shells and delicate waving flippers.

"First stop is the school for the teacher's assistant position. Some of you might have met Pat Peterson from your orientation. She has dual citizenship and teaches here too."

Noah led them to a pipeline, and they dove in, swimming another long and clear tube to get another look at the sea turtles and even more fish that were taking the same path they were, although to different destinations. Dallas steadied herself along the current, almost like she was keeping up with the turtle, swimming alongside it like they were together in the open ocean.

It had been on the tip of her tongue, but she knew the time for that would be coming as soon as the next day. She had dreamed about it since the beginning, and it was something she was seriously considering. Nothing on her Job Trials list was all that exciting, except for that one. It would be the only thing that would get her up close and personal with marine wildlife. She wondered—just wondered and hoped—if she would get to pet one of those turtles.

The turtle went about its business, and she went about hers, landing out with the rest of the group. The building they were in certainly looked like a school, although it was a melting pot of levels in just one area. Dallas noticed the preschool and nursery rooms they passed before swimming up to the second floor.

Noah passed by a cave room that had no door, the bioluminescent light snaking around a comfortably sized room with students in it, all looking like they were in comfortable seating. Dallas saw the familiar purple plum hair swimming up and down in front of a screen, showing different things. She stopped when she saw Noah and the group and gave him a pleasant smile.

"Class, we have a visitor. Hello Mr. Fendelman."

"Hi Pat."

He gestured to the group, who shyly peeked in, offering smiles to the students in the seats that were part desk, part La-Z-Boy, tails stretched out in front of them in ease.

"I've got a launchie here for you for her first Job Trial."

"Ah, wonderful! Come on in!"

The mermaid started as the teaching assistant was brought in and introduced. She seemed genuinely interested in being there, smiling at her would-be students. Dallas knew that if that were on her list, she would not be so enthusiastic. Most of her options would not be. She supposed that she was going to get the least exciting ones over with first.

Dallas waited outside the boutique while the last mermaid went in to settle. The day stretched on so far, she did not even know what time it was. She made a mental note of each stop that she would eventually have and graded them in her head based on how bad she thought they would be. Dallas knew the real reason why her listing was so random and why they just put her in places that had openings. It was definitely why she was going to be placed last.

"All right," Noah said. "Just you left. The salon is not too far from here and a short pipeline trip over."

Dallas gave a short nod, knowing that Noah was making eye contact with her and trying to show good sportsmanship. It was only temporary, and that was the only good thing about all of them. It would only make her happier when there was a time to leave.

She followed Noah through a pipeline that took them over a rose garden of red and orange coral that quickly merged with yellow, green, blue, and violet, curving above the clear window they could all see as they passed over. And what better place to have the best view of beauty?

The pipeline snaked around the building and brought them to the entrance of the business center, which was bubbling with the hubbub of different activities. She caught sight of a few mermen wearing navy blue robes and hats, carrying messenger bags on their way to the postal service. Noah led them to the entrance, and, funny to say, Dallas could smell through the water. It smelled just like a hair salon would, with strong solutions bubbling through her nose that she could almost taste.

"I've brought you another one," Noah said as they swam into a mermaid swimming by. She held a tray of colorful and intricate tools, several ending in fine-toothed combs. Her own hair matched Dallas's in the short and spiky department, only shorter and spikier, and it was bright bubblegum pink.

"Claudia, this is Dallas. She's your recruit for the week. She caused an awful lot of trouble already, so make sure you keep her in line."

Dallas internally sighed while Claudia snickered. Noah kept a straight face and gestured to Dallas with a little nod. "This should be something easy and maybe enjoyable for you. Nothing complicated or stressful. Just take it easy; you'd be surprised how much you can learn. Take care now." Noah smiled at her, and she thanked him.

With that, Noah exited the cave shop, probably all too eager to get rid of the last launchie.

"Welcome, Dallas," Claudia said. "As you can see, we have a few clients here right now. Have you ever worked in a salon on land?"

"No," Dallas admitted. "But I've done my own hair before—some trial-and-error type things."

Claudia smiled. "Understandable; we all have. I do love your hair the way it is now, though! Did you lighten the tips before you came down here?"

"I did. I had a bleach job that grew out. And now, well, I have a happy accident."

Claudia nodded. "Yeah, I've seen some accidents, and that's definitely a good one. So come with me. One of my employees is doing a cut and style right now."

Dallas followed her to hair stations occupied with merpeople, watching how all of their hair drifted in the water above their heads. The stylists simply had to go with it.

Go with the flow, thought Dallas, needing a weak joke.

It was like the water was cooperating in the job and making it easier. Claudia stopped before a chair with a tall and curvy, yet lean, mermaid with long blue-purple hair in a fishtail braid, the mini-clone to her tail counterpart. She looked to be about Dallas's age, maybe even a little older, poised and certain of her place in the world. She was combing the newly cut strands of the mermaid in the chair and instantly noticed them.

"We got a new recruit for the week. This is Dallas. Dallas, this is Sapphire."

Dallas smiled at the coincidence.

"Hey," Sapphire said. "Welcome! It's really chill here, so you'll have an easy time. I have been working here for a year since I first came down, right after I graduated from beauty school and I love it here."

"Dallas is going to help me go through our backstock and inventory, and then maybe she can join you with your next client."

Sapphire smiled warmly at the alarmed look on Dallas's face.

"You're not going to cut anyone's hair! Don't worry; you'll just do some combing and help pin hair and clean up cut hair, okay?"

"Sure," Dallas said.

Sapphire undid the apron around the client's neck, and she thanked her and left for the receptionist's desk.

"Your timing is perfect!" Sapphire told her. "So, come with me, and I'll show you around."

Dallas followed Sapphire about the store, moving down an area where they had a clear, crisp view of the great outdoors. The live painting of brightly colored plants curved in front of them and around the bend, and Dallas saw something long and ribbon-like slither inside of it. She meant to point it out to Sapphire like a kid at a zoo, only Sapphire was looking elsewhere. She was looking up, and it wasn't out of awe and wonder.

"Whoa, another one."

Dallas glanced in her direction at the red flashing lights at the front of the sub as it dashed through the sea.

"At least they don't have to worry about traffic down here the way they've been coming through."

"For what?" Dallas asked, then felt foolish when the sub turned enough for her to see and recognize the universal symbol painted on the side: the red cross.

"There have been a lot of incidents lately. Have you seen the news?"

"No," Dallas answered honestly. "Not really, I mean."

"God, look! Another one. Come here, I'll show you."

Sapphire made a detour, bringing them right in front of another window, confirming what she saw. The second sub followed the first one only a few feet away, and they both flew around to the neighboring business in the building, one that would have its own specially used entrance.

"We're right by the hospital, so we saw the ambulances come through the first time, and that's all anybody's been talking about for the past couple of days. It's so bad. You hear about those hunter/gatherers?"

"No," Dallas said.

"Yeah, they 'disappeared,'" she made finger quotes for emphasis. "No one actually confirmed it, but everyone knows that they were hunted. Something got them, and they were something's food. They're gone."

"What? What was it?"

Sapphire was shaking her head and watching the ambulances. "No one said. Pretty sure no one even knows."

Those ambulances flew in and stopped before the opened door. Merpeople in white swam out, ready to receive them. The injured were taken out from each in large sling stretchers, and within seconds they rushed to get them covered. Dallas saw small clouds of blood rise from all of them, and then more from the next merman's gently wrapped tail, spotted with cuts and gashes. Some staff used diffusers to work on getting rid of it immediately, while others got those patients safely inside.

"So... is this common?"

Sapphire bit her lip. "No, not really. And whenever it gets this bad, they send out Marine Force to take it out. Anyone is at risk going out to sea, especially Marine Force and hunter/gatherers. I heard a bunch of them took out this giant squid once. I mean, when I hear 'release the Kraken,' I would rather it be the spiced rum."

Dallas snickered, but only a little as her attention diverted back to the hospital staff frantically spraying the diffusers through the water. She watched those smears of red warp and mingle into the blue until they faded to pink and then blended into the blue altogether. Most of the staff returned to the hospital, but two stayed behind and continued to watch the seas ahead.

93

CHAPTER 12

Dallas was one of the first people to show up this time instead of the last. It was not just to redeem herself, but also out of genuine enthusiasm for that day's agenda. After looking at the sheet, she brightened inside, imagining what it would be like, genuinely believing it to be something she wanted. That feeling popped with the enthusiasm of a large balloon with the first few words out of Noah's mouth.

"I'm sorry, but due to recent events, the wildlife conservationist Job Trial is canceled."

Dallas stood there with her mouth partially open, the victim of irony.

The other merpeople in her group were also disappointed, but not as much as she was.

"What happened?" asked a mermaid who was more oblivious.

Noah was shaking his head. "There have been some incidents in the wild, and everyone is just taking safety precautions."

"Are there shark attacks?" asked a merboy near her.

"No one is saying what it is," Noah said vaguely. "But something in the wild is...well, for lack of a better word, wild. We're not sending anyone out. I'm sorry."

He looked over to Dallas.

"Sorry, Dallas, seeing as that was next on your list and where you were supposed to go today. The good news is that means you can have a day off."

"Tomorrow will I be going there, or skipping to my next one?"

"Skipping to your next one," he said. "That is, until this is available again. I'll let you know."

She gave a weak smile.

"So, you enjoy the rest of your day, and I will see you back here tomorrow."

"Thanks."

Dallas spun around and headed back in the same direction she came from, casting her eyes to the glass windows as she did. The waters were still, peaceful and pleasant enough to be a daytime sky, not a single bubble out of place or disturbance to the calm. There was no hint of movement within the coral, not even the waving arm of a starfish pressed against the glass. She looked up, hoping to catch a turtle or something—anything passing by that she hoped she would be meeting that day. Her heart was set on a dolphin or an orca.

She went through the short pipeline and made her way to the nearest Fast Eats. The refrigerated containers next to her were fully stocked with a variety of things she was still not quite familiar with, but she knew the undersea equivalent of a sandwich, picking out the foil-wrapped bundle. She was even getting used to the currency: round coins made from smooth stone that glistened in the water, easy to spot. Dallas swam out of the store with her foil bundle and a bottle of peach green tea, the tag dangling out of it not yet discolored, meaning it had been brewed that day.

There was a seating area nearby inviting her to stretch out and have her lunch, with all the time to herself. Dallas had to laugh when unwrapping the sandwich, the bread having the look and feel of a hard sponge. She had always hated soggy bread and never wanted the juice that came with roast beef. She took a big bite, already tasting the familiar favorite peppers and eggs.

Dallas ate and leisurely surfed the web on her tablet, pretending not to pay attention to the mermaids gossiping not too far from her.

"No, I heard it was huge. Long and with big jaws."

"Oh my God, like what?"

"I don't know; I'm just telling you what I heard!"

"And no one found it yet?"

"Shh!" one mermaid hushed. Dallas moved her eyes slightly to see. Another mermaid passed by with her head down, instantly noticing the others and swimming away.

"That's his girlfriend!"

The girlfriend in question wore a pinched, pained expression, her contents under enough pressure to explode at any moment. She swam through the nearest pipeline and disappeared.

"I feel so bad for her. I mean, can you imagine?"

"Yeah, but at least he got away alive."

"That's so horrifying."

Dallas scrolled past breaking headlines on her tablet, each one starting with the same ominous and vague statements. They had something else in common, too: any headline photos taken were of nothing but the blank, empty open ocean.

The sound of something sizzling danced above her head. She looked up to one of the screens placed around the Fast Eats and common area. It fought the salt and pepper static for a minute before flickering to the image of the viceroy sitting with his hands folded neatly against his tail. His eyes opened wider knowing the broadcast was working, his smile softer and sincere.

"Hello Gneiss Underway, I hope you are all doing well. It is my duty to make this broadcast addressing current events and to clear up anything you might be thinking or hearing about. It is true that some of our community members working out-sea have had some unfortunate accidents, and we as a community are doing everything we can to give them the help and attention that they need.

"We take community safety and security very seriously. We want to assure you that you are safe, and that there is nothing to fear. Certain circumstances are different for those in certain professions that take them out into the wild and come with certain risks that only those with the right training and experience can do. Our ocean home is civilized, yes, but it is still home to many kinds of other species that we co-exist with and will continue to do so. I come before you to tell you that you have nothing to fear, and there is no monster that is out hunting for us. We have the staff and the professionals trained to keep us safe at all times, and I will have more of them on duty to make sure of it."

The next Job Trial came as no surprise.

"Well," Noah said as he turned to Dallas, "you're certainly going to be busy today."

Dallas raised an eyebrow but did not ask because she did not need to. Her morbid curiosity would be answered in full.

"You have some experience, it seems."

"Yeah, I wrote for my school paper all through high school," she replied. *No, I took the class one semester.*

"Hey, that's good," Noah assured her. "Every experience counts."

Or lack thereof. What if they notice?

They headed to the pipeline that would take them over to the right business center, where a small pod of merpeople had formed a line.

"Has anything excited you so far?"

"Not really," Dallas admitted, unsure of what to say. She wasn't looking at Noah, but he gave a little nod of understanding.

"That's normal, and perfectly okay. I always get the groups that are more on the undecided side, and I like them the best. I enjoy introducing them to things they've never tried or considered before, and that most likely pairs them with a job they like."

Dallas didn't answer, and he looked at her.

"You will have your follow-up with me later after you've had a few trials to compare and contrast."

They entered the pipeline and took it all the way to the next business center. Below, Dallas could see the shadows of a particular pod passing by and taking a fork to the right. They all wore black garments and carried very long—and very sharp—spears. The last two in the group carried a bundle with a large net.

They arrived in a somewhat crowded venue, and Noah led her in the direction of her next itinerary. Instead of blocks of cubicles, there were rows of desk panels with large projected screens and colorful buttons. Merpeople at these desks typed away on their panels and scrolled through the screens to read, reread, and edit the works they had written. Dallas wished she had that in school instead of the old desktops with keyboards, where the run-down letters were barely visible.

Noah brought her to an office room in the back, where an older merwoman was talking on a headset. She talked and pressed a few buttons on her panel, lighting it up bright green. All around, at the various cubicle desks, were ongoing conversations that Dallas could not help but temporarily tune into.

"Dallas."

"Yes." Dallas jumped out of her reverie, shaking off the image of the mermen hunters practicing defense moves.

"Focus."

"Sorry."

Noah brought her to the next cubicle desk over to a merman named Gary who she would be shadowing, who did not sit in his seat for very long after Noah left.

"You came at the perfect time! We're about to do the interview," he told her, like he expected her to know what he was talking about. "Bring your tablet and come up with your own questions to ask, which I am sure you have."

When Dallas followed him into an interview room, she found out just how emphasized the "the" in "the interview" truly was.

A few others were gathered around the merman subject, whose bandages were wrapped cleanly around his tail. Dallas could see the stitches through them and peeking out at the top.

Gary reached out to shake his hand.

"You're very brave, Joe. Thank you for meeting with us."

Joe sat at an angle so his tail could remain straight. He did not have to move it. He sat up to greet them.

"Thank you for having me."

Gary took a seat, and Dallas did the same, holding her tablet and pretending to type something.

"First, off the record, how are you doing?"

Joe gave a small shrug. "I mean, I'm all right. Swimming is more difficult, but I should heal up soon."

"Good," Gary said, holding his tablet open. "Now what can you tell us?"

"Well, I'll tell you the same thing I told the lady who called me," Joe started. "We were out on a hunt, and I guess something else was hunting too, and we became competition. There was a giant school of something we were going after that it wanted as well, and it was not happy."

"All right."

"It was just...I don't know. A fish, predatory fish of some kind."

"A shark?" asked Dallas.

"I—I really don't know," Joe answered, and whether or not it was necessary, Dallas typed that in.

"And have you been to those parts of the deep before?" Gary continued.

"Yeah, I have, but that was the first time we ventured further. No one saw it coming, but when it did... I mean, it just came out of nowhere."

Gary paused as he did his own typing.

"What was the first thing you saw?" he asked.

Joe's face stayed stern. "A big, open mouth."

Dallas had no follow-up question.

"That was it," Joe continued. "Just that wide-open jaw that came out of nowhere and attacked me. Everyone was screaming. The others fought it off the best they could, and I guess it swam away, or maybe they all just grabbed me and got us out of there."

"Did you see it when you swam away?" Dallas asked next.

"Not really, no. I was in so much pain and bleeding pretty badly, and everyone was rushing to get me back and out of the blood-infused waters. It was fast, and once we got out of there, it was gone."

Joe absentmindedly rubbed the stitched wound under his bandages while Gary continued typing. She did some of her own typing just to keep herself occupied, not really sure how she could contribute to the story. She still felt chills up and down her arms like she could actually get undersea goosebumps on her scales.

"Is there anything else you want to say?"

Joe stared at nothing on the wall. "It... it wasn't a shark. It couldn't have been. It was...meaner."

CHAPTER 13

Dallas produced a big stretch, her fins sliding out of her hammock and scraping against the wall. Rolling out of bed in the ocean was the best: the surrounding waters simply carried you down in a slow, gentle dip. She swam over to the bathroom, ducking down below the ceiling and picking up her toothbrush, which she had lazily left on the side on top of the barely closed toothpaste. It wasn't until she rubbed her eyes fully awake and looked at herself in the mirror that she gasped.

Her eyes were wide awake now in her reflection as her fingertips gently brushed the sides of her face, where pieces of skin had flown off. They hung off her cheeks like saran wrap, clear flakes shedding and carelessly floating away. Down her neck and on her arms was a similar sight, scales covered in a gossamer covering all the way down to her webbed fingers. Her tail bore the worst of it, naturally, layers surrounding her in a skirt of long peelings. The flakes drifted in front of her face in the mirror in mockery, and she opened a drawer to get out her other comb.

She swam over to what looked like a Jacuzzi tub with jet holes encircling its inside, pressing a few buttons on the side before getting in. She brushed herself down in the direction of the jets with rapid strokes and watched sheets of shedding get vacuumed into the jets. Her tail needed the most attention: the layers gently getting raked off until Dallas could see its blue-green colors brighter and freshly polished, slightly reddened from her grooming activity. She swam out to look at the results in the mirror, making sure she got it all, and turned off the tub.

After finishing in the bathroom and having a breakfast of coffee and fruit, Dallas fastened her outer robe and went out the door. She felt around in one of her pockets for her tablet and almost did not see where she was going, nearly bumping into someone passing by.

"Oh, sorry, I didn't see— "

"Oh, Dallas!" the girl said.

Dallas smiled in pleasant surprise at the familiar face. "Sapphire! Hi. You live around here?"

"Yeah, not too far, just a little way around the bend at the top."

Sapphire was smiling at her in social pleasantry but was also eyeing her with concern, her lip opening mid-speech as she thought about what to say. Dallas took note of the pause.

"What is it?" she asked.

Sapphire was giving her a quick look over, and Dallas froze.

"Hey...first time shedding?" she asked, leaning in.

Dallas's hands flew down to pull her robe closer to her body.

"Yeah," she admitted quietly.

"It's cool. Listen, you got a minute? I know how to help you."

Dallas nodded. "My next Job Trial isn't for a while anyway. I just..."

Sapphire waved her hand dismissively. "Don't worry about it; it happens to everyone. Come on, you'll love this!"

Dallas pocketed her tablet and followed, Sapphire's violet braid swimming behind her head almost in unison with her tail.

"Your skin is very red," she told her. "I can tell you scrubbed too hard. It might have become irritated now."

Dallas touched her face. "I didn't think I did it that hard."

"You have to be gentle with your skin and your scales. You're not getting the grime out of your bathtub!"

Sapphire swam up the neighborhood caverns and approached her door, keying in at the pad and inviting Dallas right in. Dallas was taken aback by the décor and just how much effort and creativity went into the color schemes of pink, blue, black, and purple that adorned the artwork on the walls and pillows on the couch. She caught sight of rows of wine glasses with an iridescent finish she could only see as she swam past them, all hung up on a rack above, with the one near the end still bearing a smudge of lipstick stain.

She was set to compliment Sapphire on her home design but stopped short when she saw the one thing that surprised and delighted her at the same time. There were about five or six small fish swimming about the apartment freely, flashing colors of pearl with fins of blue and yellow.

"You've still got some spots on your back and dorsal that you missed," Sapphire explained. "And your ears. May I?" She reached out a hand holding a brush toward Dallas's back, and she nodded.

"Oh yeah, thanks."

Sapphire gently brushed the scale shedding, doing so in the direction of the fish.

"Watch this, and don't freak out!"

Sure enough, those little fish swam over and attached themselves to the new visitor, nibbling gently with tails waving in excitement like puppies would. Dallas stood still and giggled at the light tickling she felt all over her back and tail, and then they moved to her arms and finally by her ears. She scratched the tips of her ear fins once the fish left, darting this way and that on their own in the cove.

"Small fish do it to turtles and whales all the time. And other fish. They mostly eat algae on rocks, but now we showed up, and we're just other big fish friends to clean."

"That's...so adorable," Dallas couldn't help but say.

"It is. If you're out in the wild, they'll help you out whether you want them to or not, and that's always helpful. Naturally, they make much better pets now that they're out of those fishbowls on land, huh? It's helpful, but back to you."

Sapphire cringed at the scales on her tail that were the reddest, no doubt. Dallas brushed her tail, feeling both the smoothness on the outside and the irritation on the inside.

"Come on, I'll show you."

She followed Sapphire into her bathroom, which was a behind-the-curtains scene compared to the spotless museum. In fact, it was the opposite. Sapphire's bathroom reflected her day job, with a smorgasbord of scattered bottles, jars, and tubes littering the countertop and resting on the edge of the tub. There were smears of products across the sink, and with their different colors and scents, Dallas could not identify a single one. Sapphire opened a drawer and pulled out a cylinder with the lid only halfway on.

"I got this at a fantastic Dead Sea shop in the market. I could seriously spend my entire paycheck there, and I totally did a few times. Anyway, it will help with any minor irritations and keep your skin and scales glowing and healthy. Plus, it smells like coconut!"

Sapphire scooped out something turquoise and creamy with her fingers and rubbed it by Dallas's ears and gills. She handed her the jar.

"Here, help yourself! I have another one in there."

"Thanks," said Dallas, not wanting to admit that she actually liked exotic bath products, but with one touch of the stuff and the aroma it produced, she almost wanted to eat it. She bathed herself in that smooth cream with no shame while Sapphire applied something to her lips.

"So how are you liking it so far?"

"I love it," Dallas admitted. "I just... well, I'm still trying to figure everything out."

"That's normal."

"I had fun with you the other day; I did. I just don't know what's for me."

"It's totally fine. A lot of people are like that."

Dallas shrugged while massaging the coconut cream into the webbing between her fingers. "I just don't want the problems I had on land to follow me down here."

Sapphire looked at her seriously in the mirror. "They won't. They will not if you don't let them. This is a clean slate. Just remember that. You can do whatever you want and be whoever you want to be. This is a gift to us."

Sapphire gave her that advice without even asking what problems she had, as if they didn't matter. As if she might have her own she wanted to put behind her.

They smiled at each other in the mirror. Sapphire's smile was soft, but the seriousness of her tone lingered. She cast her eyes down and quickly changed the subject.

"All right, I have to go to work now."

"Me too," Dallas said, closing the jar for her. "Thank you so much."

"Oh, don't mention it!" Sapphire said as she put the things away. "Listen, now that I know we're neighbors, why don't we hang out sometime?"

"Sounds great. I'd like that."

Dallas and Sapphire parted ways after leaving her cavern. Dallas was back on track for her next agenda, taking the pipeline over to the designated part of town.

As she swam through, she caught sight of the merpeople returning, all looking the same: navy and silver clothing, all carrying spear weapons, swimming in formation. Their group stretched back to cover almost the entire pipe...like the entire force had been sent out.

❧

She stretched her tail in front of her in the inevitable waiting game. It was like she was in the principal's office, overthinking any possible outcome, even though she knew she wasn't in any real trouble. Dallas couldn't think of a single reason why she would be in trouble or receive any negative feedback, yet dread loomed over her head. In reality, the anxiety she felt was just the desire to get it over with and receive the answer she was supposed to get. Whatever that answer might be.

The cavern office door slid open, and the merman before her swam out, looking satisfied, if not just content. Dallas brought her tail back under the chair and sat up straight just in time for Noah to come out and call her name.

"Dallas, come on in."

She got out of her seat in a way that was neither too quick nor too slow and followed Noah into the room, where the door shut instantly.

His office truly was a literal "man cave" replica, styled like a working office carved into a den. His desk panel was large enough to be important but small enough to feel modest, all nestled inside, making it feel cozy and protected rather than intimidating. Dallas felt neither as she sat in the seat across from Noah, with her file pulled up on the holographic screen. Her face was expressionless... and so was his.

"How's it going with you?" Noah asked her, but instead of the folded hands and forced enthusiasm of a common authority figure, he asked genuinely.

"I'm doing okay," Dallas answered just as genuinely. "I have no complaints or issues."

"In a nutshell, that's what your Job Trial supervisors had to say about you. No one said anything bad. But no one said anything amazing either. You fall smack dab in the middle of 'meets expectations' for all of them."

Dallas nodded slightly.

"See, that's good, but it's also bad. If you did poorly in one job or two and everything went wrong, then there's no love lost because you don't actually work there and aren't getting termed. At least we'd know to eliminate that option for you. You sailed by with no process of elimination... but we didn't find areas where you excelled either. So, nothing was all that exciting for you, was it?"

"No," Dallas admitted. "Not really. Nothing was all that exciting."

Just like on land, just like in the sea.

"The only one I was interested in was something I couldn't do."

"Right," said Noah, his eyes cool blue but friendly. "So, you like wildlife?"

"I do, in general. I just don't know how to turn it into anything. Honestly, I was excited to swim with animals and take care of them."

"Yeah, that's understandable, and it is pretty awesome. Being a wildlife conservationist is more than that, though."

"Yeah."

"If that's something you want, I can put a marker next to this for you when it becomes available."

"Do you know when that will be?"

Noah paused slightly. "Unfortunately, I don't. You know, especially this job and this time, it's not a good time. There is a dangerous side to working with wild animals, and sometimes things happen."

Did they find out anything about...the things that happened?"

Noah shook his head, maintaining eye contact. "We're going to leave it to the pros who are hard at work to find whatever it is."

"Whatever attacked those merpeople."

"We're fish now. You have to remember that. We can and are seen as prey."

Noah received a chime sound on his computer indicating a new email, which he bypassed while keeping his attention on Dallas.

"That means the only ones going out in the wild right now are the ones that have to and know what they're doing. Which means, I'm sorry, it's back to making copies and cold phone calls."

Dallas groaned internally.

"And then, you're going to have to figure out what you want to do." Noah sat back in his seat, the puffs of his hair trailing back with him. "I have to tell you, Dallas, more people in your position find it the most difficult. I've seen many go back and forth between sea and land, and I have seen some go back to land."

Dallas shot up. "Never."

Noah held up a hand. "I understand."

There was a beat.

"I take it you had a hard time figuring out what you wanted to do on land as well?"

Dallas allowed an honest nod.

"I went to community college, just to go, just...for borrowed time."

"What was your major?"

Dallas paused. "Music."

To her surprise, Noah straightened. "A musician huh?"

"I had music composition classes, but mostly chorus. I was in the chorus."

She stopped herself from continuing the rest of that thought, not wanting to go down that rabbit hole.

"Anyway, I mostly just took generic classes. I worked in a resale clothing shop too before I came here."

"How old are you?"

"Nineteen. I was a freshman."

"This is normal," Noah said with a little shrug. "Normal, normal. So what? You don't know what you like until you try it. I know people who get new career paths at forty."

He pressed a button on his panel, and the holographic screen dissolved.

"Well, our time is up, for now. Do you have any questions about anything?"

"No."

"That concludes our follow-up. Painless and no big deal. We'll have another one soon, so watch for the email."

He floated up from his chair, and Dallas did the same. He offered his hand, and she shook it.

"We'll find something, Dallas. And if you ever need anything, don't be afraid to reach out to me, okay? You can call or email me anytime you want."

"Thanks."

She left the envoy's office and the envoy office area, which seemed to be more crowded now than when she first arrived. She made her way through the center and out into the common areas, where she looked around for the pipeline that would take her back to the residential building. Out of the corner of her eye, she could make out a group huddled together, and in the center was the viceroy, wildly gesturing to everyone around him.

"Get to the bottom of it," he was saying softly and urgently. "As soon as possible. I have already put the call in, and I really do not want it to come down to this. There was no body found... but we cannot scare everyone."

CHAPTER 14

ALL THE TELEVISIONS WERE on, all tuned to the news channel, where they displayed a photo of the merman. He looked like a young military recruit would: old and tough enough to be ready for the next big thing, yet young and naïve enough to go looking for danger. He had long hair that hung by his cheeks and eyes that focused on not being afraid, not being afraid at all. The text underneath the photo read *"missing for a week."*

While the news anchor droned on about how the Marine Force was on the lookout, merpeople gathered around the TVs mounted on the walls in the common areas, shaking their heads and talking amongst themselves. Many had looks of common fear and concern, while others showed anger.

"They said there were no predators before we came here!" an older mermaid hissed to her husband. "All the sharks migrated after we settled. What could possibly make any of them come back?"

"No one is saying anything," said another mermaid nearby. "Does that mean they still don't know?"

"Or they don't want to tell us," said the merman next to her.

Dallas wanted to remain rooted to the floor to watch the rest of the news, however vague the information was.

"Authorities are still on the lookout and believe that any missing merpersons at this time are connected to the recent attacks. Since then, security has increased drastically in towns all across the West and North Provinces. We are joined now by Viceroy Warren Westburn from Gneiss Underway to talk about the efforts with his community."

The camera panned over to their viceroy sitting next to the news anchor, both men looking similar so he blended in on camera. The news anchor was stiff and professional, though Viceroy Westburn had one anxious twitch of his tail.

"Viceroy, tell us about what you're doing to protect your community."

"We have learned to recognize problems whether they be big or small, and even small ones we make sure not to turn away from. Any predator encounters and attacks are not to be taken lightly, especially when merpeople go missing. We are hard at work to find any missing merpeople and get them home safely. We know that even a little extra security can go a long way."

"Do you believe the danger has increased, viceroy?"

"I believe that danger only becomes danger if one puts themselves in danger's way, actively."

The screen turned to live footage of merpeople dragging out yards of wiring and metal tubes.

"Towns like Gneiss Underway as well as Mirage Bay and others are putting up protective barriers all around the outskirts of their buildings and outdoor areas."

The camera panned over to the merpeople at work, and Dallas saw Noah live on television pick up his bundle of metal tools and look around curiously. She didn't need another minute. She swam away to the exit pipeline as fast as she could, now without a doubt knowing where they were.

She could see the flash of the lights from the news crew before anything else and hoped that would blind side the rest of them enough for her to sneak in. Dallas drifted in and picked up her own bundle of metal tubes tied together just as the news crew finished their live feed and moved on, swimming away to their parked sub a few feet away. Knowing where Noah was, Dallas joined the line of merpeople as if she had been there the whole time.

They had formed the assembly line near a bunch of small rocks, using that marker as a starting point.

"I told you it would only be for a few seconds," Noah said, swimming over to her group. "So, thanks for not picking your nose or waving at the cameras. You got your less-than-fifteen minutes of fame. Now everyone, just continue to connect those pipes until they get long enough to pass down."

Dallas got her place in the merpeople manufacturing belt to connect the pipes and pass them down. At the same time, another set of merpeople was feeding the wire through.

"And, just in case I didn't say it enough, I want to thank you all for doing this. I apologize for pulling you out of whatever Job Trial you were scheduled for today. I, along with other envoys, are working with your schedules to make sure you're back on track eventually."

"Easy labor," a merman next to her murmured. "Of course, they recruited launchies for this."

"The town is going to be safer because of you, so remember that. You're not just leaving today with a paycheck; you're leaving with a sense of security."

Noah smiled at them and himself.

"Okay, I'm done with the motivational speeches. Holler if you need me."

He scanned the workers before taking off, and Dallas was glad his eyes passed her without stopping to question. She realized she really was not late at all, or it did not matter.

Down the line, the pipes and wires were passed to merpeople waiting to receive them, both launchies and the envoys giving instructions. It became a patterned routine that was easy to get into, and whenever Dallas glanced down the line, she saw those ropes of metal being placed across the already standing metal structure waiting to receive them.

Dallas looked again at the merman who seemed familiar, standing out in the black and silver tunic he wore. His dreadlocked hair was tied loosely behind him, as the weight of the locks did not yield to the buoyancy of the water. She could make out the tattoos up and down his arms. As a human, he had some on his legs as well, but those did not transition to his tail.

Dallas became fixated on this thought for a moment, imagining how words and works of art would look embodied on scales. They would be almost pixelated or stippled and could produce different looks depending on the way one swam. He was right when he first told them all about his tail that first day: it was almost pitch black and silvery in the ocean's shimmer. He swam down the line carrying a hefty bundle of pipes and dropped them off not far from where Dallas was stationed.

"Marcus!"

He immediately turned in the direction of his name and smiled at the recognition.

"Hey hey, Launchie! I remember you from my swim class. It's Dallas, right?"

"Yeah."

"How have you been?"

"Doing good so far. Just, you know, doing the community work here today."

Marcus nodded. "Yeah, it has come down to that, unfortunately."

Now that he was closer, Dallas noticed the details on his uniform, and when he turned she could see the badge on the front left side of his tunic, the recognizable "m" and "f" designed to look like merfolk.

"That's right, I remember you mentioning you were military! And had dual citizenship."

"I am just a foot soldier rank…for now."

"So, what exactly does the military do down here?"

He helped her lift the next pipe down the assembly line.

"It's more like a combination with police; we're the protective brute force, I guess. Even though it's mostly to protect against, well, predators."

Marcus said the last line softer, but other launchies heard him, and a few craned their necks.

"We join the hunter/gatherers when they go out," Marcus said right away. "Especially now."

"Have you seen anything? Fought anything?"

"Nothing big, no. Nobody really saw anything. Taylor, though, we think he did. We think he went after it."

"The merman missing," Dallas confirmed.

Marcus nodded. "He went out and never came back, and now, well, this."

They passed another pipe down the line.

"I haven't been here since teaching swim classes to the new recruits, so I have some catching up to do. I've never seen anything like this before. Not with something that is so unidentified. We still think we know the ocean, but we don't."

Dallas's tablet lit up and chimed, and when she saw her new email, she unleashed a fit of giggles. The note was animated, starting as a scroll and unrolling to pearl-pink parchment with popping music notes, text typing from left to right as it opened:

**Get Your Sing On! This Friday night at 8 p.m. at
The Drunken Ship**
Join us all for a night of fun with karaoke and

appetizers and drink specials all night long!
Singers are first come, first served, so get there early to
get your place!
**Must be eighteen and older.*
Event by Right Up Your Ally! Event Planning

She had to hand it to her sister. Albany had only taken a few courses in graphic design, but it had paid off in full. It was the event invitations and email blasts that got people's attention the most, and she was seeing one for the first time. Dallas scrolled down to the information on the place and its address and RSVPed "going," as promised, as she assured Albany she would, over and over.

Dallas smiled. There was no doubt she would enjoy something fun and get the chance to hang out with and support her sister. Learning that the legal age for drinking was lowered in the Oceanic communities was surprising but pleasant, given it was the same in some European countries.

It must be the blend of the seas then, to be inclusive, but also allowing young people that piece of adulthood many felt was too long to wait for. Dallas looked forward to some social gathering where she would find people she knew and hide among them. As far as the event's main activity went, she would pretend to ignore it. She told Albany she might; she told her she would, probably, just to get her off her back, though in the privacy of her head, she was saying she would not and never would again.

CHAPTER 15

DALLAS SET OFF FOR the pipelines after cleaning her dishes, still amused by the convenient faucet with the built-in vacuum for that purpose. Why no one thought of that on land was beyond her.

She waited in the small line near the pipeline going out of the main community center, scanning the crowd for anyone she knew. When she rode the first pipe, she got a good look at the merpeople stationed outside, recognizing the badges on their tunics, although none of them were Marcus.

The second pipeline was a little further, at a building with shopping and restaurants. Dallas followed the pods going in the direction she was headed, all toward this end of the newly established fence. This time, there was a merman of the Marine Force stationed at this exit. He did not say much except for casual greetings. He told each one to be careful as he opened the door in the fence to the open sea, and Dallas swam out to it for the second time.

She opened her tablet to the invitation to access the GPS feature, serving like a compass to direct her where to go. The arrow hung straight but bounced a little to the left, showing her a path through some mossy rock gardens. She did not need the GPS anymore after she saw the place looming in the distance, over the horizon separating the sandy sea bottom from the rest of the big blue. It almost looked like it would above, the sails moving in a rhythmic pace like they would in the wind. The only difference was this one stayed in one place; in the very spot it first sank from above.

"The Drunken Ship" was printed on the newly made sails attached to the top and the makeshift sign in front of it, made from the rotted and fallen wood remains of the ship itself. Dallas floated there for a moment to stare at it, wondering just how old this ship was.

It surely preceded modern cruise ships and could have actually been the poster image for a pirate ship. There were some words scratched on it in another language that could have been Spanish, which made sense considering the part of the Atlantic they were in. Dallas heard the music starting up inside and headed to the entrance, a giant hole in the stomach of the ship that was either accidental or purposely made.

The lights strung along the beams above were seaweed-green orbs, bright enough to showcase the interior but dark enough to give it a mysterious cavern mood. She saw the tables all had flickering candles in sealed mason jars; the flames she saw were made of fabric and powered by an electric volt. What would be considered the nucleus of the place sat on the far left with a wide, curvy counter space and stools lined all around it. Dallas noticed the bartender right away, a large woman with fiery red hair. She took bottles off the shelves above her with ease, flexing the muscles those arms were made of. Close enough to the bar was the stage area, and Dallas first saw the flash of purple before she heard the excited squeal.

"Dally! You're here!"

Dallas swam over and nearly flipped over with Albany's greeting embrace.

"Glad you could come!"

"I loved that invitation you made. It was adorable."

Albany was all grins. "I think that is one of my favorite parts. I wish I could find a way to make my business cards animated like that. I probably could!"

"This," Dallas said, stealing another look at the ceiling light fixtures, "is so frickin' cool."

"I love this place!" Albany agreed. "I've done a few events here, and the owner is so awesome. That's her at the bar. Listen, why don't you go get anything you want and hang out for a bit while I finish getting set up? Tell her you're with me!"

"Really?" Dallas said. She watched Albany pick up one end of a banner and help another mermaid hang it across a wood beam: KARAOKE NIGHT. Another mermaid hovered over the music player and changed the stations until she found something more alternative rock, and Dallas was happy with that selection enough to go to the bar.

She did not realize she would be one of the first people to arrive, but going to see her sister gave her the excuse. The few other merpeople lingered around at the bar or sat at the tables browsing the menus. Dallas found an empty stool and sat on it with nothing else to do but pursue something new and foreign to her.

There was a menu near her that she took and opened up, taking her time reading up on the specialties of the place. There were ingredients she had never heard of and others she had, such as the flavors of sea-salt margaritas. At one point, she looked up at the sound of a blender, or what sounded like a blender.

The woman at the bar was at this machine where yellow and pink colors were swirling together. She stopped the machine when the colors were blended enough and then filled a chalice to the rim. Dallas caught whiffs of pineapple, strawberry, and coconut before the chalice was full and sealed with its top and straw. The bartender finished it off with slices of pineapple shish-kabobbed through that straw.

Dallas gave that menu another read-through and only looked up when she saw the mass of red hair right above her eye level. She froze in place, seeing the woman's eyes for the first time, because as red-hot as her hair was, her eyes were the stark opposite: ice blue. The contrasting temperatures both served the same purpose of demanding attention and setting a warning yet offering the warmth of comfort and the cool of tranquility.

"What'll ya have, honey?"

Dallas scanned the menu again. "Um, that strawberry pineapple thing smells good. I'll have one of those."

"You got it. Are you starting a tab?"

Dallas saw Albany holding a clipboard and checking things off.

"Yeah, what the hell."

"Coming right up."

Dallas's shoulders relaxed as she realized Albany was right.

When Dallas took the first sip of her first drink, every tense muscle in her body relaxed, and something hot raced through her veins. The last drink she had was out with some old friends, and she was maybe two drinks in before she felt anything. This surpassed that. It was better than on land, maybe because it wasn't on land, but either way, every problem she had coming in swam out of her pores and disappeared. She took another sip and finished it with one of the pineapple slices.

She was almost done with her drink when Albany joined her.

"How's it going?"

Dallas raised her chalice. "God, this is amazing."

Albany laughed. "Easy there, tiger."

"But really, I mean all of this is amazing."

"It is," Albany said, nodding. "I need to make sure everything is settled before I drink, though. Hey, Mickey!"

The bartender flipped two empty chalices upside down in the sink area and turned to them.

"Mickey, this is my sister Dallas. Dallas, Mickey is the owner of the place."

"Nice to meet you, Dallas," Mickey said. "You'll see "Michelle" written on all the necessary legal crap around here, but I go by Mickey."

"Dallas is a new launchie, but I think it's safe to say she's getting settled just fine."

Dallas sipped her drink through the straw until she hit the water nestled under the ice.

"I think I'm ready for another."

"You got it," Mickey said with a smile.

As the evening progressed, Dallas found herself at a table with Albany and a small group of her friends, none of whose names she remembered, but she did not care as much. She was happy to enjoy her drink and the pita bread and vegetable spread she ordered while they all listened to the musical accompaniment, some contestants better than others.

At one point, Albany was eyeing Dallas noticeably.

"What?" Dallas countered with a raise of her brow.

"Come on."

Dallas shook her head. "Not happening."

"Oh, you know I was going to ask you again, but I wasn't going to until you had a few drinks! Maybe you need another one!"

Dallas's response was to shove a triangle of pita bread and spread into her mouth and flip her off.

"My sister could blow everyone here out of the water," Albany bragged to everyone at the table. "She killed it at our school variety show!"

"That was junior high!" Dallas exclaimed, but it was not heard well through her mouthful.

"Yeah, well, you got better with age. You're good, you know, no matter what."

Dallas just chewed, playing with the straw in her drink.

Albany turned to the waitstaff and ordered another drink, then slyly looked at her sister. Dallas sighed and waved a hand.

"And another one for her."

Albany leaned in when no one was looking.

"Hey. Screw that show, okay?"

"Oh, come on, Ally, that was forever ago. I'm over it now."

She was over it, yet Dallas remembered she had still kept her old audition number sticker on her pegboard. As a reminder. As a, well, learning tool.

"You know it was rigged. They pick the sexy blonde girl from the start who has no brain and just have her voice dubbed by someone else anyway. It's a crock of shit. You're way better than that."

Dallas felt her teeth clench. It was only a year ago, but she remembered how her cold, damp palms felt on the steering wheel when she parked her car. She remembered how she made an immediate beeline to the bathroom to put the armpits of her shirt under the air dryers before she went to the registration tables. Her numbered sticker was a small name tag square that she put on her left side, a little too quickly, causing it to have a fold. She noted with invented optimism that the lime green marker for the numbers was the same color as her shirt, a perfect match she hoped would mean good luck.

When Dallas's name was called, she got up from her chair and made her way to the auditorium that was past the tables. The production crew was there, making sure everyone found their way to the right place, and they immediately matched her number to her name on her paperwork. Dallas went through the doors, knowing the cameras were turned on.

There was a single table of three people, plus others in business suits and headsets around the room. Dallas knew that first impressions made everything, and she wondered just what they thought of her when she walked through. She wanted to dress like her music style: casual alternative, someone with a little spice and spunk.

Her green shirt was not too baggy and not too tight; her black jeans were ripped at the knees, and she wore her favorite, good luck black and white checkerboard Chuck Taylors. She added enough mousse to her hair to make it almost plaster, hanging down at the base of her neck in brown and bleach-blonde sections. She even wore her glasses with a thick black frame instead of her contacts. She smiled at the judges.

"Name?"

"Dallas Dwight."

"How old are you?"

"Eighteen."

"And what are you going to sing for us today?"

"Alone, by Heart."

"Okay, Dallas," said one of them, putting her paperwork on top. "Whenever you are ready."

Dallas wasn't ready, but she started anyway, her voice skipping a bit due to her pounding heart. She tried to set her focal point on the wall behind the judges so she was not necessarily looking at them, but she could see all of them at the same time. She kept her head high and tried not to cringe when she came to the power part of the song and let her gut do the work for her. At the time, she thought the louder, the better, although she tried not to scream. When all three judges raised their hands, she stopped.

"You have a good range," another said.

"You were a little pitchy at parts, though," said the last one. "Your voice was shaky too."

Dallas kept her face stoic and nodded along to what they said, fighting to keep any emotion from escaping.

"Sorry, but you're just not what we're looking for at this time. Best of luck to you."

She had turned and left that room on autopilot, heading back to that bathroom she had been in only moments ago. She thought that was where the emotions would pour out, but all they did was sting the edges of her eyes a little bit.

Dallas helped herself to her next drink when it arrived and watched the mermaid currently on stage doing some pop number she had never heard of. At points, her mouth was too close to the microphone, and she was shouting more than she was singing. Dallas watched her body movement and stage presence, how much she leaned inward to the screen to read the words as if she were trying to close in and hide herself, never making contact with the audience at all. Dallas chuckled. She was performing on a TV screen. When this performer finished, the place sounded with weak but polite clapping.

The guy on staff went on stage with an open palm to the audience.

"Looks like we have an opening! Who's next? Any takers?"

Dallas avoided eye contact with Albany but took another long sip from her drink. Her hand shot up before she could stop herself, which caused everyone at her table to cheer.

"Come on up!" the guy said.

"Dally!" Albany cried, squeezing her arm. "I knew you'd do it! Go, go, go!"

Dallas ran her fingers through her hair and swam up to the stage, the merman pointing to the screen offstage of songs for her to choose. She lingered a moment, the edges of her eyes stinging just the same, especially when she told the merman what song to do, one she knew best. The screen came with the lyrics, but Dallas did not need them. She was grateful for the drinks because something was grounding her that was not just her desire for redemption.

The applause was polite, sans her sister's table, which whooped and cheered. Dallas took a deep breath and let the ocean bubbles calm her lungs as she maintained stability.

The music started, and she hovered in front of the mic with her hands resting on the bottom, looking at a focal point across the bar so she could see each and every audience member, but more so, so they could see her. The song started calm and serene, and Dallas began the first verse of lyrics for "Alone."

Her voice eased into those words like they were old friends, forgetting the anxiety she had the last time she sang them before a table of harsh judges. Instead, they filled her with harmony that she broadcasted to every corner of the room, the harmony that could swoon someone faster than the alcohol in their drinks.

The first verse ended with appreciative whoops from the audience, no doubt recognizing that Dallas wasn't just a drunken karaoke singer. Her semi-deep alto tones were sure to give the unsuspecting listener bumps on the back of the neck. She serenaded with this soft opening before the big number, taking the breath needed before belting out the power lines.

Dallas grabbed the mic off the stand and swam further downstage, the cheers sounding from every part of the bar. She hit every note and line, and the more she sang, the more she felt the most powerful force she had ever felt swimming up inside her. She had thought long about how everything would be underwater, but she did not give much thought to what it would be like to sing underwater.

At first, it felt like it was a lot harder, as her sound waves were pushing against the regular waves... but she did it with such ease, and it was almost like the ocean waves were making way for her. They were submitting to her and working with her sound instead of against it...like water could have acoustics. Instead of just hearing her song, she could also feel it, somewhere between a hum and vibration that was mesmerizing and massaging.

Was this how music sounded through water?

The experience was much more intimate than it was on land. It was a connection she could not have with anything else. And somehow, the audience knew it. And Dallas sang on.

Her head became dizzy with the adrenaline, the aquatic forces at hand, and not to mention the drinks she had coming together all at once. When she hit another note, this time longer and more powerful than she had throughout the whole song, she felt the vibration deep in every recess of her head that ached and made her vision fuzzy.

She blinked a few times, but her vision did not clear. As the song ended and she dragged out the final notes, she was met with a sensation that seemed to knock her back. She shut her eyes, but that did not help the dizziness at all. The audience erupted in cheers and applause when the song ended but quickly turned to gasps and shouting as Dallas fell back over in an unconscious slump.

CHAPTER 16

SHE FELT THE GROWING pressure on her wrist and fluttered her eyelids. The second thing she felt was something ice-cold on her forehead, prompting her to open her eyes and jump awake.

"Dally!"

"She's awake."

"Oh my God, are you all right?"

Dallas saw many faces peering over her, the two closest being Albany and Mickey. Albany held her wrist while Mickey put the cold thing back on her head. She groaned.

"What..."

"Dally, can you hear me? What's my name?"

"Jesus, Ally."

"Where are you?"

"I don't know, the back of the bar?"

"What's my favorite color?"

"Pink."

"What's the capital of Nepal?"

"Kathmandu."

Albany was taken aback at what was supposed to be a joke. "I think you're right."

Dallas groaned and sat up, only to be assisted by Mickey.

"Whoa, easy there, honey, you don't want to get up too fast."

"What the hell happened to me?"

"You were killing that song, and then you fainted," Albany explained. "Don't worry, though, because you were awesome, and everyone just thought you were drunk. Everyone was cheering and didn't think too much of it, and me and some of the staff helped you back here. You're a hero out there! You were out for a while."

"Are you kidding me? How long?"

"Like twenty minutes," Mickey answered. "I got someone covering the bar, and I brought you back here to rest."

Dallas took a good look around, realizing she was right about her guess in the back of the bar. She was on a couch in what looked like a storage area with shelves and a mini refrigerator. Other staff members stood around awkwardly while Dallas propped herself up on her elbows.

"You guys are good," Mickey dismissed them.

The staff members went back out through a swing door, and Dallas could still hear the music playing, letting her know that she hadn't slept the whole night away.

"So, you had a little too much," Mickey continued. "Big deal. You are one hell of a singer, and you brought the house down. If this were a competition, you would have won."

"Yeah, Dally! I told you! You just needed to get your confidence back, and you did it!"

Mickey took the cold press from her forehead and lifted a cup of water.

"Here, you'll need to hydrate yourself."

"Thanks."

Dallas took a few sips, recapping her time on stage. She had so many questions and didn't know where to start.

"Singing underwater," was all she said.

"Just like you can on land," Albany proclaimed, but Dallas shook her head.

"No, it's not. There's something different. It's like... it's almost like the sound carries differently."

Both sat silently, and Dallas laughed.

"Okay, yeah, I know how stupid that sounds."

"Sound actually travels faster and further in water," explained Mickey.

"No, I know that, that's not what I meant. There was something that happened that I can't really describe. I felt something in my head."

"The pineapple rum?" half-joked Albany.

"No, no, actually it was not the rum. No, when I was singing, I felt like it was all around me... and then I felt like it came back to me. Like it was something tangible I could feel."

"I'm sure it was because it was the first time you sang down here," Albany suggested. "Of course, it would feel weird."

Dallas shook her head again, and Mickey prompted her to drink more water. She sat all the way up now and rubbed her head, finger-combing her hair.

"You take it easy now," Mickey said. "You can stay as long as you need to until the event is over and I pay your sister."

"I took care of your bill for you."

Dallas shot her a look. "What? Ally!"

Albany laughed and waved her hand. "Don't worry about it. I took care of it. You can pay me back whenever."

"I will. Thanks."

She drank some more, and Mickey and Albany acted like they were ready to get up when Dallas said something that stopped both of them. Especially Mickey. They stared at her.

"You saw things in your head?" Mickey repeated.

"Yeah, right before I blacked out, I saw something clear as day, and I don't understand what it means. I saw this rock sort of shaped like Minnesota."

Mickey grinned in amusement, but Albany looked confused.

"Well, isn't that interesting," was all Mickey said.

"What?" Albany asked.

"You said that you could feel something in your head when you sang, and then you saw a picture of a rock."

"It's not the rum talking," Dallas insisted.

"Oh, I know. I know."

Mickey swam over and urged her to get up. "I know exactly what happened, but first I need to show you before I can tell you."

"What? Tell me what?"

Mickey led Dallas through the backcourt, with Albany in tow. They swam through another door until they were outside, and then Mickey brought them all the way to the other side of the ship where the entrance was.

"See it?"

Dallas did right away, and it baffled her. She had never seen this rock in person; she only saw it randomly appear in her head during her performance, but there it was.

"You're right, it does look like Minnesota."

"But how is this possible? I didn't even notice it when I got here!"

"You didn't need to, because you saw it when you were singing."

"That doesn't make any sense; I was technically inside and too far away."

Mickey smiled at her. "Guess what? You can echolocate."

Albany swam home with her, and Dallas didn't care at all to stay a little longer after that. She ordered a sandwich with water while Albany finished what she had to do. Mickey tended to the last remaining customers but made sure to bid them good night, inviting them back for brunch whenever they wanted. Dallas made sure to thank Mickey repeatedly before she ordered her to go home and go to bed.

She still didn't know what else to say, even after talking it over with them. She and Albany were on their way home, intrigued and confused.

"I don't know, Dally," Albany said. "It's not like it's rare; I just don't know too much about it. Plenty of merpeople can do it, I guess, but it's just a skill either you have or you don't. But this is so great! You learned something new about yourself!"

"Yeah, I guess. I am still shocked. I don't know what it means or what I'm supposed to do with it."

"Looks like you can find out. Maybe you'll get in with the hunter/gatherers! I mean, that's where that will come in handy for sure, right?"

All Dallas could do was shrug. Whatever she came up with only led to more questions.

"Hey, just sleep on it. And keep your ears open when you do your Job Trials. Look at job openings. Ask around."

"Yeah."

They passed through the first pipeline to lead them inside and to safety. The guard let them in with a nod before switching positions with another for the rest of the night shift.

"Well, look on the bright side. You did sober up."

"Ug."

Dallas didn't feel tired until she saw the door to her apartment nook, then it was like she physically relaxed into the sleep mode that would come with falling into bed. She and Albany took what felt like forever to see each other off, even though her place wasn't too far. Albany had to remind her of the dinner date with their parents, but Dallas had to tell her to remind her another time. When she had more functional brain cells.

Dallas keyed into her apartment and swayed in, heading right to her bedroom and swimming up to her hammock to collapse in it. She pulled a blanket around her but did little work to cover herself as the hammock did most of the work. It rocked her, her tail fins relaxing in the curve of the cloth, and her hair settling around her face. As she lay there, the last image she pictured in her head before drifting off to sleep was that rock, clear as when she indirectly saw it for the first time.

CHAPTER 17

IT FELT LIKE THE equivalent of the last day of school as she kept checking the time. In a way, it was better, and in a way, it was worse. On her last break from making copies and cold calls at her desk, she bought a cup of noodles from a vending machine. She didn't know how long her concluding meeting would go but wanted to prepare for more time than expected, especially with current events.

Dallas busied herself with alphabetizing the client files into the cabinets, at least grateful that her days as a glorified intern were coming to an end. It didn't matter if she finished on time. It didn't matter if she finished. She knelt by the cabinets for the last few minutes to recharge her mental batteries and get back to neutral. Without a second to waste, she got up and speed-swam to the clock to punch out, not bothering to stop in the supervisor's office for a friendly farewell. She was just extra help, after all.

Dallas got out her tablet when she left the office and entered the common area of the building. Other merpeople swam by her in their routine commutes, and it was hard to see which pipeline she was to take back. She got a good look at her map and headed to the envoy's offices in the main community building. A notification chimed in her inbox, reminding her of her meeting with Noah at 3:30, which she bypassed instantly. It never left her mind the minute she woke up that morning.

Dallas swam through the envoy's office corridor and took a seat in the common area twenty minutes early, opening her tablet for mindless social media browsing before her time arrived. The last mermaid came out of Noah's office, and Dallas sat up.

"He's ready for you," the other mermaid said to her in passing, as though Noah knew she would already be waiting. She closed her tablet and pocketed it, flipping her fins at a quicker pace.

Noah swayed in his chair with his elbows resting on the arms, greeting Dallas with a big smile.

"Well, well, well, Miss Dwight."

Dallas went to the chair and didn't sit until he nodded. She also decided that she would let him do the talking and wait to be asked a question. He studied her for a minute, still smiling.

"Looks like you have a hidden talent."

Dallas blinked.

"Now, word can travel fast, but it travels even faster when you're friends with the bar owner." Noah chuckled. "Mickey is like a mom to me."

"Oh, wow."

"Yup, and that is not something that happens often, you know."

"I didn't know," she said. "Honestly, I thought I was just drunk."

"That's understandable, especially since you discovered it by accident, but it was certainly a happy accident. You didn't act like you were anyway, according to Mickey. You just got overwhelmed with it and passed out."

Dallas rubbed her forehead.

"It's all right. It wore you out since it was your first time. According to her, everyone thought you put on the best performance of the night! You just didn't know that it would lead you to learn how to echolocate! It didn't take her long to do a search and learn that your Job Trials Envoy was me. I have to say this threw me for a loop. It certainly changed the agenda of your concluding meeting. I was all set to grill you on what your decision was."

"About all the Job Trials I did?"

Noah nodded.

"I was going to tell you that none of the ones you did seem satisfactory enough for you. I was going to say your next step was to figure out what you wanted to do, whether you wanted to investigate other temporary jobs or take the other route and look into nearby colleges. I knew it was going to be teeth-pulling for both of us, and then you go and surprise me. You really did."

"So now what happens?" Dallas asked. "I didn't know that I could do that, and I don't even know how to do it again or what it means now."

"That's all right," Noah said, his voice still maintaining a cheery tone, and Dallas figured out that it wasn't for show. Now she knew it meant a whole new ballgame. She had never seen him this genuinely pleased, at least not with her. "Of course, you need to go through training to use your new skill. It is something that is very useful and is going to open up a lot of doors for you."

"Can other people do it too? Is it like a superpower or something?"

Noah chuckled. "Yes, of course, but you're not an X-Man. Calm down. It's a natural ability, and many merpeople can do it. In fact, a lot of merpeople can do it, but not a lot of merpeople can do it exceptionally well. It's like running. Anybody can run, but some can only jog while others can cross-country sprint. So, it is also like singing, which now makes sense. There are some people who only do it in the shower, some people who only do it on karaoke nights for fun, and others who sign album contracts and do live concerts. You, my dear, are concert material."

If Dallas's eyes could water, they would have at that moment from the words she had longed to hear her whole life, only in the most unexpected circumstances.

"Merpeople have and can develop many abilities, you know, that other sea life have."

"Dolphins have echolocation," Dallas stated.

Noah gave her a knowing look. "Where do you think they learned it from?"

There was a beat while Dallas tried to choose one of the many questions in her head to ask first.

"Can you echolocate?"

Noah snickered a bit to himself.

"No, not really, and the funny part is I sing too. Well, sort of. I can sing okay, but mainly I'm just a musician, and I would much rather play for someone else singing. I had a garage band back on land when I was in high school. I'd do a few bad rocker yells into the microphone a few times per song, as is tradition. I had eyeliner and ripped jeans too, but we're not going to talk about that. The point is when merpeople try to use echolocation, it does not come in too clearly, and they can only go as far as a few feet. Those who can do it for real have no limits. And according to Mickey, you were able to see a rock way out of any normal range. You have more potential than you think."

Dallas felt like every word she spoke was a sip from a hot beverage. This was the last way she expected this meeting to go, and she felt a happiness she never thought she would feel fill her up and overflow the rim.

"So, I'm here to tell you it will be easy to get you in with the hunter/gatherers."

Noah waited for her reaction, which was just a slight raise of her eyebrow in interest.

"Hunter/gatherers."

"Yeah, it actually fits you perfectly. Hunter/gatherers go out into the open ocean to collect things, hunt for things, and search for things. They are explorers. I remembered how disappointed you were that you couldn't do the wildlife conservationist job trial. So, you like nature, and you like to explore. Bingo."

Something inside Dallas jumped, a little pop of excitement telling her it was was real and happening to her. She smiled with him but couldn't help but be distracted by the photo on his desk. He was a human sitting with his legs crossed on the floor and a guitar in his lap, grinning at the camera while craning the guitar neck.

"The first thing we need to do is get you set up for training, and we've already done that. The very person who discovered you will be the one training you."

"Mickey?"

Noah nodded. "That's right. That's how easily she saw that potential in you. She was a martial arts instructor up on land. She also trained opera singers. She used to be one herself, you know."

Dallas's eyes widened.

"She would still be pretty decent if she laid off the cigarettes as she got older, but the point is she knows her stuff and was impressed with your range, so she told me she would be happy to train you herself."

"That is so nice."

"So, just watch for an email from me when she tells me when she will be available. We will coordinate."

"Will do," she answered, feeling a new warmth toward Noah, instantly reminded of the time she shadowed a high school as a junior high student. She was paired with a senior guy who, within mere hours, became the big brother she never had. In one day, he gave her better direction and advice than any counselor she ever had in four years. Her handshake with Noah was firmer than their previous meeting.

"You really did surprise me," he said. "Keep doing it. Your true potential is going to come out here."

Dallas swam out of those offices with her mind tangled in electrical wires. She thought back to her karaoke night, her performance, and how it made her feel when she started to echolocate. She thought she would have to procure those feelings again, but this time voluntarily. Was she just going to sing a bunch of times until it happened again? Dallas tried to imagine that both hilarious and nerve-wracking scene of prepping her diaphragm like a machine. Would it be better or worse than an audition?

She paid no attention to the activity around her and didn't notice how others were swimming at quicker paces, not even the pods forming in heated alarm. She didn't notice envoys on their routine heading to the exit and being confronted by people demanding answers. It wasn't until swarms formed at the windows and the cries escalated that she broke out of her reverie and looked up.

The swarms only grew with more awareness of whatever scene was at hand. An envoy merwoman whipped out her radio to make a call and swam away. Dallas felt the sensation of being pulled in the gravitational direction of natural curiosity and joined the masses at the window, swimming higher for a better view. Her stomach curled in a curdling sick when she caught sight of what was stuck to the electric fence.

It looked like the merman was simply stuck to the fence, arms spread as if he had been knocked unconscious, but it was only when Dallas shifted her perspective that she saw it was only his top half.

Below the chest ended in a rugged, bloody stump. Tendrils of flesh, fish meat, and inner entrails floated in the water like a hundred little tails.

Shouts erupted all around Dallas and up the way to the exit, where various envoys bunched together to form their own fence.

"Remain calm!" called a man tall enough for everyone to see. "The Marine Force has been contacted and will be on site, and no one is to leave outsea!"

"You are all ordered to go home!" proclaimed another.

Dallas fell into the pod of merpeople being ushered to the residential wings and pipelines. The last thing she saw out the window was two figures swimming up to the torso and gently, carefully, moving the body off and then down with them. She watched them carry it away, the head flopping up and down with the eyes partially open, but the mouth gaping wide as if the very last thing it did was scream.

CHAPTER 18

T̲H̲E̲ ̲S̲C̲R̲E̲E̲N̲ ̲S̲H̲O̲W̲E̲D̲ ̲F̲U̲Z̲Z̲Y̲ footage, no doubt blurred enough to censor the graphic content, but it looked just like a corpse straight out of a horror movie. The camera scanned the body while the narrator talked about its injuries.

> "...teeth marks which are present around the torso where the tail was ripped and torn off. These marks are consistent with showing that the attack took place over a period of time where the victim was pursued and fought, and the predator in question made several bites, as evident in the uneven tears in other places on the stomach area."

Dallas stared at the merman, now disrobed to showcase the marks around the cause of dismemberment and death. When first found, he had been wearing the robes with the black and silver emblem of the Marine Force. No one was near him when he was attacked, at least not anyone who survived. This merman's top half was the only thing found.

"...not like the teeth one would find on a Great White, the common predator. These marks were made by something that tore instead of bit down. The identity of such a creature has not yet been made."

Dallas flipped the channel to the community network, tuning in to the prerecorded statement of the viceroy. Warren Westburn looked into the camera with a solemn, fearful expression that was almost anger.

"...everything in our power to make our community safe. We are shocked and appalled about the attacks that continue to happen without an identified predator. I have increased security around the town perimeters and business districts. As of today, I have called for more Marine Force involvement and teams involving the hunters. We will find this creature. Rest assured, your safety is our highest priority. Our hearts go to the deceased and his family at this time."

Dallas shut the TV off and regarded the lunch remains on her coffee table. There were one or two stray noodles left from her empty plate and about a sip and a half left of the green peach tea brew. She finished the drink until the straw slurped and picked up the plate to the kitchen, cleaning both under the vacuum faucet in the sink.

The last time she checked, there were no other updates, and no time changes from Noah. She timed it so that she would go to their meeting and have enough time to go to the markets to pick up a few more groceries. The new 7 p.m. curfew would take effect that night.

According to Noah's email, they would meet at his office and then be escorted by Marine Force to meet Mickey. Dallas arrived to find a line of them outside the envoy offices. Some carried long spears.

"They're not fooling around," he told her. "Anyone going outsea on official business or not will have Marine Force with them. I'll tell you more on the way."

It seemed that he had a few other answers ready for the expected questions that she did not ask, at least not yet. Instead, the Marine Force escort waited outside Noah's office until they came out.

"Ready when you are," said the man whose deep voice matched his physique. When he turned to lead them, Dallas caught a full view of the different kind of weapon strapped to his back. It looked almost like a crossbow. The arrowhead blade had something crusted on the end from whatever he last used it on, and she did not want to think about what it was.

They took the normal route with this escort, and Dallas got a good look out the window at the fence, where a team in khaki tunics gathered to work on its wiring. Something yellow flashed through the pipes and then turned back off.

"Higher voltage," she heard among a group of merpeople nearby. She swam to keep up with Noah and the escort as many heads turned in their direction. There was another envoy stationed at the pipeline leading out of the building, who regarded both the escort and Noah with interest.

"What is your business out?"

Noah had his tablet ready and showed the envoy the screen.

"Permission for echolocation training."

The envoy eyed Dallas and nodded to both Noah and the escort before opening the door to the open sea. Dallas had all sorts of scenery envisioned for this venture, including a deep cave or even dark murky waters, but was taken back to the familiar chosen venue. Another team of khaki tunics carried bundles of pipes and wiring and set up near the front of the ship, where the merwoman with red-hot hair and tail floated to watch with disdain.

"All right, so if this thing fries on my property, does that mean I can serve it up as my new daily special?"

"There will be nothing left of it if we blow it up," Noah answered as they approached the ship.

Mickey snorted. Arms folded, she regarded Noah first. "Or if I kill it first."

"Then you'll be the hero of the town."

"Then we don't have to put up with this crap?"

"Guess not, but for now, we must. And we need to make sure everyone is safe. Including you."

"And you. No more night swims."

They both opened their arms for a tight embrace, holding it for a moment before remembering Dallas.

"So, here's a familiar face," Noah gestured to Dallas.

"Welcome back, kid," Mickey greeted.

"Hi."

"I thought it would be easiest, and best, to help you practice right where you experienced it for the first time. I don't have too many customers during this time of day, so it's perfect."

Mickey grinned at her and motioned for them to follow her inside, side-swimming past a pile of pipes and wiring spools. Dallas smiled, thinking how strange it was to see the once-flourishing party bar quiet and empty.

"This is all bull if you ask me," Mickey went on as they entered the ship. "Nothing ever comes this way and never will, except for the occasional turtle or something. Even any Great White I've ever seen was off in the open blue and never anywhere civilized."

"I know, Mic. It's for your protection," Noah explained.

They were at the bar now, where Mickey smirked and pointed at what was mounted on the top, something Dallas missed in her drunken stupor the first time: the biggest harpoon she'd ever seen, needle as thick as her arm and the point ending in a slight curve.

"Does this look like I need protection?"

"You know I love you, Mickey."

"You're lucky I love you sometimes," was her response. Dallas didn't notice them staring at her until she heard Noah clear his throat, and then she pulled herself away from the mounted weapon.

"Happy now? You're scaring the launchie."

"Like Westburn isn't doing a good enough job of that already."

Noah sighed. "Come on now."

"I know, I know," Mickey waved her hand. "Listen, you, get in the back and fix that stuff on my computer. That's the only reason I said you could come. I'll take care of Dallas from here."

"Yes, ma'am!"

Noah swam to the backroom, humming to himself until he disappeared and so did his song. Mickey looked to Dallas with an arched eyebrow.

"You're probably just as surprised as I am. Truth be told, I haven't had an echolocation trainee in years."

"Really?"

"They come and go, and some have the basics and don't need the training. But when there's talent, there's talent, and you showed much more than your singing ability the other night."

Dallas saw the stage area out of the corner of her eye but did not acknowledge it, not really wanting an encore performance.

"We're going to go easy and slow," Mickey said as she led her to the stage and stood next to her. "First, take a moment to take a deep breath and focus somewhere ahead of you. It's like you are getting ready to perform because, in a little way, you are. Let's just do some breathing for a bit."

Dallas thought back to her singing lessons with amusement, now breathing in through her nose and gills and out through her mouth, watching the trail of bubbles go further and further.

Dallas made the last breath deeper and longer, watching those bubbles trail past Mickey and her outstretched finger.

"Nice one," she declared. "Echolocation is not singing or yelling, but it's very similar. It's more like producing a quick, single note that you want to carry all the way to the other side of the room, like you're performing and want the people all the way back in the last rows to hear you. And for some reason, you want to see them. You cast out frequency waves with your sound. Now, when dolphins do it, they do it via high-frequency clicks since they don't have vocal cords. When bats do it, they use a different sound. Many merpeople do the same with clicking, but others who have better skills can use their whole voices. That is where you come in. Once you send that sonic wave out and it reaches an object, it's going to bounce back and form an image in your head. Just like when you first saw the rock. Next, we're going to do some humming."

Mickey hummed next to her, and she joined in, the two creating a gentle hum. When Mickey got louder, Dallas got louder, and then she opened her mouth for a single note.

"You can feel the vibrations of the things around you, subtly at first. Try it now. Sing a single note, but keep it short, and produce it from your gut. Pretend like you are casting to that chair at that table. I want you to close your eyes and concentrate on turning that note into a wave."

Dallas made a sound, almost like an owl underwater.

"Not enough. Too quiet. Push with your gut."

She did it again, and this time it was like the exhale she released bounced back to her. As soon as she got that image of the exact size and shape of that chair in her mind, she popped her eyes back open.

"That was fast!" she declared.

"It is, and it will be for things that are closer."

Mickey swam down the tables and toward the furthest seating section of the place. "Close your eyes again and turn this way toward me. Cast a wave out and then tell me how many empty beer bottles are on the table next to me."

Dallas tried several times to emit further sonar. She focused on breathing in and making the sound, paying no attention to volume as it was not the important part here but rather the distance. She sounded it through the bar and to where Mickey was, immediately making out her form and outline next to the table with the two chairs.

"There are...four."

"Correct," said Mickey as she opened her eyes. "I think I have to fire last night's cleanup crew. Now, how about something a little harder?"

Dallas shut her eyes again and listened to Mickey's voice move away from her and around the room. "I am going to get an object and hold it, and you have to tell me what it is."

She echolocated the object Mickey was holding, coming back to her in a confused laugh.

"Is that a...huge donut?"

"You've got the shape, but you need to read all the details. Do it again."

"There's a rope on it. Is that a flotation device?"

"Right you are," said Mickey, and Dallas opened her eyes to confirm it, watching the red tail swim back up to the point on the wall where she had taken it down. "You know, in case anyone drowns here."

On the opposite side of her vision, she saw a blue tail joining the scene.

"How's it going in here?"

"She's doing very well," Mickey answered. "She's advancing faster than anyone I've trained. At least, in a very long time."

Dallas hid a smile, and Noah nodded at her. "She doesn't give compliments often."

"Am I really?" she asked.

"You are," Mickey stated. "Remember, most merpeople that can echolocate do so with clicking noises. You can use your voice, and that is more powerful. You can make sonic booms instead. You already made one before."

"So, I hope this is a good time to interrupt the lesson. I took care of your problems. You had a lot of junk in there you weren't using, so I cleared some space for you and updated your antivirus."

"Thank you, darling."

"Anytime."

Mickey looked back at Dallas.

"Well, maybe this is also a good time to ask if you two wouldn't mind helping us get rid of some leftover pizza?"

"What an inconvenience, Michelle! How dare you make my protégé and me succumb to your tedious needs?"

"Call me Michelle again, and I'll turn you into sushi. What do you say, honey? Are you hungry?"

"I'd love it, thank you."

"Doesn't look like I'll be getting any customers for lunch anytime soon, and probably not for dinner. We have to throw away whatever wasn't served yesterday, so it's on the house. I'll throw some in the warmer now. Coming right up."

Dallas realized that there was a point when she started smiling and did not stop, and it was the first time she had in a long time.

"Thanks, Mickey," Noah said. He turned back to Dallas.

"She's good people. The best, actually. It's stereotypical to vent your problems to the bartender, but she's the one that fits it. You can tell her anything and count on her for anything."

"I can definitely see that."

Noah was looking at the stage now, almost with a sense of longing.

"Man, I haven't played in a while."

Mickey came back around just then, fumbling with the watch on her wrist.

"All right, I've got a timer going, so let's squeeze a little more practice in, huh?"

Noah settled himself at a chair by a nearby table, and now Dallas had an audience.

"Now, it's not always just finding one thing. You'll need to be able to find multiple things, to scan an area to see what is there and how close or how far it is. I could scan my lineup of employees and tell how many were missing that day and who. Now, close your eyes and count the number of tables in this room."

"Twenty-eight."

"Correct. I'm going to remove some chairs, and you'll have to tell me how many and where I put them. I'll tell you when I am ready."

Dallas kept her eyes shut and started a slow inhale.

"Okay, go."

She released the sonar.

"You took out three."

She released another.

"And you put all three of them on the wall with the Fish Academy poster."

"Correct again!"

Dallas opened her eyes. Mickey floated with her arms folded and a grin that revealed she had a gold tooth. Noah's smile revealed a perfect white fence.

"That was fast, kid."

"Fast, huh?" Noah repeated. "That's great. I wasn't sure what I was going to do with this one."

Dallas smirked, but it quickly turned into a full smile.

"I think we have a better understanding of where she can belong."

"A hunter/gatherer, you said."

Noah gestured to her.

"Yep. I have scrounged up some open positions that you need to apply for. It doesn't matter that you didn't do a Job Trial there. It's a helpful boost, but it doesn't matter when you're a good candidate."

"What would I...put on it?" Dallas asked. "I mean... I have no experience at all."

"Well, that's where an envoy like me comes in. I can help you doctor up that resume. You mentioned you worked retail, so I imagine you would have done stock and inventory, correct?"

"I guess."

"Right, well, in a way that is searching for stuff."

"Oh."

"So, you are going to just tweak that resume a bit and then send that puppy out. To be honest, with your echolocation range, the first thing you apply for will probably snag you right away. There are a few groups in the area looking to fill. And then you'll be out getting lobsters and bluefin tuna and searching for clams before you know it."

"That could be good," Dallas stated.

Just then, Mickey's watch chimed.

"All right, kids, chow."

Noah and Dallas automatically took seats at the bar when Mickey went to the back. She brought out a large pan, which she held with mitts. Dallas could smell the garlic and cheese combinations bubble through her nose and leaned over the counter, curious.

Noah put a couple of black metallic coins on the counter; the surfaces etched with wavy dollar signs.

"Two of those sodas," he said. "Lemon-lime for me. And what do you want?"

"Oh, thanks! I'll have that as well."

Mickey took the slices out of the pan, already cut into the iconic triangle shapes, and put them on two clean plates.

Sea pizza was spongy and strange, but with extra salt, it added to the taste.

The last time Dallas had pizza was at the campus cafeteria: paper-thin triangles with a breadstick-hard crust. She sat at a counter eating it as she did now, leisurely, staring at nothing in particular. Only then her thoughts hung at a dead end. She wouldn't have imagined being where she was now back then, not at all, and not even close.

CHAPTER 19

"Um, I can see your bed and dressers...a pile of clothes on the floor."

Naomi gave Hugh a little shove. "I thought you said you put those away."

"What else?" Albany urged.

"Umm...Dad's computer? Mom's...uh...Mom, what is that weird brush thing on the dresser?"

"It's a scale polisher," Naomi answered, waving her tail in pride. "Look, look at this. There's more green in here now, and there might even be shades of gold if I move it differently. I got it at this beauty shop."

"Hey, that is cool."

"Well, I am impressed, Dally," Hugh said. "You really did it!"

"I feel like I am getting better and better," Dallas answered. "It was hard at first but not so bad now."

"How often do you have lessons?"

"I just had the one this week. I will have a few more, but not too much right now, as Mickey has the bar to run while she is still open. I have to squeeze in what I can while we can still get out. And then I'm going to apply for some jobs in hunter/gatherer teams."

"That's fantastic!"

"Oh, we're so proud of you!"

"Yeah, this really helped," Dallas continued, still unable to believe her luck, if it was even that. "Noah says he's going to put in a good word for me, and the training is going to help."

"See, you knew you'd find something you'd like, Dally. You will get to roam in the wild and see sea creatures. I heard some of them get to swim with the dolphins and hunt with them."

Dallas nodded after taking a sip of her drink. "That would be the best."

She brushed at the remaining sliver of burger left, debating whether she wanted to finish it.

"So, I guess you liked the burger," Naomi prompted.

"Not too bad," Dallas admitted. "It's...different but good in its own way."

"Yeah, it's grainy and textured, but you get used to it," Hugh responded. "We have been playing around with the different recipes."

"God, I miss real burgers," Dallas couldn't help but say with a little shake of her head.

"I miss chicken," added Albany.

"And ribs," said her father.

"All right, that's enough," her mother said with a chuckle. "Don't make it worse!"

"Regular meat is expensive to get and to ship down here right now," Hugh added. "But don't worry, we miss it too."

Dallas decided she wanted to finish the meal with the collard greens in the thick peanut sauce, thick as tar, clinging to the leaves instead of diffusing away.

"Well," Hugh said, looking at the clock, "we love you girls, but you know you can't be out any longer."

Albany rolled her eyes.

"They're starting to patrol the areas now," Naomi stated. "You can't be out once the time hits."

The sisters exchanged glances and got up to help clear the table of dishes, piling them near the sink even though their mother insisted they did not have to. They both went out the door with packages of zucchini bread at their parents' insistence.

Albany checked her tablet after they said their farewells, and the door shut. The lanterns above each home doorway had already lit, continuing to do so one by one down the line.

"We have about ten minutes," Albany pointed out. "I don't see any Marine Force yet."

"Me neither, but you know they are just parents who want us to be safe. It's early enough to give us the time we need to get back to our neighborhoods."

The pipeline attendant was inside the residential side of the building when they passed through, letting them in but not letting anyone leave that way. He seemed fixated on a point out to sea. Even though there was nothing there, he kept his eye trained for anything that would swim around the bend.

"This doesn't make sense if we're inside a building," Dallas said. "And not out in the ocean."

"The only thing I can think of is less movement to be seen from the outside, you know, with all the windows. We're in a big fishbowl."

Dallas pointed an arm out to nowhere in particular. "Isn't that what the fenced dome is for?"

"Yeah, even now with the view from all angles," Albany answered, casting a glance upward. "But how do we know it can stop anything that can sense movement behind it?"

The waters stayed dark, with fewer little bubbles than usual from the occasional passing fish. There were also fewer bubbles than usual from the occasional passing merperson. Those that were still out and about were few and far between.

For a minute, Dallas could almost mistake it for twilight: The still, bleak black blue that came with the night and the calming but eerie quiet that settled in. She felt used to it by now, but in their new world, it would forever be night, and not everything would be settled. Albany and Dallas started for their homes, going slowly and lingering near the curved bend.

Dallas shut off the TV and sat up. That was something this time.

Hearing the songs of the wild in this environment would never get old, but sometimes they sang a different tune. The sound that snuck in was too shrill—and too sudden—to be pleasant.

She leaned forward, craning her head a little to the left. Whatever let out that piercing shriek had been abruptly silenced, and now that silence remained. If she had been watching a horror movie, it would be akin to the scream someone made just before a knife was plunged into their chest. Or something similar, like teeth.

Dallas floated off her couch and pressed her ear against the wall of her cave home. Her fingernails scratched the surface, bubbles blowing out of her gills. Whatever it was, why would it be this close?

Was it a merfolk?

Dallas swam to different walls, trying to pinpoint where it might have come from. It did not make sense. All her surrounding area was residential and closed off due to the curfew, so even if someone was out, nothing else could be in. Whatever tried would be met with the shock of electric current that protected their community.

Dallas lifted her ear off the wall. Sound did travel faster underwater. Could she be hearing something from far away? Just how far could she hear?

Just how far could she hear?

She paced her breathing, trying to clear her mind. Mickey told her about her range and how it went further than she knew. Could she just be picking up sound as well?

Dallas moved around, trying to pinpoint which direction would point the most "out to sea." She had never thought to do it through walls. She did not even know if it were possible or not...asking herself if she really wanted to know what could be on the other side of that dome.

Dallas pressed her hands against the wall and let out a note of sonar, the light vibrations coming back to her in rough waves. She shook her head to clear what felt like mental mud, the hologram of that very wall broadcasting back. Moving her hands closer, positioning her fingers in a triangle shape to manifest a direct path, she sounded another note, pressing the wall as if she could make it malleable enough for her wave to go through it.

What came back was a blurred image, but in its center was something solid. Dallas opened her eyes. Something solid. She did it again, holding on to that image appearing in all the negative space. It returned to her, the same as before.

Oddly shaped... though it was a shape all right, and she had picked it up. The image in her mind was a dotted line struggling to reconnect and make the shape it was supposed to form, but it was long on one end. Long enough to resemble a tail. Dallas took a bigger inhale and pushed from the bottom of her gut, sending it out as far as she could feel, the hum in her throat drawn out.

There.

The dotted-line shape came back now, though every bit as hazy as the first time; it still managed to form a shape it had not before. Dolphins had a "melon" in their heads for processing echolocated images, and Dallas was not quite sure what she had, but she figured it was similar to a dark room for developing photos. Things started to form through the inky waters in her brain, bleeding through deeper and deeper until they were clear, or clear enough.

She saw that same form now, but for what it was, it was still a strangely ambiguous shape, sans the long and skinny end that was pinpointed as something's tail. But the rest of it... the rest of it was all wrong. Distorted still, a shape long enough with two pectoral fins and a head, but it was hard to tell which was which. It did not matter so much. It was all Dallas needed.

She swam around different walls, picking a spot and repeating the activity. Many times, the images came back muddied with nothing to develop. It was only one other time that she saw a repeat of that first image, though in a different form and pose to suggest someone or something else. It still was not perfect and not enough to say what it was, but she still got something.

Dallas headed to her room, curling herself up in her hammock and staring up at the caved ceiling, the curtain-type cloth covering the window. She pulled it up, staring out through the midnight blue.

If something could get in, whatever monster was out there would swim past it... She stared at it long enough for the empty blue to fill her sight and mind, and she was not exactly sure when she fell into the trance of sleep because she took that very scene with her. There was nothing to see but blue, nothing but quiet blue all around, but everything was moving like she was in a wave pool.

And for some reason, Dallas could not find her voice.

She tried to speak, to make a sound, but whatever she tried sounded gargled, and almost felt like she had bubbles in her throat...like back when she was human, simply taking a dip in a pool. Dallas tried to send out a sonar wave, but all it did was make those bubbles in her throat burn like drinking a fountain beverage too fast. Dallas pushed and pushed because something in her mind was telling her something was out there. Something was out there, but she could not see it with her eyes or with her sonar.

It only took a second, but in that moment, something did float past her window. She saw it clear as day: a hand, five fingers, webbed, with scales in the right places decorating the top of human flesh. A moment later, that hand passed her window as a solo specimen. She could even see the bloody stump where it ended.

Dallas's eyes popped open, and she sat up in her hammock, checking that window and holding the curtain away from it, just watching it for a long time.

CHAPTER 20

"I DON'T REALLY KNOW," Dallas said, giving Noah the same answer she had given Mickey. "That's just it; it wasn't a normal shape at all."

Noah had only just arrived when Mickey told him what she already had.

"This one can go through walls, apparently!" Mickey said, with pride.

Noah gave her a look that said it was not common. Dallas retold the story from last night. She left out the dream.

"Wow. How did you do that?"

"I don't know. I was trying to figure out what the noise was."

"Whales?" suggested Mickey.

"No, too small to be a whale. And the images that came back almost...almost looked like merpeople."

"But they were misshapen?" Mickey repeated.

"Yeah."

"Well, of course, they would be. I can't imagine why you would get a clear image echolocating through a wall, so that's probably why. You just saw distorted images of merpeople around."

"Maybe you did hear a whale."

Dallas shrugged.

"Anyway, the sub should be here soon," Noah said. "The driver just did a drop-off at downtown Violet Vista, so he's en route."

He kept his head down and continued to scroll on his tablet while Dallas peeked out at the fence; her only view of the open sea she could have now was through bars.

"This is like imprisonment," Mickey said, echoing exactly what she was thinking. "No one is going to want to come out like this; I am going to lose customers."

"People will still come, Mic; it's all right," Noah reassured her, looking up from his tablet. "They'd swim through ice to get your drink specials. Besides, you've got to admit the subs look cooler now."

Dallas was able to see the fat and silver fish now as stripes through the bars, wrapped in its own electrical netting. She turned to Mickey, who was hovering near the exit with them. "Thanks again for everything."

"Anytime, honey. Don't forget to learn how to breathe when you dash. See you later."

Noah swam over to Mickey and gave her a little embrace before leaving.

"You be safe going home," she insisted.

"I will; you too."

Noah led the way out of The Drunken Ship and fumbled with the door on the fence to the awaiting sub. It almost looked like a beluga whale, or one created with built-in barbed wire along with some other additions: at the nose, there were spikes jutting out, jagged and long, to give this sub creature the equivalent of a fatal bite. Dallas couldn't figure out if she wanted to laugh or not. Noah went in, and she followed.

"Municipal center," he told the driver, and they took seats near the middle.

The beluga machine set off, and Dallas leaned against the window, looking at all the Lego brick transformations of the places in the distance. Most of them had a similar rectangular shape, but others looked like they had some more "blocks" added to them. Those pipelines were too far to make out, but she knew they were similar.

"Good job today."

Dallas turned to him from the window. "Thanks."

"I know I said that already, but I do mean it. You've come a long way."

"I do feel like I am getting better."

"You have, and you will only continue to get better. Tomorrow you'll get to see it in action."

A small school swam alongside the sub and then darted in the other direction, speckled in tiny paint drops of shimmering pink and yellow colors. She needed to focus on something else besides her nerves. She tried not to think about it.

"So, I'm in? I don't have to do anything?"

"I already told you," Noah said with half a laugh. "Yes. You're in. We chatted on the phone, and I told them that you had one last echolocation practice and that you're already a master at it. It was very easy to get you a spot with this group. You'll be reporting to Clyde Whethers himself, and after meeting him in person, you'll never need a cup of coffee again in your life."

Dallas allowed herself a smile, wanting Noah to see that she was not nervous.

"You'll also never meet anyone more passionate and headstrong. Listen, he's a huge goofball who most likely worked with children in either a theme park or summer camp before he came here, and that's why he can rally troops and get the job done. His husband, A.J., is in the Marine Force, and it looks like you will be meeting and working with him too."

Dallas looked at him. "Even hunter/gatherers need to have escorts?"

Noah nodded. "I told you so. Even riding around in these machines, fish are not enough. When you do go out in the wild to work, you are still going to need someone there keeping an eye out for predators. I'm sorry that you have to experience it like this, but besides these added security measures, I do think being a hunter/gatherer is perfect for you. You'll always be out with the wildlife, searching and exploring, and that is definitely going to feed your wanderlust. Also, especially during this time, you will be contributing to seek any predators that are also out on the hunt."

The sub stopped at the municipal center, and many merpeople got off. Noah and Dallas lingered behind, being the last ones, listening to the *blurble blurble* of the beluga sub start back up again and swim out to the next stop. The fence door closed behind the last one without so much as a squeak.

Dallas was staring out into the open ocean: no bars and no glass, absorbing as much as she could before she was escorted back in, but Noah did not seem to be in any rush himself. He swam up close enough to her to share the view but let her have her moment.

"The big open blue can be our best friend and our worst enemy."

"More so the latter," Dallas deadpanned.

"Yes, it is, especially right now. Trust me, I want to go back to the way it was, and that won't happen until we're certain it's safe."

They were both looking at a point beyond the furthest coral reefs they could see, the tangle of sea plants swaying together without any disturbances to their way of life. Any fish returning to their sea anemone homes did so without an electric cage, and after watching a school of them flip away, Noah turned to her with a side glance.

"You didn't really get to test your range out in the open blue."

He looked around, then back at her with a subtle smirk.

"Hmm. Just how far can you go? Let's try it before we are ordered inside."

He pointed ahead of them.

"Can you tell me what else is in that reef?"

Dallas took a breath and exhaled a call.

"I found a starfish. Underneath that largest rock on the right, bottom right side."

"Can you cast out as far as you can?"

She did so, taking a deeper breath and sending out a vocal wave. In a moment, she looked back to Noah.

"Eighteen Queen Angelfish are passing through that reef that is ahead of the other one, the one with the reds and oranges."

"That one?" Noah pointed. "The one furthest down the line that we can see?"

Dallas fought not to smile. "That would be correct."

Noah did pause, squinting at that reef in question before turning back to her

"Well, you're just a little wielder of sonar, aren't you?"

She wasn't quite near the bulletin board when she saw the new poster, slick with fresh lamination and stuck between the ads for a babysitter and a "garage" sale. The revamped illustration of Uncle

Sam as a merperson was comical; the exaggeration of the fins on his ears made him look more like a gremlin.

Dallas thought this was done on purpose as an inside joke—whenever gremlins met water, they multiplied. That was exactly the objective of the ad.

We want YOU to join the Marine Force!
Seeking able-bodied and strong individuals. Inquire
at the viceroy/envoy headquarters.

Mer Uncle Sam kept his finger pointed right at Dallas, even as she swam away. On her way home, she noticed more of these posters, not just at every bulletin but tacked to walls and support beams, all with the same drafting point.

"Dallas!"

She spun around in surprise to see the mermaid with the long, blue-purple braid and a tail to match.

"Sapphire?" she said, surprised. "You're off today?"

"No," Sapphire answered, swimming up to her. "I got let go early."

"Really?"

"Yeah, we only had a few customers this morning, and I did my last cut and style at one o'clock, so I got sent home."

Dallas cringed. "Oh."

Sapphire shrugged. "Nothing I can do when fewer customers come in, and we get cut hours. No pun intended."

"Geez, I'm sorry."

"You get people that aren't afraid of anything and still want to yell at envoys about curfew, and then you get the 'fraidy cat idiots that want to hide in their hammocks all day. You done today too?"

"Yeah, I had my last review with Noah. And then that's it until I start my new job tomorrow."

"How exciting!" Sapphire said. "Why don't you come over and help me eat leftover stir-fry noodles and tell me all about it?"

"You know my weak spot."

Dallas and Sapphire made their way toward the residence pipeline, catching up here and there on their way to their neighborhood.

"That's pretty amazing," Sapphire said as they approached her door. "I know a few people that can echolocate, but not many are really good at it."

"Yeah, it's weird I didn't know about it."

"You discover a lot of new things about yourself once you're a merperson!"

She keyed the keypad, and they swam in through the open door.

"Forgive the mess; I went shopping the other day and found a bunch of stuff in my size on clearance, and I just couldn't help myself."

Dallas was immediately taken in by the silky silver robe stretched out on the couch, along with the rest of the loot.

"This is so pretty!"

"Isn't it? I just have to alter the bottom a little because it's too long. Rule of thumb, or rule of fin, is you don't want something that is going to be longer than your fin. Now you don't have to worry about tripping over anything dragging on the ground anymore, but you need to be able to feel the end of it and watch out for it getting caught on anything, like barnacles and coral. Coral is the worst."

Dallas mentally put that advice somewhere for safekeeping while she ran a hand down the material of the tunic, marveling over how soft it was, and how little Sapphire would have to hem it as she was tall already. Next to it was a pink skirt that went on as a belt, along with another shirt that laced up like a bodice. Next to that was another skirt on a belt that looked like a long pencil skirt.

When Dallas looked at the bottom pieces up close, she noticed some things were already altered. All the built-in bottom pieces with the snaps had already been cut out. A side glance at the empty shopping bag on the couch showed it was not so much empty, but the waste keeper of receipts, price tags, and each removed bottom piece. Dallas considered the finality of this as Sapphire busied herself in the kitchen.

"Hey, do you want a soft drink? I have Sprite and Pepsi."

"Sure," said Dallas. "Pepsi is good."

Sapphire swam over to the kitchen counter with steaming bowls, and Dallas went to join her, forgetting about the clothing stash and her alterations. She took a seat while Sapphire came back with their drinks: the cans they all knew and recognized but with the aquatic edition: built-in straws.

"Thanks!" Dallas said.

"Oh, anytime. I made too much of this the other night and cursed myself to, like, a week of leftovers."

Dallas helped herself to the vegetables and long noodles, moving the bowl only a little to get them to mix around with the help of seawater. She wrapped another nice morsel around her fork.

"Congratulations again, Dallas, really. Do you know how important you're going to be now?"

"Aww, thanks. I sure hope so. I mean, even when I was practicing, I...didn't see much."

"Did you go out in the open?" asked Sapphire with big eyes.

"A couple of times, but not enough. Just to test distance."

"What's the biggest thing you've seen?"

"A green turtle. No dolphins or anything like that. Or sharks."

"Sharks don't come around here much, especially when the town was first built, and they did all that to scare them away and make them know that a bigger, smarter fish was in town. They've always had a good grasp on that, but..."

"This thing that is out there now is...?"

"A new kid on the block that's not a shark," Sapphire answered. "And way worse."

She pulled out her tablet. "Dude, have you seen this?"

Sapphire floated around the table so that she was closer to Dallas and played a video on a social media feed.

"Someone took this out in Crosstown, which is far out in the Northwest Province, but not that far if you think about it."

Dallas saw the shaky video of someone holding their device out to the open ocean and recording what looked like the middle of a big tail, clouded by sea dust. It was a very big and long body, but very far away, swimming in the rhythmic way predator fish do while other merpeople around them made incredulous exclamations.

The video cut out with these people swimming away from there, showing nothing else.

"What is that?"

"Some people think it is some sort of eel or snake, and it is the biggest snake they have ever seen. Like bigger than a python."

"Whoa."

"So, some people said this might be the thing that has been stalking around here. Someone said something about a big eel or snake before. But no one knows exactly what it is, and anyone that gets up close and personal enough to find out, well, doesn't survive."

Dallas thought back to the top half of the merman thrown against the electric barrier, fried upon impact but dead long before that happened. Tail bitten and torn right off, with leftover ribbons of flesh and fish. She also thought about the Marine Force going out in packs, new age weapons on their backs, and putting up those posters across the whole town of Gneiss Underway, and no doubt further.

Sapphire played the video again and paused it, both of them staring at the blurred figure in the distance. It looked like a nylon stocking, stretched far with its plain color that was meant to blend in, and it was doing its job. It was like looking at the sideways angle of a tornado, the funnel that looked like it was moving slowly when in reality it was rapidly charging down the horizon to take out anything in its path in one swift strike.

Dallas and Sapphire watched the funnel swim along, almost completely invisible in the deep, only seen when its tail end would sweep behind it...like it was sweeping away the mess it just made. Dallas imagined what was on the other end, what nasty equipment it had to be packing, thinking of a large python simply opening a jaw to chomp—or swallow—its prey disappearing all the way down inside that constricting stocking. It still had plenty of room for more.

CHAPTER 21

DALLAS ENTERED THE LOUNGE and immediately regretted wearing her brand-new yellow robe that could have been a formal evening gown. Everyone else looked like they rolled out of bed in tunics meant for painting or working out. She internally sighed but scanned the faces of the people sitting around the plush chairs.

"I'm looking for Clyde?"

And to her surprise, it was the most relaxed of all who turned out to be her new boss. Clyde floated out of his chair in his own crème-colored "workout" long tunic over a marigold tail, with hair that looked silkier than her robe.

"You must be Dallas!" he cried, shaking her hand with an iron grip. "Oh, Noah told me so much about you. I am so happy to have you! Come on in and just find a seat. We're all chilling for a while and going over strategy, as we always do before we go out on a hunt. Everyone, this is Dallas Dwight, our newest employee, who has some amazing echolocation skills!"

Dallas smiled sheepishly as the room applauded, with a few whoops.

"Find a seat and just chill. I must screw around with this projector and screen for a minute, so just bear with me."

Dallas parked herself in a seat, the cushion squishing under her tail. As Clyde pressed buttons and knobs on the projector on the table, she felt an instant sense of déjà vu from her Orientation days. A moment later, a light blasted onto the cloth screen, revealing a map that looked like it was near the Eastmost consumer building where she bought kitchen supplies. There was a legend with colored dots of green, red, and brown, resembling farms or patches of something.

"So, Dallas, we go over our areas of attack and decide who is going to tackle what and where. We are a tight-knit group and rely on teamwork to get the jobs done. We're chill, but we're very organized at the same time. So, you show up here on the days you're working with an open mind and a willingness to get down and dirty sometimes. And occasionally, you might get pinched by crabs, which is something we try to avoid but can still happen. We have maps covering different levels of the ocean area depending on what we're going after. Some days we go higher up; other days, we go further down. These maps here show gardens and groves where we pick fruit and vegetables, as well as traps for fish and other things. We go in, get what we need, and always, always, echolocate and scan for wildlife. It's pretty self-explanatory."

Here, Clyde paused for a moment with a sigh.

"Now, it's unfortunate that you're coming in at a time when we don't have the same freedoms we used to."

This prompted murmurs and complaints from the peanut gallery, which Clyde immediately silenced.

"Stop it now. This is normally a free-roaming job, which is no doubt the best part of it: We would swim out in the wild. Just us, the open blue, and whatever else cares to join us. We would swim with the turtles and the dolphins without much of a care. That was taken away when this monster showed up out of nowhere and started hunting us."

Clyde's glance darted to someone in the back with whom he locked eyes.

"So sorry, but safety overruled fun. We now travel to our designated places via a sub and bring along a member of the Marine Force. It's not the same, and we try to make the best of it. And no, we don't know when things are going to go back to normal. Still."

Clyde scanned the faces in the room, stopping on a few in particular to convey his message.

"Still, no one knows. No one knows exactly what this thing is, but we're doing our best to stay safe and send those trained enough to handle it to go after it."

"So, no one was able to find it, even using echolocation?" Dallas blurted out, finally finding the opening she had been searching for.

"No," Clyde answered. "It just seems to show its ugly face around these parts whenever it feels like it. No one has found it close by. We stay within our areas, keep an eye out for any dangers, and leave that particular hunt up to the experts...which I should introduce. Everyone, this lovely man here in the back is A.J., also known as my better half, and he is our Marine Force escort today."

The burly arms would have been the dead giveaway if it hadn't been for Clyde's introduction. A.J. gave a little wave, and the emblem on his tunic was visible. It looked like the figure of a merperson standing at attention with long arms, but the more Dallas stared at it, the more she could see it was cleverly made of the letters "f" and "m" layered on top of one another. He was wearing something else underneath his tunic—navy blue and higher ranked—but she could not see it too well. It almost made it look like his chest was made of dozens of hard, black scales.

Clyde turned around again to the group. "Let's gear up. Dallas, I already have something that will fit you."

The others filtered out of the room, each shedding their tunics and leaving them on hooks on the wall. A few of them fished out large bone knives from their pockets and brought them along. They rounded the corner to an area that looked like an iron warehouse with a big door. Clyde swam up and opened it, leaning back to use his strength.

Dallas floated up enough so that she would be able to see above the heads, as one by one they went inside. She stared at the rows, and how they were all lined up. They all looked like statues of soldiers stationed against the walls. She saw how the large clam shell sat at the top like heads, with the armored shirt and utility belt and kilt at the waist. The other hunter/gatherers each approached one, taking the contents off the walls and putting them on themselves.

"Over here," Clyde jerked his head, and Dallas followed him down the row to a set that hadn't been claimed and looked smaller in size. Dallas could see it up close for what it was made of, and she was taken aback in awe. She had seen medieval garb and armor before, but never anything like this. She reached out and touched the shirt, feeling the rough crisscrossed ridges of each piece, each placed to make up the scale mail shirt made entirely out of seashells.

Clyde took this down for her first while she inspected the belt and kilt. The belt buckle was cleverly a small turtle shell that fastened on the inside. The pouches were all made of a kind of black leather, the same kind as the layered strips that formed the kilt.

"Shark hide," remarked Clyde, which prompted a surprised brow from Dallas.

"Wow."

"Yep, same as the undershirt on the mail. You put it on over your head and mind the opening in the back for your dorsal, then tie the strings on the sides."

Dallas put it on, followed by the kilt and belt. She adjusted the clam shell shoulder pieces, moving her shoulders and getting used to them while joining the others. The helmet she carried felt slightly heavy under her arm before she put it on her head.

They all looked like soldiers, knights, dutiful patrollers going out on a quest. When she caught sight of A.J. again, she made the connection of the chainmail he was wearing under his tunic. Except his appeared to be made of scallop or clam shells, black as the deepest parts of the ocean...no doubt the very places the Marine Force were trained to go.

"So, without further ado we should be ready to get out there. The sub's all ready. Who wants to drive the magic school bus today?" Clyde held up a pair of keys, and a few hands went up. He tossed them to a guy nearest to him.

"Okay, let's roll."

They all swam out of the room, with Clyde making sure he was in the back. Dallas stayed back too, watching them file out.

"You're just going to help out wherever help is needed today. There are extra sacks in the sub you can take."

Dallas had the helmet on, pushing it back and forth to get used to the feel. As hard and a little heavy as the clamshell was, it did have something spongy and light around the head and neck area to make it tolerable.

"You'll get used to it," Clyde remarked, putting on his own. The clamshell used as a helmet was very practical, with the bottom half cut out to fit a merfolk head. It just looked like an ordinary clam shell, open and cradling a head inside. The gentle goldfish wash of Clyde's skin made him look like a golden pearl.

The group went through a pipeline out the East end and then out the pipeline to the fence where their sub monster machine waited.

Dallas took a seat, disappointed that the ones near the windows filled up and she was stuck in the aisle. She heard her tablet chime and took it out to find news headlines that could not have worse timing: **"Five Dead in Crosstown, More Remains Scattered in Northwest Province.**"

She browsed through each one, scrolling through them. Any pictures were of the Marine Force emblem uniform and none of any other evidence. Carnage is too graphic to show, but one could get the idea visually.

Marine Force in Crosstown Never Came Home

A pod of five Marine Force troops set out for a hunt in the town of Crosstown in the West Atlantic, Northwest Province, where some claimed to have seen a very large eel-like creature that matches the general description of the wanted predator.

When it was believed they were late in returning from their hunt, it soon became known that they had not returned at all. A second pod went out only to find some remains of their comrades in the few pieces that were left, alongside weaponry lost in mid-battle. The remains have been taken in for further study and possible identification, but it is confirmed they are of the missing troops sent out last Friday.

Dallas looked up from her tablet and peeked over the shoulders of the merpeople in the seats ahead and all around her at the next troop going out for a hunt. She looked out the windows to the stretches of ocean and vegetation scattered on the ground that looked like bones: old, with patches of seaweed growing all over, long discarded and camouflaged after the rest of the body was eaten.

The next time Dallas looked up from her tablet was when the metal whale started to slow, and Clyde turned from the front in a slow-motion whirlwind of his marigold hair.

"Okay, the field trip's over."

She tried to get a good look out any window but had difficulty with everyone getting out of their seats and wanting to see as well. Clyde and A.J. got out of their seats first to lead the rest of them out.

"You know the drill, everyone."

Row by row, they filed out of the sub until they bunched in a group around the designated stop. It looked like the middle of a coral reef garden: brilliant colors of yellow, red, and green, with little rocks in different geometric shapes to serve as markers. Dallas could see and feel the heaviness of the ocean around her, the wild living things present in every anemone, wave, and in the sands below their fins.

She could hear every breath she exhaled through her gills, the bubbles echoing and disrupting the stillness.

The group dispersed, with merpeople swimming to all opposite sides, while A.J., the assigned Marine Force authority, swam out further than anyone else was allowed to. Dallas heard the clicking sounds broadcast from all angles of their makeshift circle, even some that had graduated to calls equal to the song of the whales.

"Do your thing," Clyde said, swimming past her.

She turned to a random point where the ocean was darkest. She inhaled and cast out a ring of sonar, getting the same image reported back to her. Dallas gradually kept inching her way around the invisible perimeter, doing the same and getting the same result. The next one she sent out gave her the image of A.J. swimming back to their area, and in moments he did so, holding his harpoon out at his side and ready.

"Clear," he announced.

Then the work began. With sack bags slung around their shoulders, they all scattered in various directions and disappeared behind rock formations and into coral beds. Clyde pointed Dallas in the direction of a particular garden formation with its own familiarity. She smiled at the pyramid roofs, the tiny protective fences built around them, and the way those little roofs were pulled back to reveal what was inside.

Dallas approached to reveal a branch filled with red apples, each bigger than her fist, lined all the way down and almost filling the bottom. She got to work picking them, feeling the smoothness of each skin, and admiring the shine of the candy-red color. Was the color more vibrant against the starkness of the dark sea, or were they altered in some way during growth? She filled the sack with the largest and ripest apples, pulling the pyramid hatch back to close it.

She repeated the process with the other little huts, pulling back each pyramid top to reveal new surprises. There were potatoes, tomatoes, green beans, strawberries, oranges, and pineapples, all in their oxygen-converting greenhouses proving themselves worthy of their land counterparts. She soon learned about the sections that separated the fruit from the vegetables and that there was more than one in different places, but she focused on where she was for the time being. Occasionally, she would look up at passing hunters/gatherers with their own cloth sacks, and she noticed that some had different weapons.

Two mermen swam past her with their cloth sacks slung over one shoulder and something long and sharp on their backs. They were close enough for her to make out the spear-like needles at the top, and once they reached her section of the garden, they separated and swam off into the distance.

From where she was, she could hear the clicking, and then a long-range song echoed out into both sides of the abyss, down to what looked like a deep trench. One merman turned to the other and gestured for him to follow, and then they both took off in a flash toward that trench. In a moment that was not planned and entirely spontaneous, Dallas found herself following them.

She took off in the direction of the mermen, watching the fins of their tails wave up and down at a quicker pace in the distance. Both removed small stun guns from their utility belts and held them at the ready as they dove down. They also had something else in their hands that she could not see too well from where she was—and when her sonar sounds came back to her, she saw an image of netting in her head. Dallas pumped her tail to pick up speed and sent out another blast.

The more they descended, the more light she lost.

She wondered if she would be close enough to pick up whatever they had sensed, finding it difficult to focus when she wasn't sitting still and there were two beings far enough in front of her to block that path. They stopped abruptly; their tails coiled in front of them in defense.

The mermen held their guns pointed out in front of them, lifting the netting high.

Dallas ducked behind a rock when the hunters stopped, making sure that she was obscured and unfound. They were in a much more open area, but with a small archipelago of rocks. Here, the hunters floated around it, edging closer. Dallas stuck her head around and sent out her own echo, the image coming back to her filling her with intrigue. Somewhere in those rocks was a creature that could either be a small snake or a large worm, flashing tiny, bright red and blue orbs like LED lights.

Within seconds, she saw it for herself... something darted out of the abyss and whipped at the two hunters. It was long, black, and slick, with pulsating red and blue lights just near its eyes in the ocean's darkness. She noticed a smaller whip dangling from its chin, thrashing out against the mermen, its end a feathered, glowing bulb. They held the netting while aiming their weapons, each firing an electronic zap that landed in different places around the rocks, missing the creature as it sprinted among them.

Dallas leaned out a bit more, struggling to get a better look at this thing that resembled a deadly black snake. The only way anyone could see it was by the spots that occasionally lit up here and there, making its movement difficult to pinpoint. They would have to rely on echolocation to catch it, if even their sonar could detect it.

In an instant, the sea-snake proved that to be wrong. Within seconds, bright blue bioluminescence lined its entire body, showcasing its monstrous form. It was a radiating skeleton with a head and a mouth curved with tiny fangs, a trap filled with tiny needles, a xenophobic nightmare born from the deep.

The mermen now had their advantage. They shot and shot and moved about as the creature flashed blue repeatedly until one of those shots landed. The sparks lit the creature from blue to yellow, from its jaw all the way down the rest of its serpentine body. It curled into a slight horseshoe shape as it froze, allowing the currents of the sea to carry it above the grainy ground. One hunter wrapped it up with his net while the other lifted his head to the distance.

"Where's the other one?"

The blinking lights that appeared next to Dallas answered that question.

She gasped and fell back, the slithery tail slinking through the water and opening and closing its mouth. Even up close, it was difficult to make out until it chose to reveal itself in flashes of horror, but Dallas didn't need echolocation to know it was there. Up close, she could see how black and smooth it was, slick without any scales and shiny as if it were leather.

Its eyes were blank orbs, almost holes, with the bioluminescence dotting them on the sides like a distraction. Dallas doubled back again, keeping her eye on it while the mermen swam around the rock piles and sent clicks out in opposite directions. She froze as she watched this creature dangle its chin whip, searching for smaller prey.

This glow snake, this eel, this long fish—whatever it was, it was undoubtedly not looking for her, but she did not think it was harmless. It drifted behind her, the hunters echolocating the area and only picking up that rock and the others.

Dallas did not know what came over her, but without a second thought, she flipped her cloth sack and let loose a sea of apples, potatoes, green beans, and peppers. The black worm jerked with interest at the peppers—small, red, and could be mistaken for something else—and darted out to investigate. In a move that felt like slow motion, she flipped that cloth sack again to make it swallow those floating peppers and the unsuspecting creature, pulling the sack closed as it took notice of its new surroundings and thrashed against the cloth walls. It had ample enough room to swim, but now only due to some missing produce.

Dallas held the bag as it glowed fluorescent, cool blue on and off, like an oversized firefly, and abandoned her hiding place. She swam out to the hunters, who finally noticed her and, especially, what she was holding.

"I, uh..."

"What are you doing down here?"

"Did you...?"

"It was behind me."

The mermen reached for the bag, looking from the bag to her, and she could not tell if they were horrified or impressed.

"You caught it just like that?"

"Did it attack you?"

"No, it barely noticed me; it went after the peppers. Probably thought they were shrimp. What is this thing?"

One merman held the bag while the other carefully opened it enough to stick his gun in to stun it. The glowing and the wiggling subsided. They kept the bag open enough for them all to peer inside and shine their pearl orbs to view that second catch.

"That's a black dragonfish. We catch them for their bioluminescence and venom."

Dallas stared at the creature, its jaw partially open and eyes as blank as black holes.

"The only ones that really exist are the females, and this is the biggest they ever get. The males are as small as your thumb and are really only good for fertilizing eggs. These girls are masters of camouflage in the deep and have the rare use of these red lights. You saw how they light up."

The merman took the creature out of the bag and gave it back to Dallas, wrapping the fish in his own netting.

"Thanks for your help. You might want to get that food before it all drifts away."

Dallas looked back at the escaped apples, potatoes, and green beans and swam back after them, netting them in her bag as the hunters left the area. Once she swam back up, she saw the hunters talking head-to-head with a small group, Clyde among them. Clyde's head turned to face her as she arrived, his brow raised.

"Well, nice work," he said.

"Thanks," Dallas patted the bag to make sure she got all the food back, pretending to distract herself with it. She wasn't sure if she should say she meant to do that, but how could she have said she went after the black dragonfish on purpose?

"You fit in just fine."

Dallas smiled, happy that he and the others mostly had their attention on the black dragonfish.

CHAPTER 22

"We need all of you to sharpen your eyes today," Clyde started. "We have run out of supplies for our blasters, so it's time to go find some cuttlefish."

Dallas searched the back recesses of her brain to match the image to the familiar name. What she remembered was something that looked like a small squid, not really a fish, and similar to an octopus. She continued to think about it as Clyde and some of the others gathered nets from their supply bins and the smaller stun guns. Everyone went to get their gear on, with Dallas's muscles protesting under the weight, even though it was a little lighter.

Clyde and A.J. ushered the team out to their sub. They were the last ones on the sub as usual, giving the nod of safe approval before they rode out. Dallas stared out the window at the various forms of coral and rock formations that passed. It was the differing textures, colors, and shapes that made her sigh in both amusement and annoyance at the challenge.

When their sub stopped in what seemed to be a jungle of coral and tall weeds, Clyde got up first while unraveling his net.

"All right, keep your senses sharp now."

They piled out, with Dallas fumbling to get her tablet untangled from her netting. It was still set on the webpage she had opened for a refresher. The picture was still there of the common cuttlefish as it would be seen out in the open ocean. She knew she would not get to see it like that, but just wanted to become more familiar with its shape.

So, she sent out a wave, outlining all the rocks and weeds in their every rough bump and pronged end. She sent out another wave, tracing the outlines sharper this time in search of anything that might appear within its form. She swam through the area, ducking down and allowing the tall sea grasses to tickle her as she passed before arriving at the open area. Dallas lowered herself to the sandy sea floor and sent out another echo wave, searching with both her mind and her eyes for any signs of movement beneath the sand.

Nothing wavered, and nothing surfaced. She swam further out, where she joined some of the others looking beyond where they could see. The flick of a fin to her left sent her in a determined, confirmed direction.

She followed the small pod that was now forming while casting out another wave to see if she could catch a glimpse. The outline that returned to her brain was fuzzy as it kept moving. It was like a piece of coral had detached itself and floated away, but she got it. She dashed ahead to keep up with her teammates, who were already holding unraveled nets. Sure enough, the cuttlefish officially introduced itself.

The floating rock piece broke away, its frilly skirt wiggling in the water, and its tentacles brushing in haste. Suddenly, that gritty and speckled texture wavered to reveal the smooth, gelatinous skin of a little squid, with tentacles in front of its face resembling an old man's long beard.

The cuttlefish's eyes fluttered in a most strange way with their "w"-shaped pupils. They looked like slits that at any moment could burst open to reveal giant reptilian eyes, the kind that could rotate 360 degrees to see everything around them. It was what Dallas expected from something known as the chameleon of the sea.

The merman ahead of Dallas opened his net, and the others nearby quickly swept in, netting the cuttlefish while it twisted and writhed in protest.

Many kept their distance while still observing the creature, its tentacles petting the net and shifting to match the rough brown colors. Dallas leaned in just as everyone crowded around when, all of a sudden, a thick black cloud erupted and bled through the water. They jumped back but continued what they were doing as much as they could, for within seconds the clear blue waters around them diffused with the dark ink.

What seemed like a small puff soon grew large enough to spread all around them, as far as any of them could see. Dallas waved her hands in front of her but realized she was making it worse. Soon she couldn't see the other merpeople around her as they chatted. She swam back, using her arms to feel around her while she made a sonar wave.

Instantly, it showed her the merpeople around her as well as the cuttlefish in the net. She swam back far enough until she was out of the ink cloud and could see through the bleary blue again, wiping her eyes. As sudden and alarming as the ink release was, the other hunter/gatherers dealt with it and treated it as amusement. One of them saw Dallas and smiled at her.

"Just think," he said. "When you're in the *deep*, deep, that's what it looks like."

"It's pretty basic, really," Clyde said as he turned the safety off. "You use this trigger here to fire the volts. You never need to worry about the harpoon too much; it is mostly for bigger game, and you don't use it until the game has already been stunned. Your firing options are over here with this switch, and you can flip from single fire to auto for schools and bigger groups of things. It's just like a stun gun, and all that happens is you feel a little tingly with shots. Any questions?"

Dallas shook her head.

Clyde aimed the gun at the rock and fired, a yellow-green spark hitting its middle, and then handed it to her.

"Go ahead, get a feel."

Dallas took the gun, which looked like a cool upgrade from a Nerf gun spray-painted black and loaded with electrical wiring in an organized chaos of coils. She aimed and fired, pleased by the very little kickback and the tingling aftermath running up her arms.

"Pretty cool," she said.

"It sure is. We assign these out to those that are to be hunters for the day, usually randomly. At the end of the day, you just bring it back to get charged."

The hunter/gatherers had already split up from exiting the sub, the gatherers swimming out to the gardens and the hunters going just a bit further.

"We never hunt alone, so make sure to always stick with your team. There will always be a Marine Force officer out with you guys, so don't worry. The others will show you the ropes, and you all work together to catch stuff. And, from what we learned about you handling that black dragonfish, you shouldn't have any problems."

Dallas smirked. A.J. swam by with another Marine Force officer and told Clyde they were going to make their rounds.

"Sounds good. Dallas, you go with A.J. to join the other hunters."

Dallas put the safety back on the gun and hoisted it on her waist near her back, almost awkwardly at first as it rubbed against her dorsal fin. She met up with the other hunters gathered furthest from the sub, forgetting all their names. A.J. drifted out to scan the area, and when he came back, he had a smile on his face.

"We got ourselves a nice bunch of squid."

"Squid. Yum," said the mermaid hunter nearest to her. "Let's go get 'em."

Dallas sent out her own echoes as she swam with the hunting pod, seeing that wiggling blob of squid swimming around in pursuit of fish. The team dashed out, clicking and humming to maintain that school's location, and swam in formation. Dallas kept up with the pod in exhilarated glee, feeling the rush of the waves past her as she got her first real taste of what it felt like to sprint.

Her tail and fin pumped on autopilot as she dashed up and down until she could see the wriggling mass of squid for herself. The hunters split up to surround it, A.J. floating above them to keep the entire area scanned.

"Everybody fire!" someone shouted.

Dallas unlatched her gun and fumbled with it while the others were ready within seconds, blasting electrified shots that zapped into the wiggling creatures, their legs curling and jerking before falling straight. As Dallas swam closer and trailed the squid, pale with orange spots here and there, those tagged flashed a brilliant bright green in the shimmering water. Their tentacles wavered, and they squirmed, several breaking away from the mass and getting blasted in minutes. Dallas raced around the stunned squid to spot the live ones, watching the other hunters go after them.

Soon, she echoed their activity and took out her net to collect them, studying the squid with fascination. They were almost gelatinous, as if they were made of Jell-O, with bits of fruit floating around to give them the occasional splash of color.

"Longfin squid," said a passing merman, sheathing his gun. "They are the most common and are delicious. You'll never get fresher sushi than right on the spot."

Dallas snickered and fastened her net shut, hearing the chorus of clicks and hums around her. A.J. sent a wave out in the distance and then paused where he was. Dallas still had her gun out, watching him as he moved his to the front of his chest and stayed still. The others were rounding up the squid and searching the nearby areas. She joined him with care.

"What do you see?"

He kept his eyes on the distance.

"So far, nothing. But things can appear at any time. You always have to be prepared."

"Are you ever really prepared?"

The corners of his mouth straightened. "No, not always. But knowing what's out there is key because if you can avoid it before it comes to your area, that is always the best action to take. If you see something out there, but it's far enough away, minding its own business and not going after anybody, that doesn't mean you have to go after it."

"The hunters all coexist."

"That is it, exactly. Never ever go after something you shouldn't be going after. You don't attack unless there's a threat present."

"Right. They made sure to pound that into our heads."

A.J. lowered his weapon, and Dallas noticed the safety was still off.

"And that's something you will never encounter or worry about. You leave it to us."

They continued to watch out into the blue, and at one point, Dallas looked at A.J., noticing for the first time the strange shape of his back. She furrowed her brow, knowing it was not the tunic nor the armor that made it look so... rugged. Bumpy.

She could see right where his tunic and armor started at the base of his neck, and the skin exposed showed masses, ridges, and crevices that formed anything but smooth flesh. When he moved slightly, she was able to see that his dorsal fin was not all that smooth either, curling over to its side like an orca's would in distress. Dallas did not dare move her head any more to reveal her staring at him, believing that these battle scars wanted to stay hidden.

"You ready? Let's head out."

Clyde rounding up the troops broke her out of her reverie. She adjusted the buttons on her leather pouches, the strip of leather holding her bone knife in place. Ahead of her, she heard the light clicks and gentle hums of those scoping out the area.

"Clear," said one.

"Clear," agreed another.

Dallas thought to do the same, sending out her own sonar. When she got nothing back, she thought to do it again, as far out as she could go, farther than any of them could go.

Dallas stopped short at the image that came back. Just as she had received through the cave walls of her home, she was seeing that ambiguous dotted line shape once again. She blinked as though that would help bring it into focus.

"Uhhh...."

A.J. turned around first, being the closest to her. She could see his eyes under the rim of the clamshell helmet, zoned in on her, looking both intrigued and worried.

Dallas sent out another wave while A.J. waited. The two of them staying behind caught the attention of the others, if her extended sonar sound did not already do so. She could not really answer when they all asked her what she saw.

"It's...a bit blurry."

"What is it?"

A.J. appeared next to her. "Can you tell me the shape you're getting?"

It was just like before, the same strange form that did not have a clear shape.

"Long-ish. Blobby. It's just thick with fins. That's all I can make out. It could be anything."

"Sounds like it," A.J. answered. Clyde appeared by them in a minute.

"Well, you can send out your sonar pretty far, and that's good. Whatever it is, that means it must be far enough away that we don't need to worry about it."

"I've seen some humpback whales around lately," A.J. said encouragingly. "Beautiful and big, but the smaller they appear in echolocation, the further they are."

"Right, right, it's just... I don't know."

Should she say that the outlines were different and this was a different shape than last time?

The troops piled out and headed back to their sub while Dallas held on to the dotted line image that looked nothing like a humpback whale.

The next book she pulled out had more pictures in it, and they were striking enough to keep her attention. The terrifying spider crab was the size of a dog, with long, prickly legs. She actually cringed a little imagining what it would feel like to encounter one, to feel the rough scratches of those legs teasing against her flesh before it attacked. They were at sea-ground level, though, and wouldn't be floating up in her echolocation range anyway. Still, it was that rough, irregular shape...

There was one of a long, slick barracuda with sharp, scissor-like teeth, along with whales, plenty of different sharks, all fish or mammals with the same oval shape. No, no, that was not it.

Dallas surveyed more of the spines on the shelf. She found it absolutely joyous that she could keep swimming up to the higher ones without the use of a rickety stepladder. She really had no idea what she was looking for. She pulled on the spine of a book so brightly silver it could have been made from aluminum foil, smiled at the picture of the moray eel on the cover, and took it all the way out.

Dallas stacked her other book on top of this bigger one and swam around until she found the seating areas. The plush chairs here resembled heads of lettuce with the centers cut out, open flowers waiting to consume someone in comfort. Dallas chose one facing the adjacent bookshelf and parked with her newest finds.

The plush chairs here resembled heads of lettuce with the centers cut out, open flowers waiting to consume someone in comfort. Dallas chose one facing the adjacent bookshelf and parked with her newest finds. It was like a repeat of biology class, and she never pictured herself doing this for enjoyment, but there she was, poring over paragraphs about all the fish and creatures she had already encountered and the things she had not. The picture of the bamboo coral was almost like a snowy Christmas tree. The porcupine crabs looked like pink branches filled with long thorns... she did not want to imagine feeling one scratch her stomach if she swam too close to the bottom. Octopuses were also a unique shape.

She read on about octopuses, shapeshifters of the sea that can change their colors and blend in with their surroundings, much like cuttlefish. These creatures are very intelligent and have strong instincts when it comes to evading predators. Dallas knew that if she cast a sonar ring at some coral, it just might come back to her revealing eight curling legs. She did not see an octopus.

She turned to the index, finding the pages she wanted, and then read all about the different kinds of predators. They mostly took her to pages of sharks, with more species than she thought existed. How could there be so many, and how could there still be so many more?

Page after page, all that long oval shape of a creature swimming headfirst just like merfolk, though sharks like fish swim side to side and mammals like whales, dolphins, and merfolk swim up and down. Dallas tried to revisit the image sketched in her head, the rough dotted line that took no shape but was still there and kept coming back.

CHAPTER 23

THE SUB DROPPED THEM off somewhere new that day, stopping just before the garden of mini greenhouses that blended with the rock formations. When Dallas got off, she took longer to explore the area, not even finding a place of business or civilization as far as she could echolocate. She could see nothing but groves of produce hiding in plain sight and the wide nets of trapped lobsters and shrimp.

She set off for the mini greenhouses on the left and opened her cloth sack, harvesting the biggest oranges she had ever seen. The two Marine Force officers assigned to them that day swam up ahead, already casting out their sonar as far as they could. She bagged a few oranges—only a few—before the two Marine Force officers flew back to the group, waving their arms and shouting for them to get back in the sub.

"Go, now!"

"In the sub, in the sub!"

Clyde flew out of the grove he was in and circled all the gardens. He herded those nearest to him and went to do his rounds with the others. Most did not need a second command. Clyde and the two Marine Forces split up, the male going to the left and the female going to the right.

"What's going on?" a mermaid tried to ask.

"You're safe, just get in the sub," the female officer answered.

"All gatherers get inside!" called Clyde. "All hunters with weapons follow forth!"

Dallas barely had her bag tied back up before he came around to her section and ushered them away. Clyde followed the gatherers back into the sub and shut the door. He counted all the heads present out loud, ignoring questions until he was done.

"They... they found bodies not too far ahead."

Several exclaimed. Dallas glanced out the window to notice the hunters and Marine Force swimming ahead.

"They found bodies, but nothing else. There is nothing out there anymore... at least that is what they are going to make sure of. Whatever happened did its damage and left."

"What happened?"

"What was it?"

While the questions fired from all sides, Clyde adjusted the controls on the side of the sub that would activate the electric wire on the outside.

"There are two merpeople, said to be other hunter/gatherers. They are... they are pretty torn up. They're not from Gneiss Underway, and we don't know who they are just yet, but we're going to let the Marine Force take care of that once they find identification. We are going to stay inside to be on the safe side."

Out of habit, some merpeople ducked down but kept their faces high enough to see out the windows, looking for their group coming back or the inevitable monster that was in the very spot they were. They just did not know how long ago. The hideaways in the sub perked up once they saw their team of six hunters coming back. Clyde turned off the electricity and pulled the door open.

The hunters were pale in the face but unharmed, eyes wide in alarm but lips pinched in forced calm.

"They're putting in calls," one guy said. "It's a merman and mermaid both in their forties with hunter/gatherer tools that were found too. Their IDs say that they are from Rose Canyon in the North Province."

"How bad are they?" someone in the back asked.

"Ripped up," a quiet girl said. "Just torn all over."

"How many were there?" Clyde asked.

"Well, just the two," the guy answered. "But those might just be the ones that were left over."

After a solemn silence that needed no further questions, the two Marine Force merpeople came back. Clyde popped the door open, but they did not come in.

"We got the medical examiner and coroner on their way. They are sending out a shared location to our tablets and yours."

"We will go to protect the bodies until then."

"Thank you," Clyde told them, shutting the door back and watching the Marine Force go back to the kill site. He stayed put, watching his tablet and waiting for the notification status of the arriving parties.

While the others talked amongst themselves and threw out their own guesses about the known monster's identity, Dallas leaned against the window. She systematically moved her elbow enough to press the button, watching the window slide down at a glacial pace and disappear into its slot.

The waters inside the sub got a little cooler, probably to everyone's liking, but Dallas did not feel warm. She leaned her head out as far as she could and sent out a sonar blast, clean and quiet but already rippling through as far as she needed it to go.

The images that came back to her looked like the graphic images she saw online and on the news. She could make out the outlines of the bodies, but she knew they were a mess. They were barely in one piece, torn so much they were hanging by fish-scale threads. One of them, the male, had most of his arm ripped away so that he did not have a hand anymore, only strips of flesh that could resemble long, chunky fingers.

Dallas was getting better at focusing her images, but these were details she was sorry to see. She sent out another wave, assessing the bodies and the Marine Force idly pacing while protecting them from any other predators, their spears and shields right in front of them, tails wavering behind them in anticipation, on alert.

Dallas read the email and then looked up, focusing on a point on the wall so she could read it again and find different words.

She read it over once more, her fingers sliding from her tablet until it slowly sank in front of her face in mockery, refusing to go away.

> Due to the severity of recent events, all hunter/gatherer positions are temporarily suspended until further notice. This is done to ensure the safety of all in the best way possible. This was a difficult decision to make, as it affects not only the employees but also the markets relying on fresh supplies. Measures will be taken to have items from various farms shipped out to markets. As of this day, employees will receive their next pay check

at the end of the week, but further payments are still in negotiation. We appreciate your patience and understanding at this time.

Her tablet continued to ping with notifications: news reports on the community and the latest attack, information on the individuals found and the state of their bodies. There was another notification from Viceroy Westburn himself.

Gneiss Underway Citizens:

I am, as you are now, shocked and terrified by the recent events. We are doing everything in our power to keep our community safe and are enlisting more Marine Forces. The losses we have suffered are nothing short of tragic and horrible. Words cannot express what we are all feeling, but we are in this together.

We will be issuing a new quarantine ordinance effective immediately. As such, all outersea businesses will have to be temporarily suspended, and no merpersons are to be outsea. No one is allowed outsea at any time or under any circumstances except for Marine Force and even envoys are to have special permission.

Dallas skimmed these emails to pick up all the same words, phrases, and dates and times. She closed them out and violently pushed her tablet away from her, letting it float dismissively next to her on the couch as she slumped and hid her face in her fingers.

And the pinging and chimes never stopped.

She scowled and grabbed it, finding a plethora of text messages from her parents and sister.

Yeah, I'm laid off, but temporarily, she typed back. *That's all I know right now.*

Dallas tossed her tablet aside, not wanting to look at it anymore.

The ringing in her ears steadied for a couple of minutes, and at one point it was no longer due to the notifications from her tablet, but rather the activity in her brain that struggled to make sense of it all. She could shut off her tablet to get rid of the outside noise, but it was even worse that she could not shut off her brain to silence the inside noise which proved to be louder. She ignored the screen lighting up and covered her eyes.

I have only been at my new job for, what? Five minutes?

Dallas glanced up to stare at the refrigerator and cabinets in the kitchen, recalling from memory the contents of both and how long she could make each last when it came down to it. She had almost become an expert on that some time ago in her dorm during her last time on land. A sting of annoyance pinched her stomach at the thought of having to go back to that. She told herself she would never have to live like that again.

She opened the Currents app, pressing the icon that looked like faces floating in waves, which took her directly to her profile page. Ignoring her news feed for the time being, she started to type out her own status update:

> Well, I got the official email today that I have been "temporarily suspended..." I CAN'T BELIEVE this

is happening to me. I finally feel like I am getting settled, and then this happens! I had a job for five minutes, and now I am back to sitting around with nothing to do but exist until who knows how long. Of course, it has to be MY job that is too dangerous because of a predator out there somewhere. OF COURSE. What am I going to do now? So much for finally getting settled. I know I'm not the only one, but if anyone has any insights or leads on anything right now, please let me know.

She hit the post button and watched as the icon of current waves animated while it loaded her news feed. Scrolling through familiar names, she recognized that the layoffs were exclusive to all who had jobs outsea. Within moments, she received a few comments on her post that were nothing more than sincere empathy. Dallas smirked at the nice yet empty gestures until the next comment gave her cold fins:

Noah Fendelman commented:

Call me.

She closed out Currents and opened her contacts list, her fingers wavering. She hit Noah's name and took a deep breath.

He picked up on the second ring.

"*Noah Fendelman.*"

"Uh, hi. It's Dallas."

"*Hi, Miss Dwight.*"

"Hi," she said, grateful she did not have to see whatever look was on his face.

"*I know this sucks.*"

"Yeah..."

"You should have also gotten an email going over your pay details. Did you?"

"Not a detailed one, no."

"Okay. I know Clyde is working on that and should be getting that out soon. Listen, do not worry. I know this is the last thing you wanted to hear right now, and you should also know that it is happening to everyone whose job requires them to be outsea. It is for everyone's protection. You're better off bored than eaten, you hear?"

"Y-yeah, I know."

"So, relax. You will be getting a basic pay for the time you're off. Clyde is working on all of this. It will be based on your average hours for the week. I am working with him on his budget and for those who qualify for paid time off, so they get that first. We are going to make sure you are taken care of. Clyde will keep you posted with everything soon. He's just swamped right now."

"All right."

"Hang tight."

After they hung up, Dallas viewed the new activity on her post and in her news feed. She put her tablet down and turned on the TV for any kind of distracting stimulation. Every new notification ping! brought her back to her tablet with news that was all bad and never changing.

She maintained this repetitive loop for the remainder of the day, magnetically drawn to every new thing that came her way while wanting to avoid it. It was something to do while she had the television on as background noise, set to everything and anything that was not the news.

CHAPTER 24

Dallas pressed the bell button on the keypad by the door. The door opened without the need for the intercom, as she was expected, and she swam in.

"I'm in the kitchen!" Sapphire called.

Dallas swam right into the kitchen, where her friend was floating at the higher cabinet, putting away plates.

"I put it off for too long, so of course I had too many to clean," laughed Sapphire as she placed a stack of plates on the shelf. She shut the cabinet and turned around, widening her eyes upon seeing Dallas.

"Girl, you weren't kidding!"

"Yeah," Dallas said, snickering. "Seriously, I can't believe it got this long this fast." She ran her fingers through her hair as it drifted up and down in front of her face. "I look like a wet mop now. This cavegirl life."

Sapphire drifted over to her and smoothed out strands of her hair as long as they could go.

"When was your last cut?"

"I don't even know. I've been doing nothing really this whole time, and it just went wild."

"I hear ya. Sapphire to the rescue. Follow me to my lab."

Dallas went with Sapphire to the bathroom, where she had already set up a chair, the sink adorned with assorted bottles and tools waiting to be used. Dallas flopped down in the chair and tucked her long shirt around her tail, placing a small bag on the floor.

"You're seriously a lifesaver."

"No, you are. You're giving me work, technically."

"Well, at least you can work from home and have clients whenever you want. You don't need to go anywhere to work."

"That is true, but I still miss going to the salon to see Claudia and everyone. It's not the same."

"Do they know when they can have you back?"

"Not yet. Fewer people are using the pipelines, which means fewer paying customers and fewer employees getting paid."

"Well, you got me and this hot mess." Dallas finger-combed her hair that went way past her neck. Sapphire wasted no time grabbing the first items from the sink: a comb and small bottle, in order they stood. She combed out Dallas's hair a few times while spraying product into her roots and combing it down to her ends. Dallas caught a whiff of coconut and saw thin silver lines highlight down her hair strands.

The more Sapphire combed, the more her hair strands started to stiffen, revealing just how long it had grown. The front part of her hair formed into a slick slope sticking straight out.

"So, what are you thinking? Like, two inches?"

"Sure," Dallas replied. "Maybe more. I want it back to the pixie cut I had before with the spiky ends."

"Sounds good, that was definitely cute. You've still got some green to pull that off again."

Sapphire's fin touched the small bag resting against the chair.

"Is that what I think it is?"

Dallas smiled under her hair shield. "Mom's zucchini bread, just like I promised."

"You're the best!"

Sapphire measured and combed down Dallas's hair, cutting it here and there until that part was short enough to barely cover Dallas's face. She combed forward another section to repeat the process.

"So, any news on work yet?" Sapphire asked while adding the silvery product.

"Nope. Clyde has been great at keeping us updated, even though most of the updates just say that nothing is happening and nothing is changing, which is annoying. No news isn't good news."

"That's like that with everything."

"I know; they haven't even said anything more about this thing yet."

"No. Apparently, the Marine Force is increasing in troops, and they are going out in bigger groups and bigger subs, but no one is finding it. At all. No one is even close enough with echolocation. It just comes out whenever it feels like it. But like, the story that was spreading about it being spotted in Coleman's Cove was fake."

"Fake?"

"Fake; it was a humpback whale that was just passing through and minding its own business. It's not a whale. I was hanging out with my friend Cece the other day. She lives in Mirage Bay, and she told me how people freak out and literally think it's anything that swims by them and call the Marine Force."

"Wait, when were you in Mirage Bay?"

"Before the quarantine and curfew order."

"I was gonna say."

"Yeah, I at least got to hang out with her before all this happened. But you know that snake thing might just be a rumor, too."

"What about the video of that?"

"People are saying someone just filmed an eel swimming and pretended it was a big sea snake far away."

"What?"

"I know, but if you think about it, it has to be. It just doesn't sound possible. There are sea snakes, but like giant ones that are just eating merpeople up? I don't think so. I don't know what to believe. That's just so prehistoric."

She changed her long tunic to one with bigger pockets, grabbing the book on her table to put in one of them. Her tablet went into the other as she swam out the door.

Any merpeople who were out and about, not many at all, apparently were in absolutely no rush to go anywhere. Some came and went as per their usual routine, while others stopped to gossip among themselves. Dallas swam through her cave neighborhood until she reached the pipeline leading to the municipal center, where she overheard the envoy merman there asking too many questions.

"We're just going to the garden burger place!" exclaimed the mermaid in front of her. "We're going to eat, and then we'll leave!"

"I'm picking up the shelves I ordered," a merman said.

All mundane answers led to the closest pipelines, and no outsea businesses. When Dallas moved up the line, she already had her library book out.

"I am going to the library to return this."

"Remember, most public places will be closing early due to curfew."

Dallas just nodded and waited for him to open the pipeline, diving in with gusto once it was ready. When she arrived at the municipal building, all she saw was a sea of black and silver, and a few navy and silver speckled among them. Overseeing.

The Marine Force was sweeping every corner and corridor, moving in rotation toward the outer pipelines, their long robes syncing with their tails. Their clamshell helmets bobbed up and down, resembling bullets ready to shoot. Envoys were stationed around, no doubt acting as both guards and information centers.

Dallas swam past all of them without making eye contact, and without any of them grilling her on her whereabouts. It was a little after three, still early enough in the day for regular activity, allowing her to swim down to the library without a fuss. The library was a nook carved in the cave walls, a particularly tall place no doubt for its tall stacks of product. The sleek marble transformed from blue-black to ash white as she entered and got lost among the labyrinth of bookshelves.

The reference section was closer to the back. Dallas dropped off the latest book she had finished in the return bin and set out for where she had last left off. She still got practically nowhere, finding the same sections and chapters on certain kinds of animals. No mysteries confirmed. Nowhere did she read anything about gigantic sea snakes that wasn't folklore or anything similar.

But it was always a moment of excitement to uncover anything new. She loved everything she read and those little discoveries about her own backyard that she had yet to explore for herself. There was a book about the creatures of the deepest deep, the ones that humans had never seen, drinking in every word on every page.

Her favorite was the anglerfish, with its hanging lure of bright light that, at the right moment, would reveal the rows of large teeth.

Dallas browsed over the history section, picking up books on ancient marine history and prehistoric sea civilizations, just like the books she had in school growing up. She considered the pictures of early merpeople, more pronounced in fish characteristics than mammals before evolution.

Dallas ran her tongue over her teeth, slightly sharpened at the ends but not to the extent of the reptilian bites of their ancestors. She browsed over their ancient warfare, the very replicas of hunter/gatherers they had today. In one photo, there were mermen and merwomen holding long spears ending in spiked bottom jaws, long and curled almost in the shape of a scythe. It was a wonder as to what kind of creature that came from and she was almost envious that they did not have them now.

Dallas read on about the prehistoric monsters that existed under the sea at the same time the giants of the land ruled the Earth. The Megalodon was the equivalent of a dire shark, its gigantic size and aggression matched only by its bite, which could break whale vertebrae without a second thought. Since sharks are known for shaking prey back and forth once they get a good clamp on them, it only made the bite more effective, rendering another dire beast helpless.

The Mosasaurus was a large, sleek reptilian with a long jaw that ate other plesiosaurs and was very fast in the water. One of Dallas's favorites had to be the Dunkleosteus. This super soldier came equipped with its own natural armor plate covering its head, face, and thorax, believed impenetrable. This fish had bone-like teeth structures to perform iron-heavy bites in milliseconds. Twenty-six feet long, it looked like a massive bullet shot through the ocean.

Dallas flipped ahead to ancient weaponry, marveling at how big teeth were not the only things they stocked up on. A hidden weapon was venom collected from various creatures and soaked onto teeth blades. She loved the pictures of the ancient hunters and warriors wearing the best thing they had for armor over their heads, made to cover their entire bodies: remains from the Dunkleosteidae themselves, becoming miniature versions of them.

Dallas tried to imagine how her ancestors did it, especially with beasts bigger than modern-day buildings.

All they had to work with was whatever nature provided, and they made it work. They strategized and used their smarts where they lacked size and strength to take the monsters down, working in large groups and setting larger traps. They had the use of their venom weapons to help take on the big beasts. She had learned all about how they formed civilizations in undersea caves and made themselves hidden. Living underground helped...sticking their heads out to echolocate to scan the area and then swimming out into the wild when the coast was clear, willing, and ready.

Now, their weaponry and technology were advanced. Now, they had fewer—and smaller—predators to worry about. But predators still existed.

CHAPTER 25

DALLAS FOUND THE CORD to her charger and fed it to her tablet, the blinking red battery icon turning back to green in relief. She let it float on the counter as she replayed the long conversations she shared with her parents and then her sister. They had been the same, repetitious, and dull information that they all shared with no real updates, but they were all equally happy that everyone was safe.

The same held true for work and life in the community in general. The old saying was "no news is good news," and yet awaiting the time to go back into the world to function did not make it so.

Even when one did get news, it was so vague and absent of substance that it did not even need to be said. The last email from Clyde, copied to the supervising envoy, was really just an employee "check-up" and assurance that they would keep them all informed.

As the weeks rolled on, life inside the goldfish bowl proved to be tense. Like too many fish kept in the same bowl, they tended to become restless and anxious, darting around at the glass windows in vain attempts to see anything outside. Only this outside had a protective fence built all around it, side by side and above, so that the only view was through vertical bars. One afternoon, the fish in this bowl clumped at these windows.

Dallas and Albany found themselves in the middle of them, nearly dropping bags of parental produce gifts in the escalating alarm. After picking as much as they could for their own food supply, they graciously had more than enough bags to bestow on their daughters. Now, they struggled to keep hold of them as merpeople swam around them and responded to what someone else was looking at through the window, through those fence bars.

"It's the Marine Force," someone said. "Looks like they're carrying someone!"

"Someone's hurt."

"Move, let me see!"

"How bad?"

Moving with the current of natural curiosity, Dallas and Albany made their way to the windows to get their own glimpses, swimming almost as high as the ceiling to see out.

"They're coming this way," Albany said. "Oh my God, they've got an officer who is bleeding pretty badly!"

This current moved to the opposite windows as the action did. Naturally, the first and only responders were the envoys stationed nearby. They hit the panel to open it before the officers arrived, immediately swarming them in a protective pod.

"We found him swimming for his life! Already called the hospital," one of the officers holding the injured said, though they were all speaking at once.

"Everyone stay back and give them room to pass!" cried the closest envoy.

Now, inside the municipal center, everyone could see the merman, his bleeding tail wrapped in his robe and another officer's robe lent to him. The blotches of blood trailed all the way down those makeshift bandages...as well as through the water.

Envoys flew left and right as they all tried to get the closest diffusers and bring them back to the infected areas. The Marine Force and the injured merman swam off, his eyelids fluttering up and down, muttering inaudible things under his breath. Other envoys flew to the pipeline outsea to diffuse the waters there, spraying it as far as it would go and as far as they dared to go. More members of the Marine Force swam out as well, armed with larger harpoon weapons.

"Oh my God, Dally."

"This just keeps getting worse."

Any envoys not outsea diffusing the blood away formed a chain by the pipelines and called out for everyone to stay back and exit the area. Dallas could still catch a hint of the metallic smell of blood in the water and knew any creature would be getting it full throttle, and from far away.

The sisters continued on their way to their own homes, Dallas balancing her bags on her arm as she keyed into her apartment and swam inside.

It was not long after putting away the abundance of food and subjecting herself to mindless social media browsing that the television in her living room area blinked on. Dallas's eyes glanced up at it expectantly, the one visitor to come at any time but only for emergencies.

Viceroy Westburn sat before the camera in his office, blinking and taking a few breaths before he realized he was live and began to speak.

"Hello, Gneiss Underway. I come to you with reports of recent events that we are all still recovering from. It is troubling to say that more attacks have happened, and while we are doing everything we can, the predator is still at large.

"We have set up traps. We have diffused the waters leading to and around our community with the strongest scent masker. Our Marine Force troops make their rounds and send out sonar in pursuit. This creature is not staying in one place for long. We could say that it is distracted, picking up scents and hunting around communities wherever it happens to find pods. Now, the individual on the Marine Force who has been the most recent victim of the attacks has been hospitalized. He is in critical condition, not stable enough to describe the predator he encountered, and we still do not have enough information on this.

"Now, for my next announcement on the matter. We are going to continue with the security measures we have been practicing, but it has come to our attention that there needs to be more enforcement. Recently, our Marine Force troops came back with the missing school ID of a resident named Patrick Flowers that has yet to be claimed. This individual possibly came from Gneiss Underway or Mirage Bay, as it was found somewhere in between. This can only mean that someone has been outsea and has broken curfew... and it is possible the predator out there has claimed another. We are losing both Marine Force officers on the hunt and civilians who are not taking safety seriously. This cannot go on any longer. I have made the decision to put the entire town on lights out.

"Starting at once in all buildings, all bioluminescence lighting in common areas and pipelines will be shut off. All outsea lantern fixtures will also be turned off to decrease visibility to this predator. The only exception is in your individual homes, which can be turned on but only on lower settings. The electric dome coverings will still be operational, and any businesses shut down will act as traps. You should all have emergency glow pearls available in your homes, and if not, I will enlist some envoys to send some out. Until this beast is caught, taken out, and no longer a threat to anyone, we have to do whatever it takes to keep ourselves safe."

The viceroy's address ended with well wishes, never breaking eye contact with the camera until the television flickered and the channel went off. At about the same time, Dallas saw the blue and green lights all around her fade, dimming down to only a very subtle spread of color lingering in the waters. She got up and swam into her kitchen, right over to the window overlooking the cavern neighborhood.

Dallas could barely see out as the lanterns went out one by one, any bioluminescence leading to the pipelines fading until the blue all around was so dark it was almost black. She couldn't see past the next apartment. All she could see was the curious and concerned reflection of her own face, the way her eyes looked so much larger...forming wider, deeper puddles to adjust to the darkness, almost an unrecognizable new creature of the deep.

When Dallas pulled her eyes open, she was convinced it was still night. Up and out her ceiling window the ocean remained a patch of blackened blue that leaked into her room. She reached for her tablet to tell her the time, and lifted her head in surprise: 11 a.m.

Her first thought went to the twenty-four-hour no-lights policy and how seriously they were enforcing it in all common areas, though quickly put aside when Dallas noticed that she had a new email.

She sat up in her hammock, letting her tail wave and not fully committing to getting up yet, opening her email account to see a new one from Clyde.

Fwd, fwd, from Clyde Whethers

Hunter/Gatherers

Team,

I am sending you this latest news as a head's up. These are going out to all hunter/gatherer teams and will affect all of us, even if it does not affect you directly. The deciding factors range and are all personal and particular. If you have any questions or concerns don't hesitate to reach out.

-Clyde

Dallas scrolled past the forwarded message parts and grapevine of emails from and copied to other people until she got to the original from the Marine Force Recruitment office.

Effective immediately:

The West Atlantic Provinces of Gneiss Underway, Mirage Bay, and surrounding areas have instituted a draft into the Marine Force for persons in military, law enforcement, and hunter/gatherer positions. All those drafted are to report to the West Atlantic branch for duty.

Dallas got tangled in her hammock trying to get out of it, the end of her blanket covering her face and she fought to get it off. She still felt all the words already stuck to her, and there was no way to get them off. She forced herself to read the rest of the email, to process all those words into a complete sentence so she could know exactly what was going on. And she did, her heart hammering in her chest.

CHAPTER 26

Nothing.

Yet.

Just as the last day, and the few before that.

It still became her new routine to wake up that way, opening her eyes to her tablet positioned right under her pillow. One morning, she awoke to an email that turned out to be spam, but it still jolted her and managed to make her mouth dry under the ocean. Dry enough to make her tongue stick. After that, she was had been unable to even close her eyes again.

Dallas's new routine also grounded her to her living room area. She started slowly, having the first meal of the day and continuing to scroll social media sites on her tablet, all while feeling the pins all over her body of the news that could possibly happen at any given time.

I'm new, ish. Too new. They would probably go after more seasoned veterans first.

She ate another part of her bagel, some kind of berry. Blueberry? It was not something to notice. While lifting her arm, she examined it, flexing. Skinny, she was probably too skinny, not fit enough.

The Currents news feed varied from hoax predator sightings to those just using the space to complain. They got creative, she would give them that, seeing new photos circulate of the Stick Figure behind bars with sad faces. Of course, there were others. She scrolled through, seeing for a second the Stick Figure in a Marine Force uniform. It started as a joke, but then soon the same image was circulating on official Marine Force posts.

It was hard to tell what was real, and what was not. Names were another thing to look for. Friends, friends of friends, anyone who made that post making *that* announcement. It had been friends of friends, and friends and family of co-workers. Dallas paused mid-bite, even if it was a small bite, no longer wanting to continue eating. *Sean?*

Sean.

A few years older than her, had been at the job longer. Quiet and always on the patrol. Dallas clicked on his profile to read his full status, and there it was. "*I got the draft!*" Came the first sentence, and through the written words Dallas was trying to find the tone in them. Was this the excited Sean that came when he caught all those crabs at their last outing, or the scared Sean when he told all the new employees about his first encounter with a Great White?

She checked her email.

Again. And refreshed, again, just to be safe.

Her territory, her grouping, were already on the radar.

Dallas let go of her tablet, allowing herself to slump on the couch.

Her shoulder was sore, again, as she had been slipping into the bad habit of sleeping with her arm up and over her head, fingers grazing her tablet by her pillow, ready for it even in her sleep. She rolled it, wincing, feeling like the waters around her were as thick as molasses. On the floor were two weights, right on her pile of magazines. Many merpeople had a variety of these in their homes to help hold things down that were light enough to float. Dallas got up.

The weights pulled down on her arms, and when she lifted them, she watched the crooks of her arms as she cranked them up and down. It didn't take long to feel the pull. She had to at least be able to get through these if she were to tolerate heavier ones, and longer regimens. After a few counts, her tablet remained quiet of any notifications, now default to a glowing screen saver at rest.

Everything was okay, as long as she still saw that screen saver.

Dallas kept up a few more rounds, stopping when she wanted to, eyes trained on the empty plate sitting on the kitchen counter. She closed her eyes now, inhaling and exhaling a light vocal wave to mentally read everything on the counter: the plate, the fork, the container of coffee with the lid on top not closed all the way.

Again, now, the further areas of the kitchen: Her hooded tunic over the chair by the table, the library books on the counter. Dallas sent out another wave, stretching as far across her apartment as she could and just hitting the wall by the front door. Her sonar came back to her almost instantly, light tingles she could feel at the space at her forehead, the frustration at being enclosed.

Dallas opened her eyes. Her apartment was not very big, by a longshot, but it was also not very small. She had not practiced. Last time, at work, she *was* able to pick up that school of fish. The one no one else could see, but she did, and it was because of her the other gatherers that day swam out into the blue and came back with full nets. She could go further, cast out a wider net, and tell them all what's out there.

The jingle stabbed her in the ears, really, forgetting just how high she set the volume, and in her startle, Dallas dashed over to the couch where her tablet lit up in alarm. Dallas fumbled with it, her heart sinking to see the new message in her inbox. And where it was from.

From Clyde Whethers

Fwd, fwd, fwd, from the offices of the West Atlantic Marine Force

Team,

As per the official email sent out by the Marine Force recently, they have concluded with the draft selections and will not be sending out anymore. If you have not received a draft notice, no further action is needed on your part. For those that have been selected you will be notified for your first summons date as was already stated. And since I am one of those people, I will be joining you at training.

As far as work goes, we are still figuring things out on our end and when we can go back to being operational. For right now, things are tight and the focus is on aiding the Marine Force. Thank you so much for your patience, we are trying our best and should have answers soon. Feel free to reach out if you have any questions or concerns. -Clyde

Dallas only skimmed the next part of the email, before going back to the meat of it. She stayed floating by the couch, her tail swirling underneath her. A part of her wanted to collapse on it and let go of all the tension she had in her back. But she didn't. Her shoulders fell in the relief that she felt, but they also fell in a way that made her cross her brow in confusion. She did not expect to be disappointed.

The orbs were drifting down and all around like fireflies in a night sky, wavering slightly like the dark shadows they were attached to. There weren't many merpeople out, and those who were restricted their activities to necessities rather than wants. Her excuse was a mixture of both.

Dallas glanced down at her own oversized pearl in her left palm, adjusting the straps around her wrist. With her other hand, she stroked it until the blue light awakened, groggy at first, until it grew large enough to cast its own haze. And then Dallas was just another firefly in the mass. She curled her fingers around the pearl, rotating her wrist to cast the light around her and determine her direction.

The lanterns hanging from doorways remained dark, no light conjured, dismissed from their duties.

Dallas looked toward the home around the corner, where almost no light activity had been seen at all. She checked the messages on her tablet, opening the one she had sent to Sapphire earlier that day to see what she was up to. Recently, Dallas received a notification that her message had been opened and seen, but there was no reply. She glanced at Sapphire's door and dark window, disappointed, before swimming out of her neighborhood.

The municipal center was home to the main firefly orbs swimming around, with stationary lights in the corners revealed to be envoys keeping watch. The further Dallas went in, the more she could have sworn she was not inside at all. The dark mass of the outsea ocean matched the very same inside the building so closely that it felt as though the glass walls were not there. And without the usual operating light pollution, the ocean could be seen for miles. Or it would be, if not for the fence.

Even through vertical viewpoints, Dallas could catch glimpses of the outsea, but not the entire seascape. She spotted rock formations standing out like the shadows of giant creatures, perched and still, waiting to kill. But those rock formations were the only things out there—nothing else alive, nothing else moving in the quiet waters.

Along the fence, Dallas noticed a few of those orbs patrolling back and forth: the Marine Force officers spying through the bars. The lack of light gave them the advantage to see out where something else could not see in.

All around her, merpeople occasionally called out to one another, adjusting individual lights to see who was there, to recognize the face of each swimming shadow and confirm they were friends. Dallas sideswam small crowds and made her way to the pipeline leading to the marketplace building. The envoy merwoman stationed there instructed everyone leaving to turn off their pearls at once. Dallas complied and joined four other merpeople, sailing through nothing but calm and quiet seas in the protection of a tube.

She readjusted her pearl light once they landed and made her way to the market stores to browse any Fast Eats. She sighed with indecision, her only real choice being to get out of her cave. Her tablet pinged, and she opened it to another new news article.

> The ID card of a college student named Patrick Flowers was found on Wednesday near the recreational buildings. This is in violation of the town curfew. He has since been added to the list of those missing with no other information. Any family and friends of this person need to contact the authorities immediately regarding his whereabouts, and if lockdowns are going to continue to be broken.

> Since the lockdowns were issued, no merpeople have been outsea, or are allowed outsea, except officials traveling in subs. Viceroys from each town and district want to continue to enforce lockdowns by any means necessary to drive home the seriousness of the situation and the real danger that is still out there. Anyone who goes outsea alone is not safe.

Dallas closed the article after reading about more missing merpersons and the scientific testing of the waters for bloodshed. Out of the corner of her eye, she saw rose lights standing out against the teal of the bioluminescent pearls. They belonged to a sign above a restaurant blinking the name "Mixin' Bowl." She swam up to it to read the menus posted by the door, waving her pearl to get a bigger light. She shook it, and shook it some more, rubbing the top that would summon a genie.

A moment later, a brighter pearl appeared, swimming next to her, attached to a merman.

"It's not a Magic 8 Ball, Miss Dwight."

She looked up to recognize both the voice and face, now illuminated by a pearl brighter than hers.

"Need some help?"

Noah reached out to her, and she surrendered. He loosened the straps on her wrist and pulled the pearl, wrapping the strap back around her palm and then sliding the pearl back down.

"Use your fingers to roll it," Noah said, demonstrating with his own. The flashing teal light reminded Dallas of the bowling balls rolling down the lane during glow-in-the-dark event nights. "Forward for more, backward for less."

"Thanks!"

"There, now you can actually read the menu."

Dallas rolled the pearl, and the bioluminescence brightened. The first thing she could see better was Noah's face. The stubble she last saw on him had developed into a small, pointed shrub at his chin.

"You look like you've never been here before."

"I haven't," she answered honestly. "I mean, I am now that I have all this free time."

Noah let out a little snicker in understanding.

"It's one of my favorites. You pick whatever you want in each category, and they mix it all up for you, cook it, and serve it. Easy-peasy, and there are just too many options."

"Well, noodles are one of my greatest weaknesses."

Noah grinned. "You feel like joining me?"

Dallas shrugged slightly. "Sure."

They entered the line and viewed the menu options, picking things here and there. Dallas watched her bowl fill with egg noodles, mushrooms, tofu beef, carrots, peapods, sesame seeds, and topped with spicy teriyaki sauce. The bowls were placed in strange blenders behind the counter, mixing and heating them simultaneously. Their orders were passed to the pickup counter, bowls topped with their respective covers and everything secure.

After paying, Dallas picked hers up and peered through the clear covering, spotting tiny specs of sea salt keeping the food. She saw Noah holding his bowl in one arm and two bottles of cucumber water in the other. He moved his head in the direction of the seating areas, and she followed, glad to see the inside cave lanterns around the tables and chairs were all turned on to a decent setting.

She watched Noah turn off his pearl and move it to the back of his hand; she did the same, both opening their bowls and stirring the contents with chopsticks.

"I felt like getting out today," Noah started. "Normally I hide in my office or my home, and I need to get away from emails and phone calls."

"I understand," Dallas replied, spreading the thick teriyaki sauce around the noodle bed.

"Well, I am supposed to be doing follow-ups anyway. How are things going for you, despite everything?"

"Well, about the job in general, I—enjoy it." The truth in the sentence pleased Noah and surprised Dallas as she heard how it sounded out loud, even though it had its disclaimers.

"I mean, I would enjoy it more if it were as it normally is."

Noah was nodding between mouthfuls of noodles, while Dallas dug into hers, wondering just how much she wanted to tell him. If she should tell him.

"Any updates on anything?" she asked casually yet hopefully.

"Any updates on anything?" she asked casually yet hopefully.

"No, the viceroy is still panicking, as he should be, as he finally had to admit that there was a problem. It just took more merpeople getting killed for that to happen. Us envoys are stuck answering the same questions over and over with the same vague and unhelpful answers, mostly to the panicky ones who won't stick a fin outside their homes."

"Fun."

"Loads. We're in communication with viceroys and envoys from neighboring towns, though, trying to keep tabs to know if or when this thing hits the immediate radar. But anyway, what have you been up to?"

"I've been spending most of my time at the library."

Noah smiled between bites. "That's a good place to be."

"I've just been really into reading about marine life, what's out there, and stories about ancient civilizations. I just can't get over how they were able to survive down here with so little against giant prehistoric beasts that could swallow a hundred merpeople at once."

"Well, that's why they were so happy to come on land after the dinosaurs were wiped out. They built some impressive underground sea cave burrows where they lived and built their entire communities. I've seen pictures, and there is even a replica at a museum I've been to. It puts groundhogs to shame. There were even life-sized jaws of Megalodons."

Dallas's eyes lit up.

"We could use a tip or two from our ancestors at this time. But it's in our blood, it's in our bones, it's in our fins to be top dog. We've come to take the sea back. And so far, we've done pretty well. Except, you know, the fear of the unknown that is still out there and will be for some time."

Dallas nodded, taking a large mouthful of noodles, needing her mouth to stay busy so that they did not betray the thoughts she was having, the ones she still needed to process and put together, and even figure out if that was what she wanted to do.

CHAPTER 27

She flipped to the next page, where she saw a simple illustration of the paragraphs she had just read. The almost reptilian, ancient merpeople were snug underneath the sea ground, peeking out of openings. The wavy lines drawn from them all the way out to a behemoth fish represented their sonar radar, getting both that creature and another a bit further out. She considered that range, that skill of sending it out while staying obscured—also considering about how their casting exercises went to cover that much area for such large creatures, and just how far out they were willing to go to get something even farther...

Dallas read on about the different traps they would make, the secret places where the merpeople would stay hidden in their concealed forts, and the convenient holes cut out on the top. She lifted her face from the book, and in her soft, clamshell-like chair, stared at no particular point across the library shelves and imagined it for herself.

What it must be like to send out waves of echolocation, knowing exactly where the creature was and when it was going to come, and then collectively, everyone thrusting their weapons through the holes to strike it, to impale it and injure it enough to take it out. Venom-soaked tooth blades helped. They initiated the power of sneak attacks, of striking secretly guerilla-style. It was not always about being the biggest and the strongest.

Dallas's fin poked out of her clamshell chair, waving leisurely as she immersed herself in the next chapter filled with more hunting techniques. The ancient civilizations were all hunter/gatherers; each and every one was raised to be so and took control of their environment. They knew the sea. They understood what was there and how to work with it. All Dallas knew was whatever she read in books, whatever she saw in photos of both past and present, the creatures of the deep hiding just as they all were right now.

All around her in the library, the bioluminescent lanterns were dimming, dimming, until they went out completely. But she never saw this, for her eyes were shut, and she was playing images and scenes in her head of those ancient merpeople going to battle, weapons raised and swimming together as a massive army pod.

Those scenes of historical merpeople versus beast warfare instantly faded, the chimes of various notifications from her tablet breaking her out of that dream and sudden deep sleep. Dallas uncurled herself from the spiral of slumber, completely snug inside the clamshell. She opened her tablet to mostly ignore and bypass things that were unimportant; but the important thing was the time. The library was empty of everyone, except for her. The clock read after 11 p.m.

She cursed and pushed out of the chair before retreating inside to think about it. No one else would still be in the library, but she had to consider where the Marine Force would be patrolling.

Her excuse was innocent yet still stupid enough to warrant some consequences if she got caught. But she wouldn't.

Dallas turned her tablet notifications to silent, putting the screen to sleep and closing the protective covering over it. She unwrapped her pearl from her palm and tucked it into her skirt pocket. With both hands, she pushed on the top of the clamshell cushion over her head until it peeked open, and then she sent out a sonar wave.

It bounced off the bookshelves enough to reveal clear paths with no one in them, and Dallas set off. She navigated through the bookshelf labyrinth in the most satisfying zig-zag echolocation she had ever tried, the fuzzy-to-clear outlines of each one in the dark materializing all around her until she found the path to the main door.

Dallas swam up to the control pad and simply pressed the button to open it. It was not a problem to do so from the inside, of course, and it shut and locked the moment she swam out past the sensor.

She pressed against the wall, flattening her tail and holding her tunic down so it wouldn't move either. In the foreground of the main resource center, she could see those tiny blue orbs. One was all the way over to the left, slowly making its way to the one standing still on the right. Two others were coming in from the far right, stopping a bit, no doubt to chit-chat.

Dallas drifted down to her stomach, touching the floor, and pushed along, steadying her breathing so she made as few bubbles as possible. She echolocated walls, sofa chairs, posts—any obstacle that she could position behind and use as markers. She stayed still, she stayed low, she tracked the patrolling orbs and made her way from obstacle to obstacle. The tricky part came when she got closer to the pipeline.

They would know when someone opened it. They would see her once she got out in the open, pearl light or not, or catch her with echolocation when she came out from behind the obstacles. The best she could do was wait until they were all out of range at the same time.

Dallas sank behind a sofa chair and peered around the corner. The pearl orbs separated down different hallways until they both disappeared, and without a second to waste, she moved across the floor. The pipeline was within reach, but she stayed low, reaching an arm up to activate it and ducking through before any of them could come back.

Coming out the other side would be even more difficult, so she stayed by the door, snug along its outline so that no one would be able to see her rogue tail out in the pipe and bust her. She saw mostly darkness in the main center, with the patrolling orbs at various spots in the distance. Dallas steadied her breathing, knowing that the outburst of bubbles from her gills would no doubt be seen, so she timed the directions of those orbs and waited for them to be out of sight before she pressed open the door.

Dallas stayed low and echolocated walls and seats while swimming across the room, having too much confidence about being out in the open until those orbs came back. She froze and pressed herself to the floor as they glowed in the nearby hallway, close enough to make out the outline of the Marine Force merman making the patrol. She held her breath and imagined herself as flat on the floor as possible, wishing she could bury herself in it like a stargazer fish does in the sand.

The orb continued down but did not pass in front of her, lingering a bit before moving on and giving her a second to split. She darted out and jerked back as another orb was making its way in from somewhere else. In an instant, Dallas flew to the pipeline door that led out to sea and exited, throwing herself against it as that orb light came back around.

The outer fence surrounded the building, the only thing separating her from the wild sea, the waters too dark to distinguish the bars from the gaps. She floated there, nondescript and motionless, as the watch guards passed, still trying to make out the gaps. Dallas drifted over to the fence and touched the bars, pushing her nose to it just enough. Her ancestors were able to do it through small openings such as this, focusing their radar to a narrow path.

She sent sonar out, messy at first as most of it bounced off the fence. She leaned in and worked on her breathing to a deep inhale and elongated exhale, making that wave narrow enough to fit. The image that came back was massive, thick, and round, big enough to be a whale, though it was not quite a whale. Dallas leaned back. There was not anything else on her radar, but she was on the other side of someone else's.

Within moments, the pearl orb lit up next to her, and she jumped, jerking back from the fence as the light illuminated the merman attached to it.

He held the pearl in his palm, and the blue light mingled with his eyes and the grays in his hair and beard, the waves in the water and the light making their own currents on his face, resembling tiger stripes. Her heart sank.

"Oh, you are in serious trouble, young lady."

"I— I—"

"What reason do you have to not only be out after curfew so late but outside the building?"

Dallas stayed frozen as the guards inside made their rounds once again, but Liam never broke his stare and made sure she stayed pinned. His hand lingered near his radio, no doubt moments away from alerting the others of his discovery, but yet it still only lingered.

"Whatever your reason, it's not good enough."

"I fell asleep!" Dallas blurted out.

"Fell asleep... Where?"

"In the library, in one of the chairs that I curled up in and just got too comfortable. I fell asleep, and when I woke up, it was closed and after curfew, so I mean, I left."

"And no one noticed you."

"No."

"You don't have your pearl?"

"I do..." Dallas admitted. Liam got it.

"How did you get all the way out then, and out here without seeing or being seen?"

Dallas was still keeping her body flat and small, and if Liam did not have the pearl and did not echolocate that area, she knew that she would probably not be seen at all.

"Very, very carefully. I...made sure of it."

Liam's response was amusement, but it did not show on his face. Instead, it formed as sparkles in his eyes.

"Carefully, huh?"

Dallas sighed on the inside.

"Well, I can echolocate."

Liam had a raised brow. "That's how I found you."

His arms were now folded, more interested in Dallas's explanation than busting her.

"So, then what exactly brought you out to sea, so close to the fence that you were practically going through it?"

"Well, I wanted to just get home safely without anyone noticing, and I wanted to practice echolocating through narrow obstacles. I read about how the ancient civilizations built those underground burrows and used them to sneak attack huge predators. I just...I just wanted to see if I could see...anything."

Liam lowered his pearl and even adjusted the settings a bit.

"You aren't going to see anything but the open blue."

"I did see something; I thought it was a whale, but I know it was one of the subs."

"One of the subs?" Liam repeated.

"Yeah, I could tell by the metal make."

Liam just stared at her for a moment.

"That left here a while ago. A very long while ago."

Liam took a glance out through the bars, and Dallas did as well.

"You're telling me that you can go that far?"

She only shrugged, not denying it at all.

"I can. Yeah. But I have been out of work for so long that I wanted to make sure I could... I could still do it. I am a hunter/gatherer."

"*Liam, what's your twenty?*"

Liam pulled his radio out and pressed the side button.

"Outside by the fence."

"*You have not passed by in a while. Everything okay?*"

"Yeah," Liam said, keeping his eyes on Dallas. "Nothing to worry about. I am just having a discussion with someone."

"*Ten-four.*"

Liam put his radio back. "I'm supposed to write you up for breaking curfew," he stated. "But I also realized that if you were out on patrol with the crew and something was out there right now, you would be the one to know sooner than any of them."

Liam took a side glance at the fence and the sea beyond it, then back to the windows.

"I'll escort you home. Come on."

Liam increased the light setting on his pearl again as the other guards did another lap, no one noticing to stop or come through the outsea door. He led Dallas to the same door she had come out of, swimming inside and paying no attention to the guard who turned at his presence and then turned again upon seeing he had company.

"I am taking care of it," Liam told the guard before he could even ask. "Carry on."

After telling Liam her neighborhood, he led her straight to that pipeline back. They stopped at the resident caverns, where a few home lights here and there were turned on. Dallas bashfully turned to Liam as she took out her key card.

"Thanks," she said, wanting every meaning in the word to come out, for all the reasons, the reasons he understood, since he gave a little nod. Dallas did not go in just yet, lingering a minute.

"Don't worry, you're off the hook. Just make sure you leave the library at the right time and sleep in your own bed, okay?"

"I will. Um..."

"Yes?"

"The Marine Force, are they..."

Liam considered her, believing he knew what she was going to ask.

"They've finished their draft. If you didn't get one, you're safe. I have been getting that question a lot."

"Are they taking volunteers?"

Liam's eyebrows jumped.

"You want to volunteer?"

Dallas nodded now, sure. "I'm not the strongest, but I am strong in echolocation. I think I can help. I want to help. I want to, just…"

Liam kept his eyes on her, reading her, and she hoped that she was not giving off any insecure vibes.

"If you truly want to, you should."

A voice in Dallas's head told her not to slouch, her backbone trying to remind her that it was there.

"I do. I have skills. I should use them."

"Okay. Seeing as how I am an envoy that handles military affairs, I think this is something I can look into."

"Really?"

"If it works out, which it probably will, I might see you in about a week or so."

Dallas paused at the door. "A week?"

He smiled. "You got that right. I'm former military myself, so guess who the training coach is?"

Liam held back the laugh on his lips, but once again, his eyes did the laughing for him.

CHAPTER 28

SHE DID NOT EVEN need echolocation to find the base.

The moment Dallas swam past the trough and a school of fish parted like curtains, she could see all of them. They were spread out, arms stretched, and tails extended as well. Many held weights and routinely lifted them up and down, bubbles of relief blowing out of their gills once they set them down.

It was easy to tell which were the regular Marine Force and which ones were the volunteer recruits. Those stood off to the side, grouped together, not necessarily knowing one another but merely sticking together with that one aspect in common. She recognized some, including Clyde and some others from her troop but not all, mainly hunter/gatherers with the muscles to prove something.

And certain ones thought they were on the same level as the Marine Force, those buff athletic guys with smirks on their faces as they looked around the area and sized them all up. She wondered if it mattered which were drafted and which were volunteers...and if it would give her a higher regard.

Dallas closed her official email, shut her tablet, and went to join the group. She positioned herself in the crowd, neither pompous nor shy. Ahead of them was an obstacle course she had already visualized repeatedly, starting with the low slabs to swim under, the high slabs to swim over, and the narrow trench to go through. There were rock formations arranged in a maze, creating a race to see who could find the way out first.

There was no telling what lay inside the maze.

The course occupied most of the designated training area. Dallas could see various heights of hoops to swim through at the end; the farther down, the smaller the hoops.

"Welcome, everyone."

Heads and bodies turned towards the merman swimming above the gathering so everyone could see him, beard drifting along the military jacket he wore. It was not of Marine Force colors, but with color faded with so much age it was no longer black but not yet gray, with a few stitches near the sleeve.

Liam observed them all, sizing them up more subtly than they did one another.

"Most of you here know the drill."

A few confirmations scattered amongst the crowd.

"If you're a newly minted Marine Force member, you're more familiar with our training grounds. If you're a hunter/gatherer, not so much, but you possess many of the same skills, which will come in handy. If you don't fall into either category, you're here because you've got some moxie and are looking for a way to channel it. I can tell you that you're in the right place for that."

Liam swam over to the beginning of the course. Scattered weights littered the ground around it, none in their proper place; they looked as if they had been tossed down in haste.

"For those of you who don't know me, I'm Envoy Liam Owen. I got my sea legs in another way before I came down here. I served in the U.S. Navy, where I was lucky to train new recruits, and now you're lucky to be with me. I thought I retired to the sea, but now I'm a living irony."

He gestured behind him. "You'll all be going through this in no time, don't worry. But for now, we're going to work out those muscles of yours."

Liam smiled, a smile he had held back for so long.

"I never thought I'd say these words again: drop and give me twenty!"

Dallas thought back to gym class and was instantly amused to be doing push-ups with the help of buoyancy, sinking into the sand with each descent.

They swam laps, pumping their tails and bending their bodies to navigate around curves and bends. She was able to tell the difference immediately with the trained professionals with each whirlwind spin, showing off and dashing above the rest of the group.

The shrill sound of Liam's whistle signaled them to stop and join him by the hoops.

"Line up in threes and dash through them as fast as you can. Begin!"

Dallas felt the protesting muscles in her fins but expertly flapped them as she moved forward, racing the two others in shifting equality. She straightened her arms in front of her head with one hand over the other in true diver's fashion when she passed through, fins brushing the hoop edges in a light scrape.

When she joined those who had finished, she had an up-close view of the labyrinth they were to navigate, the blunt and shaved ends of rock where pieces were cut into pathways.

Liam floated over the group.

"Line up the same way you were before, in threes. This is your first echolocation exercise, and it's fairly simple. Find the walls, find the paths, and find your way out in complete darkness. This is not a short maze and depending how fast or slow you are, some of you will no doubt find one another and use teamwork to get out. Your time starts now."

Liam's whistle sounded and the groups of three swam into the maze at different entrances, their tails disappearing behind the walls. Liam sent more in bit by bit, but before Dallas swam up to her entrance, she sent out a light wave that revealed a wall not too far inside. So, when her turn came, she rushed in and immediately turned left, the light from the open ocean fading with each stroke.

Dallas stretched out her arms in front of her as she cast another blast, receiving the bounce back of a wall a few feet ahead and another path down her left. She swam a little faster as the blue around her turned to black.

Being completely blind in the water was not frightening, at least not in closed quarters, and all she could rely on was her strongest sense. She felt the bubbles around her as she exhaled, tickling her neck like the nibbles of little fish. When she reached up to scratch her gills, she was surprised to find there was, in fact, a little fish. She sent out a small sonar barely above a hum as she sensed the little creature fluttering around in her mind.

There it was, something she could see as clearly as a photo developing in a dark room. The pure outline showed every ridge and slope of its fins and the teardrop shape of its tiny body. Dallas cupped her palm precisely where it was and felt it flutter about her hand, kissing her palm in greeting a few times before taking off. It would find its way out in its own time, and it was a wonder to know how some things could survive in the darkest depths...and for how long.

After her first day of training, Dallas felt sore in places she didn't know she had, the pull of stretched muscles like rubber bands tightening to strong, thin lines. Her tail throbbed all the way to her fluke, and she felt those muscles straining each time she pumped through the water. She went home and heated up a quick dinner of a tofu burger patty and mixed vegetables, knowing she was too tired to stretch out in front of the TV.

She headed to her room instantly, dimming the bioluminescent lighting to none, letting the natural blanket of the sea cover her until she wrapped herself up in her hammock. Sleep came almost instantly as her body welcomed the stillness. It was rewarding and peaceful at first, until Dallas sank into a dream that made her move around again.

This time, her dream brought her swimming through giant hoops, never-ending and changing in size. The hoops were all so far away, and she was swimming extremely slowly to reach them, no matter how hard she tried to go faster. In her dream, she pumped and pumped until her tail hurt, only to look down and realize that she had no tail at all, but rather human legs.

Dallas pushed and pushed, swimming as hard as she could with her arms, not knowing why she had turned back into a human but somehow knowing it was important to make it through all those loops. Each time she passed through one, it became smaller and smaller, until she reached the very last one, lined with barbs or spikes, looking like the final challenge.

It wasn't until she finally reached it that she discovered those were neither barbs nor spikes. Once her weak human body swam through the loop, it clamped down on her with an iron-clad bite.

Dallas flew out of her hammock, twisting in her blankets that first wrapped around her waist and then started their slow descent into the ocean water over her head. She fought her way out of them, grabbing her pearl by her dresser and flipping it on. The light blue glow revealed that she was back to having a tail, all intact. She ran her hands down her scales, where mere seconds ago she had felt deep puncture wounds.

The next day, they were all told they would be wearing armor.

Dallas was taken aback. No reason was given, and they were all ordered to get fitted. They all lined up, some speculating that this could possibly be the start of the hunt, though others denied it. Dallas went with the alarm the others had, and told herself she shouldn't be, it was just like protocol at her job. Her old job. Her hopefully still existing job.

The group swam around to the warehouse building behind the green coral reefs, the same one where she had echolocated the fish swimming around moments ago. Fish, and nothing else. There, the Marine Force members worked to size up all the volunteers and draftees and issued their gear.

Dallas felt the upgrade from her hunter/gatherer armor, noting the weight of it in quality and seriousness. The scale mail vest was made of scallop or clam shells, with matching shoulder pieces—though a bit larger. The utility belt had more slings than pouches to hold for more weapons...as Dallas got one handed to her that already had a small gun in a holster. The leather kilt was accompanied by other large clamshells with rough edges, already poking at her back and tail when she tried it on.

"It's a bit big, but it'll do," the Marine Force mermaid said, looking at the way the kilt hung lower on Dallas' waist. She then handed her the signature leather tunic, the one they all wore, with the official emblem on the left side. Dallas worked the armholes over her shoulder pads and let the back sections fall against her dorsal. She was given the helmet, which she held at her waist out of habit. She kept adjusting the turtle arm guards, irritated that they were long enough to touch the ridges of her arm pectoral fins and kept scraping.

Once everyone had their gear on, they were ordered outside. They were given weapons.

"You've no doubt worked in armor before, so it's important to get used to wearing it while you're on a job outsea," said Liam. "We're going to begin with a few warm-ups... and then you'll all start some new training."

Liam blew the whistle, and they all started with push-ups, then laps around the arena. As Dallas swam her laps, she caught sight of what was in the middle, and what that new training would be. Makeshift targets were stationed in rows, waiting for them when they finished their warm-ups.

Everyone lined up when Liam blew the whistle, and they were all directed to station themselves at a target. Dallas stared at her target, which resembled a body wrapped in a garbage bag. It reminded her of that movie where a killer dumped a body in the ocean and was caught with the help of merpeople who found the evidence.

"Now, welcome to combat."

Some cheered and expressed appreciative outbursts.

"You're going to learn some basics that come with the territory. You have weapons for hunting, but let's not forget the biological weapon that might still be new for some of you: your tail."

Dallas watched the others practice their hits. On her turn, she struck the bundle and found it was squishier than pounds of seaweed. She angled her tail in front of her again as Liam drilled into them to watch their balance, practicing the moves they were taught but also threw in a few of her own. She struck upward in an uppercut, hitting with the very middle of her fluke, and delivered roundhouse slaps to the sides.

Dallas drifted a few inches back from the target and made slices across it, first from the left and then from the right. The very ends of her fins were more the equivalent of nails than blades but enough to scratch.

"Now, float on your backs and strike with your fins only. Kick and slash and stay horizontal."

Dallas executed this move while keeping her eye on the target from the side.

"We only use this move against a mer opponent and smaller prey, as it is the perfect block, but we never ever use this defense against large sea creatures! It only makes it easier for them to swallow you whole! Be mindful!"

The troops continued their target practice before Liam ordered them to line up in front of the weapon racks.

Dallas scanned the rifle-shaped weapons before her and knew from the additional knobs, wiring, and contraptions that they were much more involved. Liam took one from the rack and floated above the troops so they could see him as he held it out.

"Your more advanced, yet basic stunner. Designed by the finest aquatic technology companies this side of the Atlantic, these little devices have enough oomph in them to slow down a ravenous barracuda or a tiger shark.

Now, keep in mind that stunners are designed to stun, not kill. For situations that require a complete takedown, there are different weapons for that. With these, you can stop something up to ten feet away if you echolocate it first and can determine its location before it knows where you are. Some of you hunter/gatherers use something like this out at sea, so you should know how to use it. Here is a demonstration."

Without further warning, Liam aimed the stun gun at the target dummies behind them. A shot of yellow-green, electrifying rope impaled three of them in a row, jerking their makeshift heads back to mimic the sudden loss of movement.

Some of the troops reacted with short gasps at witnessing it for the first time, while others smirked with familiarity.

"Like I said, fairly basic. Now come and get your own."

One by one, they retrieved stun guns from the rack, but instead of returning to the target dummies, they followed Liam to another area where a large trench stood in the middle of a great divide. Some members of the Marine Force were positioned above it, tails up casually, yet they were all holding something.

"You are to swim through and hit as many targets as you can. Most of them will not be tied to stakes in the ground, you know."

Dallas held the gun in various positions until it felt right. Not fully prepared when the whistle blew, she went anyway and flicked off the safety. She got about a tail's length in before the guards above started tossing targets her way. They were dummies made of the same material, tossed and tied together but creatively twisted to have their own fins and jaws.

Dallas threw out her practice shots and watched them bounce off the trench walls, cursing to herself and hoping no one noticed. She steadied her arm and the weight of the weapon against it as she fought to regain control of the hand-eye coordination she used to have...but that was back in her college days of playing video games. Of course, hand-held console controllers were much easier to use, and all the buttons were close together. It took the right timing and usage of X, Y, A, B, and Forward, Back, Left, and Right on the directional pad. Aiming a weapon in a video game only meant pressing the right button, not actually lifting it and aiming.

Still, Dallas pressed those buttons mentally in her head as she lifted, aimed, and caught one of those "swimming" fish targets right in the head. Her gun buzzed, zapped, and the target fell against the wall.

In her mind, she imagined the hit points bar of the targeted enemy drop down to nothing, and she grinned.

CHAPTER 29

Silence from the other end of the phone. From all three of them. Dallas's tail curled underneath her.

Say something, one of you.

"You did WHAT?"

"Are you serious?"

"Dad," Dallas started. "Mom. It's all right."

"What made you do that?"

"Dally, you're going to get yourself killed!"

"Are you crazy?"

"Guys!" Dallas silenced, adding a half-laugh to her tone to lighten the mood. "I mean it, it's not bad at all, and it's actually just like work. We do training drills and practice shooting and echolocating, which is a skill I have now and is something I have to grow anyway. It's literally no different than being a hunter/gatherer, except it's actually way safer because we're surrounded by soldiers and it's a bunch of people from my job anyway, *including* my supervisor."

"But you weren't drafted?"

"No Dad, I volunteered."

Silence again.

"Wow, Dally. I couldn't do that. You're tough."

"Thanks Ally."

"You are. You're so brave, but you know, we still worry about you."

"I know Mom, and don't worry. I am surrounded by protection. It's not like I am going to fight this big monster by myself. And if I'm on the team that helps take this down, well, who knows."

"That will definitely look good for you."

"Yeah," Dallas admitted, to her family, but something she had to say out loud. "It will."

"So, you go out then?"

"Not really, not yet. We have just been doing training patrols, short and easy routines."

"So, are you on call?"

Dallas brushed the tab that came up on her tablet at the top, another notification that wasn't a notification, and just meant nothing for the day.

"In a way. But it's not like a surprise."

Dallas rubbed her forehead as her mind wandered, daydreaming about things that never happened while completely tuning out her show and missing what was happening. She took one last sip of coke and put the cup next to her plate on the table, still smelling the leftover smears of ketchup littered with speckled tofu chicken breading. She was about to close up the potato chip bag when a sharp siren noise broke her out of her reverie.

She first looked to the TV to see whatever action was taking place. There was no action except for characters talking, and the dialogue was nothing that warranted excitement. The siren sounded again and Dallas looked at her tablet lighting up and buzzing. Soon enough, the show officially cut out and resorted to the same scrolling text.

> This is an emergency broadcast update for a predator watch. All merpersons are to retreat from windows in common areas and seek safety in covered areas at this time. Turn off lights, and all pipeline traveling will be put to a halt until further notice. No one is allowed out at sea except for approved Marine Force personnel.

Any lazy state of mind and body that had settled in her, so much so that it felt like weight, dissipated. Dallas sat all the way up as she read the mirroring message on both her tablet and television screen. And without her control, the bioluminescence around her started to dim until it was nearly out.

Even the television screen lost its cast of light over her table. The light she had left on in the kitchen seemed to go out almost completely, turning to a pale blue to match the water. She got up and immediately swam to the window in her kitchen.

Merpeople were swimming into the neighborhood caverns, and some still had their glow pearls, hastily lowering the brightness on them as they made it back to their own homes. As far back as she could see, there were envoys stationed to herd the masses out of the pipelines. She swam to another window, the one near her entrance door that would give her another view.

Her tablet pinged, right on time, and she went back to get it, opening simultaneous text messages.

Roll out, team! Meet at the front entrance with any weapons you have. We will distribute more once we're all gathered. This is not a drill.

Dally, are you home?

She sent:

I'm fine... Are you? You're not at the greenhouses, are you?

Seconds later, there were two pings.

We are home, and no, not after curfew. We left the greenhouses earlier during the day and are done now.

We heard a few envoys were a little more panicked and telling merpeople this is not a drill. Are they sending you out?

Dallas listened to the shouts of the pipeline envoys barking orders at merpeople to move along.

Yeah. I've got to go. Please be safe! Don't worry.

Another ping.

Dally, they think it's close...

She texted Albany back:

So did they see it?

Someone saw something. They didn't say what it was. It might be it. But it's just too dark.

She swam back to the window with the same view as before. From beyond, there was nothing else to see or make out at all. Dallas got the idea that she could have a better view. She swam to her bedroom and went up to her ceiling, still able to see the bars of the fence around the dome, but nothing through it. It was difficult even making out the bars of the fence in the pitch blue-black, but what she couldn't see started with shouts, followed by flashes of lime-green lights.

Dallas bolted back to her living room and rushed to the other window, where she caught a glimpse of one of those lights. Pressing her nose against the glass, she watched as the line streamed by in the distance. The range and voltage power levels were higher than the weapons she had used.

Then came more shouts.

The burst of bubbles from her gills came in short spurts as the water through the bars grew darker. The dark mass passed through and disappeared somewhere else, confirming its size and elongated shape.

Dallas doubled back from the window and swam around to the other ones in her house, seeing nothing there, and nothing anywhere.

She swam to her door and hit the keypad to open it, keeping her tablet in the inside pocket of her tunic to muffle the sounds and light. When she shut it behind her, her eyes had to adjust to the dimness of the neighborhood caverns.

All along the rock the blue and green bioluminescence looked like the glow on their last lifelines of power, fading here and there and smearing into one another to almost have no light at all. Dallas noted the pearl lights of the envoys had also dimmed, and she observed the way they were swimming purposefully along the main community center, driven by desperation and fear.

"Send more to the south end!" she heard a cry from ahead. "The south end! Echolocation radar is confirmed!"

"It's a snake!" someone else shouted. "It's a huge snake!"

More pearl lights dashed in that direction, and even more formed pods to the pipelines out at sea. Dallas swam down and over to the windows, where all the guarding envoys were making their way to station at the pipelines. A pod of Marine Force soldiers moved forward, several weapons in tow. Dallas could hear their calls of echolocation as they exited the pipeline to the sea, and she made her way to get in their line.

As she peered through the window near her all she could make out were the bars of the fence. The spaces between them revealed the bleak ocean world outside. Once the Marine Force was out, the sparks flew. Dallas saw jolts of green and yellow lights while hearing the other guns firing, yet all they did was sail past without hitting a target. She jumped when something did hit, and not the target she expected.

Instead, it was much closer.

Her entire body twisted to the other side of the building she could not see. Whatever it was, it was big enough to send jolts of lightning through the bars of the fence and into the building. Within seconds, lights all around completely zapped out.

Dallas waved her hand in front of her face repeatedly, realizing there was no longer any kind of power. Above her, the TV monitor emitted a short-circuited cry before going dark. Outside, the bars went as black as the sea surrounding them. Her eyes darted this way and that as the Marine Force troops and any stationed envoys inside all lit up their pearls, setting them to higher brightness. They dashed around, shouting orders to each other and over radios. Outside, the troops continued to swim around, casting out their sparks.

The next thing that hit made Dallas jump higher than before.

Her ears echoed with the clanging crash that happened only a few feet away, the smash and crackle of each inch of glass as it shattered. Her head spun in the sudden whirlwind of noise, and it took a moment for her to collect herself, while the Marine Force troops already outsea actively swam toward the disturbance. To whatever had broken the fence bars. To whatever had smashed the window. To see just how far it had gotten in.

The wave of merpeople overpowered the area, and the ringing in her ears drowned out all the screams and shouts among the crowds and envoys. Dallas held onto her head as it bobbed in the water, trying to regain control of herself and her mind while letting her body get carried away by the current. She swam away with everyone else back to their neighborhoods, out of the way and safely tucked away. She didn't even know there were emergency doors. Those closed behind them, keeping them all inside.

Back in her cave, there would be safety watching from her own windows. She stared out the one in her kitchen, not seeing the pearl lights or the firing shots of the troops. The only thing she saw was a shroud of darkness, and only after staring at it for a few seconds did the end of the shroud slim down to an elongated tail swimming away, disappearing within a few blinks.

254

CHAPTER 30

Dallas rounded the corner out of the neighborhood caverns with their pearl lights ablaze.

They could see the sections that were taped off and the signs with construction zone language and icons right before them, along with their own emergency pearl light stands. A few merpeople wearing white tunics swam around the work site carrying frame parts and tools. Along the border of the window were loose screws, and the rectangle where the window used to be acted more like an open door.

Dallas caught the reflection of the old window placed in the corner, and her heart froze when she saw the size of the crack for herself. It took one hit big enough to spread into a supernova of ugly, sharp branches. Something had impacted with enough force to cause that damage. The sound echoed in her head from the first time she heard it: the glass cracking all the way, and then just enough.

"Geez," Albany said, shaking her head. "That glass is strong, and it still made a mark."

The windows were close enough to the spot where she had been camping that night. If she had looked up at just the right moment, she would have seen the monster. Seconds later, it would have come through the window after her.

"Who was even around here when it got in and smashed against the window?" Dallas asked. "And if it's so big, how come no one saw it?"

"Because it was all dark, Dally. The ocean by itself doesn't have light. Everyone was all over the place once the fence went out. We are all just so, so lucky. Not lucky enough, but still."

They swam past the scene of the crime, getting a good view of the other one being patched up out at sea. From their own light stands, they could see a new assembly line forming with new pipes and coils of wire, with the damaged goods piled to the side. They made their way down to the community center, lit by more emergency light stands, but still only providing light to their own sections. Dallas inhaled and let out a hard breath.

"What's up there?" Albany asked.

"A few envoys floating around asking questions and holding radios."

"You're getting so good at that."

"I mean, I am not expecting to find anything else."

The light above pointed to the bulletin board on the wall. The sisters stopped to view the notices posted there, most if not all old news, with the newest news put up in haste.

Dallas stared at the poster of the drawing, the crude and comical rendering someone created of the terror. It looked like a cartoon cobra with big eyes, angry eyebrows, and an open jaw. The end of the tail curled around it, accompanied by text. This image multiplied and appeared on posters, signs, and online notices as the official visual mascot for the creature, even though still no one had truly seen it. Dallas shook her head. It was such a science fiction nightmare, but what else would explain that tail flipping away from the scene of the crime? If it was all accurate, the front and the creature's ugly face would be just as terrifying.

She messed up the side strings, tangling them before undoing them to set them right and re-tie, knowing that she should have done this before putting on the helmet, and now it was blocking her vision. Dallas took a moment to check that both sides of the clam shell mail shirt were tied and secured while everyone lined up. She smoothed out the kilt, hoping no one noticed that she had put some candy bars in the pouches.

The way they were rushing about, no one would care. Not even Clyde, who had lectured her on leaving candy wrappers out at sea and had given her a speech about sea pollution. In fact, his usual teasing manner was gone, and there was a new tenseness to his jaw. His orders to the group were short and crisp.

"Come get your weapons," he said. "And don't forget the ink blasters on the bottom row."

The situation churned in Dallas's stomach. No one said anything, and no one asked because they did not need to. When her turn came closer, and when she finally stacked up on the blaster, the standard stun gun, and the more advanced bullet pistol, she had to double back to see who was in line a few merpersons behind her.

"Sapphire?" she said, both surprised and confused.

Sapphire brightened at her greeting. "Dallas!"

"You volunteered?"

"Yeah," Sapphire said. "I feel like every time I swam through that hallway, there was a new poster up. This time I thought, why not?"

"Geez."

Dallas marveled at how blasé she seemed to be, like a giant sea snake did not just crash into the glass windows where they lived.

"Yeah, it was kind of a last-minute thing," Sapphire explained. Upon getting a better look at her, Dallas realized why she did not recognize her friend at first. Her usual sparkling eyelids smeared with bright greens and blues had nothing on them, and instead, there were darker circles underneath.

Dallas read that tone the way it was supposed to be. "Did you...?"

"Oh, I still have a job, of course! Technically. It's just...in limbo. I haven't been to the salon in weeks."

"I'm sorry," Dallas said.

Sapphire shrugged. "So, whatever, I was bored. Ready for a little excitement. And they called me soon after I put my application in."

"Of course they did. It's an all-hands-on-deck situation," Dallas said. "Especially now."

She eyed the rest of the volunteers, who now wore their armor with seriousness, floating around and awaiting orders. Not too long ago, when they had just started out, they joked and laughed, poking fun at how they looked in the gear. Now they looked like soldiers. They held onto their spears at their sides, trembling with the reminder of what it meant to wear them.

"It's...pretty serious now."

"It'll be all right," Dallas found herself saying, though she needed convincing herself.

"Don't think I've ever seen a creature so big before," Sapphire replied. "Except for this one whale that wasn't even fully grown and wasn't even trying to eat me."

"We're going to stun it and blind it so fast it won't be able to. It will just piss it off at best, and then we'll all storm in to zap it," Dallas hoped she sounded confident enough. "What that fence would have done if the power hadn't gone out." All Sapphire did was mumble in agreement.

"They fixed the window," Sapphire recalled. "But the new power line for the fence? It's so bright we're practically asking for something to come!"

"All the more reason for it to get zapped next time it comes," said a mermaid near them, pulling her hair out of her eyes from inside the helmet. "Then we don't have to go out on these suicide missions anymore."

Clyde and A.J. swam to the front of the room while slinging harpoon guns over their shoulders.

"Come on, let's roll," A.J. announced, with the Marine Force leading the way and the rest of the hunter/gatherers and volunteers bringing up the rear. Sapphire joined Dallas and the rest of the group, smoothing out her tunic and under armor that fit perfectly to the rest of her body. Even the armor complemented her curves and could not hide them. It seemed like anything Sapphire wore just morphed and molded to flatter her, while anything Dallas put on automatically added more buoyancy.

Dallas made sure that her stun gun was in her right pouch for easy access, with the handle sticking out just enough for her to grab it quickly. In her left pouch, she shoved the ink blaster. She and Sapphire found seats near the back of the sub, with Sapphire leaning her arm against the window.

Once everyone was in and settled, A.J. and Clyde stayed near the front. A.J. held his tablet, which Clyde kept glancing at.

"So, here's what's going on. We are going to be following a lead from some sightings reported on the south side. The good news is that it couldn't have gone far. The bad news is that it couldn't have gone far. All right? Everyone understand what this means?"

There were some general murmurs. Clyde glanced at the tablet again in case that changed.

"This could be it."

Dallas swallowed a few times, but she still could not get rid of the lump that sat stubbornly at the back of her throat, just like the thought that sat at the back of her head. They rode past different coral reefs and other business buildings that weren't connected to the main metropolis of Gneiss Underway. Several stood alone, with their own fenced-dome protections, and some were connected with separate pipelines, but the sub was taking them further than that.

Dallas recognized some of them from the province maps and in slideshows whenever they went out on a hunt. The further they went out, the less she recognized. Clyde and A.J. were next to one another at the front, and occasionally, they would point to somewhere vague out the window and talk amongst themselves. The next thing she knew, Clyde was leaning out of his seat to say something to the driver, and the sub was rolling to a stop.

Everyone tensed in their seats, sitting up and stretching their necks to see what they could see. Dallas leaned over next to Sapphire at the window, but there was nothing but blue. She craned her neck, expecting a few lone fish or the flora of sea plants, but there was almost nothing.

"Where are we?" Sapphire asked.

Several curious heads were asking the same question. Both Clyde and A.J. unfastened their seatbelts and floated up the aisle for everyone to see. Clyde held his helmet, while A.J. already wore his.

"This is the area of the reported sighting," he announced. "We're going to file out. You are not to do anything unless ordered to, and you are to stay quiet. We keep moving until we catch it on our echolocation radar. If we get a confirmation on the target, we can guerilla-style surround it and stun it. Is everyone clear?"

"Yes," they all answered.

Clyde just gave a little wave of his hand. The group lined up to disembark the sub, where they grouped around nowhere in particular. Ahead, Dallas could make out something in the shape of a mound in the sea sand, which turned out to be a long-lost sunken ship of some sort. It did not look like an ordinary ship at all; it looked instead like something flying through space. While she was curious about the ship, the others were casting out their own sonar, all coming back clear.

Clyde and A.J. led the pod. They swam on for a while through those mostly uncharted waters with nothing to do except wait for any orders. No one talked much, aside from the occasional comment about the lack of fish or other sea life, aside from something scuttling in the sands below their tails. Some had their stun guns and blasters out already, holding them by their sides, though most still had the safety on.

Dallas became startled by the beginnings of a black cloud streaming in front of her. She doubled back and checked her pouch, taking out her blaster and noting that her safety was on. The cloud grew and revealed who it had come from.

"Sapphire?"

"What?"

"It's you!"

Sapphire cursed as she spun in place, further spreading the ink cloud in front of her and all around the rest of the pod. Everyone cried out, swishing this way and that to avoid the cloud, and the pod broke apart as the ink cloud spread.

"What happened?" came Clyde's voice through the ink, increasing. "Who did that? And why?"

"It—it was an accident!" said Sapphire, still holding her blaster. She ended up squeezing it again, resulting in another burst. "Oh shit!"

"Spread out!" Clyde called. "Spread out, and let's try to get away from all of this!"

Everyone began talking and yelling at once, with Clyde asking for silence more than once.

"It's okay, it's okay," Dallas reassured while Sapphire spouted out more choice swear words. "It happens. You just really have to be careful with your safety on this one; it's easily triggered and very sensitive."

Clyde told them all to echolocate as far as they could while Dallas was consoling Sapphire.

"We need to get out of this area!" Clyde was saying. "We just gave away our position to something that probably eats squid!"

"I'm sorry!" Sapphire was saying amid the yells.

"Everyone, follow this way!" A.J. called. "Use echolocation to keep in line and aim for the ship that's up ahead. It's big enough for us all."

They swam through the thick black cloud that engulfed the entire pod and almost the entire surrounding area. The last time Dallas saw Sapphire, she watched her shove her gun back in her pouch and try to cover it with pieces of shark leather from her kilt. The blackness filled in everywhere so much that she could not even see her hands in front of her face. Dallas forced herself to stay calm for the sake of her friend, who she could hear blowing out exasperated bubbles next to her.

She echolocated for the ship, now seeing it closer in her mind. It really did look like it should be flying through space and not floating in the deep sea.

"Almost there," A.J. called. "Need confirmation on our surroundings. Clear?"

"Clear."

"Clear."

"All clear."

As the black faded from black blue, they could see the ship for itself in its strange Saturn-shaped form.

"We're going inside," Clyde ordered. "Until the area clears."

Dallas watched A.J. push on the door that opened almost instantly, and the pod piled in. Dallas and Sapphire were somewhere at the end, but not quite. She continued to console her, assuring her that it was all right, not even paying attention to where she was going or where she was. As Dallas followed the group, she heard the outbursts of gasps ahead of her, and they were the types of gasps she had not heard in a long time.

Dallas's head broke through, and for the first time in months, she met air.

The skin on her face burned with frozen shock. She opened her mouth and heaved in the air at the same time her gills constricted against her neck. As she blinked water droplets from her eyes and adjusted to the strange, lighter shade of dimness, she saw the inside of the ship and just how far up it went to create the dome that held it all there. The rows of seats lined up by the walls with a separate room for the pilot, all the chairs in adjustable sections to accommodate the two different body types.

Dallas continued to heave, throwing out a cough here and there as all the others did the same. Then she saw just how much water was there. Clyde, A.J., and the senior Marine Force had pushed themselves up onto the ship floor.

"We're not all going to fit!" Clyde called, his voice hoarse and scratchy in the stale air. Both hands were at his gills. "You all need to get all the way in."

The chattering teeth, the coughing, and the dry heaving sounded all around the ship.

"You need to come all the way in," Clyde repeated raspily. "And we're going to have to...deal with this for a while."

Dallas, like the others, considered this. Their hands went to their bodies, their tunics, and the kilts they had and would have as clothing. They hoisted themselves out of the small pool of ocean that was in this ship. Dallas floated there while she allowed everyone else to pass her by, realizing that she did not see Sapphire.

"Sapphire?"

As the last in the group passed Dallas and their heads broke the surface, she looked down to the pair of eyes under the water that had not yet surfaced. Or they already had. Sapphire's eyes were like a cornered animal, wide and terrified in headlights. Dallas ducked back down into the ocean pool, floating down to where Sapphire was hugging herself by the ship's door, already closed by the last member that entered it.

"I can't..." she shook her head furiously. "Dallas, I can't!"

"What's wrong?" Dallas swam closer to her friend, who in return seemed to back closer to the door.

"I didn't know that this...I didn't know that we would...I can't ever, ever go back to that! I can't ever do that again!" With each word, Sapphire's voice cracked like pieces of Styrofoam breaking off in bigger and bigger pieces.

"What's—"

"I can't!" Sapphire cried, waving her hands. "I can't! I just can't!"

"You can't do what?"

Dallas turned her head to Clyde, speaking to the group, unaware if he knew they were not up there.

"What are you talking about? What's wrong?"

"I can't be here."

"What do you mean?"

"Dallas? Sapphire?"

Dallas jerked her head toward Clyde's voice calling to them. When she looked back, Sapphire had taken off and swam frantically through the ship's door.

CHAPTER 31

Dallas broke through the air surface like a torpedo and hoisted herself up to the ship's floor level, coughing and gasping for air, breaking out into shivers.

"Clyde," she coughed. "Clyde!"

Clyde's face appeared from the small crowd he was with. He went up on his hands and then dragged himself over to where Dallas was sitting, with the fluke of her tail still in the water. She pressed all of her fingers to her gills as she struggled to form the words.

"Sapphire...took...off."

Clyde's face sank. "What?"

"She...swam away."

"Why? Where did she go?"

Dallas kept shaking her head. "I don't...know. She just...freaked out...she's gone."

On hearing this, both Clyde and the other Marine Force members were already on their tablets. They fumbled with them, and then A.J. answered his incoming call.

"Yes," A.J. answered. "A mermaid, mid-twenties, with blue-violet hair and a tail named Sapphire, most likely heading back to Gneiss Underway in West Province. Recent. Very recent. I am going to send you those coordinates."

He paused, giving Dallas a quick glance.

"No explanation was given. Thank you."

He hung up and turned back to her.

"Okay. They're on it. They're on their way now."

A.J. went to speak with Clyde and the other Marine Force members, leaning in to see their tablets and responses.

"Yeah," he was telling them. "One of our volunteer members just left the area unsupervised and seemed to be in distress. We don't know why, we don't know where she went, but it's dangerous to be out there alone. A.J. just called in reinforcements."

Dallas couldn't make out most of the conversations. She was too busy trying to figure out what happened. Her fins flipped in the small pool of ocean, keeping grounded to something comforting and familiar.

Dallas kept rubbing her gills, feeling like the moisture was already evaporating. Just when she wondered how long they would stay in there, they were meant to believe it would be long enough for them to adapt and change in the air. What did she mean she can't ever be that again?

A.J. and Clyde approached her, sliding on their tails and hitting the water next to her. "Let's go," Clyde said. "We're going to find her. Pile out, head back to the sub!"

Dallas didn't bother asking any questions. She pushed herself back into the ocean along with the others, and she noticed that it was even before any of them had begun to change. The minute she was submerged again, her skin bubbled with warmth. She opened her eyes back to the water and let them sharpen as her gills burst out in relief.

The group exited the ship door in a single-file line, weapons close by but not drawn. They were relieved to see that most of the ink was gone, although some smoky black tendrils remained. The water seemed to seep back into her brain, mostly filled with thoughts sloshing back and forth, giving her an unwanted headache. She heard the calls of echolocation from the rest of the group all around her like echoes.

"Clear," came one, from somewhere on her right where the ink was darkest.

"Clear," came another, from much further down, someone she could not see quite yet.

Even so, some held their stun guns poised and ready for defense. Dallas kept one hand on hers at her side while she echolocated, counting the starfish on a rock and the tuna swimming up ahead. But nothing bigger—whether half-mammal or whole fish—or anything else.

They met the deep blue and nothing else. They boarded the sub and made their way back down the route they had come, scanning the windows while Clyde and A.J. checked their tablets. Radio messages came in but added little of true value regarding either target.

Dallas kept her eyes on the seascapes passing by, training her gaze to watch for even the slightest movement. Anything blue or violet caught her eye automatically, even though a part of her knew that Sapphire would not be there. She would be gone by then, assuming she was halfway home.

The further they traveled, the more she began to wonder why they hadn't caught up with her yet, and the sickening worry began to churn in Dallas's stomach. The radios and tablets pinged, beeped, and murmured voices came from and into them. The last call that came through made Clyde raise an eyebrow, staring at nothing. He and A.J. leaned in, and Dallas's stomach continued to churn.

"They found her."

Clyde's tone made her jerk out of her seat.

"...escorts now. Area surveyed," A.J. was saying.

Dallas stuck her neck out into the aisle.

"...wounds to the head, and no other signs of trauma."

"Clyde!? What happened?"

He turned to get out of his seat and address the rest of the group.

"Everyone, Sapphire has been found. She is alive, but she was discovered unconscious with a head injury. She is near the kelp gardens off Limestone Way. The search team found her and is bringing her to the nearest hospital. She had no other serious injuries, and we're grateful someone found her when they did—"

"Oh my God! What caused her head injury?" Dallas interrupted.

The voices coming from the radio told Dallas she was not the first to interrupt. Clyde maintained a cool expression, but there was no mistaking the horror breaking through.

"We don't know that yet, but she's lucky. It seems like she just missed something. And apparently, so did everyone else. It's gone."

Dallas lingered at the doorway when she saw the way Sapphire lay.

Still on her back, eyes closed, arms crossed idly over her chest. She looked like a sarcophagus, a hollow form, but there was still life inside. The monitors waved in the rhythmic formation they were supposed to, but that was all the movement in the room.

Dallas saw her stomach rise and fall, releasing little bubbles from her gills, and one exhale that could have been a sigh. She swam into the room and approached her friend, whose head was wrapped in so much bandage that only a few stray strands of violet stuck out. The bandages barely covered the tops of her eyelids, which flickered a little, fighting to open.

"Hey Sapphire," Dallas said quietly, fighting a lump in her throat. "Not sure if you can hear me, but I hope you can. I wanted to see you and make sure you're okay."

Sapphire's arm moved slightly, and it wasn't the movement that caught her attention. Dallas furrowed her brow and leaned forward, her mouth opening in confusion and surprise as she reached out to take Sapphire's wrist carefully. She was able to make out the lettering on Sapphire's hospital bracelet:

Flowers, Patrick

Sex: M

Dallas retreated the moment she read it, and in that very instant, Sapphire stirred awake at the sudden touch. She looked at Dallas looking at her, both sets of eyes wide with alarm. Dallas raised both her hands when Sapphire pulled her wrist under her arm.

"Oh my God, I—I'm sorry, I—"

"Don't, it's okay," Sapphire's groggy voice raised a pitch slightly as Dallas continued processing it all. She searched for clues all over Sapphire's face, looking for something she just did not see before. Sapphire's nose and chin were a bit pointed, giving her a pear shape. Her skin was flawless, giving that pear a smooth texture without any stubble that carried all the way into her neck, which was missing any sort of bump. Her voice was not princess-high, nor was it bass-low. She was thin but still had some muscle in her arms.

Dallas could see them outlined in tension as Sapphire cradled her braceleted arm as though it were the injured part of her.

"It's just my dead name," Sapphire said quietly.

She looked at Dallas. "I still had to use it for a while, still so legally for now, but I thought most of those days were behind me. Some things were just harder to transfer and took forever, and still are taking forever, especially when you move from land to sea and get a different body with a different identity."

"I had no idea," Dallas admitted.

Sapphire played with the edges of the bracelet, a finger pushing underneath it, driven to tear it off.

Sapphire formed a small smile. "I had to come clean. You know the missing I.D. they found? That was my old school I.D. from freshman year that was in my bag. I forgot I had it. I had to come forward and say it was me and that I wasn't missing or dead."

Dallas put her fingers over her mouth.

"Listen," Dallas said, shaking her head. "It doesn't matter. You're still not missing or dead, and that's the point! You made me worried sick!"

Sapphire relaxed her arm a little while acknowledging Dallas, her face still forlorn yet comforted.

"It doesn't matter about any of that stuff. All that matters is that you're alive."

Sapphire's smile spread to her ears. "Thank you. Thank you for...understanding."

"Yeah," Dallas continued. "But you still scared the shit out of me."

Sapphire's smile faltered then, her hand brushing the bandage on her head.

"God—"

"What?"

"Dallas, I saw it. I saw it. I—I saw the thing everyone is looking for."

"You did? Clyde said something was on the radar, but no one got a clear match."

"Oh, I know I did. It was... I don't know how to describe it. It wasn't really a snake. It was long like one and had this mouth that made it look like one, but it didn't have fangs or anything like that. It's like the teeth were on the inside, and I couldn't see them, but it was gigantic and absolutely terrified me. But it didn't see me, so I swam like hell, and I was so scared I crashed right into this big rock and hit my head."

Dallas, in her own head, was piecing together the descriptions into a funny mental drawing.

"I was close but not that close, and I seriously did not see it at first, but then I saw this super long body just...move. And then I saw the eyes, and it opened its mouth up and down like it was getting ready to go on a hunt."

Dallas just stared.

"But it didn't see me, that's the thing. You know my stupid ink blaster gun? Well, I guess the safety switch was still stuck, so it shot out a huge pool of ink that stopped it from seeing me. But I didn't stick around after that; I swam like hell, and the ink probably stopped me from seeing that rock. It probably saved my life."

"Clyde, A.J., and the rest of the troops didn't find anything. They didn't catch anything on the GPS radar, and no one echolocated anything. It was long gone."

"You got away safe."

There was a beat.

"Sapphire, you saw it."

Sapphire gave a little nod.

"Okay, so it was very long and had a head that made it look like a snake but wasn't a snake. More like an eel; its teeth were on the inside..."

"It had red gills."

"So, it was big?"

"Gigantic. And long."

Dallas drew that picture in her head, one she tried to match with every one she ever saw in library books.

"You saw it. That's our monster. You have to tell everyone what you just told me."

"I will; I just wish I had a better description. It was so fast."

"So what? It's the best one we've ever had. It's actually the only one we've ever had thanks to you. You're the first one to see it. And I think I know what it is."

CHAPTER 32

Liam looked from his monitor screens back to Dallas, Sapphire, Clyde, and A.J.

"You think so?" he asked.

Dallas nodded. "Oh yeah, I do. It just makes perfect sense."

Liam flipped the monitor screen so that they could all see the creature: long and gray, averaging six to seven feet long, body curved like a whip that looked like it could curl and snap, tail ending in an elongated feather instead of a fluke, mouth opened in a fangless grin...until one looked closely at the rows of hidden, inverted teeth lining the inside of its gums.

The four stared at it without a word at first.

"Well," A.J. broke the ice. "We can see where people thought it was an eel or a snake."

"It's not, and it's not a shark, even though it has the shark name," Liam said, reading the webpage. "Frilled shark. An eighty-million-year-old prehistoric monster that's still around, even nicknamed a 'living fossil.' Jesus. Look at this thing."

The photo showed the creature with an open mouth, almost up close and personal, body curved around it like a snake of the sea. They could see those hidden teeth lining the inner mouth, the secret trap for its prey.

Dallas pictured that thing biting into something, into someone, and tearing them to shreds.

Clyde's fingers held his chin like he was trying to keep himself stable.

"It makes sense."

"It makes sense that no one has seen one before."

"Is this what you saw?" Liam asked Sapphire.

Sapphire nodded. "That's it. That's definitely it."

"You got that close?" Liam asked. "Close enough to see it but far enough away to swim away?"

"I did."

"You're very fortunate."

"She is," Dallas said. "She saw it closer than anyone else ever has. When she was describing it to me, I remembered reading a little bit about it in a prehistoric book once."

Liam's eyes stayed on the webpage as he continued to read the article from National Geographic, the image of that prehistoric living fossil intimidating them from the screen, mouth open in mockery, in challenge.

"Does Viceroy Westburn know?" asked Clyde.

"Oh, he's about to. I am shooting him an email now. And I'm copying the rest of the envoys and Marine Force sergeants," Liam answered as his fingers moved over the keys. "It won't be long before we go on our intended mission. They will be sending out more troops where it was last spotted. But now we await further instruction."

Further instruction came with a meeting exclusive for Marine Force and hunter/gatherers. This meeting was, of course, to be held in the larger meeting hall. The seasoned and high-ranked Marine Force officers sat in their reserved section in the front, waiting expectantly. Dallas swam in with her team.

The room turned their attention to the front when a merwoman envoy swam up to the podium, followed by Viceroy Warren Westburn himself. He wore a tunic that shimmered blue and green, short on the bottom as if he had outgrown it but saved it for special occasions. The two buttons near his stomach were left unbuttoned.

"Hunter/gatherers, Marine Force, envoys, welcome. Thank you all for coming out, as we have much to discuss. A lot of activity at the viceroy headquarters had to shift in order to be more prepared for you today and for the events to come. Viceroy Westburn certainly has a lot to discuss! So, without further ado, here he is now."

She waved her hand and backed away from the podium while the viceroy gave a little nod and approached it. In his hand, he held a small packet of paper with edges already curled this way and that. He looked out at the crowd as if acknowledging who he was talking to first, instead of taking on the persona of a televised talking head.

"Welcome, everyone, and thank you very much for being here. We have made progress, and finally a more stable kind. We now have a better idea of what we are up against, but unfortunately, we are not one hundred percent sure about it. That is how things are, and how they will always be. We have done some studying and placed some phone calls, and I am happy to say that we have a special guest here today who knows a little more than we do. From The Oceans Through the Ages Museum in Pink Sands, East

Province, I am pleased to introduce a special guest who is with us. Please welcome marine biologist and paleontologist, Kendall Wadsworth."

Everyone applauded as a round merwoman flipped from her seat in the front row to the podium. Her tail was thick, but her fins were flimsy and delicate, reminding Dallas a little of a bumblebee in the way she swam. Her hair was short enough to bob along with her, reddish-brown like her tail and the cardigan-like tunic she wore, with tight sleeves stopping right where her arm fins began. She approached the front holding a small notepad and smiled at the audience, looking over at an attentive envoy merwoman who turned on the projector.

"Hello!" Kendall started, jolly as a kindergarten teacher. "Thank you all so much for having me here. The moment I got a call saying that the mysterious predator making the news was confirmed to be a frilled shark, I was more than happy to step in to share what I know. Frilled sharks are rarely seen and not well-known, especially on land, since any confirmed sightings and catches have spanned years apart. We do have a section in our museum dedicated to prehistoric sea creatures that are still alive today, and this one is one of them! I'm going to show you what it looks like up close and personal."

The envoy merwoman flicked on the projector screen to introduce everyone to the creature, captured only by photo.

This image was clearer than the one they first looked up in Liam's office, and it looked more like a real creature than something that could have easily been a painting. It was the monster hybrid of an eel, a snake, a lizard, and a shark all in one. Its head was more lizard-like than fish-like, oval yet flat, plain with the exception of what it hid inside its mouth. Its body was long and gray, with gill slits blood-red like claws slashed through its flesh. Its eyes were dull and opaque, looking like peeled grapes. They seemed to stare at nothing and everything at once.

"They were initially categorized as sea serpents and were called eels as well until they were finally classified in the shark family. Supposedly, this is where the first sea serpent legends originated. You can see where this creature is...different. No one notices its teeth at first until it opens its mouth wide enough. It has twenty-five rows of three hundred barbed tricuspid teeth! They're all shaped like tridents and go into the mouth inwards as opposed to outwards... and this is where it gets deadly. Once the frilled shark gets a chomp on something, the only way to be released from its teeth is to move forward, further into its mouth. Naturally, this is not the first response of some poor creatures. The first and most natural response is to pull away, and that causes those teeth to rip faster and further."

Kendall was pointing to the mouth in the picture, not seeing the frozen looks of horror and recognition around the room as they remembered those who met their fate, now understanding why.

"It mainly feeds on squid, preferring things that are softer and squishy. It has six pairs of frilled gill slits; the first one is more like a collar, and the rest have these bright red fleshy tips. And this is where our frilled shark gets its name."

Kendall pointed. "Now, not too many have been seen or recorded in the sea, but even the rare sightings show that the frilled shark is not a fast swimmer. If anything, it hovers and floats. Scientists believe that its body works like a snake. It can coil its body and lash out quickly, and even twist and turn to get away from or wrap around something."

Near the front, one of the Marine Force mermen raised a hand.

"If this thing is slow, then how come no one has been able to catch it yet?"

Kendall pointed to the slide again.

"See its color? It is in gray, dull colors that blend in with the ocean surrounding it, especially since it lives in deeper, darker waters. And since it swims slower, it is hard to pick up its movement. That makes it practically invisible."

CHAPTER 33

THEY LINED UP MOSTLY in silence, holding the newer and larger stun weapons to their chests. Dallas steadied hers while she waited for the others to get off the adrenaline spiking with nerves. In a few moments, Dallas was also joined by Mickey. She held her gun on her arm like a pro, the only one who was a clear picture-perfect poster child of the Marine Force, even in a volunteer uniform. She stood with her chin up, cool as a cucumber, turning her head to the right to give Dallas a little wink.

"I've been shark hunting before. This thing isn't all that big; it's going to be a piece of cake."

Dallas snickered and let herself relax a little, but it was brief until Mickey's next words.

"Besides, you're going to be the most useful one here."

And those little fires she had swallowed down rose up again to her throat.

"Well, I'll try," she said.

Mickey shook her head. "I'm telling you, you're a natural hunter."

Dallas's chin rose until it was at the same level as Mickey's.

A.J. and Clyde came out as the last ones from the sub, swimming to the front of the group. Both wore matching charcoal-gray robes with shimmer, sleek as dragonfish. Underneath, they wore their shell mail armor, bulky, rough, and thick enough to protect. With them, they carried a bundle of netting, and a particular bundle in a particular shape.

"This is our spot," Clyde stated. "Radar indicated it was not too far from here and should be easy to find. Marine Force troops are in neighboring areas in the next surrounding towns in the event that it gets away. We have plans to surround it. Everyone remembers their part in this plan, correct? Do not shoot or strike or flee unless told to. Do not make any sudden movements, and do not be a hero. Only shoot when needed; otherwise, you'll risk missing and make it angry enough to attack. Wait for it to be subdued, and then we move in. Clear?"

"Yes," everyone answered.

A.J. looked to Clyde, the twinkle of pride passing back and forth in their eyes.

"You did good with your team here," A.J. stated.

Clyde bit his lip. "I did my best."

He turned to his team, relaxing his lip into a more serious, straight line.

"Move out! This is it!"

The Marine Force and hunter/gatherers swam out as one moving force, a deadly school of trained hunters in a long single line, ready to match their foe. They swam through a kelp forest, letting the slimy tendrils brush them as they passed—the last canopy of protection before they were in the open ocean. Several members already had their stun guns turned to the switch on the side as the waters started to darken.

Soon, the sandy bottom began to curve, and the pod followed that curve down, down, and further down. One by one, those lights on the guns flicked on, snapping like eyes opening wide awake and alert.

The eyes all drifted apart as the pod started to spread; each aimed in a particular direction. The Marine Force members at the front of the pod cast out their songs of sonar, and the empty abyss answered back in echoes of clicks and hums. One light pivoted and nearly blinded Dallas as it focused right on her.

"Hey, get up there," came Clyde's voice. "Can you cast farther than them?"

Mickey nudged her, and if it were light enough, Dallas would have seen her smile and wink.

"Farther than them? I don't think so."

"I think you do," Clyde answered. "Here, come here."

Clyde drifted back so that others swam ahead of him in line, and he took Dallas's arm to escort her to the front. The Marine Force troops there raised their lights and clicked, hummed, and sang, keeping their heads turned to the distance.

"Any readings?" Clyde asked them.

"Nothing but some fat fish," one answered.

"What can you see?" he asked her.

Dallas couldn't really see the troops turn to her or what their expressions were. She cast out her sonar, keeping her voice steady and low and long.

"There is a trench up ahead."

"A trench?" came the surprise from more than one Marine Force member, and there was no mistaking the stabs of envy.

"Yep," A.J. answered from out of nowhere. "She has further range than you."

Both A.J. and Clyde allowed Dallas to drift closer to the front.

"All right, what's in the trench? Is it in there?"

"Hard to tell," she said. "It seems empty."

"Then our frilled monster isn't in it, and that probably means it's out."

They continued to cast their light beams and echolocation throughout the dark underpass, occasionally greeted by smaller glows of light in the distance. To the left was a tiny bulb bobbing up and down. It reeled itself in enough for the light to reveal what was casting it out: a jaw full of spiked teeth.

"That's a good sign, isn't it?" someone muttered from behind Dallas. "It would probably be fleeing for its life if it saw something bigger."

"Predators of predators. They all have them," A.J. commented. "But we're not sure if this one has one."

The pod swam as low as they could, monitoring the sandy bottom and any rock structures along the way. They used echolocation ahead, all stating it was clear.

"Make our way to the trench," Clyde declared. "That's where we will set that up."

They kept their guns cradled in their arms yet positioned, bioluminescence beams bright enough to see but subtle enough to conceal. Dallas kept her eyes forward, but occasionally, something stirred below, causing her to look down. Puffs of sand kicked up here and there from something that slept below. She focused on the radar ahead and surrounding, not wanting to be confronted by something that had to be more than one.

They moved fast enough so that, in that event, any eyes opening in the sand would miss them and simply go back to sleep. Dallas stopped echolocating when the trench in her mind started to focus on the horizon, two towering structures as a pronged tuning fork as thick as they could see. Clyde and A.J held their netting between them, drifting higher than the group as they approached the trench. Then, as ordered, the Marine Force took the front and swam ahead. Clyde turned to them as they all stopped before it.

"Stay behind, and close," A.J. instructed the group. "We are going to set the trap while the Marine Force goes around the bend to do a quick scan. You all stand by. According to the radar, it could be close. This could be where it lives. Move out."

Clyde and A.J. swam through the narrow opening of the trench, inviting and welcoming only to prey. Dallas watched the others split up and hang around the bend while she stayed put to watch the activity inside. A.J. and Clyde unraveled one clump of netting, shaped like an egg and almost looking like it had been stuffed with one until Clyde pulled it apart, revealing that it was indeed filled, but with something much softer.

The netting wavered and squished as tendrils of seaweed poked through. Clyde made a point to add to the squishing as if he were reshaping it back to what it was or what he wanted it to be, while A.J. pulled out other types of tendrils: ropes tied together into long strands.

"Let's tie it onto there," Clyde suggested. "Once it snags it, it needs to be secure enough so that it can't get away."

Dallas oscillated between scanning the area visually and with echolocation, glancing back at Clyde and A.J.'s bait. It was far enough inside and tied around, its loose tendrils waving casually in the water. She watched them open vials of something they had taken from their knapsacks and diffuse it through the water before swimming all the way out. Dallas caught a whiff and doubled back as they continued down past the trench. Other hunter/gatherers nearby turned their heads, coughing and gagging.

"God, that's rank," one guy said. "It will smell it from a mile away."

"That's the point," another replied.

A.J. and Clyde swam out, catching up with the other troops stationed just ahead. Dallas watched them talk, and a few of them swam apart to echolocate in different directions. She sighed and held her gun, catching a glance of Mickey chatting with the Marine Force troops. She listened to the echolocators sending out more waves of sonar before doing her own, extending as far as the pile of mismatched rocks that only she could see.

That was all she could perceive until she did it again.

Her lips parted, mimicking a fish getting snared on a hook. Dallas sent out another wave with more force for greater distance and nearly dropped her gun when a full, long shape formed in her mind. A smiling, open mouth, as if it were aware of its company and pleased to see them. She hit the bioluminescence trigger on her gun, flashing the signal once, twice, three times, allowing her excitement to dominate.

Sure enough, the rest of the guns responded with those same flashes, and any merperson on the ocean floor retreated above the trench. Dallas waited for Clyde and A.J. to approach her.

"You got it?" A.J. asked.

"I definitely do."

"Which direction?"

"East," Dallas replied.

"Get to position now! It will pick up the scent at once!"

Dallas cradled her gun and swam to the top of the trench with them, hardly able to hold back her smile, though her hands were shaking a little. Even from there, she sent out sonar waves to keep tracking, seeing those still-shot frames of the eel-like shark getting closer to their location.

The ripples in the water formed the shape. From the depths, the dark images from Dallas' mind focused into a living, moving picture of something slithering. Something moving slowly enough to remain concealed but with enough gusto to be noticed.

The head emerged from the deep, an ancient sea serpent with gummy, shapeless eyes. Its jaw opened and closed in anticipation of its next meal. It came to them now across the bend, its entire body undulating like one long tail. Everyone stationed above the trench saw the silver snake and its blood-red frills at its gills that gave it its name.

The deep slits could have been the aftermath of a brutal encounter with another beast, but only a few glances down its body proved it had already endured several. Wide, long, short, and jagged slashes decorated its sides in irregular patterns, each at different stages of healing. It was clear these were not just marks from other beasts.

It swam on, the silent predator of the deep, its body moving so slowly it seemed almost stationary, disappearing into the current. Dallas could see the tension in the Marine Force members as they clung to parts of the rock, helplessly waiting in the stillness. The creature made no sound, no ripple, no stream of bubbles out of place. It was as if it could glide across a mirror and leave no reflection, only the bland gray of the ocean, absorbing it and making it disappear.

Dallas observed that tail wave side to side, imagining how it could coil and spring to attack. She very much did not want to witness that.

She held her breath as she watched the slithery shark make its way inside the trench, the fanned end of its tail fin picking up speed and anticipation as it followed the scent trail all the way to the desired bait. A few feet away from her, on the edge, Clyde had his right hand clenched in a fist, with A.J.'s right hand clamped around his left arm.

"Steady," one of them whispered, but she could not make out who.

The frilled shark found the bundled netting and opened its mouth, snatching it in its teeth within seconds.

The two shots that went off made Dallas jump, and both Clyde and A.J. cursed.

"No, not yet!" Clyde hissed. "Who did that?"

The yellow-green beams grazed the top of the beast and cascaded into the wall above it, but it was enough to make contact. The frilled shark thrashed at the searing burns, and as its body coiled and recoiled, it could not move or free itself from the bundled netting. It pumped its body and opened and closed its mouth, but like Velcro, it only snagged the netting further down its barbed teeth.

The next shot that went off sailed over the top of its head and crashed into the rock wall. Its tail beat against the bubbly rock formations, causing some to break and float down into the trench while the hunter/gatherers and Marine Force all increased the bioluminescence settings on their weapons. The yellow-green lights popped and cast as far down into the trench as they could go, but all they illuminated were those rocky walls. They listened and heard no more sound.

The disturbance in the sand had since quieted down, settling back into place right around where the bundled netting still lay, yet torn down the middle.

Everyone instinctively ducked while casting their light all around the area.

"Where is it?"

"Anyone see it?"

"Stay still, stay calm!"

A.J. and Clyde made their way along the trench wall.

"The only place for it to go is down," A.J. declared. "And that's where it gets darker."

Clyde cursed and slapped his hand to his forehead.

"And what's down there? Someone, all of you, come here. My echolocators."

It was mainly Marine Force troops and more advanced hunter/gatherers, but Dallas automatically answered the call without thinking.

One guy stretched his neck out to make the call, while another lady nearby cupped her hands around her mouth for dramatic effect.

"It can't be gone," the guy stated.

"It is," the lady answered.

"No," Dallas said. "It's not."

This time, she was in the front.

Clyde and A.J. were still by her side, along with Mickey close behind, followed by the other troops, who more or less avoided eye contact with the mere volunteer who had never even seen half of their province's predators. They swam further down, trench rock walls on either side of them serving as a protective barrier or an enclosing trap. They swam cautiously as one.

"Tell me again," A.J. said to her.

"Fourteen miles," Dallas answered. "It slithered faster than we thought. And...this trench is very...rocky. Irregular. It's more like a cave than a trench. There are a lot of open areas, it seems."

"Stay on it," he ordered. "Don't lose its track. Tell us immediately if it changes route."

Dallas stared through the mid-deep waters, the amoeba-shaped rock walls all around them varying in size, shape, and depth. She focused on steadying both her swimming and her breathing as she synced them together, sending out waves.

"Walls. Rocks. It's heading left now. It... it... it's going inside a hole."

Clyde and A.J. both flicked on the higher settings of their guns and aimed the beams into the distance, the rest of the troops following suit. The moment their yellow-green headlights lit the way, they could make out more than just the rows of stalactite teeth that formed up the new cave's open mouth: Tiny fishes, and tiny wriggling centipede-like worms swam in front of and around them, blind to light and used to the dark and not troubled by it at all, or by the oncoming company.

They swam in and out of the stalactite structures, some with double-pointed edges. The team flashed their lights left to right, scanning the area to see if any of those stalactite rows suddenly opened and closed in anticipation of prey and lunged.

"Is it ahead?" Clyde asked her again.

"Just beyond this part of stalactites," Dallas replied. "It went there, through a hole in the left side of the wall. It is still there...moving slower. There are other openings that lead to it."

"Right then."

Clyde turned to the pod.

"Time for a new trap."

As Clyde and A.J. separated the pod into smaller groups, Dallas stayed put, knowing perfectly well that she would be her own group. She turned her head to the group for a moment before focusing back on what was in front of her...what was ahead of all of them.

Dallas furrowed her brow as she cast another ray, finding that she could not only "see" the rock formations beyond but also what was around them. She realized that her radar was a straight shot and only stopped once it hit something. Now, she cast again to get the full picture in her head, allowing her to see and describe it. It was nothing less than a small cave maze, and with every obstacle, there was another opening.

"Surround this area," A.J. ordered. "Everyone move out."

He and Clyde held their guns with the beams aimed directly at the protruding cave teeth. They moved forward, and once they passed the checkpoint, the pod split into separate groups.

"It's further in," Dallas reported. "It's got to be after something in here."

She waited patiently as Clyde echolocated as far as he could, not picking up the target or its location. She remained quiet and pretended not to notice, keeping her light low enough to see a bit of everything. They passed the last curtain of rock teeth, and she pointed out the small opening to their left.

They moved, not quite together yet not quite separate, the light from the open ocean fading behind them. The darkness closed in, and all they had were their gun light beams. At one point, Dallas looked at her gun, then at the hazy shadows of the cave formations, and shut it off. She hoisted her gun back into its holster and kept her hands down at her sides. She listened.

She sent out sonar...drawing out the map in her mind. This became a pattern she advanced on each time, her mind creating the blueprint of the cave with every irregular shape, nook, and cavern. And she had it.

Dallas swam forward and found the opening, moving in just enough to get a layout of what was inside. In what she could see, she made out small, dull fish swimming almost directly in front of her face. She was taken aback when she encountered them up close, discovering they had no eyes: slick and smooth, devoid of any facial features except for the small slit that opened into a mouth. They resembled the Swedish fish gummies she would have at the movie theater, and like now, she only knew them from how she encountered them in the dark.

Now, watching how they swam around creatures accustomed to moving in complete darkness, was how she needed to act.

Dallas sent out another sonar wave and then retreated from the hole.

"It's close," she said. "It went further in, but it's still close."

Dallas leaned back a little more, then some more, doing a side-swim away from the opening. At first, she thought they all followed her lead and turned off their lights as well. She doubled back just enough to check on them.

"Clyde? A.J.?"

The only living things that mapped in her mind were those eyeless fish.

CHAPTER 34

Her first reaction was to panic and shoot out of the cavern for the nearest opening, but she kept herself rooted. Her hand went to her tablet, but instead, she sent out another sonar wave as far as she could push. All she got back were those walls and rock formations she had navigated around. She was deep in. The others could not have gone far, but she could not lose track of their target.

Dallas turned back, seeing the hole of the cavern nook before her and the increasing bubbles exhaling from her gills. She stuck her head in again to assess the situation: the grooves and rocks protruding from the ceiling and sides...and small flecks floating in disturbance in the distance. Dallas swam all the way into the opening toward those flecks... and the next sonar confirmed the creature was just beyond that, swishing its tail back and forth in a wide, open area.

It was on the hunt for something, but what?

It chilled her gills to think that perhaps it was on the hunt for a who.

She sailed through a forked opening between three large stalactites, with what little light that filtered into that cavern forming a triangular beam, its point ending in the middle of nowhere. To her right was more stretch of the cavern; to her left were more boulders arranged at different levels, blocking her view and radar. She quickly assessed the right, found more openings, and headed for them.

Dallas held the maze in her head, irregular and sharp, with some too-small spaces. Some led out, and others did not. Some curved around bends; some went lower, but all had one thing in common: they were long and thin enough to accommodate a six-foot-long living fossil. And an average-sized mermaid.

She hovered behind the rocks below once that image came back to her almost full-sized, curved around, with its head facing her direction. She ducked behind those rocks.

Can this thing smell me?

She flattened her tail against that rock to make as few waves as possible.

No, sharks only come after you if they smell your blood. I'm good. I'm good.

She recalled those shows she watched on National Geographic about wild animals on the hunt, and how the predator stalked its prey in a slow, exhilarating fashion until the time was right to pounce. Dallas needed to ensure she was the predator, so she stayed low, and each wave she sent out showed her monstrous prey in the same position as before, only this time its head changed direction, no longer concerned with what was behind it.

Dallas felt the chills dance down her scales, wondering if there was an undersea equivalent to getting goosebumps, as she echolocated as far into the cavern as she could to make out the nooks and where they led. And that was when she imagined how it would unfold.

She rose from her hiding place and ducked behind other rock formations, meandering through the sharp obstacles, heading for that one special nook that was small enough, just right, just for her. She swam to it and through it, peeking her head out just enough to freeze in place and marvel at what was before her.

There was the outline of the creature, long and sleek as a monstrous sea serpent, its feathered tail end fanning the water behind it as if it were waiting. Waiting to catch something, or waiting for something to approach? For something to come closer for it to catch? Through the semi-darkness, she could make out its gray fish color, dull and camouflaging, flashing a little silver whenever it slithered. Its head turned and positioned near her right, mouth open in what someone not knowing better would interpret as a grin of realization, of knowledge, of excitement.

Dallas echolocated to the cave nooks near her quickly and drifted out, staying low, barely brushing against the spiked obstacles.

The sound of her tablet pinging and vibrating at her side made her want to skyrocket to the cave ceiling. She grabbed at her tunic pocket with both hands to cover the sound and the light, ducking behind a rock.

> Where are you??

She shielded her hand over the screen while taking a cursory peek back at the gaping frilled shark.

> I'm inside another part of the cave, and I'm on it.

Clyde's "typing" bubble appeared after her response.

> Stay put! We are trying to find our way around here. Don't move and don't do anything stupid!!!

Dallas put the screen to sleep and shoved it in her pocket once again. The creature showed no signs of alert and was now uncoiling its tail to swim in a straight line somewhere. Going back to her mental outline, she first looked to her right and then her left, getting the images back in her head so she could confirm her strategy.

She followed it, staying low and ensuring she was far enough away. She waited, impatiently, for it to go where she thought it would go, where she wanted it to go, then she pulled out her tablet again.

> I need all of you to stay put. I have it in plain sight, and I know this entire cavern's layout. I know what to do.

She knew his response would come post-haste.

> You need to come find us ASAP!

She decided to give him a final thought.

> It will be caught.

Dallas shut her tablet and secured it away, drawing one of her guns and making her way toward the open space ahead. She stayed low and stuck to the stalagmites, ducking behind them and peeking out enough to send out more sonar waves. She drifted closer, close enough for the images in her head to appear live in the scenery.

Around the neck of a pointy rock, there. There was that beast closer than she'd ever seen it before: something taken straight out of a science fiction novel, less beast and more like a living weapon: long and silver like an enlarged sword, its deadly edges hidden in plain sight. Its pectoral fins rested in anticipation until it could strike and slice, its grin stretching past its pale and undead eyes.

Dallas held her gun and practiced her aim, using all her concentration to keep it steady and find the perfect target. She adjusted the settings to the lowest frequency, glad that Clyde and the others were not there to see her do so. Her tail rubbed against the rock she leaned against, searching for the perfect spot until she felt the pinch against her scales. In a swift motion, she scraped her tail against the side and cut just enough to create a small cloud of blood.

Dallas winced but stayed put, her fluke fanning the waters to send them traveling as best as she could. She high-tailed out of there to retreat, doubling back just in time to see the monster's face turn in her direction, and in no time, it opened its mouth in an even bigger smile as its company was revealed.

In seconds, she saw it twist and coil before dashing out, its body a lethal spring with flesh-tearing Velcro for a mouth.

She turned around and dove out of the cavern, making her way toward the one hole that was just the right size, the one she noted earlier that was supposed to be an unknown hideout. But first, she dashed behind a wall as the frilled shark made itself into a spring again to lash out.

It opened its mouth and lunged for her, smashing its head against a stalactite so hard that it sent black silt snowflakes swirling around them, turning the scene into a television screen that suddenly lost signal and picture.

Dallas saw that area fill quickly with dense matter, the still waters of the abyss disturbed so much it thickened. She curled into her own coiled position to hold onto her bleeding tail as best as she could while she echolocated the creature in the silt smoke. It smashed against the rocks again as some of her blood still lingered nearby, and that was when Dallas picked up her stun gun and fired a shot.

It hit the frilled shark in the head, just enough to disorient it, and Dallas was not sure if the shriek that echoed off the walls came from her or from the creature. It returned to its senses and lashed out just as she sprang out of the way. She found that hole with her sonar as the silt masses thickened and smothered the waters all around her, slithering in just as the frilled shark slithered to gain on her.

Dallas rolled away from the hole just in time to feel the earth-shattering THUD that sent her flying, flipping her around to see the massive snake head protruding through the hole and opening its deadly bear-trap mouth. Dallas stared back at the rows of backward, snagging teeth and swam out of the way before she could see just how many there were.

The only thing she saw were the severed remains of the rope netting the hunter/gatherer team initially set for it, torn right through like it would any soft cephalopod. The hole was just big enough for it to fit its face halfway through, leaving the rest of it to extend and flex in determination. With enough force, it could be through that hole in no time.

She cursed at the pinging of her tablet.

"You're going to get me killed, Clyde!"

Dallas sprinted behind another rock near another hole, its insides already mapped out in her head.

I'm fine. I am on it. Nobody come any further. Trust me, just wait!!

She fanned her tail out, whipping back and forth to create a new blood trail for the beast to pick up. The ring of rock around its head started to deteriorate with each lunge, clumps of stone raining down until they were big enough to make the whole thing break away. The frilled shark opened its mouth as wide as it could as it charged toward Dallas's injured tail, but she was already inside the other cavern, navigating her way up and around.

Darkness surrounded her. In her head, she saw the cavern's layout and knew where each wall and rock obstacle was, but all she saw were the ocean water walls without light. She stayed to the right and kept her hands on the rocks there, knowing that the creature could not fit through the hole on the left that she came in. But it would try.

The first THUD jolted from the left side, a few spaces behind her, making her jump and grasp a jagged section of the wall.

She kept going, slithering in and out as a second THUD sounded again, this time closer, almost close enough to hit her. Dallas climbed to the top and made her way out of the opening there, her hand on her gun pocket as she located the frilled shark's exact position.

She shot out of the hole and aimed at its open mouth.

The electric green and yellow rays sizzled its palate, momentarily lighting the area around it so she could see the vibrant and angry green flashing in its eyes. She shot again, enough to make it slow down for just a while longer, then she made her way to the other side of the cavern.

She found the openings there that would lead out and echolocated just beyond that, seeing exactly what she thought she would see. As the frilled shark slithered in place to regain its consciousness, she hid behind a pile of rocks and dug out her tablet.

> I need all of you to come toward that opening closest to you and A.J. Surround it and get your guns ready. I am going to come out first, and it will be right behind me.

Dallas pressed at the bleeding wound on her tail until she saw those black-green eyes come back into focus and stop right on her, its jaw wide open as if it could swallow her whole. She fled from the rock and made her way to the hole she was already closer to. She stretched her arms out, pointing her hands toward the hole and making sure that everyone on the other side saw her first.

Dallas jolted out of the hole in time to recognize a more lit area and the members of the team present and accounted for. Many shouted for her and exclaimed about her leaking tail, but she pivoted and drew her gun, turning the setting all the way up.

The explosion of broken rock bits and the discharge of electric rays happened almost simultaneously. The head of the monster burst through the hole, bringing the rest of its gigantic snake body with it as the gun beams fired from all different angles. It jerked and shook at each shot, zapped into different positions and shapes until it took on its final one, belly-up in the shape of a rainbow. The snare-trap mouth opened all the way this time, loose and flapping on its final hinges.

CHAPTER 35

"LET'S GET YOU ALL a little closer together; try to squeeze in from the sides."

The merman backed up and raised his camera, almost as large and ancient as he was.

"Okay, that's better. Where's our girl?"

Someone gave Dallas a little shove.

"Get in the front middle," the cameraman instructed her.

Dallas kept her bashful smile as she moved down a row, holding on to her flowing yellow tunic, which was a bit too big but was the most decent thing she had in her closet according to her mom. It was almost long enough to cover the bandage wrapped around her tail, but they stressed that they wanted that to show.

"I think I got a good one now. Smile!"

The group congregated, holding their poses while Viceroy Westburn leaned in a little more and smiled a little more, this smile more genuine than the last few photos taken. His smile remained after the picture was taken, assessing the group one more time. His smile was mainly for Dallas.

The merman put his camera down and switched to a tablet with a stylus.

"Great! You're all done. Now I'll just need Dallas for the interview part."

Everyone left the room, the rest of the team exiting one way and talking with the viceroy while Dallas was invited to another space. They went to a room that looked like a corporate meeting room, complete with a long table and swivel chairs. They occupied only one corner, yet the formality was still there.

"Wow, I can't believe it. You were with us during your Job Trial, and look at you now!"

Dallas's mind had to rewind. She knew the merman looked slightly familiar.

"You probably don't remember me; I sat a few cubicles down from you, but I was always out on a lead and wasn't in the office too much. I'm Dave."

"Oh, yeah!" Dallas forced herself to say. "I remember. I wasn't at my desk that much either. Mostly at the copy machine."

"Yeah, how crazy is that? Looks like you found something that worked for you. And now look at what you ended up doing!"

Dave made some notes on his stylus but kept his attention on her.

"All right, so you decided on being a hunter/gatherer. How long were you working with this pod before you volunteered for the Marine Force?"

"I am not sure. Not very long at all."

Dave scribbled.

"What made you want to volunteer?"

"Honestly, I was just...bored. You know when they suspended jobs, I had to do something."

"Do you like being a hunter/gatherer?"

"Well, yeah, I do. I love being out in the open ocean, just...exploring."

"But you liked being with the Marine Force too. Going after things."

"Well, I just really wanted the...freedom. Looking and searching for things and seeing what I would find along the way. I love the idea of being out and doing whatever I want, but with the curfew and all the limitations that came with it while the frilled shark was out there, it was anything but."

Dave's eyes raised in surprise and interest.

"It was frustrating, and I felt like I wasn't getting the full serving of what it should have been. So, I joined the Marine Force when they were searching for volunteers, especially since I fit the profile, hoping to satisfy that."

"Did you join with the intention of going after the frilled shark?"

"No. I honestly didn't think it would be us. I honestly didn't think it would be me."

"Your team and envoys had a lot to say about that. They said you were quite the dark horse."

Dallas gave a little nod and swayed a bit in the swivel chair, but not too much to convey discomfort.

"So, let's talk about what went on in there, in those deep-sea caves. I want to know everything. What were you feeling? What were you thinking? Were you scared? Did you panic at all? How much of that was planned?"

Dallas's answer had become well-said and well-rehearsed, having had to repeat it to all who asked since they got back to Gneiss Underway, beast trophy in their netting. She relaxed with the knowledge that these questions were all being published, and she would not have to keep repeating it, although nothing would be more grilling than it had been with her own family.

"I realized that I had made people afraid," she started with honesty. "My boss, my coworkers, friends, my family, and everyone that found out what I did and what could have happened. Of course, they would be, and anyone would be. And, of course, I was scared at times, but most of the time, I wasn't. I wasn't scared because I knew what to do. I became too focused. I knew the entire layout of the caves and what opening went where and how I could use it to my advantage. There were places I could fit, and the frilled shark couldn't. I could see the entire thing in my head like a map, so I worked with it."

Dave kept scribbling, stopping once in a while to correct sloppy handwriting.

"It was your skills in echolocation. Your very impressive skills in echolocation."

"Yeah."

"And you could see the entirety of the caves, and you knew where the frilled shark was at all times, even when it did not know where you were."

"That's right."

"Did you know where the rest of your team was?"

"I did when I got closer to the way out and there was nothing blocking the exit. I knew where they were and told them to stay there."

"And so, you got the frilled shark to chase you out, and you brought it to them."

Dallas nodded. "I did."

"You cut your tail to make it chase you."

"Yeah. It was the only way. The point wasn't to just attack it until it was killed. The point was to trap it and then catch it."

The reporter made more notes.

"Why didn't you kill it on the spot? Surely you had the weapons for it, but you barely used them."

"Well, even if I were successful in taking it out all by myself, it would have been a very unhappy time for me and for everyone else to have to drag a six-foot-long animal out of there."

"I see... So, does this mean that you will be ready and willing to face other sea creatures you encounter?"

Dave looked at her through one eye while his snow-white bangs covered the other, almost looking like the frilled shark did when it looked at her from the side, waiting for her next move.

"I think we're both always, and never, ready."

That was the last thing he wrote down before looking back up at Dallas and thanking her for the interview. He was all smiles as he scanned the notes on his tablet, and they both left the room to make their way back to the lobby. The reporter approached Viceroy Westburn and chatted with him while Dallas tried to figure out what she wanted to do with herself.

She swam among the merpeople hanging around and saw Clyde with Liam and Noah, his back to her, arms gesticulating in what looked like anger. She stopped, feeling the tingle of a bad feeling. She swam behind other merpeople to get close enough, just enough to tune in.

"She doesn't deserve this!"

"Yes, she does! You need to stop it," Liam was saying. "Right now."

"She should not be rewarded for a happy accident."

Liam jerked his chin forward, bringing his voice lower and sharper. "She was thinking like a soldier. She displayed more courage and quick-thinking than anyone and saved the community."

"She disobeyed orders!" Clyde said, his voice raised. "She put herself and others at risk by doing whatever she felt like, and she could have gotten killed! I had a plan. She was the only one who went against it."

"But your plan did not work, so someone acted on something else that did work. One of your employees has some great talent. That is all. So, get your head out of your ass and swallow your pride!"

The merpeople shielding Dallas moved to split up, forcing her to retreat and find someplace else to hide. She pretended to be involved in the conversations of others, head down with her heart thumping and looking at her tablet, pretending to be looking at something.

Anything but Clyde.

She looked out the nearest window, observing the groups of workers stationed around the center, lingering near as the rows of fencing came down, taking her back to when they were all going up. Some merchildren swam outsea as far as they dared to go, still peeking through the bars, chasing each other in rapid bursts of bubbles.

"All right, come on," Clyde's hurried voice came to the group. "We have a lot of work to do and fewer hours today to do it. Let's move."

Dallas stayed near the back, pretending to be engrossed in her tablet.

Not long after she finished her late breakfast, down to the last few gulps of tea, the news came on her television right on schedule. Dallas perked up and grabbed the remote to turn up the volume, barely floating off the edge of her couch.

Oh God, they're going to show the photo. I probably have hair in my face.

"...now with Viceroy Westburn and the hunter/gatherer troupe responsible for the capture of the terrifying frilled shark, most notably the mermaid Dallas Dwight, who successfully kept tabs on the creature by means of her echolocation skills."

The camera switched from the news anchorman to a group photo of the hunter/gatherer troupe with the Viceroy, followed by an individual headshot of Dallas. She cringed and tugged at the ends of her hair, cringing even more at the dumb tunic she wore. *God, it's like a yearbook photo!*

"Viceroy Westburn, along with other neighboring towns, are relieved and happy to see that the danger is over, and the communities can feel safe again, though many safety precautions will still be in place. Marine Force troops have been stationed at town limits outsea though have since decreased some of their security. Many outsea jobs have gone back into operation, though the traveling pipelines will remain restricted for the time being."

Her phone buzzed, and she immediately knew who it was, a smile forming involuntarily.

"Helloooo?"

"You're on TV!"

"I know, Mom."

"You look so good! Look at you!"

"Ah, thanks, Mom."

"We're very proud!"

"Thanks, Dad."

"People keep talking about it. You know you're like a little celebrity around here now!"

Dallas felt a pinch in her stomach.

A little celebrity around here now.

Her supervisor was probably thrilled.

"It's really weird, but yeah, I still can't believe it."

The news continued, moving on to the progress on other towns. There were photos of fences still up, security locks in place. It showed footage of envoys guarding intracity pipeline systems and merfolk lining up to use them.

"Things are going to get back to normal," her mother promised, echoing the attitude of the news anchor, the viceroy, and anyone else she encountered. They were all so certain.

CHAPTER 36

DALLAS ENJOYED WHAT SHE could of her day off, while she had one, away from others and away from all the noise. She spent the early part of her day on her couch, drinking tea and browsing through her Currents app, staying involved without directly participating. Businesses everywhere were throwing an abnormally large number of specials and events with buy-one-get-one offers and new menu options for restaurants.

Dallas scrolled to the news bulletin from the official Gneiss Underway page, the post from the viceroy announcing that the community had opened itself up to the next arrival of launchies. She stared at it. All it was, was a photo of Viceroy Westburn in his office smiling, along with some bulleted facts about the town, as well as tips and tricks for a smooth transition, including reminders to get your after-injection cream to stop the itching from the first batch of scales!

It never mentioned the attacks, the lockdown, the deaths, or even the capture of the frilled shark itself. She almost wanted to laugh. Almost. How could that even be a secret?

A message from Sapphire interrupted her thoughts:

Hey girl, you still going tonight?

Dallas paused, searching her brain for the time, place, and event she evidently committed to.

> Going where?

Sapphire was typing.

> The Drunken Ship! They're doing like a soft reopening tonight! There's a special on popcorn shrimp!

The tide that rolled into Dallas's stomach at that moment was warmer, something she missed, something simple and free, and it was something she wanted to grab back. Something that she needed to wash over her feelings of anxiety and dread.

Yeah, she found herself typing.

And some hours later, Dallas was able to see for herself just how grandly open the town had become. She left her home to an array of merfolk coming and going. She frowned as she passed the neighboring caves where, for the past couple of weeks, there had been at least two envoys, if not Marine Force, stationed there, and now there were none. When she reached the municipal area, she did not see any at all. She cast a glance out the window to the big open blue, quiet and beautiful, but also waiting. Their crystal aquarium was almost completely back, and they were about out of the cage for good.

Dallas rode the pipeline out from the municipal center and into the open sea, where she could see construction workers continuing their work on the dome. They carried pipes off and down, adding more to the piles littered about the seafloor, with small schools of fish swimming in between them in their newly opened freedom. She greeted the open ocean with a long-exhaled sigh as she made her way down the unofficial pathway. And, out of habit, she sent out some radar.

The screenshot pictures she received back were overwhelming at first, showing pods of merfolk outsea and the occasional small fish. They were so abundant they practically blended and merged together, creating strange hybrid shadows.

The Drunken Ship already had patrons mingling outside in small groups, drinks in hand, and cheerful chatter nearly drowned out by the music inside. Dallas swam past, glancing for any other familiar faces before heading inside. By default, she made her way to the bar and found Sapphire at a riser table with stools.

"There she is!"

"Hey, Sapphire!"

Sapphire had an open menu and passed it over with new bubblegum-pink nails, longer than her last ones. They chatted while browsing the menu, Dallas perking up when Sapphire mentioned her work schedule.

"So, you're back!"

"Yeah, actually, I'm booked this whole week! I am so glad to be back. Don't get me wrong, it was fun to be an unofficial Marine Force, but only because it was for a little bit. You know, get out and get some exercise."

"I'll bet Claudia is happy to have you back."

Sapphire nodded. "She is. No one else cleans and organizes the storage room like I do. So, how are things with Clyde?"

Dallas shrugged. "Not that good. He hasn't talked to me."

"He's got a bruised ego."

"I guess."

"He's just jealous!"

"He said if the frilled shark didn't kill me, he would have himself."

"I know this kind of personality; he wants to be in control all the time and hates it when he can't be. I dated a guy like him once, and it got annoying super fast."

"I know, I know. I guess he isn't used to someone winging it. I can see that, but like I told everyone, I was all right. The rest of the team congratulated me and really showed me support and praise. No one else acted jealous. Even his husband gave me encouragement! After the interview and the photo at the Viceroy's office, A.J. told me that I could perhaps be a Marine Force soldier someday."

"That's wild!"

"It is; it's just... work is a little uncomfortable right now. I'm just staying out of his way for a while. Now that we're back to just hunting crabs and bluefin tuna and the usual stuff, he just acts like nothing happened."

"Yeah, I think that's it. That's good, though, that you're back to normal now that everything else is getting there.

A waitress came by and took their orders. Dallas turned to Sapphire as she applied lipstick, using a small compact mirror. In the reflection, Dallas could see just how much she was smiling with her eyes.

"How did other things go with you?" Dallas asked.

Sapphire looked back at her now with a real smile. "It was easier than I thought."

Dallas nodded in understanding.

"I thought maybe I was making a big deal out of it because I didn't know how people would react. But no one did. Everyone was cool and supportive about it when they found out at work. I mean, of course, Claudia knew when she hired me, she knew my legal name, but she respected my wishes and was the biggest help when we talked to everyone. They all say they are happy I wasn't eaten. And it's like it went back to normal."

"Oh, that's great."

"No one was surprised, and they acted like it was nothing. I can't tell you how much of a relief that is."

"I'm so happy for you, Sapphire."

In the middle of pineapple rum drinks and popcorn shrimp baskets, Dallas got up to use the bathroom. The buzz she caught from her drink settled in nicely and didn't show itself until she got up, floating all the way up to her head just as she left her seat. She made her way to the bathroom, hoping that Sapphire ordered that other basket of fries.

On her way back, Dallas was either focused on everything at once or nothing at all, swimming on autopilot and so out of tune she barely noticed who had been calling her name.

She stopped short as her name echoed in her ears and turned to face the caller, opening her eyes wide enough not to look too inebriated. Mickey had come out from behind the bar to give her a hug.

"There she is, the crazy little hero!" Mickey said.

"Hey, Mickey!"

"How are you, honey?"

"Just glad to be back out again."

"You said it! I don't remember the last time I had so many customers!"

Mickey's conversation, as well as the others buzzing all around her, flew in and out of her ears. She listened to all of them and none of them. While Mickey droned on about the capture of the frilled shark and the news and the town's rebranding, her ears struggled to focus, but her eyes did not. She caught the tablet of a merman sitting at the bar, scrolling through a news article.

Vicious Attack at Mirage Bay

Marine Force are on the lookout and patrolling after an anonymous resident of Mirage Bay claimed to be attacked by something near a coral bed, claiming it had been camouflaged and they did not see it.

"...Dallas?"

Dallas shook out of it and refocused her eyes on Mickey.

"Sorry, what?"

"I know it's so loud in here, honey. I was asking who you're here with?"

"Oh! My friend Sapphire: she put another order in for us."

"I'll leave you to it then. I'll check on you later!"

"Okay, bye!"

Dallas gave him a little nod and swam back to her seat. Not only had Sapphire broken out the second basket of fries, but she had also ordered her next drink, dipping her shish kebab of pineapple and maraschino cherries through the slush.

"Girl, I thought you fell in. I was going to come in after you."

Dallas sat down hard and was glad that Sapphire got her another round. She flipped the lid back and took her own swig.

"Damn, honey."

Dallas put the cup down and squeezed her eyes at the brain freeze.

"You okay?"

Dallas opened her eyes to Sapphire's raised eyebrow.

"Sure, I'm fine! I just bumped into Mickey at the bar, and we were chatting for a while."

It hurt to talk, and it hurt to hear, and Dallas was only happy when they cranked the music up. She needed whatever conscious brain activity she had left to think about what she just read. It stuck to the frontmost part of her mind, clear as a post-it note, though Dallas didn't mention it to Sapphire out loud. She swirled her straw in her drink the way she swirled her thoughts in her head like clockwork, revisiting one point to the next.

Dallas woke up completely wrapped in her hammock, turned down and facing her floor. The corner end of her blanket was wedged between the fins in her fluke, and her arms were pinned bent to her chest. She looked like an upside-down sarcophagus. Dallas pushed and wiggled herself free, her blankets de-ribboning themselves and her hammock twisting back into its rightful position. She floated in place, trying to recall the events of the evening, vaguely remembering swimming back with Sapphire, though it was blurry and muffled.

Opening her eyes completely and setting her head right and awake, it seemed like in her dream, she was being chased by a giant blowfish made of many different colors and at least a thousand arms. She yawned, looking at the clock on her dresser to see it was well past one in the afternoon. She finger-combed her hair and made her way to her bathroom.

Mirage Bay, she thought. *Not that far from there.*

She checked her Currents app, browsed people's stories and various news items, and continued to scroll as she made herself some oatmeal with cut-up strawberries, then set the water on for coffee. Dallas kept scrolling while she had breakfast. At one point, she entered "Mirage Bay attacks" in the search and kept looking until she found it:

> Some in Mirage Bay claimed to be attacked by something near the coral reefs while traveling out to sea. The first attack was a few days ago on sixty-year-old August Hubble, who was going to visit her son. "I don't know what it was!" Hubble proclaimed. "But it grabbed and scratched my tail. It was something that had very long tentacles or claws or something." Another attack happened days later on thirty-two-year-old Steven Shooke, a postal worker, who claimed something similar. "It looked like something that just came out of the coral," said Shooke. "Something just came out and grabbed me."

No creature was found or reported.

Dallas searched other articles that reported similar things, and they were similarly short. She thought of one thing, and one thing only, as she finished eating: she wanted to go on a little outing.

She put her empty coffee cup in the sink next to others she'd neglected during the week, but found she had to put them off once again for something that needed her immediate attention. Dallas searched for her messenger bag hidden among debris in her room and then headed out. When she left her neighborhood, the traffic was about the same as before. All she did was mind the map and her general knowledge of the area. She reached the pipeline that would take her there and rode it out with the other travelers going on out-to-sea business—whatever that was. Dallas reached the end, exiting the pipeline and into the open blue. Everyone else went their separate ways, but for the moment, she was still.

Dallas was between buildings, spread out enough for more open space yet close enough together to still be considered the city and at the outskirts of Mirage Bay. She swam past these on her path outward, out to sea completely, sending out a sonar pulse or two. Some merfolk were here and there, along with a sea turtle or two. Dallas swam on, turning toward some coral reefs once she saw them, though she did not pick up on anything else. She settled among the reefs, alone, letting the smaller creatures scuttle in and out without being bothered. It was just the solitude she needed.

Dallas took a deep breath, feeling the pull from the inside of her chest, and sent out her radar as far as she could reach. Her gills fluttered at her neck as bubbles poured, and she focused on the point ahead of her, wherever that was. She could feel the strain in her head, and as the picture came back, she did a mental scan of the usual shapes. The usual fish, mammals, tiny fish, big fish, and merfolk all spread out at a distance, until she caught sight of an unusual shape.

Dallas tried to grab it mentally and hold it there. It was the shape of everything and nothing. She sent out sonar again in that direction, ignoring everything else that came back to her but that shape. It was misshapen in a way that it could have been clumps of rocks or something rough, but the way it moved told her it could have been something else. It moved with four long fins—very long fins—appendages akin to a squid, but this was no squid.

Whatever this was, it moved with quick movements, not slow and fluid ones. Like something that waited for the right time to move. Like something that waited for the right moment to attack. Dallas cast again; the image now came back to her smaller.

It was moving away, however far away it was, and was now going further. Those shapes pulsed in and out. Dallas reached into her bag and pulled out her notebook and a pen, sketching what she had in memory.

What she saw looked like a weird, fish-like squid with four long fins and a clumpy, misshapen body. She studied the fins, particularly the pectoral ones—the ones that looked like they ended in a few separate appendages. Whether tentacles or something else, they could be sharp. They must have something sharp if merpeople were claiming it grabbed and scratched their tails.

CHAPTER 37

THEY ALL SET DOWN their netting sacks on the seafloor while Clyde punched in the keypad to open the door. The warehouse door grumbled and slid open like a garage door before settling at the top and stopping, letting out one last mechanical grunt. They filed in.

"Okay," Clyde started, swiping through the spreadsheets on his tablet. "The orders for the produce are over here. The fruits and vegetables go in these trailers over there labeled 'Millman and Oats Grocer.' Oh, coffee beans, coffee beans, who had the coffee beans? Those go in that trailer because they're going to the same building anyway with the grains and rice. Oh my God, we didn't forget crabs, did we?"

"Nope," Dallas answered, tugging on her net full of squirming, wriggling, pinching creatures. Most of their legs poked out like they could swim away. "I got 'em."

Clyde sighed. "Yes, good, thank you. Let's get all the seafood collections together, as they're the biggest this time."

Dallas grabbed the crab net with one hand and the tuna net in the other; the rope indents from both still molded in her palms, going right back into place. She learned early on to net what weight she could carry, but sometimes still went over that limit out of drive. She usually didn't care, and that day especially, she didn't care when she had too much on her mind.

They started busy and stayed that way. Dallas barely got a "hello" in before the troupe was ushered out to sea to bring in all the new supplies needed. She didn't get a chance to ask the question she wanted to ask anyone—not a single person. Of course, no one else was asking either.

She waited with the others by the submarine trailers, and when her turn came, she swam inside with her loot to stock it in the organized categories. When Dallas swam out of the trailer to nowhere in particular in the warehouse, she noticed a few merpeople talking to a merwoman near the front who looked familiar. They looked toward the back where Dallas had come from, necks craned and watching Clyde move crates of snails.

"Hey, Clyde? Someone here for you."

Clyde peeked up from his tablet and swam over to the newcomer, stylus still in hand. The merwoman wore a long jacket that went down almost to the base of her fluke, and she held it closed in shyness, as if she wished it would cover her completely. Dallas frowned as she stared at this woman, trying to place her.

"Hi, Clyde, I'm not sure if you remember me. I've called a couple of times but was unable to reach anyone. I'm Kendall Wadsworth from the Oceans Through the Ages museum. Remember I came to talk about the frilled shark?"

Bingo.

"Oh, yes," said Clyde, shaking his head. "Of course. I'm sorry; we have been out at the crustacean farms. What can we do for you?"

Kendall kept a shy smile as she squeezed the edges of her jacket.

"I would like to know what became of the frilled shark."

Clyde's eyebrows twitched, but he fought them back. "Well, as you know, we brought it back in one piece after—"

He turned around until he found Dallas floating there.

"After Dallas here fought it, manipulated it, and brought it out—basically got it captured. We brought it to a safe place and were thinking of keeping the jaw for a display at the Viceroy headquarters and using the—"

"See, I want it. For my museum."

"Oh!" Clyde's eyebrows rose along with his voice. "Oh, well that makes sense. But we don't think it has been fully...decomposed yet."

"But you know where it is?"

"Yes, we do. It is a little way out."

"I would love to have that jawbone as a display. It's so rare. I hope we can work something out."

Clyde kept his face even and stoic, but even Dallas could see that he was considering it. "I would have to talk with the Viceroy on this, as I know he had the idea to keep it and put it somewhere, but why don't we touch base again?"

Kendall's grip on her jacket relaxed as she smiled and nodded. "I would love that; thank you so much."

"Thank you for coming by!"

By the time Kendall swam out of the warehouse, most of the crew had gathered around to witness the conversation.

"So," a merman close to Clyde started. "Are we going to let her have it?"

Clyde shrugged. "You know, I really don't know. I don't see why not, but it's not really my call. The only thing I know is that no one is going to want to go get it."

There were laughs of agreement, whatever that meant. Clyde did not say anything else on the matter and brought everyone back to loading up the shipments.

As Dallas helped with nets and crates, she found herself inching closer to Clyde, looking for her opening. Normally, she made sure he was surrounded by others when asking any question, and the subject always stayed on that day's haul and packing. Clyde never mentioned anything else, about anything.

They were in the back of the warehouse with the last crate of lobsters, just the two of them. An electric charge went down her tail when she lifted her head and addressed him.

"Clyde."

He barely looked up, fumbling with the lock on the crate. "Yeah?"

"Have you, or anyone, picked up anything else on the radar lately?"

Clyde raised himself up and pushed his hair out of his eyes. "No, what do you mean?"

He was upright completely now, knowing that he could and would believe her.

"I've read some things in the news about other attacks close by, in the Mirage Bay area," she explained. "Of something else."

"Oh."

She had her notebook out and ready and flipped to the page of her amateurish sketch.

"When I was out there, I sent out my radar, and this is what I saw."

She held the notebook out like an ancient tablet of truth, watching Clyde's reaction and trying to keep hers neutral. He frowned, fingers at his chin in a pensive study.

"Merpeople claimed that it camouflaged with the coral and grabbed them, and they couldn't find it. No one could still find it."

Clyde's brow furrowed further as he tilted his head this way and that to consider Dallas's drawing.

"I don't think this is anything."

Dallas's heart sank. "What do you mean?"

"I know what you're talking about. It's not connected to the news about Mirage Bay. Many are actually saying that it was a cuttlefish or octopus that surprised them, and that was that. It's nothing."

He pointed to her drawing. "So, as far as this goes, what you saw from very far away is probably a sea turtle."

Dallas frowned. "A sea turtle?"

"It's distorted and exaggerated in places, but yeah. When you pick up on things from a distance, the further it is, the less clear it will be, so it could make it look like something it is not."

Clyde turned her notebook sideways and showed her. "Look, those long appendages are their flippers. The body is the shell. You noticed it swimming, so you probably got different angles, and that's probably what got you confused about the whole outline. What's all over it could very well be barnacles. They constantly attach to turtle shells."

"But... but..." Dallas couldn't get her next thought out.

"Look," Clyde said. She looked at him. "You are an excellent echolocator. And if there is something out there dangerous to be wary of, you would be one of the first people to listen to. But you don't have to feel like you have to sound the alarm about every little thing you find, or think you find, especially things that are far away and minding their own business and not presenting any harm. If no one else is concerned, that means you don't have to be either. Got it?"

Dallas took the notebook back.

"No crying wolf."

She knew that it wouldn't be possible to have every single creature of the ocean identified and printed in a book.

Still, Dallas couldn't find anything new or out of the ordinary with her latest hoard.

Any pictures of turtles all looked about the same... She searched for squid and octopuses. Nothing satisfied.

No crying wolf.

She had to let it go.

It was time to leave, and she needed to return all the books by their due date. She had three books this time and double-checked her room to make sure there weren't any more. The last time Dallas did a library run, she lifted the blankets in her hammock and found a rogue book nestled in the folds where she had once fallen asleep. She looked in her hammock again, at her nightstand, on top of her dresser, and among piles of clothes to check that this time the number was, in fact, three. She slung her messenger bag over her shoulder and left the house as a boat would do in a no wake zone.

The window washers moved at a faster pace than she did, brushes sweeping up and down like waves on the shore to clear away clumps of green algae nestled in the corners. Some flakes fell away as she passed the windows on her way to the library, the same trek she always took. To her disappointment, she could not spend that day there. After dropping her materials in the outside chute and heading to work, she eyed the Fast Eats she would pass on the way. On impulse, she made that pit stop.

Nothing raised anyone's mood faster than coffee.

Her mocha order filled to the brim, cream and chocolate chips added before it was sealed shut. Dallas held the instant warmth and joy in her hands, feeling it pass through her fingers. She took the first sip and allowed it to recharge her batteries, giving her the needed fuel-boost. She smiled as she held that comfort beacon, the only thing that could energize her for work that day and help her forget everything else.

Dallas swallowed that gulp, the roof of her mouth tingling as the scalding liquid stripped away a layer of skin. She scratched it with her tongue, leisurely swimming to work. She did not even notice what was sticking out of the sand until her tail kicked up some dust around it, covering the jagged point. The edge scraped her fin and jerked her tail up. She swam up, fanning the dust away to reveal what had scratched her; it was just a rock. She tried not to think it could be anything else.

CHAPTER 38

THE WEEK WAS DULL until Friday, the day Clyde said he wanted to have a team meeting to go over a few things. Dallas sat with a seed of anxiety in her stomach that only grew the longer the day went, wanting it to travel up her throat and float out of her mouth already. They all sat around for a while after lunch, relaxing in the meeting room and taking their time throwing away their trash. Dallas even picked at the chips she told herself she would save for later but found herself still reaching into the bag for a few more.

"So, we reached our quota for the week, which is good," Clyde said from his laptop. "Everyone is happy and there are no problems. But, on to the things I needed to address. First, it has been confirmed that the new farm broke ground in Cloveland."

Several cheered.

"Yeah, finally! We will get more leeway when traveling to the South Province and we got ourselves that expansion. Second, matters regarding the frilled shark remains."

The seed of anxiety dissolved, burning up in a new train of thought. Dallas was conditioned to perk up whenever that word passed her ears, even if her name wasn't connected to it; it already was. She would always have that connection.

"The Viceroy has claimed ownership of the teeth but otherwise is not too concerned about where the rest of it goes and is open to it getting a good home. This brings us to the museum owner, Kendall Wadsworth. They went ahead and told her that it's hers, much to her protest that the teeth were already claimed. The Viceroy managed to talk her down and explain that for safety reasons it would be best to have artificial teeth modeled and dulled down.

Other than that, he is okay with it getting a good home, but it is not going to officially come from us. We can't, as a pod, break away from our routine and do something separate, as it will be an independent transaction. So, this is sort of an extra thing, and I am supposed to open it up to all of you to see who would be interested in doing it."

"I'm going to get the frilled shark jaw?" someone asked.

"Yep. The rest of the carcass was just food for whatever came to the free meal. All that's needed is to go get it and bring it to Kendall."

"Where is it?" someone else asked.

"At a dumping ground in the wild, a spot for that sort of thing where nature could do its thing. We know where it is; it's just in the middle of nowhere."

The white noise filled the room, and Dallas felt every single pair of eyes turn on her, except for Clyde, who more or less looked anywhere but at her.

She sat up. The decision was in her head before she voiced it.

"I will," she said.

Clyde half-smiled. "I knew you would."

When Dallas pulled up the navigation on her tablet, she zoomed in and out on the map to figure out where it was. Clyde had told her verbally, but that does nothing when working to get a visual. She sighed with the frustrated realization that comes with the phrase "what did I get myself into" as she traced the route with her finger.

No wonder no one else jumped on it.

According to Clyde's description, it was not that far and given the size and shape of the target, finding it would be easy. She just had to get there first. It wasn't like she had pressing plans on her day off, anyway.

Having free access to the storage closet and supplies gave her a new sense of freedom when she opened that door and realized she had free range of anything she could want. Netting was important, of course, to collect, but soon her eyes drifted to other things on other shelves. She already had her armor and approved weapons, but that didn't stop her from browsing the other items.

They were larger and on higher shelves for safekeeping, all arranged in rows like a shop display. She pulled one off the shelf, long with a delicate design on the side and a groove where an arrow would be placed. She unfolded the leather-like strap, knowing how to adjust it for where it would be worn, the visual in her head from pictures of their ancestors in history books, balancing the crossbow on one arm while fitting the arrow with the other.

Dallas gently put it back next to the others, other crossbows in different sizes, as well as harpoons almost bigger than she was. Dallas had never seen anyone take those out, not even Marine Force, not even for their last expedition. She wondered what occasion they would be used for.

The basics were equipped: a blaster and stun gun in her utility pouches, and a spear she attached with a strap to her back. Dallas felt ready for...whatever was to come, if it were something she could even predict. She was going to meet the monster again, or at least its remains, and there would be others she could encounter along the way.

Dallas took the pipeline out of the municipal center, merging between business merpeople. Some looked her way casually, with some of those looks lasting a bit longer due to her publicized recognition.

There she was, armed and ready to tackle something new. She made them wonder, and that wonder gave Dallas a little ego boost. She avoided eye contact as she swam through the next building but held on to that thought with warmth. There was that small spotlight to make her aware of her own sense of self and existence and would never forget how it altered her life.

Now, she was wearing clamshell armor and carrying a stun gun in her pouch. Dallas noticed each pair of eyes, each new look of recognition, and from that moment on it caused her to double-check her hair and tunic for wrinkles before walking out the door. It transformed into a sense of being seen that she did not have before and still could not get used to.

She exited the building and took to the open sea. She saw the substation Clyde had pointed out to her, the very one she would take. Dallas swam right past it without so much as a pause, just her and the open ocean, taking that sub's line for herself and herself only. The current drifted into the path she was taking, sweeping her along with it.

She remembered times on land when she went to the beach, even walking past seafood restaurants, finding the smell of fish unpleasant and crinkling her nose. Now, it was something she had gotten used to, and in that moment, it was something she looked forward to smelling—a scent she could only experience in the sea, something wild and natural and alive.

It wasn't necessary to echolocate if she were hunting for fish, for when she passed over the fluorescent reefs, the fish of matching colors darted in and out, making themselves known, but only for a few seconds, dashing away from potential harm and leaving a trail of tiny bubbles. Dallas swam through rock formations and small island landscapes, taking a moment to practice her whirlwind spins.

Her fins twisted as her body did, and her hair wrapped around her face with momentum as she shaped herself into an arrow sailing through a donut-shaped rock, slowing down and bending back to fish shape to admire her accomplishment. It was the best one she had ever done, away from any group exercises and critical eyes. Ahead of her spanned more of the open blue, and an echolocation scan told her that was all it was.

Dallas pulled her tablet out to assess the rest of the path and swam in the corresponding directions, inching closer to the point in the path where the sea floor curved into a downward bend. She drifted to the slope and followed it as the blue around her grew darker. She had her pearl orb ready, palming it on; the gentle frost color offsetting the darker end of the color spectrum, illuminating her new surroundings.

She sent out a sonar wave: picking up rocks, small fish, and other worm-like creatures meandering through the deeper waters. Soon she was joined by other forms of light and did not need any other way to search for them as they made themselves known. Up ahead on her right, tiny red lights flashed on and off before revealing the full blue-green outline of the long, slick form of a black dragonfish.

She scanned the benthic floors where the bottom was and where the Marine Force troops did the drop-off. Clyde had mentioned decomposition once or twice, or a few times, but did not provide any more insight, and Dallas assumed she would just be searching for the remains. She echolocated for the frilled shark body, bypassing all rocks that were remotely the size and almost the shape, until she came across what could have been it. But it couldn't have been.

Dallas paused and sent out another sonar wave, confused. There was the confirmed outline of the frilled shark corpse, but there was something else. It came back to her almost like the body of a gigantic paramecium, blown up under a microscope and planted on the ocean floor. This entire body was wiggling with hundreds of tiny appendages. She palmed her pearl orb to higher settings and swam in its direction until she could see the thing for herself.

The first thing the light picked up was that open jaw.

Now, however, it had nothing left but its stark-white frame outlining where its face used to be. The sunken holes of the eyes seemed to stare at her once again, as if to recognize her, while frozen in its former sneering smile, displayed its most powerful weapon that it still possessed. Dallas immediately saw the rest of the body—or what was left of it. The cartilaginous form was now worn down like the wax of a candle melted into uneven lumps. She saw what was feeding on it.

At first, she could not place those wiggling appendages until she approached the six-foot decaying corpse herself. They resembled the undersea version of long, bluish-purple slithering leeches, and they were still hard at work. They tied themselves into knots and pushed the knots down their bodies for leverage. They tore chunks of meat and penetrated in, wiggling their tails as they plunged into the body to eat it from the inside out.

She recalled a page in a book where the description matched this very scene, a snapshot from history trapped in time to carry on into the present. There was no mistaking that she was witnessing a scene from millions of years ago, as there were still things that had not gone extinct, including both species right in front of her.

The name "hagfish" did not seem fitting for these creatures, as they did not resemble fish at all to anyone who might see them, but here they were. The body of the frilled shark had been brought to this spot for proper disposal, and they were just finishing the job.

Dallas sighed as she approached the corpse a little closer, her nose crinkling in disgust at the flakes floating up from the torn meat. She watched the area around the neck and headed for an opening—any opening.

The hagfish wiggled and slithered their way around, and Dallas now understood why no one wanted to do this. She reached out and narrowly missed one, jerking her arm back before it could realize she was there and react. She reached for the netting she had tied to her knapsack, opening it up as she moved closer to the jaw, stalling for time while the hagfish moved about the enormous buffet.

She hoped it would be as easy as simply scaring them off with sudden movement, but as she waved her netting in the water, they seemed indifferent to the new waves. Dallas watched them flutter about inside the carcass, unwilling to spend the entire day watching them clean off every speck of meat, and simply started to drag the net over it with care, watching the bottom loops snag onto the tricuspid teeth hooks.

Just as they had the first time.

Dallas pulled the net up slowly, as if putting on a knee-high sock, but only got as far as a little over the head.

She ducked away in time for a stream of silver to surround the top of the net, lingering in its own long and silky shape as it expanded in the water. With another attempt came another release from a hagfish as it jerked around the body, its tail twitching in defensive mode. Even with their defense mechanism, they got out of the way. Dallas yanked the netting further up with more determination, even as the hagfish released more slime, streams of milky mucus shooting out from them like cans of silly string, now enough to surround the waters all around her.

In reaction, Dallas dropped the netting the first time she moved her hands and felt that slime between the webbing in her fingers, now completely coating her hands in new goo. She scraped and pulled at the jelly trap stretched between her fingers and clinging to her arm fins. It felt like something had sneezed all over her.

The protein was opaque mucus that stretched into clarity as it expanded, reminding her of the time she spilled Elmer's glue on her desk in first grade and did not clean it up right away, instead wanting to watch it dry periodically throughout the day. The more she struggled to get it off, the more it populated, as the hagfish kept bumping into her in alarm, forming a flowy white skirt from her abdomen almost all the way down her tail.

Dallas flung her hands through the water aggressively, but all it did was create gooey fins down her fingers. She shook the disgust out of her mind and refocused on the task at hand, grabbing the net again to put it around the head. She managed to separate the jawbone from the rest of its decaying flesh, pulling the net all around it until she got it secure.

She flung that netting closed just in time for the hagfish to release more slime, forming a cocoon that threatened to envelop her and infiltrate her pores. Dallas dashed away from the area with her acquired item, holding her hands up to cover her gills. As she swam away, the slime followed, attaching itself and almost swallowing her up indefinitely.

CHAPTER 39

She soared until it was light enough to leave the deeper waters. Once in a clear area, she got a good look at herself and the aftermath she was wearing, clinging to every scale and dangling from every fin. Dallas kept the net with the frilled shark jaw looped around her back, along with the turtle shell shield that would not have helped, as she put more effort into trying to get it off.

Several silky tendrils drifted away, but others remained stuck in moist and cold grips all around her body. Dallas swam over to a rock she thought was gritty enough and began to wipe it off, rubbing against it, knowing how stupid she looked in case there were any other merpeople in the area. Most of it came off but Dallas did not want to care so much anymore.

She pulled out her tablet to access the area and determine the best way to Kendall Wadsworth's museum. She did not think to echolocate the area just yet, but when she looked up into the distance, she realized she did not have to. She froze in place as she watched it swim, close enough for her to identify it as a shark.

Dallas lowered herself behind the rock a little more but peeked out enough to see it. It was not a great white, but another type. Bull shark? Nurse shark? She could not tell from there and did not want to find out. The shark steadied itself in the waters ahead of her with its nose pointed to the left, no doubt on the lookout for a hunt, and a mermaid was not going to be on the menu. Dallas cursed and backtracked to the hidden dark from which she had come to reroute.

She sent sonar waves to find other ways out, returning to the carcass buffet and swimming a little past it. There was a small drop-off that took her deeper than before, believing it would snake around and lead her away from the shark's vicinity. She swam further into the dark, drifting down into an open abyss that might extend deeper than she thought.

She did not see any flickers of bioluminescence, no eyes and teeth combinations looking to snatch a small bite of anything else, but still, she sent out more waves. When Dallas lingered, her tail resting behind her with no committed direction, she felt compelled to send her inner sights downward. There was something she partially picked up, and there was no way it was just rock formations. It was too smooth.

She sent out another sonar wave, aiming directly beneath her and propelling herself as high as she could when the shape returned to her. It almost looked like a rock, the way the head was round, but the rest of it was not. When Dallas sent out her sonar again, she saw those long arms floating in anticipation, especially two in particular that were longer.

Dallas doubled back just in time for one of those arms to shoot out from below, long and red pink with rows of lethal suction cups. With eyes as big as dinner plates, there was no doubt it saw her before she even reached that area. They had the biggest eyes known in existence, and she recognized them from an illustration in a book, not wanting to stick around to confirm it in person.

Dallas jerked back as the second arm took its turn, knowing when it was going to strike from the angle in her echo vision. She swam back to where she had come from, taking short breaths, hugging her arms tight across her chest, and getting the hagfish slime back in return.

She looked in the direction where the hagfish were and immediately made a beeline to find them.

She swam back up the small slope just as those arms were gaining on her, bringing the rest of the beast to pursue this bigger fish. The tentacle arms slapped against a rock as Dallas dove back toward the decomposition feast, the last place she thought she would be happy to see. She grabbed the closest wriggling sea leech she could and squeezed around its middle, right where the glands were.

The moment the webbing sprayed out, Dallas aimed it all for her chest, back, clothing, and every square inch of her tail. She released the hagfish as it furiously tied itself into a knot and smeared the mucus all over herself, sparing her neck and above. The squid itself was merely a few feet away, the reddish oval-shaped head and spaghetti tentacles squirming for a meal. It was a baby giant squid, but still a giant at about ten or fifteen feet, and still bigger than her.

She raced back to the open drop-off she had come from, with its arms still lashing out.

Dallas screamed when she felt the arm whip around her waist, and just as quickly slide all the way down her tail until it had nothing but a grip of goo. The second arm followed suit, and this time grabbed her a little lower, ending in the same result. Dallas turned and witnessed the feeding tentacles open and close in their new mittens of mucus in defeat.

Dallas's heart raced, and her fins were sore from flipping so hard. She swam backward, keeping her eye on the squid as it remained in the same place, reevaluating its plans until a new one was made.

Dallas screamed once again at the larger head that just emerged, wide and hard as a boulder.

It was a mallet coming in to strike, and strike it did, sailing through the water out of nowhere and opening up to reveal a set of teeth. The sperm whale caught the squid right as its bottom jaw opened just enough to crunch down, pumping its tail in joy as it sped away with its newfound calamari. The squid's arms and tentacles flailed on the side of its gigantic frame until they began to slow down and then hung limp out of the whale's mouth.

Dallas leaned against a rock as she watched the whale swim away until that mallet head grew smaller and smaller, bringing her heart rate and breathing back to as steady as she could manage. She kept her hand on her chest to will herself to a relaxed state, squishing hagfish slime in the process, and then Dallas started to laugh.

She did not seek out the museum as soon as she landed at Pink Sands, but rather, a bathroom.

The closest place turned out to be a donut shop with brightly colored blue and green rings decorating the window display. Dallas quickly made her way to the bathroom before the stares could linger on the mermaid covered in sticky goo with a strange-looking bone in her netting.

She was relieved to see that this place had individual bathrooms and shut the lock. On the left was a blue, glossy bowl with jets lining the inside, and on the right was a tall structure with a sprinkler head and dispenser. She went to the right and turned on the head, pulling on its spiral hose as it vacuumed up and down, picking up every ounce of slime.

When she thought she was clean enough, she helped herself to the cleansing scrub from the dispenser and worked it into her scales, using the hose for another minute before heading out.

The buildings here were small and spaced close enough together with clean pathways in the sand, one leading to another and leading out to common swim traffic and dug so deep they looked free of the common grit and grime from the ocean. They were pale in color, which made the pathways easier to see.

Dallas.had her tablet out with the map, already matching up the very path she was on. She joined the swim traffic of merpeople, some swimming either on the path for closer destinations or swimming above to reach further places. While making her way through town, she stopped looking at her tablet and instead continued down the end of the road. The buildings all took on the same shapes and color schemes in the commercial part of town, and she turned right as she scanned them for the one that would not follow this pattern, echolocation not even needed.

The first thing about it that was not a square or in the colors of blue, beige, brown, or black was obvious. It looked like a giant sugar cube shaved into a one-sided pyramid. Dallas swam up this slope, amused, knowing this was the equivalent of climbing a flight of stairs. The sign at the top gave the establishment its name, as though it was needed, in a salmon color that looked like it had been much brighter once upon a time.

The entrance was a pair of double doors accompanied by glass windows on each side, and she could see a small line at the reception kiosk for admission. Dallas opened the door and bypassed the line, feeling the stares the minute she swam through with the prized item behind her back.

The receptionist darted her attention to Dallas and stopped mid-sentence with the customer in front of her. "Oh, yes?"

"I'm here for Kendall Wadsworth."

"Oh, okay. Just a sec."

Dallas hung back and immersed herself in the informational posters clinging to the walls, the lists of exhibits, and the map of the building's layout. They started at the top of the pyramid and worked their way down to two more levels, the very bottom level an entire exhibit of the ancient civilization that used to live there millions of years ago. She mentally moved down, down, down the map in the flow of traffic from prehistoric fish skeletons to displays of ancient merpeople and the evolution process.

"Dallas, wow!"

Dallas turned just in time for Kendall to swim up to her, and she only went behind her to keep her eye on Dallas's back.

"My God, look at it! Come on, let's go to my office."

Kendall led Dallas to a door on the right that said "staff only" in chipped gold letters and shut the door behind them, taking the opportunity to poke her finger through the netting to touch the bone.

"You've made me a very happy woman."

"Glad to."

They swam to her office with matching navy blue plush chairs. Dallas didn't sit, remaining upright while Kendall re-shut the door behind her. She took the netting off her back and opened it.

Kendall's eyes grew and glistened the more she scanned over the bone, reaching out to brush the outline of the jaw and braving those teeth with a light stroke.

"Just, wow, I can't believe this. I am so happy someone was able to do this for me. Thank you so much, Dallas!"

Kendall changed her focus from the jawbone to Dallas, peering at her with concern.

"What... what happened to you?"

Dallas smoothed her hair and brushed her cheeks; imagining the cuts and bruises she might have received that she was too busy to notice.

Kendall was looking at something around her waist.

"What is that?"

Dallas turned her gaze and twisted her torso enough to see the globs of slime leftover on her lower back, hanging off her shark skin kilt.

"Hagfish," Dallas answered.

Kendall's brows went up in recognition and understanding.

"I got most of it off."

"Not to worry. Seems like you went through a bit of trouble to get this, didn't you?"

"Not...too much."

"So, you got it while the body was still...decomposing and brought it here in one piece without any problems. I can't tell you how much I appreciate that. I know they are going to make a mold of the teeth, but this head is just so perfect."

Kendall was swimming around to her desk in the middle of the conversation and picked up her tablet.

"Okay, what's your Cashflow email?"

Dallas told her, and she typed it in. When finished, she turned to look up at Dallas with a knowing smile.

"You don't know what this means to me, this rare piece of ancient history that is still around, and I appreciate you taking the time and effort to go get this for me...and especially since you're the one who helped get it caught in the first place."

Dallas's tablet pinged with the deposit notification, and she took it out to see, nearly dropping it with the gasp that escaped her mouth as she saw, and had to keep blinking to keep seeing the amount of two thousand dollars.

CHAPTER 40

MOST OF THE TIME she ignored the bulletin board or silently appreciated it when she passed it, but today she wanted to read that article again and see that group photo and her position in the front row, smiling to avoid looking too pompous or too shy. Her interview followed the introduction and backstory paragraphs on the creature and then the initial capture itself, with her headshot looking like a forced yearbook photo.

Q: Were you scared?
A: Not really. I mean, I was, but I was more focused on what I could do and what I had to do.
Q: So you had a plan?
A: I didn't until I got in there. I had to figure out the lay of the caverns first and how I could use them, and how I could go places the frilled shark couldn't.
Q: They say that you have very advanced skills in echolocation and you have the longest range out of anyone on your team, even the Marine Force! Was this a skill you have been practicing for a long time?
A: No. Actually, it wasn't. I didn't even know I had it until I tried it, and then as I practiced more, I just

got better and better at it. It has become something that comes naturally to me, and I really enjoy getting better at it. I love to explore, and I feel that it is a part of me I always had but did not know or see too much of until I became my mer self.

Q: That is very impressive. How did you tell your team what your plans were?

A: I really didn't. I found their positions through echolocation and had them stay at the exit where I could have the frilled shark chase me out, and then they could get it.

"Still regretting your photo, Miss Dwight?"

Dallas spun around and, by habit, ran her fingers through the front part of her hair.

"I rest my case."

She scowled a little, but only a little, half regretting stopping so close to the envoy offices.

"Day off again, huh?" Noah asked.

"Yep."

"Well, you seem to be in good health for someone who has been sick the last two days."

Dallas froze, keeping her face stoic. Noah smirked at her.

"I talked with Clyde today."

"Uh..."

Dallas expected Noah to say more, but instead, he waited for her response. She wondered if he knew something she did not.

"I went to get the frilled shark jaw and deliver it to the museum lady."

"Yeah, I know that."

"I—just needed some personal time after that, that's all. I needed a mental rest."

"Was it that straining for you that you had to call in sick twice?"

Dallas straightened her back. "Straining? No! I actually enjoyed the challenge of being out in the wild and dealing with wild things, like hagfish and squid and some other things. It's not like I get out much anyway... and I was just tired and wanted time to myself. Really."

Noah considered her for a minute.

Dallas tugged at her messenger bag to balance the weight of library books and noticed the bag that Noah had around his shoulder was not a bag.

"You...play?"

"Yeah, I am going to The Drunken Ship tonight. It's an open mic night. Good to let loose and do something relaxing. I thought I'd warm up a bit and hang out with Mickey."

He let that sentence hang in the air, and Dallas was not sure how to respond.

"Come by if you like."

Dallas looked at him as his tone changed to make those words stick. They were the gentler and more relaxed kind, much more than the business-casual tone one had during business hours. This was the tone that came after, the voice people were apt to listen to more, which was the very reason Dallas gave a little shrug and said, "Sure."

With no familiar faces, yet, the only option was to lurk at the bar.

On stage was a stand-up comic whose routine involved a dramatic pause and turn of the head to the audience before he delivered each punchline. Dallas could not make out half his words when he spoke too loudly into the mic, but that was not where her attention was. She waved her tail under the stool and caught sight of the red mane at the end of the bar making its way down.

Mickey grinned at her.

"How you doin', honey?"

"All right! Here for the open mic night."

"Good, I hope you get up there. There are a lot of open slots."

Dallas laughed. "Sure, maybe after a Captain Nemo's Ale."

"Coming right up."

Dallas scanned the area casually and then turned back to the comic by default. Out of the corner of the stage was the ruffling of the curtain, and then a fluke from the side. Noah flipped back the rest of the curtain and swam out from the backstage area. Dallas's arm jerked in the first instinct to wave but held back. She watched him to see if he would notice her or if he were looking for her. He swam by the bar and looked up to meet her eyes, instantly connecting, and all she had to do was rest her cheek in her fist and wait for him to come over.

She pretended to check her tablet and put it down once he sat next to her.

"So, you did make it."

"Yeah," she said. "Why not? Good atmosphere. I needed to get away from my TV anyway."

Mickey appeared a moment later with Dallas's beer, the bottom of the glass still frosted. She took notice of Noah and the way he sat on the stool: half-on, half-off, with his tail trying to decide which direction to rest.

"All right, you, do you want something yet?"

"Nah," Noah said. "Not yet. Maybe wait until I get closer, or I don't know. I'll see."

"Okay," Mickey said with a little grin before moving on to the next customer.

Noah sighed and finger-combed his hair.

"Remember, I told you I haven't played in a while?"

"Yeah," Dallas said after a sip. The honey aftertaste lingered on her tongue, and she liked it very much. She couldn't bring herself to say that it was her first beer.

"Well, I haven't played in a while. I couldn't just jump into it. You, though, it doesn't bother you?"

"No," Dallas stated truthfully. "It doesn't. With me, I always feel like I am in control. That is, except for the last time when I did more than just sing."

Noah snickered. "Maybe you can help me out tonight."

She lowered her bottle. "With what?"

The next act came on stage, which was two merwomen setting up microphones while someone prepared their musical track accompaniment.

"Well, I can't decide what song to do. I know a million of them, of course, but maybe it would help if I had someone else, maybe someone who can sing along."

Dallas burst out laughing. "Okay, so that's why you invited me out."

"Hey, no, not completely. I mean, I only thought of it when I saw you. You don't have to if you don't want to, but, you know, seeing as how you enjoy it and you're good at it. What do you say?"

Dallas took a longer drink.

"Guess I don't have a choice!" she said. "I mean, you've helped me, so I don't see why I shouldn't help you."

Noah gave her shoulder a squeeze before realizing he did so, pulling back instantly.

"Thanks so much. I mean, you're not going to echo-blast and faint again, are you?"

She glared at him.

"Just kidding."

The merwomen on stage did their own song number, a duet Dallas did not recognize.

"When are you supposed to go on?"

"Two more after this."

She jerked her chin at him. "Well, that's a bit soon. What were you planning on doing if I wasn't here?"

"Being awkward and nervous."

Noah listed off a few of the songs that he knew and then went on to ask her if she knew the lyrics. Dallas perked up at one.

"Yeah," she said, pointing. "That one. I definitely know that one!"

Noah smiled. "Okay. That's it then. How about we practice a little? Bring your beer with you."

Dallas picked it up with a laugh and followed Noah to the makeshift backstage, which was nothing more than a cloth drapery pinned in place. He led her over a pile of cases on the floor, where she recognized his guitar.

"Okay, let's do a quick run-through and make sure you know all the lyrics."

"Oh," Dallas started. "Don't worry, I do."

They ran the song once, just in time for the last act to exit the stage. Noah held on to his guitar and slung the strap around his back. When Dallas followed him to the entrance, he took a moment to turn around slightly—not all the way, but just enough for his chin to reach his shoulder, and not enough to look at her.

"Hey... thanks."

Dallas waited a few moments before responding, "You're welcome," just before the guy on staff announced the next act and pulled the curtain away.

"So, we have an addition to this act here," the guy introduced. "Music and lyrics with Noah and his friend Dallas. Let's give it up for them!"

The bar audience responded with the appropriate applause while Noah squeezed the neck of his guitar. They both clumped next to the microphone for a minute while he leaned in.

"Thanks, everyone. We'll be performing 'What's Up' by The Four Non-Blondes."

Noah darted away from the microphone, leaving it all to Dallas while he took a breath and started the intro.

Dallas came in at her cue, channeling that smooth rock tone. She cradled the mic while Noah cradled the neck and strummed. Starting off smooth and easy with gentle "hey, yay, yays," Dallas sang like an old pair of pants that she always had—comfortable and a perfect fit with just enough wear.

Gradually, she packed more punch into the chorus, just as Noah strummed those strings a bit harder at the same time. They performed better than they had in practice, and out of the corner of her eye, she tried to catch Noah's expression.

All she could see was the way his grin widened with each strum. Mostly, she focused on a point on the wall where she could connect with the audience. There were plenty of smiles there too, and as they finished the number, the bar erupted in applause and "woots."

Finally, Dallas looked right at Noah as he rested his guitar on his tail, returning her gaze with an understanding that words could not explain.

"Let's hear it for them!" the staff guy called again as Dallas and Noah took a bow and exited through the stage curtain. On their way, a few people high-fived them.

"That was great," Noah said. "That was great! You were great."

"That was," Dallas admitted. "Hey, I mean, nothing like a little impromptu performance, huh? It was fun."

Noah put his guitar away in the case. "You are more Linda Perry than Linda Perry," he said, getting a laugh out of Dallas. "Let's celebrate with some drinks."

Face-to-face at a small table in the corner, where they could still see the stage but mostly chose not to, Dallas mostly drank in Noah's words while she held her new beer bottle.

"But you weren't nervous," she pointed out. "You nailed it once you relaxed and got into it."

"Thanks. But still, I told you, I haven't performed live in front of an audience in a really long time. You helped me up there, so I owe you. I just don't feel like myself sometimes, and that really does it for me. I feel more like myself when I can do what I really want to do."

Dallas felt and heard those words click in her head—the very ones she herself had not said out loud. For a moment, they didn't say much else, simply allowing the next singing act to fill the background noise. Something else was building inside Dallas; somehow, hearing Noah's insecurities invited her own to come out of hiding. She let them linger before they overflowed from the rim of her mind, thinking there was no better time than the present.

"I know how you feel," Dallas blurted out. "I haven't really felt too much like myself lately, and sometimes I just feel really held back. Like I'm not living up to my full potential. Finding ways to channel that is important. I just... wish I had more."

Noah's eyes softened after the rush of stage time and the consumption of alcohol, but Dallas knew that was not all.

"I thought you liked being a hunter/gatherer."

"I do; I do; it's not that. Not completely."

"What is it?"

"I wish I could...do more. I mean, I like my job, but I wish I could do more of what I really want to do too."

Noah leaned forward. "So, what is it you want to do?"

Dallas took a breath all the way down to her deepest core. All the thoughts that had been swirling around in her mind for the past couple of weeks and months finally changed direction and headed for a finish line. She looked at him, really looked at him—someone who was not that much older than her, but the common ground was still fresh.

"You know how I did the thing for Kendall Wadsworth at the museum and got her the frilled shark jaw?"

"Yeah..."

And then Dallas, for the first time, spilled all the thoughts she had been having for the past few months, coming together in simple sentences. She surprised herself to learn just how easy it was to say and knew it would not have been so if the conversation had taken place in Noah's office.

CHAPTER 41

DALLAS OPENED UP HER tablet and searched the news again.

It was usually the first thing she did, mostly skimming over articles about new movie theaters opening and classes for merfolk getting dual citizenship on land. Nothing else she thought she would see. She browsed another site with different postings. It was a site floating around the Currents social media pages called "Posters for All," dedicated to every kind of job posting from babysitting to an opening in a CPA firm. She scanned these posts for about five seconds before something caught her eye. The keywords for a particular post read "searching for" and "hunter/gatherer," so she clicked on it right away and read the description:

Oracle, Orleans Oceanic District
Gulf of Mexico, North Province

Doctor seeking research on and information on different kinds of venom, looking to collect as many specimens as possible for pharmaceutical development. Need someone willing to travel and collect specimens to fit the doctor's needs. Atlantic and Pacific. Please reply to message with experience. Thank you!

- Trudy, Medical Assistant to Dr. Cecile DuFresne

Dallas's brow raised in intrigue, though not in consideration. That was quite the swim. She hadn't even been to all parts of the North Province, let alone the other parts of the Atlantic. Still, she couldn't help but feel disappointed that it was not closer. It certainly seemed like the type of thing she could do and the type of thing she should be on the lookout for. Dallas bookmarked that page, deciding that she could use it as an example. She entered "hunter/gatherer" in the search box and browsed anything local, which was not much. She came across one about an hour away via sub:

Cloveland, South Province

Textile company seeking a hunter/gatherer to find and collect kelp to be woven into tunics. Reply with work history.

She shrugged and bookmarked that one too. Dallas ran her tongue over her teeth, feeling the grime of the waffles and coffee, and realized she forgot to brush them. She made a mental note to update her resume later and headed to her bathroom to start the day's routine that she had put off. It wasn't until a few brushes later that her tablet lit up with Albany's name and picture. She hit the jets in the sink to suck away the toothpaste and then answered the phone while still holding her toothbrush, thinking that she had taken a couple of days to respond.

"Ally, hey."

"Hey! I'm sorry I didn't get back to you sooner!"

Dallas wiped toothpaste from her lip. "No, it's all right."

"I have been SWAMPED. Everyone and their mom wants to plan parties right now that there is no more frilled shark."

Dallas rolled her eyes, even though Albany could not see her.

"I've actually got Piper Hammond's baby shower today."

Dallas blinked at the name. "Hammond? Oh! Marcus's wife!"

"Yeah, you know them! They were both swim instructors during my OAC classes."

"Yeah."

"It's funny you were asking if I could hang out, because actually they want to invite you to the shower."

Dallas's brows jumped in surprise. "Me? They do?"

"Yeah, you know I talked you up, and their little daughter Harmony is a singer too and she wants to meet you! They said to bring you if you're not doing anything. I mean, you don't have to if you don't want to, but I figured you wouldn't say no to free food."

Dallas snickered. "Of course! I need to get out a little bit anyway," she said out loud. *And to ask for your help with something,* she thought to herself. Normally, she probably would not have, but all signs were pointing to this being the opportunity to talk to her sister and get her insight.

"Great! I'll send you the address!"

"All right, I'll text you when I'm on my way."

Dallas grinned, her bathroom mirror reflecting that smudge of toothpaste on her lip.

"Okay, bye!"

Dallas put her tablet on the counter and swam to the tub. She took a quick scrub with the pink salt soap that smelled like grapefruit, and then, after setting off those jets, she ran a comb with conditioner through her hair. She started to feel hungry again but ignored it. There was no doubt Albany would have the caterer start the party right on the nose, as she usually did with her events.

After putting on her blue tunic with the shorter sleeves, she left her house and made her way through the neighborhood, ensuring she took the right pipeline from the municipal center. Marcus and Piper Hammond were close to the library.

Dallas smiled at the pink balloons tied to the door handle and the ribbon decorating the doorframe. She rang the buzzer and, within seconds, the door opened.

"Hi!" cried a high-pitched, enthusiastic voice. Dallas caught a whirr of black violet and hundreds of braids before she was tackled.

"Harmony, stop that! Give the poor girl some breathing room."

Marcus appeared in the doorway just as Harmony released the surprised Dallas.

"I'm sorry," the child said, flashing Dallas a smile with one missing tooth.

"She's just excited," Marcus explained.

"No, it's okay! I'm glad to be here," Dallas said.

"Come on in," Marcus said, giving Dallas a fist bump. "How are you?"

"Not bad."

"So, this little guppy, as I'm sure you know, is Harmony."

"Nice to finally meet you, Harmony."

"She has been excited to meet you after Albany told us how good of a singer you are."

Marcus brought Dallas into the house, where merpeople were holding drinks and hanging out in the living room. Tables were all set out and decorated in pink and white. Dallas saw the cake already on display. "It's a girl!" sat on top in fat letters with a purple tail sticking out, lined with darker pink icing.

"We told her three times not to touch it," Marcus said with a laugh.

"But Mommy promised me the first piece!" Harmony insisted. "And I get to eat the tail because it looks like mine."

A mermaid came around the corner, and Dallas immediately knew she was meeting Piper. Aside from her protruding belly stretching her scales and tail, Dallas could see where Harmony got her dark violet tail and a skin tone that was a purple wash over smooth cocoa all the way up to her eyes. Her own hair was also in hundreds of braids, but they had all been braided into one woven plait that barely went down her back.

"And this, of course, is my lovely wife."

Piper smiled. "Okay, you're Dallas."

"That I am."

"Yeah, you sure do look a little like Albany. I can see it now. She's in the kitchen right now. Come on."

Dallas followed the Hammonds until she found her sister, clad in a blue buttoned tunic shirt with her logo in red across the left: Right up your Ally!

"Hi Dally! Oh, cute shirt! Okay, the caterer is putting the food together now and should have it all out and ready in time for everyone else to get here. And then we'll do the games."

They got to enjoy lunch quicker than they thought. Everyone filled their plates with breaded fish, potato salad, and rolls. Dallas got a spot at a table with Albany and the Hammonds.

"It almost tastes like chicken," Marcus joked, prompting a laugh from everyone at the table but Harmony.

"What does chicken taste like?"

Dallas looked at her in surprise.

Piper smiled. "We'll get some soon when it becomes more available. It's, well, it's like a gator, except gator is much chewier."

"Oh," Harmony said.

Piper turned to Dallas, her expression curious as she realized it.

"Harmony has never been on land."

Dallas nodded. "Oh, I see."

"She was born in the sea and spent all her eight years down here."

"I forget about that too," Albany admitted.

"I'm gonna see land someday," Harmony declared. "I'm going when I get bigger. So, I can walk with my legs. Is it weird? Do you fall down a lot?"

Marcus chuckled. "Babies do a little when they learn to walk for the first time. Don't you worry; we won't bring you to transition until you're older and ready, okay?"

"Okay," Harmony said, looking around the table at all the grown-ups who had walked on legs before, no doubt trying to imagine it.

"Raising a first-generation mermaid the first time was definitely interesting," Piper said between bites. "Now, we'll have another one."

Harmony, next to her mother, leaned in close and gently smoothed a hand down her belly.

"Don't worry," everyone at the table heard her whisper. "When you get big enough, I will already be big enough so then I can teach you everything."

She patted her mom's belly, and everyone around the table pretended they didn't hear and resumed their own conversations.

The "Guess the Name" game turned out to be a version of Hangman, revealing the new Hammond's name as "Melody Laine Hammond."

"We swear, it's a coincidence that Harmony likes music and can sing," Piper joked. "We don't know which side of the family she gets that from. Who knows what will happen with this little Melody?"

Albany helped cut the cake and hand out slices. Dallas mostly watched Harmony and the way she paid extra attention to her mother's belly, enjoying the sight of two sisters having a conversation that was only for them.

They were among the last to leave, with Marcus settling payment for Albany, and Harmony telling Dallas about all the songs she sings in choir at school. They left the house, both overfull from the late lunch and the dessert of ice cream cake, with Dallas still having small crumbles on her tunic and chest scales.

"Aren't they so cool?" Albany said the moment they swam away. "I knew you would get along with them."

"They are. What a cute little family."

"I know! Harmony made me melt when I first met her! Thanks so much for coming along; it was a good excuse to invite you to a party."

"I had fun."

"Piper and I hung out more once she got on maternity leave, and we became fast friends. Did you know she's in the Marine Force too?"

"No kidding."

"Yeah, that's how she and Marcus met. I had Marcus for the OAC Swim training too, so then when I came down here and saw him a few times, he put me in touch with the missus when she wanted to plan a shower."

"That's too cool."

They swam along home, Dallas waiting for the perfect opening.

"I am so proud of you, Ally. You know, you are really inspiring."

"Aww, I am? For what?"

"For being you. For being a self-starter and go-getter. You can stand on your own two feet. Well, you know what I mean. You're so independent."

"Thanks, Dally. It wasn't easy to begin with, but it was perfect timing to still be living with Mom and Dad for a bit before I could go on my own."

"That's the thing... Ally. I need your help."

Her sister turned to her, amused and surprised.

"You need my help? With what?"

"I came up with an idea. An idea I have been thinking about, doing some of my own...'things.' It started when I got the frilled shark jaw for the museum lady, and it got me thinking. That's exactly what I want to do."

"Okay," Albany said, looking at her now.

"I need, like, all the advice in the world from you because I got to talking to Noah, and I realized just how serious I was and how much I want to make this happen. But I need something else too that you have that is very specific. Can you get me in touch with your friend from ClickPrints?"

Albany broke out in a smile wide enough to show the line of a dimple in her right cheek, the one she only reached when she was really happy.

"Dally, whatever you're planning, I want *in*."

CHAPTER 42

DALLAS WATCHED THE POSTAL sub drift in and make its way to the start of the cavern. When it came around to her postal box, she noticed the blue and pink envelope the postal merman slipped in, and she flapped her tail up and down in excitement. As soon as the sub circled around to the rest of the neighborhood, she dashed out to retrieve the thing she had been waiting for, what seemed like eons.

She pried open the little ClickPrints box to find the collection all wrapped up, fighting with the wrapping to show her exactly what she wanted to hold in her hands and see up close and personal:

Dallas Dwight
"Wielder of Sonar"
Freelance Hunter/Gatherer Expert
wielderofsonar@wayword.com

At first, she was skeptical about using the midnight blue color in fear it would blend in with the sea too much and get lost easily, but her bright gold lettering made it stand out, complete with the glossy wave design starting from the bottom left and going up to the top right corner. When held and moved at the right angles, those rings lit up, looking like a sonar wave in action.

Dallas moved the card package repeatedly to watch the effect with giddy squeals. She got the smaller bulk print of two hundred cards to start with, knowing these would last a while. In the package was a promotional card offering her fifteen percent off her next order. It had no expiration date, and she did not really know how or where she would be distributing cards.

She went back inside with her goods, keeping the cards with the box so she knew where they were at all times. The orange-pineapple smoothie drink still sat on the coffee table in the living room where she had left it earlier, so now she sat down to resume enjoying it and resume her earlier activity.

Dallas put the box down on the table and picked up her tablet, pulling up the browser to the saved document she had obsessively written and rewritten.

> My name is Dallas Dwight, and I am a hunter/gatherer from Gneiss Underway, in the West Atlantic in the West Province. I have been a hunter/gatherer for less than a year, but the experience and drive that I have had in that short time make me worthy of freelance work. My echolocation range can go out to about a hundred feet. Recently, an unknown predator has threatened the area I live in, and I served as a volunteer in the Marine Force, where I single-handedly led to the capture of a frilled shark. The newspaper article is attached for reference.

I took on the task of fetching the bone remains of the frilled shark for museum curator Kendall Wadsworth at the "Oceans Through the Ages" Museum. I went out on my own and not only located the jaw but managed to fend for myself against other predators with my growing knowledge about the open ocean. My passion for the wild makes me a contender for exploration and survival.

Dallas smirked at the cover letter, proud of her accomplishments in general, but also in how she crafted it just a teensy bit more colorful to make it sound the best. She pulled out a single card from the box and took a picture of it, adding it to the CV along with one more thing: the link to the newspaper article.

She made sure it was a big enough version so they could see the picture, even though she still hated how dorky she looked; she needed to be seen. The last thing to do was leave contact info and make sure her card photo was in the right place, and hit save, knowing that everything she already had would be enough.

She sat back and finished the pineapple drink, now ready to browse Currents and the ads she had already saved. She pulled up the home page and was about to access her bookmarked pages folder when a new article headline froze her in place.

Her finger hovered over the scroll bar on the right-hand side as her brain processed the words and the description, while she reformulated an image in her head. She stopped short at the words "barnacle beast" that appeared in more than one news headline:

'Barnacle Beast' Spotted Again in Rolling Rocks Valley

Hunter/Gatherers Claim to See Mammalian Creature Near Texan Provinces

Growing Urban Legend 'Barnacle Beast' from the Gulf of Mexico

Dallas clicked on the first article, leading her to a piece from a newspaper in one of the Texan-influenced provinces:

> There have been reports of an unidentifiable creature seen in the Rolling Rocks Valley. The creature is described as large for a fish but small for a whale, with no telling if it is a mammal or fish, having an abnormal, tall and skinny shape with long fins.

> Witnesses state that this creature looked like it had a massive growth of barnacles all over its body, which made it hard to identify. "It looked like something that woke from a long sleep on some coral, covered in things growing all over it," says Jane Arnold of Rolling Rocks. "I saw it traveling to Barkmen Brush from afar."

> Other witnesses claim to see such a creature not only covered in barnacles but also having some sort of

slime-like substance. "It has to be venomous," says Gerald Lane of Rolling Rocks. "My wife and I saw something swimming very fast, and it looked like there was a yellow slime that came out of it. That should be enough to tell merpeople to stay away from it."

Dallas speedread one article before moving on to another, scanning similar information and many more claims of having seen a large, monstrous thing. She clicked on more to find a visual, but so far none.

One website included an artist's exaggerated rendering that looked like it belonged in a graphic novel: a large, blobby-looking thing with boils all over it, each resembling a mini volcano erupting yellow pus. Its face was a crude cartoon with a wide, fang-toothed mouth and demon red eyes, complete with an angry eyebrow "V."

Dallas leapt up, dashing to her room to find the notebook she needed. She brought it back out and opened to the page of the sloppy sketch she made not long ago...of the thing she echolocated not long ago: the large, blobby-looking thing with something like appendages or boils sticking out all over it. It could not be barnacles because barnacles did not produce slime. Dallas felt her insides spreading with ice, freezing her chest like she drank an Icee too fast, settling right over her heart. She knew that was no turtle.

Dallas put in "Gulf of Mexico Barnacle Beast" as her next search in her home browser and watched the results multiply, all speculation, all saying the same things.

Child Attacked by Clawed Creature Near New Gill, Gulf of Mexico Province

Seven-year-old Ari Marsh was playing on the school playground, swimming through hoops when she saw something strange. She described it as looking like a little whale covered in sea sand, barnacles, and seaweed. Before she knew it, the creature lunged at her and tried to grab her with its long claws. Thankfully, the child was uninjured but traumatized enough to rush to her teacher to tell her what happened. By then, the creature was gone, and the only description available was what Ari provided. Authorities searching the area did not find such an animal but are urging merpeople to be on the lookout.

She pulled up a map included with an article that showed the Gulf of Mexico and the surrounding provinces of Mexico and Texas, with red dots indicating reported sightings. Most of them were near Texan communities. She browsed through the maps and reports of more recent sightings, noting how those red dots seemed to have originated from the Caribbean and, before that, the Atlantic. She bit her lip. The most recent sighting was in New Gill, near another town called Oracle.

Oracle.

Oracle?

Dallas felt the ice in her chest instantly melt with the new heat she was feeling.

She returned to her bookmarked tab and rapidly scrolled until she found it, confirming her suspicion. It was Oracle. She scanned all the way down the ad until she found the phone number and instantly pressed on the phone icon.

Dallas's heart pounded as it rang. It pounded even harder when someone picked up on the fourth ring, leaving her unsure of what to say.

"Hello, Dr. DuFresne's office."

"Hi, um, I'm calling about your ad for a hunter/gatherer?"

"Oh! Yes! You got the right person. My name is Trudy, and I posted the ad."

"I'm interested in learning more about it. I'm a hunter/gatherer looking for...some extra work."

"Well, we're looking for someone who knows their way around and can navigate easily. Have you handled venomous sea creatures in the wild before?"

"Yes, I have. More recently, I caught some black dragonfish, and other times I've caught lionfish."

"How long have you been a hunter/gatherer?"

"Not long," Dallas admitted. "But I caught a frilled shark. Alone."

"A what? I've never heard of one of those. Where are you located?"

"West Atlantic. Gneiss Underway."

A pause.

"Oh! Are you willing to come this far? To Oracle in the Orleans Oceanic in the Gulf of Mexico Province?"

Without skipping a beat, Dallas answered, "Yes."

She left the house with her lunch pack at her side; her mind filled with different conversation scenarios of what Clyde would say.

The others were all in the lounge area, scrolling through tablets and casually chatting while waiting for the rest of the team to filter in. Dallas put her lunch away and saw that it was still too early for her to punch in, so she headed to the office in the back room, where Clyde was typing away on the computer.

"Clyde?"

"Yes?"

Dallas entered the room, tablet ready. "I want to talk to you about vacation time."

"What?" Clyde said, with hints of a laugh. He turned to her, wiping his forehead like the thought hurt his head. "Vacation time? You don't get vacation time since you haven't been here a year, and those accumulate over time."

"I just will need a few days, tops. Nothing big."

Clyde regarded her, no doubt her recent sick days hanging in the air between them.

"For what?"

"I was thinking of going to the Gulf of Mexico, the Orleans Oceanic district to see a friend."

She paused, letting Clyde gather his thoughts, not volunteering any other information.

"That's probably not going to happen right now."

"Why not?"

"Because a lot of our routes finally opened back up and we need to get back on track to make up for lost time and lost supplies we all had to make last. We need all hands on deck right now."

"I see that, but—"

"I get that things opening back up slowly but surely also means you want to get out more, I do, but this is not a good time."

"Okay...I'll...maybe figure something out for later."

Clyde gave a little nod and then returned to typing, not taking his eyes off the screen.

Dallas left to check the time clock, parking herself right there until it was time to clock in with nothing to do but think. Though she was sure of everything, she needed to stop and figure out her next moves. It was easy to go about the day, focused on the tasks at hand while forming a soft plan in her head. She gathered shells, not caring if she scooped up the small ones along with the big ones.

At one point, Dallas was suddenly hit with an idea, unannounced, nagging at her brain, making her stop what she was doing and whip out her tablet. She opened the icon to her Wayword email and started composing a message, keeping it short but covering all the basics. She then attached the articles, all the ones she found that were at least consistent, and sent it all over.

Throughout the rest of the day, she took her tablet out for a minute just to check for a response. Whenever she was alone, she kept the pouch on her belt open, always resting her hand near it. Any waking opportunity she had, she would sneak a peek, only to be met by the blank screen and unchanging icon of her Wayword email.

Dallas held on to a net of fighting lobsters, echolocating the surrounding area to scan for any more. The area around her remained empty and blank, nothing but blue with nothing to swim around or hide behind. She gathered the netting to swim back to the rest of the team, not entirely trusting the quiet.

For now, she had to take it easy and keep her cool. As promised, she arranged the phone call with her family.

"*Well?*" came Albany, the ever-enthusiastic optimist.

"Clyde won't let me go."

"*What?*"

"*Why not?*"

"*What did he say?*"

Dallas talked over the three of them.

"...something about needing all the staff and doing more routes and stuff and not a good time. I just..."

"*Did you tell him what it was for?*" asked Mom.

Dallas cringed. "I feel like I can't. He'll think I'm nuts."

"*What do you want to do?*"

"I know what I want to do," Dallas answered quietly.

"*Do not quit your job,*" her dad had said almost immediately. "*You can't rely on these separate gigs completely. Not yet, and not now.*"

"*You need time to grow your client list,*" Albany reminded. "*And if it ever takes off well enough, then you can consider it. But you need to start slow and work your way up. That's what I did.*"

"*You can do as many as you want and as much as you can. You can work around it!*" her mother chimed in. "*But maybe right now if it's not going to work out you should just wait until the next gig. Your father is right. Do not quit.*"

Dallas kept all these thoughts in addition to her own, taking them with a grain of salt, but knowing to stick to her instincts. She had kept it to herself that she already received the phone call from Trudy officially offering her the job; All she wanted was to swim freely with nothing but the open ocean, but she had to pull on those reins. Those new cards burned a hole in the box they sat in.

CHAPTER 43

She opened the stand on her tablet and propped it up on the couch vertically. Lying on her stomach with her tail bent over her head, her fin looking like an awning, she adjusted the stand to a more acute angle and started her search.

The first things that came up were general destination websites with photos of hotels to stay at and "just like on land!" marketing proclamations. There were sections on Mardi Gras events and tourist appeal year-round. Dallas admittedly got sidetracked, pulling up photos of merpeople in traditional Mardi Gras attire altered to undersea equivalents.

They wore long, sequined robes complete with matching glittering "stockings" on their tails, with headpieces and jewelry adorning their necks. There were pictures of oceanfront restaurants holding similar décor, the glittering green and gold ribbons laced around their patios while merpeople held abnormally shaped vials and glasses filled with different colored liquids, topped with floppy stems of seaweed.

Perhaps, she could think of this as a vacation as well. Dallas clicked back to her other search results and scrolled through the websites and articles that mentioned the Orleans Oceanic District or the Gulf of Mexico. She pulled down another book and flipped to the back index to find the corresponding pages. The information in this book was vague, giving her the basic flora and fauna just like the previous sections.

Dallas scanned pages on different whales even though she was not convinced of pinpointing one. There were pictures of whales and different types of dolphins, but all their flippers were proportionally short compared to the rest of their bodies. She still could not imagine any of them reaching out to anyone or anything in the way it was described. Kids tended to exaggerate, and really anybody could, especially when startled and describing something. There was no such thing as a whale with long arms.

Dallas looked up sections on barnacles to read about the different things they attached to. It was mainly whales, turtles, and crabs. She pulled another book from the shelf and flipped to the section she wanted, reading mostly the same information. Frustrated, she put the two books she had back where she found them. Nothing mentioned anything about yellow slime.

She picked it up on the first ring.

"Hi, Sean, thanks for calling me back!"

"You're good. So, you say you want the eleventh and twelfth covered?"

"If possible, yeah, if you can swing it."

"Yeah, I can do both."

"Really?" Dallas's voice squeaked a little more than she intended. "Sean, that's great, I, thank you so much."

"No problem, I could use the extra money. I'll send the email for the shift change."

"Thank you again. Oh, I have to go, Lydia's on the other line. Talk to you later!"

"*Bye!*"

Dallas hit the button, smearing it a bit with ketchup paste.

"Hey Lydia!"

"*Hi Dallas, what dates were you giving away?*"

"Well, Sean is taking the eleventh and twelfth. Do you think you could do the thirteenth?"

"*Yeah, that's good. I can do that.*"

Dallas's stomach bubbled more than when she drank the carbonated beverage.

"I appreciate this so much."

"*Of course. Do you want to send the email or should I?*"

"Could you please?" went Dallas's voice, again raising to a higher, begging octave.

"*Yeah. Everything okay?*"

"I'm fine, just want to take a small trip, not really a vacation but I don't have vacation time, so, just a couple days. No big deal."

"*Oh, Clyde wouldn't let you go?*"

"I mean, I guess we're busy right now, so he wouldn't just let me take off. But it will only be a couple days."

"*Okay.*"

"Thank you again, I'll return the favor!"

Dallas pulled her tablet away from her ear, seeing the ketchup paste and smearing it away. It had only barely touched her plate, and she had barely begun to eat before she started to get responses. Dallas popped the chicken nuggets in her mouth and pulled up her calendar, officially marking the dates that she had, all corresponding with the already given days off.

Before she finished chewing, her email notification pinged, and she took it out, opening the new email message she had been awaiting from Kendall Wadsworth:

Re: Gulf of Mexico

Hi Dallas!

That is great news! I'm so happy to hear that you're branching out to challenge yourself and help others. I know that you'll deliver to others the same way you delivered to me!

About this barnacle beast thing you described, I have to say it does not ring a bell. It doesn't describe anything that would exist in the Gulf of Mexico or even in the Caribbean Sea, or anywhere at all. It doesn't seem real. This could be an urban legend, you know, things that merpeople conjure up from time to time. If it is a real animal, it might just be exaggerated. Merpeople, especially newly transitioned merpeople, experience a new fear of the unknown when they come down here and tend to see things for what they are not, which sounds like one of the articles you sent me. I'll do some research to see what I can find out. Don't give up.

I'll talk with you later!

-Kendall

Dallas took a long gulp of her Coke and then started to type a reply, backspacing sentences and starting over a few times.

But the frilled shark turned out to be real.

That was all it took, really. Just one to see something and then pass it through the grapevine until more saw it, and then and only then was it seen for real. There was really nothing else to do. Nothing but get through the next few days she had left to work. Which reminded her...of something she needed to do while she still could.

The time said it was 4:16 p.m. The offices closed at five o'clock. Dallas shoved the last chicken nugget in her mouth and swam her plate over to the sink, piling it on top of the other two, waiting for her when she had the time, but she never did.

Dallas navigated the pipeline to the municipal area, knowing very well she had this small window, and it was now or never. She ducked around passing merpeople in a hurry and was able to get by mostly unnoticed to some of the envoy offices. She stopped in a hallway where the storage rooms were, retracing by memory to find the one she needed. Dallas swam around the corner to the door, only to cup the handle in her hand and feel it click.

She cursed and pressed her forehead against the glass, window shopping from what she could see from the outside. If only it was clear enough to see what was further in the back. She lifted her face to scan the nearby offices and the other doors that appeared to be open.

Pulling herself away from the locked room, she made her way to an office she knew would be open, where its occupant would most likely still be. The nameplate on the door read: "William Owen," and the bioluminescence diffusing through the bottom of the door. Dallas raised a fist, giving herself a second, and then gently rapped.

"Yeah, come on in," came the voice from inside, and Dallas pushed the door open.

Liam lowered his glasses to the tip of his nose when he saw her coming through the door, his tone perking up in interest.

"Well, Miss Dwight! You're not the visitor I was expecting. But that's a good thing, because everyone else has been up my rear, and I would rather not see them. What can I do for you?"

"Well, actually, I was wondering if I could get into one of the storage rooms."

"Which one?"

"The...weapons one."

Liam lowered his chin and kept his gaze on her over his glasses. He folded his fingers.

"Okay, also not what I was expecting. Are the hunter/gatherer supplies running low? Did Clyde send you?"

"No," Dallas said, resting her hand on the chair before his desk, which was topped with a long-sleeved tunic he might have shed and kept there. It gave her the opportunity to squeeze something soft.

"No. I... I would like to look through and check something out for myself. I am doing some traveling. A lot of traveling, actually, so I'll be out in the open ocean."

"And whatever weapons you have in your storage just wouldn't cut it?"

Dallas shrugged. "It's not that, really. I just want to be...prepared."

Liam's eyes smiled before his lips did. "Prepared, huh?"

"Yeah..."

"Whatever it is you're doing, you don't want anyone to know what you're doing."

Dallas was not really ready.

"I'm not really...doing anything. I am just going out on my own... I'm going out alone to a new place I don't know, so I want to be able to take care of myself and...be safe from predators."

It was his eyes, really, the way they were positioned behind the glasses that were protected yet out enough to be open. Like a secret, safe place that let something in and kept it safe. She reached into her pocket and pulled out a card, showing it to Liam. He took it and viewed it with interest, almost with pride.

"Something I'm doing. I'm going solo."

"Interesting..."

"Not officially. It's just a side thing for a while. I am doing some independent missions. It's something I wanted for a long time and didn't realize it. I'm just...trying it out. A little at a time. Maybe something I can grow over time."

Liam looked back at her and lifted his wrist with her card, then pulled back like he was changing his mind.

"Can I have this?"

Dallas smiled. "Sure."

"Maybe I can pass it along and sing your praises."

"Thanks."

"So, you're going to have to tell me more. You're going out on your first supposed mission?"

"I am," Dallas answered, catching sight of the pictures hung on the wall behind Liam. One was a military group photo where his beard was only starting to gray. "Out in the New Orleans district. There's a doctor there wanting different collections of venom."

Dallas looked over to the next picture of Liam next to a tiger shark with a proud grin.

"I...actually have read about something else that's out there."

Liam crossed his brow. "You read about what?"

"Some sort of...beast. It was described as a barnacle monster. It's popped up in news articles about people who have seen it, and it attacked merpeople. And it's been seen in the area I'm going..."

Liam studied her while she waved her hand to let the rest of the sentence finish itself in both their heads.

"I need to be prepared."

"I understand. Now, you need to slow down a little here, Miss Dwight. You're a little fireball, and while you have proven yourself, I can't just give out higher-end weapons to someone who has not been trained on them or has experience using them. I would not want to put you in greater danger should something happen with a bigger gun, and you hurt yourself, or are unable to hit your target and it comes after you, which is one of the worst things to happen—"

"But I need—"

Liam held up a hand.

"I am not trying to be a ball buster here. Trust me when I say I am not discrediting you as a hunter. I just don't want you to get in over your head. Now, that being said, I will be happy to get you upper-grade stun guns and blasters that you have used and were trained on when you served with the Marine Force."

Dallas made a small nod.

Liam turned behind him and went to open a cabinet, searching through a few drawers.

"Do you believe it?"

"Believe what?"

"Believe in this barnacle beast?"

Liam turned around from the cabinet empty-handed.

"Truth is, down here, no one knows what to believe."

"Exactly."

"The only thing I know is once you get better with your skills, in time, you'll be able to go after anything. And I think you'll get there. The advantage you have now will help you... and whatever is out there, you just might find it before it finds you."

She grinned.

"Looks like I don't have what I was looking for around here. When do you leave?"

"Next week."

"Okay, I should be able to get something then. I won't let you leave unprepared."

"Thank you."

Liam retrieved her card from the desk, holding it up.

"You got it, 'wielder of sonar.'"

CHAPTER 44

SHE PAUSED THE VIDEO, flipping the fish over so that the back faced her, and played it again. The woman in the video did the cutting from the tail up along the dorsal, and Dallas zoomed in to see just how close she got. She played it again to watch the entire process before picking up the knife to copy it.

Although the fish was dead and safe to handle, she still wore gloves. She held the head while she sawed the spines off the dorsal one by one, watching them fall on the cutting board. The video continued with the other parts on the pectoral fins and the single spines on the pelvic fins, the narrator explaining how the venom came from the tips.

Dallas fanned out the fins and cut off more of these spines. When the video moved on to the next step, Dallas stopped it. She focused on cutting off all the visible spines and placing them in a pile on a square of parchment, and then folded the parchment around the bundle and took it to her freezer, adjusting the temperature to be a little lower and putting it in its own compartment. When Dallas returned to the cutting board, she resumed the video to its next part: cooking preparation. This would be a new one for her.

She cooked the meat and added butter with a cupful of Brussels sprouts. As she ate, she tried to keep the memory of the taste in her palate to tell her parents and her sister that lionfish tasted just like a white flaky fish, similar to mahi-mahi, for the next time they talked, and she could tell them about it.

It was not a strong or different taste but distinguished enough for them to be in high demand both on land and at sea. "Delicious and invasive," they were called, as aquaculture launched several campaigns encouraging hunter/gatherers to hunt them to curb the overpopulation. Now, she could agree with it. The meal was an added bonus to the more important thing she collected from the lionfish.

After finishing eating and cleaning up, Dallas relaxed on the couch to browse on her tablet and look for any new notifications. The icons all remained static. A creature of paranoid habit, she opened her email again to reread the last correspondence she had with Trudy:

> Thank you so much, Dallas! We are looking forward to meeting you. You'll find several inns and motels in the area that are very highly rated. I would recommend the King's Den Motel. The owner's name is Pamela, and you can tell her I sent you. She can work out having you there for as long as you need while you are doing this job for us.
>
> Dr. Cecile is very busy, so you will be in touch with me primarily, and when you come, she will meet with you. I can tell you she is already impressed with

your knowledge of various venomous sea creatures,
so there is no doubt you can get us what we need.

The email above that one was Dallas's confirmation from the motel to check in at noon and to be sure to tell Pamela when she arrived. Dallas scrolled up and down again, all the boxes checked off, with not much else to do. Now, she debated a little on sending Trudy an update that she had already gotten a head start on the job.

Her tablet chimed with a notification she was not expecting.

> **When are you going?**

She sat up a little and saw that Noah was continuing the message. The typing text disappeared and started up again. Her thumbs hovered over the screen as the typing continued, but no message was final yet.

> **My sources told me it was pretty soon.**

Dallas typed in her message.

> **I don't want too many to know about this.**

The typing text bubble wavered.

> **It's okay, you're safe. Your sister mentioned it to me. I just hope you were able to get things sorted out for you.**

> Yeah, I got some shifts covered at work and got the time to collect myself and get everything straightened out.

> I am really happy for you. And I'm proud of you.

Then it was Dallas's turn to type a few sentences before backspacing and starting over.

> Honestly, I am happy that I told you about it to begin with. You sort of helped me come to terms with it out loud. Thank you for that, in case I didn't thank you enough.

Noah was typing.

> No, you did. And you're welcome.

Dallas waited for the typing text. She gave it a minute, trying to form new sentences in her head as his next message came through.

> Just promise me one thing.

> What?

Noah typed, backspaced, and then typed again.

> Don't be too brave out there. Promise me you'll make it back.

I will.

You better. Because I won't find a better duet partner.

She sent a smiley face icon.

Anytime.

Noah was typing again, and then again, and kept backspacing, and then the text came up that he was typing again. Dallas waited, but no more messages came through.

Dallas had a habit of making a list and checking it not twice, but thrice, as this list was usually in her head, and sometimes she became forgetfully paranoid. She did at one point pack her bag and then take it all out to recap and pack it over again, even though there were not too many things in it. Her knapsack folded over at the top and then fastened with a little button over the front, just like that, no added effort to seal the top with overflowing items.

Dallas found this amusing.

On land, one would overpack outfits to bring on trips with the notion that more options were always needed, and you just never knew what the weather would be like or what you felt like wearing. This was different in sea life.

Dallas's knapsack mainly sonnsisted of toiletries, her wallet, tablet, orb, charging pod, and only one extra tunic. She adjusted the straps on her turtle shell shield for a comfortable fit. She wore a scale mail shirt and a utility belt with calabash gourds—one holding lionfish venom—as well as pouches for the weapons she had to bring: her stun gun and ink blaster. It would be too much to bring the long-range gun and even the swordfish spear, because apparently, there would be something better.

Dallas opened the email again, because reading it always gave her thrilling flurries:

From: Owen, William
Subject: Your weapons request

Dallas,
I've got just the thing you need and could ever want for your upcoming gig and many, many more, I'm sure. Shoot me an email when you think you can stop by; I'll be doing paperwork in my office for a bit. Trust me when I say you're going to like this. Oh, and this needs to stay between us...

Later, kid,
-Liam

CHAPTER 45

After an hour or so, she pocketed her tablet and set off with a rush of adrenaline, leaving her gear behind for this errand.

She made her way through the neighborhood and common areas before reaching the pipelines, becoming instantly annoyed at the traffic waiting to ride. Eventually Dallas joined a small group and urged the currents to carry them faster. Someone in front of her was wearing a tunic with bright green stripes, which made her think of the bioluminescent tools they had seen on TV.

One science-fiction show featured giant gun blades that spun and shot out tiny, deadly pellets at rapid speed. Dallas might have gotten a bit ahead of herself envisioning how to wield something like that. When she landed, she made her way to the envoy offices and passed a few Marine Force officers she had seen before on the hunt, giving them casual nods of acknowledgment.

She turned her head away from them as she approached Liam's wing of the offices, not wanting to see them recognize where she was going and develop curiosity.

Liam's door was slightly ajar. She rapped on it lightly, but her knocks opened it for her, and she saw a Marine Force merman with Liam at his desk.

"...so, just so you're aware, we can...come in, Dallas."

She opened the door wide enough to enter and then let it rest against the wall.

"But sir…"

Liam held up a hand.

"You have nothing to worry about. Did you need anything else?"

"No, sir," the merman answered.

"All right," Liam concluded. "I've got an appointment now, so I will be in touch."

The merman saluted him.

"Yes, sir."

When he turned around, he gave Dallas a look up and down with a touch of surprise and interest. He made a polite nod before leaving and actually shut the door completely behind him.

Liam winked at Dallas, and she raised a brow.

"Don't mind him; I am taking applications for sergeants, so I think he got the wrong impression here."

She giggled while Liam pushed himself out of his chair and swam upward to his higher bookshelves.

"I'm glad he shut the door too, because I was going to ask you to do the same."

As Liam's chalky gray hair floated around him, she noticed a tattoo on his arm beneath his short-sleeved tunic that she hadn't seen before. It was the Stick Figure flexing beefy arms. Dallas always found it endearing to see the personal touches people made to this figure to personalize and promote their own version of that symbol of pride.

By itself, the icon remained simple and represented everything it could. Liam had his own beefy arms to match; his top form had remained the same. When he turned around, those arms were holding a chest. It was so brand new that the lock almost cast a golden glint against his monitor lights, looking like a sunset disappearing into the water. He drifted down and over to Dallas with his own golden glint in his eyes.

"This is very rare. When you see it, you'll understand why."

Liam held the chest out to Dallas, and she took it, feeling the smoothness of the wood and the care put into something that would carefully conceal and house another item. Dallas placed the chest on the desk and lifted the lock latch, opening the top of the chest all the way back in a dramatic reveal of hidden treasure.

When she peeked inside, she looked at the small item and didn't recognize it at first. It looked like a small, ordinary harpoon, complete with a handle and a tube-like covering that resembled a decorated armband. Dallas examined the end of this harpoon and then it clicked.

Her eyes jumped to Liam's as she reached for it and pulled it out to see for herself. Her jaw dropped in awe at the discovery she was meant to make.

She held it by its decorative body as she examined its deadly end: the rows of tricuspid teeth were tiny but lethal once they sank into their target, leaving no means of escape. She took a finger and, with the lightest touch, brushed down those rows of teeth—destructive little Christmas trees with sharp, protruding branches.

"Oh my God, it's a..."

Liam nodded.

"And it's made from..."

Liam nodded even more.

"You bet. It's the very one."

Dallas turned it over, exploring every bit of it. She reached a hand inside the tube and felt the pull trigger and coiled chain, pulling it back out to brush the tip once again.

"Holy crap, it's beautiful. It's...oh my God."

"It certainly is," Liam said.

For a moment, Dallas continued to marvel over it while Liam did as well, appreciating seeing it for the first time again and recognizing her excitement.

"It's only fair that you have it."

"It?" Dallas asked, looking at him. "So, is this the only one?"

"No, no, there are more. Not that many, though. As you remember, we had a conflict with that museum owner about the jaw and the teeth for a reason. Viceroy Westburn knew the Marine Force and hunter/gatherers were looking for new and unique materials for new weapons but were out of options.

Once we got these teeth, thanks to you, it was obvious it was the answer everyone had been looking for. They made these hookshots and passed them off to advanced Marine Force troops and hunter/gatherers leading envoys. They had no problem giving one to me when I asked for it. They thought I wanted it for my own reasons, but the truth is, I immediately knew you had to have one. No contest."

Dallas lowered the hookshot, watching Liam's eyes almost glaze over, as if those same signs of emotion could be read underwater. She wondered if hers were as well. Without thinking about it, Dallas dashed to Liam and squeezed him in a tight embrace. He responded with a squeeze one degree tighter before parting and moving his beard out of the way.

"Do you know how to work one of these?"

He reached a hand out, and she gave it to him.

"So, you felt the handle and the chains wrapped up inside, right? You pull that, and then the chain shoots it out as fast as seventy miles per hour. It goes as far as the chain does, which this one I believe is like fifty feet or so. It has both firing and retracting functions. Whatever you shoot this sucker at, it will hitch right on, and your target is as good as caught. You can use this against anything you're hunting and, well, frankly, anything that tries to hunt you. It's not just a weapon, either. It's also used for grappling. Latch this to any rocky fixture anywhere if you want to get somewhere further, faster. It could save your life."

Dallas smoothed her hand down the top.

"Can we try it out?"

Liam let out a hearty laugh.

"I thought you'd never ask! Let's go out back!"

The pipeline that brought her out to sea pushed her out in a rush, but the moment Dallas met the open blue, she felt everything around her slow down.

Anyone else that left went about their way, but she did not—not right away. She drifted away from the building until she could get that scenic view, the one that could give her enough of a 360. She turned, noting all the rocky landscapes and rainbow gardens of coral, the landmarks beyond of various buildings. The pipelines connected some, and then further, the metropolis part stopped, calmed down to scattered communities and businesses. Beyond that lay the endless stretch of the mother ocean.

Before Dallas could make her way to the substation to go out to sea, she heard the chimes from her messenger bag, startling her; this was not the notification for an email or Current message. It was the phone ringing. She swung her bag at her waist and retrieved the phone, seeing Kendall Wadsworth's name pop up.

"Hello, Kendall?"

"Dallas! So glad I caught you! Do you have a minute? I need to tell you about something!"

"Yeah, yeah," Dallas said, catching the urgency in her voice and forming some of her own. "What is it?"

"They found some more bones from the remains."

Dallas waited. "More?"

"These bones are not mer."

Dallas frowned. "What does that mean?"

"They called me. They took pictures of the pieces and sent them to me, and these bones are something I have never seen before! The pectorals, the fins, the torso—they're all LONG. Dallas, this describes your barnacle beast. Whatever it is, there are more of them."

Dallas pressed her tablet to her ear, feeling bubbles pop in her chest.

"I'm sending you the photos now. You have to look at the pectoral and fin bones and how long they are, and how they end, it looks like they could have tentacles. The part of the torso they found is super long, just like the appendages. It describes exactly the thing that you saw."

Dallas pulled up her email, clicking on the pictures Kendall sent and hearing her exhale on the phone as she waited for her to see them. Dallas stared at those photos of an extraterrestrial burial scene. She stared at the separated bones laid down together, as well as the part of a skull that was intact, the rest crushed in, with the left eye hole bigger than half of it. Though incomplete, it partially formed that outline—the very one.

"Oh my God."

"I think that you were right."

"I knew there was something...I just... But what is it?"

"I don't know, and neither does anyone else."

"Well, it's definitely not a turtle! Or a whale, or a squid, or..."

"No, no vertebrate even has such a complex skeletal structure."

Dallas exhaled. "Whatever it is, it's in the Gulf of Mexico."

"And you're still tracking it."

That wasn't a question.

"Yeah," she said. "Yeah, I am."

Dallas ran her hand over her hair, pulling her fingers through a few knots.

"That means that whatever these creatures are... they were in Gneiss Underway."

"And no one saw them because—"

"The frilled shark saw them first."

The bubbles in Dallas's chest popped some more with ideas of what could have been, what already was, and what could happen next.

Up ahead, she caught movement. It was massive and moving quickly, circulating the west part of Gneiss Underway's urban neighborhoods.

"I'm going after it. Especially now."

"Keep me posted!"

"I will, and I have to go now! Thanks Kendall!"

"Find it, Dallas."

Dallas hung up as she fought to catch up to what was ahead of her...determined not to miss it. She pumped her tail, bypassing sea stones and bunches of weeds while keeping it on her radar. It loomed in the distance, and Dallas noted its size as it sailed through the sea. She pumped her tail faster, knowing that she had to catch this one, without delay. There were rock islands ahead, things to be used to her advantage.

Dallas felt around her turtle-shell shield for the hookshot attached to her bag strap and pulled it out, timing and aiming carefully. She pumped her tail a little faster and got it right. She fired off the shot, the chain shooting out like the graceful tail of a shooting star.

The barbed wire teeth were tiny, which helped them sink into small spaces, such as the nooks and holes in the rock formations. Dallas found her target the moment the chain hooked on; it performed its reverse effect, sending Dallas sailing through her former line of fire. The sensation lasted only seconds, but in that brief time, Dallas realized it was possible to fly without air. The waters rushed past her gills so quickly that she almost couldn't feel them, and her fins flipped along with the current.

She reached the end of her grapple and felt around the device for the release, just as Liam had taught her to dislodge it. It only took a few short swims from there to catch up to the sub and board it.

The Caribbean and the Gulf of Mexico would come soon enough.

ABOUT THE AUTHOR

Jackie Sonnenberg has a thing for creatures that hide in the dark, and it shows. With a background in the haunted house industry as an actor and a costume maker, she learned how to make her worlds merge in the most unique way possible. She is known for dressing as and appearing as her book characters for events and conventions in an interactive style of marketing, introducing people to her stories by first introducing them to the characters. She has won costume contests and creative awards in fiction and character design. Jackie lives in Orlando, Florida, where she is surrounded by creativity and imagination. Check out her worlds at jackiesonnenberg.com.

THE END?

Not if you want to dive into more of Crystal Lake Publishing's Tales from the Darkest Depths!

Check out our amazing website and online store or download our latest catalog here.

We always have great new projects and content on the website to dive into, as well as a newsletter, behind the scenes options, social media platforms, our own dark fiction shared-world series and our very own webstore. Our webstore even has categories specifically for KU books, non-fiction, anthologies, and of course more novels and novellas.

Readers...

Thank you for reading *The Fathoms Below*. We hope you enjoyed this novel. If you have a moment, please review *The Fathoms Below* at the store where you bought it.

Help other readers by telling them why you enjoyed this book. No need to write an in-depth discussion. Even a single sentence will be greatly appreciated. Reviews go a long way to helping a book sell, and are great for an author's career. It'll also help us to continue publishing quality books.

Thank you again for taking the time to journey with Crystal Lake's Crystal Cove Press.

You will find links to all our social media platforms on our Linktree page: https://linktr.ee/CrystalCovePress.

Follow us on Amazon:

MISSION STATEMENT

Since its founding in August 2012, Crystal Lake has quickly become one of the world's leading publishers of Dark Fiction and Horror books. In 2023, Crystal Lake officially transitioned into an entertainment company, joining several other divisions, genres, and imprints, including Torrid Waters, Sinister Smile Press, Crystal Lake Comics, Crystal Lake Games, Crystal Cove Press, Crystal Lake Kids, Memento Mori Ink, and The House of Shadows & Ink on YouTube.

While we strive to present only the highest quality fiction and entertainment, we also endeavor to support authors along their writing journey. We offer our time and experience in non-fiction projects, as well as author mentoring and services, at competitive prices.

With several Bram Stoker Award wins and many other wins and nominations (including the HWA's Specialty Press Award), Crystal Lake puts integrity, honor, and respect at the forefront of our publishing operations.

We strive for each book and outreach program we spearhead to not only entertain and touch or comment on issues that affect our readers, but also to strengthen and support the Dark Fiction field and its authors.

Not only do we find and publish authors we believe are destined for greatness, but we strive to work with men and women who endeavor to be decent human beings who care more for others than themselves, while still being hard-working, driven, and passionate artists and storytellers.

Crystal Lake is and will always be a beacon of what passion and dedication, combined with overwhelming teamwork and respect, can accomplish. We endeavor to know each and every one of our readers, while building personal relationships with our authors, reviewers, bloggers, podcasters, bookstores, and libraries.

We will be as trustworthy, forthright, and transparent as any business can be, while also keeping most of the headaches away from our authors, since it's our job to solve the problems so they can stay in a creative mind. Which of course also means paying our authors.

We do not just publish books, we present to you worlds within your world, doors within your mind, from talented authors who sacrifice so much for a moment of your time.

There are some amazing small presses out there, and through collaboration and open forums we will continue to support other presses in the goal of helping authors and showing the world what quality small presses are capable of accomplishing. No one wins when a small press goes down, so we will always be there to support hardworking, legitimate presses and their authors. We don't see Crystal Lake as the best press out there, but we will always strive to be the best, strive to be the most interactive and grateful, and even blessed press around. No matter what happens over time, we will also take our mission very seriously while appreciating where we are and enjoying the journey.

What do we offer our authors that they can't do for themselves through self-publishing?

We are big supporters of self-publishing (especially hybrid publishing), if done with care, patience, and planning. However, not every author has the time or inclination to do market research, advertise, and set up book launch strategies. Although a lot of authors are successful in doing it all, strong small presses will always be there for the authors who just want to do what they do best: write.

What we offer is experience, industry knowledge, contacts and trust built up over years. And due to our strong brand and trusting fanbase, every Crystal Lake book comes with weight of respect. In time our fans begin to trust our judgment and will try a new author purely based on our support of said author.

To date we've published around 300 books, and with each launch we strive to fine-tune our approach, learn from our mistakes, and increase our reach. We continue to assure our authors that we're here for them and that we'll carry the weight of the launch and deal with third parties while they focus on their strengths—be it writing, interviews, blogs, signings, etc.

We also offer several mentoring packages to authors that include knowledge and skills they can use in both traditional and self-publishing endeavors. This includes Shadows & Ink Creators on our The House of Shadows & Ink YouTube channel and our Crystal Lake Academy.

We look forward to launching many new careers.

This is what we believe in. What we stand for. This will be our legacy.

**Welcome to Crystal Lake Publishing—
Where Stories Come Alive!**